# Cometh the Hour

## Annie Whitehead

## *Acknowledgements*

This book has been a long time in the writing. I began the first draft back in 2012, but have been sidetracked, by no means unpleasantly, by other writing projects since then. I suppose though, that like all my novels, the story began to form while I was still a student under the guidance of Ann Williams, and so once again I must thank her for her inspirational teaching.

I am indebted to Julia Brannan, Lisl Zlitni, and Joshua Desbottes for their help, suggestions, diligence and eagle-eyed perusal of the manuscript. Any remaining errors are entirely my fault. I must also express my gratitude to Cryssa Bazos for her insight about one aspect of the design.

My thanks go to Cathy Helms of Avalon Graphics (www.avalongraphics.org) for designing the cover and producing the map of the ancient kingdoms, and to Lin White at Coinlea Services (www.coinlea.co.uk) for her skill and endless patience while producing the family tree.

7th Century
**Britain**

*o*

PICTS

DÁLRIADA

STRATHCLYDE

LOTHIAN

BERNICIA

RHEGED

MAN

DEIRA

ANGLESEY

ELMET

PECSÆTE

GWYNEDD WRECONSÆTE

LINDSEY

MERCIA

POWYS

MAGONSÆTE

AROSÆTE

MIDDLE
ANGLES

EAST
ANGLES

GWENT

HWICCE

CHILTERNSÆTE

EAST
SAXONS

WEST SAXONS

KENT

0  20  40      80 KM

# *Royal Houses Family Tree*

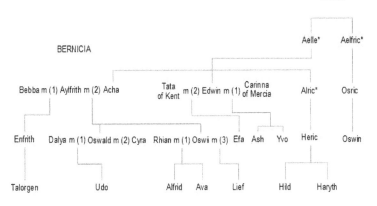

DEIRA

BERNICIA

Aelle* — Aelfric*

Bebba m (1) Aylfrith m (2) Acha | Tata of Kent m (2) Edwin m (1) Carinna of Mercia | Alric* | Osric

Enfrith | Dalya m (1) Oswald m (2) Cyra | Rhian m (1) Oswii m (3) Efa | Ash | Yvo | Heric | Oswin

Talorgen | Udo | Alfrid | Ava | Lief | Hild | Haryth

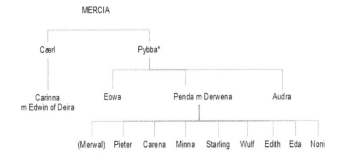

MERCIA

Cærl — Pybba*

Carinna m Edwin of Deira | Eowa | Penda m Derwena | Audra

(Merwal) Pieter Carena Minna Starling Wulf Edith Eda Noni

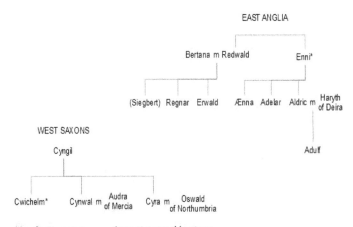

EAST ANGLIA

Bertana m Redwald — Enni*

(Siegbert) Regnar Erwald | Ænna Adelar Aldric m Haryth of Deira

Adulf

WEST SAXONS

Cyngil

Cwichelm* | Cynwal m Audra of Mercia | Cyra m Oswald of Northumbria

( ) = foster sons        * = not named in story
[Real historical names are listed in 'Author's Notes']

## *The Royal Houses – Dramatis Personæ*

*Bernicia*
King Aylfrith the Cunning
Enfrith, his son by first wife, Bebba
Talorgen, Enfrith's son by a Pictish princess
Oswald, Aylfrith's son by Deiran princess, Acha
Œthelwold 'Udo', Oswald's son
Oswii, younger brother of Oswald
Alfrid and Ava, his children by Rhian of Rheged
Ecgfrith 'Lief', his son by Efa of Deira

*Deira*
Edwin
His sons, Ash and Yvo, by his Mercian wife, Carinna
Efa, his daughter by his Kentish wife, 'Tata'
Acha, Edwin's sister, abducted by Aylfrith of Bernicia
Heric, son of Edwin's murdered brother
Hild and Haryth, his daughters
Osric, cousin of Edwin
Oswin, his son

*Mercia*
King Cærl
Carinna, his daughter
Eowa and Penda, his nephews
Audra, their sister
Merwal, Derwena's son, and foster son of Penda
Penda's children by Derwena: Pieter, Carena, Minna,
Starling, Wulfhere 'Wulf', Edith and Eda, Ethelred 'Noni'

*East Anglia*
King Redwald
Siegbert, his foster son
Regnar and Erwald, sons of Redwald by Bertana
Their cousins: Ænna, Adelar, Aldric
Adulf, son of Aldric and his wife, Haryth of Deira

# *It begins...*

*AD604 - The kingdom of Deira*

The midsummer sun was falling, staining the sky with an ever-darkening red tint. A good portent, it foretold the spilling of blood. Aylfrith the Cunning of Bernicia slipped from his saddle and raised his arm, signalling to his men to get into position. He looked at the royal palace on the high mound beyond the line of trees and as he brought his arm down he paused; from so far away it seemed as if all he had to do was to reach out and the palace and all the lesser buildings within the compound would fit neatly into the palm of his hand. He smiled. In reality it would not be much more difficult to take it.

The realm of Deira stood temptingly close to his own kingdom and had rich pasture full of well-fed cattle. If he could conquer Deira, he would be king of all the lands north of the Humber. Since Aylfrith had only one son from his first wife and no prospect of reaping any more from that particular furrow, he was ready to justify once more his reputation for guile. This was one occasion where a pitched battle would not serve him.

The Deiran kings had been more prolific than Aylfrith and there were too many adult males of the royal line. The only way to ensure that enough of them died this day was to catch them off guard as they feasted, when their weapons were hung not at their belts, but on the walls of the mead hall.

All around him, his men had settled into position and were waiting, spears, swords and axes ready, for his signal.

Aylfrith brought his arm up once more, looked to his left and to his right and pointed towards the hill.

The fire in the great central hearth had been stoked and the little slave-boy who had been tending it curled up beside it, to rest until more logs were needed. Shadows danced on the wall, thrown by the flickering flames glowing from the cressets filled with expensive oil. The scop, who was both poet and musician, was quietly plucking the strings of his lyre, his head bent low over the instrument as he listened to the tuning whilst warming his fingers in readiness for the king's command for him to sing and play.

Two small children who had been ushered to bed were peering out from a curtained bed box at the side of the hall. At the mead benches the king's coterie, his kinfolk and other members of his war band, were settling down after their meal for an evening of drinking, riddle-solving and tale-telling. The children peeping round the curtains were waiting; official boasting might ensue, with the scop acting as judge and referee, particularly if the boast was challenged and the resultant show of strength turned into a fight.

Edwin of Deira wiped the blade of his sæx, the knife he'd used for spearing the slices of meat, slipped his thumbs under his tunic belt and tugged, trying to release the pressure on his belly. The meal of boiled lamb, fresh summer cheeses and soft summer fruits, all washed down with sweet wine, had left him feeling replete but a little uncomfortable. He tried and failed to suppress a belch.

His brother, the king of Deira, was sitting next to Edwin on the king-stool, with his young son Heric on his lap. The eight-year-old boy was toying with the gold ring on his father's finger, turning it so that its jewels caught the reflection of the firelight.

The king jabbed a teasing finger and spoke to Edwin.

"Eaten too much, little brother?"

Before Edwin could answer, young Heric halted his contemplation of the gold and garnet ring. "Uncle Edwin, will you be too fat to take me riding tomorrow?"

Edwin had only been eleven years old when his nephew was born and he had always thought of the lad as a younger brother. He ruffled the boy's red-gold hair. "Would I let you down, Heric the Fearless? Once I give my word, it becomes the truth."

Seated to Edwin's left, his cousin Osric snorted. "That's not what I hear from the women; they tell me your word is no more likely to stand than other parts of you."

Edwin acknowledged the crude witticism with a slap on his cousin's back. "And what would you know of women, eh?"

Edwin glanced across the hall at the royal women who were no doubt engaged in their own light-hearted conversation, gently and affectionately deriding their menfolk for their own amusement. Acha, sister to Edwin and the king, was sitting with her hands in her lap and a demure half-smile on her face. She was not laughing at the jokes; either she did not understand the comments of the married women, or she knew that she should not, at sixteen, have any comprehension of their allusions to the goings-on of the marriage bed. She would have to learn soon enough, for it was her destiny to marry a king or prince of another kingdom and thus take the glory of the Deiran blood to add to another dynasty.

Next to him, as if reading Edwin's thoughts, Osric said, "You will miss her more than any of us."

Edwin shrugged, able to acknowledge the truth of his cousin's words but attempting to brush away any hint of sentimentality. "My brother is so much older; Acha and I are nearer in age."

Osric was not so easily fooled. "If it were simply a

matter of age then she and I would be the closest. She is your little sister and you take care of her." He took a sip of wine and smiled. "I recall the day she and I stole some fresh loaves. Your father found out and you took the blame for her. Not for me though; oh no, I still got walloped."

Edwin laughed, grateful to be able to deflect his thoughts away from the contemplation of his sister's imminent departure. He glanced once more at Acha, gave her a full, open-mouthed smile and looked down to resume his drinking.

The only warning was a scream. The great oak door was thrust open, the slain guard toppled backwards into the hall and Aylfrith's men trampled over the body as they rushed into the room. The door-thegn attempted to challenge them, standing with his arm forward in a defensive pose. He received a blow so powerful that it slashed through his left shoulder, sliced down to his pelvis and all the way to his left knee.

The hearth-thegns leaped to their feet, throwing wine jugs and punches, stabbing with their sæx-blades, dodging axe blows. Edwin and Osric stood side by side, slashing and thrusting with their short-bladed knives, trying to reach the swords and spears by the wall. Their purpose was to hold the fighting near the door, to protect the king and his heir and with Woden's grace, repel the intruders. Edwin's personal hearth-thegns, the brothers Lilla and Diethelm, stood close by, fighting as best they could whilst attempting to protect Edwin's back.

The space within the hall was cramped and not conducive to swinging weapons and punches, but as long as they could form a barrier, a human shield to prevent any more of the enemy from passing through the doorway, they would keep the advantage, but this would mean a delay in getting to the weapons on the wall.

Edwin looked at Osric, jerked his head in the direction

of the weapons and Osric nodded. "Go."

Edwin lunged to the side of the room, tucking and rolling as he went, hoping that as he stood up he would be close enough to grab a sword or axe. There was no time to turn round but Edwin was sure that Osric was doing his best to keep a bottleneck at the doorway, to stop any more Bernicians pouring into the hall. He reached up and snatched at a sword; not his own, but it would do.

Half-turning, he swung the blade in a downwards slash that caught one of the aggressors across the left shoulder. Driving the weapon deeper into the neck, Edwin pushed out with his foot at the same time and the man, dying, fell backwards. Another rushed at Edwin and he held the blade out in front of him, shoving hard to penetrate the other man's stomach.

Slashing and slicing, he made his way back to Osric to help him contain the number of adversaries in the hall and keep it to as fair a fight as possible, but for every two they felled, three more came through and before long the only thing to slow their progress was the increasing jumble of bodies that impeded them as they surged forward.

Tiring, they fought on and at last, after Osric had stabbed his sæx straight through the eye of the next man through the door, Edwin noted that no more followed him. For better or worse, all the Bernicians still alive were in the hall and the doorway was clear.

Edwin chanced a glance behind him and saw that whilst they had been engaged with holding as many of the rabble as they could, the ones they had missed had inevitably gained ground and the bastards had moved round the edges of the hall. The king was slumped in his chair, eyes wide, blood pumping from the opening in his chest. His son, little Heric, was cowering by his feet. Edwin shouted to Osric and his cousin promptly took a roll and a dive, reaching out to grab the terrified boy.

He could not be sure that his cries of "Get him out" were audible above the clang and clamour, but Edwin's last view of Osric was of his valiant cousin shielding the boy with one arm, slashing with the other as he made his way through a gap in the door and, gods willing, to freedom.

Nodding with satisfaction, Edwin turned again. Acha had been there, moments before, sensibly barricading herself behind one of the benches. Now, he could not see her. The king's wife lay lifeless on the floor where only moments before, Acha had been crouching.

Edwin looked quickly round the hall. The massive cauldron which once hung above the central hearth was upturned, its contents splattered across the floor. The pile of logs, tended so diligently by the little slave-boy, had rolled and scattered. Wine and ale cups and pitchers were on the floor, some still spinning. The curtained bed boxes were empty, the curtains hanging shredded and blood-stained. Completing his scan of the room, Edwin turned back towards the door and glimpsed his sister as she was dragged outside.

Yelling, he lunged forward and with his anger now barbed with worry, he fought to get out of the hall. A barrel-bellied man advanced towards him and Edwin put his head down and ran, butting the enormous belly and shoving with his shoulder. Beyond, another Bernician came at him, brandishing a hand-sæx and shuffling from side to side, trying to anticipate which way Edwin would swerve to get past him. Edwin feinted to the left and as the man copied, he brought his own short-blade round and caught his opponent in the side, jamming the blade up towards the ribs and thrusting hard. Yet another was coming at him, but this one tripped on one of the spilled logs and Edwin dodged as he crashed to the ground. Leaping past him, he lurched towards the door and ran through.

Gasping, chest burning, he took but one moment to stand still and focus as Lilla and Diethelm burst out of the hall to stand beside him, and in that moment he saw his beloved sister being lifted onto the back of Aylfrith's horse, barely given a chance to steady herself before the beast galloped away.

Panting, Edwin stood, knowing he had but another moment to decide what to do. Catching sight of Osric and Heric in the woods and counting from rough, half-snatched memory the number of Deirans left alive in the hall, Edwin sprinted with his hearth-thegns to join what was left of his kin in the sanctuary of the woodland.

Aylfrith had taken a royal princess of Deira and Edwin guessed that he would use the purity of her blood to establish his own dynasty in the newly conquered kingdom and merge the two Northumbrian realms. He had ridden away, yes, but not far and he would be back. Such a raid was more than a mere border squabble; the nature of it made clear Aylfrith's intention to eradicate the Deiran line and supplant it with heirs from his own seed. Edwin and Osric were in danger and not strong enough to defeat him. Not yet.

There was no daylight left by which to navigate, no light by which to see the fear in little Heric's eyes, but even in the warmth of the summer night, Edwin could feel the boy shivering, his hands shaking as he clung to his uncle's legs. Even if they chanced a night in the forest, the boy would not sleep. Edwin grunted. "To Elmet."

Osric agreed, his voice cracking on the short word. "Elmet."

Only yesterday, Edwin had teased his cousin for the fractured tones of his voice which occasionally still betrayed his ongoing passage from boyhood to manhood. Now the voice was broken by a sob. All in the turn of a day they had been reduced to the role of dispossessed refugees, the only surviving members of the House of Deira.

The British kingdom of Elmet, where the people known as the Loides lived, bordered Deira to the southwest; if they moved quickly and, Edwin thought with a stab of angry regret, it should not be hard for them to travel swiftly enough since they had no belongings to carry, they would reach the edges of the neighbouring kingdom before too much of the new day had passed.

Thus the remnants of the Deiran royal family and hearth-troops made their way to the crossing on the River Wharfe which marked the boundary, with Heric gulping back his sobs and trying to live up to his uncle's teasing epithet for him, attempting, at the age of only eight, to be 'the Fearless', despite having been orphaned and made homeless, while the adults clung to the hope that King Ceredig of the Loides would give them sanctuary. The British kings were no friends of Aylfrith, so their chances were good, but to make sure, they stopped and worshipped briefly at every wēoh site, the roadside shrines where travellers could offer prayers and leave gifts for the gods.

As dawn broke pale over the retreating indigo of the night sky, the three princes and their retainers set their blood-stained, mud-stained boots onto the western bank of the river.

Wandering from settlement to settlement, they asked enough questions in faltering British and hand mimes until they ascertained the whereabouts of the king. Heric was distracted by the curved walls of the buildings that he saw within the stockades of the massive hill forts and began asking questions about these strange round-houses. Osric took on the task of furnishing him with as much information as he had regarding their British neighbours, the better to keep the boy from dwelling on his loss. He told him what he knew of their strange ways of worship and how they prayed to a god whom they called 'Christ' who he thought had been found in Ireland and now, apparently, resided in every man who believed in him. Heric entertained himself after that, staring at every person they met to see if this Christ god was hiding inside them.

Along the way, they received food and shelter from a bemused local population. Edwin had neither the time nor inclination to discover whether the hospitality was freely given. He demanded sustenance at knife point, no longer willing to trust anyone who was not bound to him by blood. He slept little, not daring to abandon Heric to danger should he, as uncle and protector, succumb to indulgent slumber.

They found Ceredig, king of Elmet, in his fortified settlement of Leeds. Walking through the palisade gateway, they were stopped by the guards and divested of their remaining few weapons. Language barriers aside, Edwin knew that it must be obvious that they were no raiding party. Whatever the British opinion of the savage Angles they would know that they would not bring such a young child with them into battle, nor would they come so inadequately armed. They shambled through the enclosure and were brought to the king's house where the ageing, beaver-toothed Ceredig eyed them with suspicion.

Through an interpreter, a man who had spent some years as a Bernician slave, as well as hand gestures and enactment, Edwin explained what had happened. Whenever Aylfrith's name was mentioned, Ceredig's eyes narrowed and he screwed his mouth in an expression of hatred but he listened at all other times with a look of detachment.

It became clear that while this old man might sympathise, he was in the business of self-preservation and did not have the foresight to see that if he helped Edwin against Aylfrith, it would make his own kingdom more secure. No, Ceredig would act only if his kingdom came under direct threat and it was obvious that their salvation lay elsewhere.

The old man's features quickened when Edwin, frustrated, promised gold and riches in return for his support but, deliberately or not, Ceredig misunderstood and accepted the offer of gifts in payment only for his hospitality and for providing sanctuary.

Edwin decided to waste no more time but to push Ceredig's offer to its limits. "Will you give shelter, then, to my cousin and my nephew?"

Ceredig frowned. "Not you?"

Edwin muttered under his breath. "Oh, I would not wish to trouble you." But realising that sarcasm would not translate well, he raised his voice and said, "No. But when I return, you will be richly rewarded for your kindness."

The old man's eyes twinkled and Edwin knew he had found the measure of this grasping king. He swallowed his disgust, aware that open contempt would not help him, but he was of the opinion that avarice and cowardice were quite often inseparable bedfellows.

Turning to Osric, Edwin led him to one side and said, "I give Heric over into your care. I know you will guard his life with your own. When I have raised enough men and weapons, I will be back. Until then…" His voice cracked and he had to stop talking.

Osric clasped him by the forearms and nodded vigorously. "Yes."

Edwin turned to look at the small band of men who had travelled with them and, without his asking, they began to separate into two groups, one to stay with Osric and the heir to the Deiran throne, one to journey with Edwin in search of the means to destroy Aylfrith and restore the kingdom of Deira. They were bound to the cause unto death. Edwin embraced his cousin, hugged his nephew and, with Lilla and Diethelm as ever by his side, strode from the hall without a backward glance.

## The kingdom of Bernicia 605

The tearing pain had been as brutal at the end as it had been when he had first thrust himself into her. The waves had crashed on the rocks below the great fortress at Bamburgh and when the contractions had speeded up to synchronise with the ebb and flow of the noisy sea, Acha had screamed in an effort to silence the swell of the sea and drown the pain.

As she laboured to bear forth the fruits of his violence, she had cursed Aylfrith and prayed that the child would wither and die like a putrid apple left to rot long after harvest time. Acha had left gifts by the tree, at the shrine dedicated to Eostre, in the hope that the goddess of the spring would be benign and allow her to leave this world even as her son came into it. But perhaps she had not offered enough. Certainly all the offerings the previous year when the harvest failed had not prevented the folk suffering from heat and drought the like of which no man could remember.

Acha had done what she could to help the poor, but it was precious little, riding out when she could with carts of bread from the royal food stores and the remains of last summer's cheeses. She had stayed awhile with some of the mothers while they buried their starved children. And yet her own sacrifice to the Mother should perhaps have been bigger, bloodier, for her child was born and she was alive.

Acha stared at the purple, bruised little face and as her tears dried she remembered that Eostre was always a loving and generous goddess. He was born on Eostre's festival day, when the day and night were the same length and he was healthy, despite all her prayers and curses.

Gradually, as the bleeding lessened and she recovered,

by means of short naps and the ministrations of Nia, a British slave-girl who brought her honey-flavoured biscuits to build up her strength, Acha was suffused with a mother's love and somehow detected that she might one day, with the goddess' help, find a way to endure and perhaps even overcome her circumstances.

Aylfrith entered the chamber with his eldest son trailing behind him. He strode to the cradle and said, "He is too small. Sickly. You will have to do better than that."

His son, Enfrith, laughed and repeated the word like an echo. "Sickly, sickly, sickly."

Acha felt a surge of protective love rush through her. How dare they be so cruel to such a tiny creature? She could not bear for him to become another helpless victim of this violent man.

Aylfrith said, "You will name him after me. But he will be known as Æthelfrith."

Silently appealing to the Mother for help, Acha stared back at him. For the nine months she had been his 'wife', she had suffered on a nightly basis his bouts of rampant arousal that were fuelled by his beating her, and she had been the target of daily taunting by Enfrith, who hated her for supplanting his mother, Bebba, blamed her for his mother's death last Yuletide and took pleasure in witnessing her degradation. He was a nasty ten-year-old, stocky with reddish hair, who resembled his father in more than looks. Now he was teasing her son before he had spent one day on the earth. No, she decided, there would be no more Bernician boys running around this palace.

Her baby was small and had a tiny crop of the palest hair; he was more her son than thick-necked Aylfrith's. They might be deep in Bernicia, but she was a Deiran princess and her fair son would have a Deiran name. In her weakened post-partum state, somehow she managed to muster some inner strength and she looked her oppressor in the eye, telling him quietly but firmly that the boy's name was Oswald.

Aylfrith laughed at her boldness, promised that he would have her again soon and left her alone with the newest, perhaps only, living member of her family. Despite the pain, despite the bleeding and ignoring the exhaustion, she sat up and went to the cradle, picked up her son and brought him back to bed with her, kissing the top of his head and asking forgiveness of the Mother for ever harbouring hopes for his suffering. From now on, he was her world and he would know nothing but the purest love.

\*\*\*

In Mercia, the Eostre celebrations were nearly over. The yew tree was still draped in its finery, but the adults had dispersed. The little boy had an uninterrupted view of the shrine and he stepped closer. "Look, not touch," he said, nodding and fixing his face with a serious expression. A hand grabbed his, a gentle tug. He looked up and smiled a child's grin, revealing both sets of tiny white teeth. "Carinna not cross, not yell?"

"No, my sweet youngling, I could never be cross with you." Carinna dropped to one knee and allowed the boy to put his arms around her neck. She stood up with him still clinging on.

"Want Mumma," he said, squeezing her neck. "Mumma not here again? Where Mumma? Me and you play now?"

Carinna smoothed the hair from the child's forehead and planted a kiss there. She placed him back on the ground, and squatted in front of him, bringing her face level with his. "Your mumma is resting; she's tired. You have a baby brother. His name is Penda."

*Part One ~ The Years of Exile and Wandering*

# Chapter One

*The kingdom of Mercia 608*

Carinna held her aunt's hand as the older women worked to bring the baby forth. Carinna had not been concerned at first; it was her kinswoman's third child and the previous births had been uncomplicated. The existence of two strong, healthy boys meant that this labour should prove easy. And yet the midwives looked worried and Carinna, even at the young age of seventeen, had witnessed enough births to know that all was not well. It had been too long, the baby was not the right way round and the labour had been well advanced before the women had succeeded in turning it. The contractions were strong, but the mother was weak and could not help them by adding any force by pushing.

At last the baby crowned and then arrived in the world, but it seemed as though the breath left the mother at the precise moment that the child took its first deep inhalation and began to wail.

Carinna clutched her stomach as if she had been winded; her aunt was dear to her, but clawing at her heart even more strongly was sadness for the orphaned boys. Carinna's father, King Cærl, would look after them well, for they were the closest heirs to his throne, but they were only six and three and far, far too young to be without their mother.

Wiping her sweaty palms down the front of her dress, Carinna stepped from the murky birthing chamber and leaned against the wall. Immersed in her pool of grief, she was slow to hear the commotion and only saw the stranger once he had been escorted almost to the doors of the palace. But notice him she did, for he was tall, standing half a head taller than his companions, he was unusually blond even for an Anglian and his eyes were uncommonly blue, as if painted onto his face with woad, and sparkling in the morning sunshine.

He had travelled far; his clothes were dusty, his unshaven face was smeared with grime and his hands were raw and chapped as if he had spent a long time riding. Visitors appeared frequently at the court of King Cærl and it was not unusual for leaders of local tribesmen to come bringing tribute or requesting military help, but this man was different, for he came with only a handful of retainers and yet was richly dressed.

His cloak was pile-woven, giving it a shaggy appearance and it was fastened with a thick gold brooch, studded with dark red garnets. The garment showed that he had once been a man of means, but it was odd that he should be wearing such a warm cloak in the summer months, as if he had no other. There were garnets too on his belt buckle and his scabbard was fur-lined, yet the sword sheathed therein was devoid of any jewels or decoration as if he had either stolen the scabbard or the sword was not his own. He wore a necklace, but it was grimy and she could not tell if the beads were painted earthenware or glass. His hair was below his collar but looked as if, rather than being indicative of a fashion for a longer style, it had simply not been cut for some time.

She watched as he walked; his bearing was such that he was used to being served and whatever his current circumstances, this was a man who was once of some importance.

Before he entered the hall, he looked across the yard, taking stock, it seemed to her, of all the defences, even lifting his fingers and surreptitiously counting the number of stalls in the stables, the number of guards on the wooden wall by the boundary ditch and, with a glance at the smithy, assessing the number of weapons waiting there to be repaired or altered. Finally he looked across at the bower houses and stared at Carinna. He smiled at her, even in his obvious weariness, and she smiled back. He was acknowledging her rank, just as she had spotted his.

Only after he had disappeared inside did she look down and remember that this day she was dressed in plain-spun, her dull garments befitting her role as one of the birthing-women, and that her fine robes were still folded inside her clothes chest. The stranger had smiled not at her rank, but at her.

It was but a second of respite, for all too soon she was redirected to her sad task when little Eowa and his even littler brother, Penda, came skipping from the bake-house, chewing on chunks of freshly baked bread, the younger boy demanding to see his new baby sibling and the elder one calling for their mother.

Edwin, with Lilla and Diethelm following a few steps behind, entered the great hall and bowed low before King Cærl of Mercia, chief of the people of the Iclingas. The king was older than Edwin but he was still a young man, with a full head of straw-blond hair tied back and crowned with a simple band of gold which stretched across his forehead. He was unmistakably a king but either he was not rich or he avoided ostentation, because he wore little else in the way of jewellery. Edwin hoped that this man was a different proposition from the creaky ancient who sat on the throne in Elmet and cravenly prevaricated about the best time to attack Aylfrith.

Edwin had travelled the length and breadth of Elmet and to the lands west of its borders, persuading, haranguing, even threatening where necessary, rallying men to his cause and painting for them a picture of what would happen to them if Aylfrith was not stopped. But every time he returned to Ceredig and told him how many warriors were now willing to take up arms, presenting him at the same time with the small amounts of tribute he had managed to accumulate, a few head of cattle, some deer and wolfskins, the old man sucked air through his increasingly toothless mouth and bleated about the cost, material and political, before consulting his most trusted warriors and informing Edwin that the time was not auspicious.

Losing patience, Edwin had decided to widen his search for help and try his luck at the court of the Mercian king. At least here they were Angles, like him; not that a shared ethnic identity had stopped Aylfrith, but at least there would be no language or religious barriers to hamper negotiations.

He approached the dais and after the formalities, began his speech, so well-rehearsed during his journey. Cærl nodded slowly, acknowledging every point: Aylfrith's domination would spread, bleeding like an untended wound, until someone found a binding strong enough to staunch it. He controlled Deira, which bordered Elmet, whose southern borders touched on the northern reaches of Mercia. With an old fool ruling Elmet, there was no effective buffer and make no mistake, Aylfrith would come south eventually.

Cærl squinted through hooded eyes. "I know nothing about you."

Edwin said "You don't need to. All you need to know is that Aylfrith killed my kin. I am his foe, you are his foe, that makes us friends."

Cærl of the Iclingas nodded again, but he said, "How can I know that once you have your kingdom back, you will not leave mine to the Bernician wolves?" Edwin opened his mouth to protest, but Cærl put up a hand to silence him. "I already have the answer, Northman. I have no sons and no one to pass my kingdom to other than the sons of my dead brother. I do, however, have a daughter. Beget some Northumbrian sons on her and I will look kindly on helping you."

Edwin summoned enough self-control to suppress the automatic sigh that such a suggestion induced. It came as no surprise that there was a price attached to Cærl's help. At least he hadn't immediately held out his hand for gold, but considered the political advantage to be gained in return for his promise of military assistance.

Had Edwin's life stayed on its predicted course then sooner or later he would have had to take a wife for political purposes, but now, it would be a distraction at best, a burden at worst. Edwin would have preferred the option of moving on if assistance proved not to be forthcoming, to leave with no ties to bind him should he need to plead at yet another king's court, but Cærl had already sent the steward to fetch the princess. Edwin would have to continue to dance the appropriate courtship steps, while trying to find a way out of marrying the girl.

The guest-seat, always reserved for special occasions, was brought out and placed on the dais, he was bidden to sit and a slave-boy poured him a cup of ale.

Edwin drank, gestured for more and was only vaguely aware that the king's daughter had entered the hall. He put his cup down on the table and wiped the back of his hand across his mouth as he looked up.

His hand remained briefly where it was, halfway across his face, as he paused and realised that the comely woman he had stared at in the yard was a daughter of royal birth. Perhaps this task would not be so burdensome after all. The honey-coloured hair looked darker in the firelight and he could no longer see the freckles which were dotted across her nose and upper cheeks, but her delicate chin and slightly upturned nose were still discernible.

The girl walked slowly towards her father, looking straight ahead, but as she passed the table where Edwin

31

was sitting, her eyelids lowered briefly, as if she might have given the visitor a quick sideward glance. She greeted her father with hands outstretched, using the clasping of hands to pull him towards her and as the king bent his head and leaned in, she whispered in his ear.

The king's expression changed and he clutched his child to his chest. His tears fell, running in channels until they disappeared into his beard. He stood up, still holding his daughter to him and, with his arm around her shoulder, he announced to his hearth-men that his kinswoman had died in childbirth.

Amid the ensuing wails from the women present, the calls from the men for ale to drink to the deceased's memory and shouts for the scop to come forth and sing her life-song, Edwin noticed a nurse who walked timidly into the hall, a small boy walking by her side and another in her arms. She searched with her eyes until she saw the king's daughter and then hurried to take the children to the dais.

The princess saw them, disentangled herself from her father's grip and ran to the centre of the hall. Crouching down, she folded her arms around the elder of the boys and hugged him tight, before standing up and taking the younger child from his nurse's arms and cradling him to her own chest.

Edwin, watching, felt his stomach lurch. For more than three years he had been wandering, driven by his anger and propelled by his desperate need for vengeance. Now the charity and compassion, etched so beautifully on this woman's face, for children who were not of her own womb, filled him with an overwhelming need for physical comfort that went far beyond that offered by the whores he had encountered on the road.

## The kingdom of Mercia 612

They were sitting at the hearth together: Penda, Eowa and their little sister, Carinna and her husband Edwin of Deira, and their little boy, who was nearly two. Penda's brother said that this new little boy would now be the heir, but Penda pretended not to care, because he didn't really understand. All that he knew was that, of the group, only the little boy was laughing, reaching out with chubby hands to roll a ball of hardened dough across the floor until it came to rest, butted up against the flanks of one of the hounds sleeping by the hearth, and then scrambling to retrieve it without waking the beast. Whenever the boy got too close to Eowa, Eowa pinched his arm, thinking that no one could see him.

Edwin's bright blue eyes were narrowed in a frown. He was never one to laugh or even smile too often but this day he seemed unusually glum. Carinna was big and fat with her new baby, due any day; at least, that was what she told Penda every time he asked, or sometimes she would say, "*One day less than the last time you asked me, little man*," and she would smile her lopsided smile, the one that made him sure she loved him more than any other of the children, although Penda sometimes suspected that the other children felt exactly the same way. He didn't mind, because it simply confirmed his belief that she was possessed of magical powers. And Edwin shouldn't mind either and he should be happy about the baby.

Penda had been chided often enough for speaking out of turn, but had never been able to work out exactly when his turn came around. Edwin and Carinna were, in his eyes, his parents, and he didn't think he needed to wait his turn at all when speaking to them, so he asked Edwin outright what was wrong and while he waited for the answer he snuggled in to lean against Edwin's lower leg, enjoying the comfort he always gleaned from being supported by such a strong man.

33

The reply, when it came, was puzzling. "My sister has given birth to another son."

Penda said, "That is good news, is it not?"

Edwin frowned, as if he did not know the answer. He gave no direct response and said instead, "How old are you?"

"Seven. I shall be eight at the next feast of Eostre."

"The same age as Oswald. Almost to the day."

"Is he your kinsman? I should like to meet him, for we are nearly kin, are we not?"

Edwin laughed, but it was a short, sharp noise, like the one that Eowa made whenever Penda bested him at wooden sword-play. Eowa would splutter, *"I let you win. And anyway, I am the one who will be king so you need a good sword arm to be my hearth-thegn. So hah!"* And that was the same noise that Edwin had made at the thought of Penda and Oswald being kin. It was very odd.

"Don't you like your sister's son?"

Edwin reached down and ruffled Penda's hair. He said, "I hold no hatred for Oswald, or for this new child of hers, but I am worried for my sister. I do not think that she wanted to have the children."

Penda caught his bottom lip between his teeth and thought hard. He couldn't understand how wanting a child or not wanting it had any bearing on things. Once a man and a woman agreed to be bound in marriage the babies arrived less than a twelve-month later. If anyone had any say on the matter then surely it was the goddess Fríge?

Edwin smiled. "Let me say it another way. My sister was only sixteen when bad King Aylfrith the Cunning rode to our hall and took her away. She did not want to leave her kin or her home and now she lives far away, where she has no friends. She does not even know if I am alive or dead and I fear that she is lonely and afraid."

Penda looked across to the other side of the hearth

where his little sister, Audra, was playing with a wooden gaming-piece. When he cried for his dead mother on the day Audra was born, Carinna had hugged him tight and told him that, just as she would watch over him, so he must watch over his baby sister and make sure that no harm came to her. He was sad to hear about Edwin's sister and he shook his head, because he didn't want to think about such horrid things happening to Audra. He gave what he thought was a suitably grown-up, empathetic gesture, rubbing Edwin's leg and finishing the action with a manly pat, and then went to lie on his stomach next to Audra, joining in her game and taking turns to try to make the gaming-piece spin across the floor.

As the children fell asleep either in their beds or by the hearth, Carinna tucked their blankets around their shoulders. Walking over to where Edwin was standing, she tried to reach her arms around her husband's body, but her swollen belly made it impossible. Instead, she stood tall, pushed her backside out to make as much room as possible and gave him a kiss.

His mood had plummeted with the arrival of the messenger from Bernicia and the poor emissary who had travelled with the news had suffered a tongue-lashing which was ill-deserved. The man risked his life bringing information in and out of the northern kingdoms and it was hardly his fault if the tidings were not always joyful. But Edwin had been instantly contrite and she was not cross, for she knew how much he pined for his lost kin. Her unborn babe kicked and Edwin laughed, in spite of his obvious sadness.

Carinna decided to take advantage of the moment to restore his good cheer. "He is in a hurry to be with us. If the midwives are right, you might find yourself sleeping in the hall with the men tomorrow night."

He leaned in as close as he could and nuzzled her ear. "Then we should make the most of this night." Asking in whispered tones after her comfort and being assured of it, he told her he loved her.

"Ah," she said, "Love, is it?" She was smiling and though he could not see it, she hoped the gentle teasing was evident from her tone.

Between continued kisses he said, "Yes, but only from daybreak to daybreak."

She knew that in the moment of its being said, he meant every word, but she could no more forget his reason for being in Mercia than he could. He had allowed himself to be distracted, to return her affection, but she knew this latest information from Northumbria had brought his thoughts back to his task. The news had cut him and though the wound was slight, it would open out and fester as the misgivings found their way into his soul.

## *Tamworth, the kingdom of Mercia, Easter 614*

On the dawn of the day which would be as long as the night, the Iclingas of Mercia gathered not in the great hall, but by the yew tree where the temple held shrines to several deities. Within, the sanctum had been decorated and prepared according to Carinna's instructions. The temple belonged to Cærl, but it was the duty of Carinna, as the senior female of the royal house, to oversee preparations for any religious festival or ceremony. The flames which had been burning all night were extinguished, no longer needed now that the spring sunshine was appearing on the horizon.

The king was dressed in a wrap-over coat, with silk braid brocade in spun gold round the collar, part of the ceremonial regalia of the cult of Woden. The high priest stood by the shrine dedicated to the goddess Eostre, reciting incantations while offerings to the deity of spring were brought forth and placed on and around the shrine.

The gifts represented birth, fertility and growth and came in diverse forms; dried seeds, spring blooms, an early lamb and carved figures of men and women, fashioned from one piece of wood, showing the couples with intertwined limbs. Children chosen especially for the purity of their voices sang while the adults danced and drank toasts with purpose-brewed apple-wine in thanksgiving for the awakening of the earth.

They proceeded to the nearest field, where the high priest sprinkled water from the well over the ground. Edwin tried and failed to stifle a yawn. His youngest boy had been up in the night, screaming and rubbing his face and it was clear that the child's latest tooth was being bothersome. Sometimes the privilege of having his own separate sleeping quarters away from the main hall had its disadvantages and he remembered with wistful longing his life as an unmarried man, sleeping in the hall with the other young men. Carinna, as royal princess, could simply have had the children established in rooms of their own, under the care of a nurse, but she insisted on sleeping with them. She was never happier than in her role as mother, even to children not her own.

He looked at her now as she handed a small gift to Penda, who always took extra joy in celebrating the feast of Eostre, given that it also marked the passing of another year in his life.

Edwin had not known the boy's father but he must have been a tall man; Eowa, at twelve, was already as tall as some of the men at court and Penda, although still possessed of a boy's physique, was a strong sapling and looked set at least to match his brother for height. Edwin wondered if there had been some Welsh blood poured into the mix at some point, for Penda was darker than most Anglian Mercians. His hair was a dark, ruddy brown and his eyes were a shade of deep hazel.

An inter-racial relationship would hardly have raised an

eyebrow on either side of the border in the marches, for as Edwin had quickly learned, the Mercians were, for the most part, on friendly terms with their Welsh neighbours. It was another reason why Cærl had so readily agreed to assist in a retaliatory raid on Aylfrith who had given many of the old British kingdoms cause to hate the Bernicians.

With his thoughts turning once more to the north, Edwin's indulgent smile faded. Penda worshipped him, in a manner similar to those who now prostrated themselves to receive the blessings of the goddess. Edwin had done little to deserve this adoration, having wielded his sword and spear recently only in preparation for war and never in the act itself. There were no hearth-songs written for him and so far, no acts of heroism that would ensure the immortality of his name.

If Penda loved him for anything, it was his role as a substitute father, a role which Edwin had been happy enough to play, especially as Carinna was so fond of the lad. But he was an ever more frequent reminder that somewhere in the most northerly point of the Anglian kingdoms, a pretender to the Deiran throne was being nurtured by Aylfrith, being primed to usurp the rights of the true Deiran line, which had not been eradicated but still flourished, albeit in exile. As Penda grew nearer to manhood, it merely highlighted how close the bastard boy Oswald was also coming to the point where he would attempt to fulfil Aylfrith's ambition.

Carinna looked over her shoulder, unerring in her ability to sense when a loved one was troubled, met his gaze and, patting Penda on the shoulder, took her leave of the boy. She made her way towards her husband, took him by the hand and led him to a quieter place. "What is it?"

There was no point in dissembling, for she knew his moods and expressions too well to accept any dissimulation. "A message came last night, from Elmet."

"And it is bad news?"

Edwin sighed and rubbed his chin. "It is good news, for those whom it involves. My nephew, Heric, has taken a wife, and she has given him a daughter." He fell back to the comfort of his own thoughts, which needed no censoring, nor to take account of sensibilities.

Little Heric 'the Fearless' was eighteen and a father. Only last month Edwin had received the belated news that his cousin Osric had a child, a three-year-old boy he had named Oswin. Edwin had been an exile for ten years. King Cærl was good at making aggressive noises but he now had the promised grandsons and still he did nothing. For the love of Carinna, Edwin had willed himself to believe that her father would implement his part of the bargain but he could deceive himself no longer.

He felt gentle pressure on his arm and covered Carinna's hand with his own, stroking it as he played for time, trying to find the right words. For if he were to stand any chance of putting his displaced family back together again…

"You are leaving."

He looked down at her lovely face and saw the beginnings of tears in her eyes. He had not meant to fall in love; it was a complication which he had never anticipated and he had naively thought that he would be able to walk away once he had fulfilled his obligation to Cærl.

"I have been wasting time here when I should have been fighting."

He flinched as the pain flashed across her face.

"We have held you back, I know."

This was not honourable; it was like hurting a butterfly, pulling off its wings by way of thanking it for brightening a summer day. He had no words.

She continued. "I know that you have to leave, but please remember, as I will, that for a short time, you laughed and loved without cares. These years have been better for you than you know. You will look back upon them one day and be thankful that you took the time to rest awhile."

He had thought his very core to have been rent beyond repair when his family was attacked and scattered, but this felt like the wound, still unhealed, was being sluiced afresh with acid wine. She would be his undoing. Her words pricked him deeper than a thorn and his response was vocal and instant. "Come with me."

She turned round and joined him in observing the gaiety; the colourful costumes, the young girls with garlands of spring blossom, the old women who had no doubt attended her birth and the three motherless children whom it had been her duty and pleasure to care for, and he knew she was tallying up the value of everything that she would be leaving behind.

He was not even sure that Cærl would agree to their taking her sons with them, even with a promise to send them home when they came of age, but he knew Carinna would not leave without them.

She turned back to face him and said, "I will try it. But will you promise me that I can come home if I do not like it?"

Now it was his turn to feel the wet heat in his eyes. "You have my word on it."


Penda knew that he was shaking because he could feel the quivering of his shoulders underneath the firm but gentle pressure of Carinna's hands. His voice was wobbly, too, but he hoped that if he pretended it wasn't, then she wouldn't notice. "He should not be doing this," he told her.

Carinna knelt down, without releasing her grip, so that Penda was lightly dragged downwards until he was seated on the ground beside her. She hugged his head to her chest and said, "Think about how you would feel if you had not seen your little sister for ten years. Surely you must understand why he has to go."

Penda said, "But he is making you go with him and you will be far from your home and your kin. You will be like her."

Carinna took a deep breath and it pushed Penda's head out a little way before he was able to rest it once more against her body. She said, "I know it seems like two sides of a round pebble but there is more to it than you know. Edwin is torn. You are still a child, so all I will tell you is that whilst I am not happy to leave, I am happy that he wants me to go. One day, I hope you will understand."

It might very well have been two sides of the same argument, but Penda didn't believe that Edwin was torn. Carinna wasn't saying that Penda was wrong, only that Edwin wasn't wrong either. But since Penda was the one who was hurting, as far as he was concerned, that made him the one who was in the right. "I hate him," he said and, even knowing that he was too old for such behaviour, he wriggled free from her grasp and ran off to the woods, where he could sob without being seen or heard.

Aylfrith of Bamburgh watched while his steward counted out the gold pieces and handed them to the messenger. "So, he's on the move again?"

The messenger put his payment in the leather pouch hanging from his belt. "Aye, my lord. Last seen heading eastward out of Mercian land."

"And we can guess where he's going." Aylfrith rubbed his beard and frowned. "I can't take my hearth-men down there. If I am right, Edwin is about to make friends with a king too mighty even for me to take on. It will have to be done by other means."

Acha, sitting by the window light and trying to

concentrate on her sewing, fought and lost against the urge to gasp. She had been overjoyed to hear that her brother was not only still alive but thriving, if the messenger could be believed, and Edwin really was travelling with a wife and children, but it was as if a candle had been lit only to be snuffed out, for it seemed that by moving, Edwin had placed himself in danger once more. Nia, who had held her hand through both of her confinements and rarely left her side except to look after the boys, patted her hand before squeezing it. She would not dare to speak in front of the king and Acha would not have welcomed any platitudes, however well meant, but a gentle touch of support was like water for a parched flower and she smiled her gratitude.

Enfrith was sitting next to his father and now he leaned back, put one foot and then the other up on the table and crossed his ankles. He laced his hands behind his head and arched his back in an indulgent stretch. He said, "He should have stayed where he was. Now we know for sure that he has some sons and he has forced us to act."

He was nineteen, old enough to have learned some compassion and yet his heart was already cold. Acha was shocked enough to forget her customary self-preserving silence. "You would not harm children?"

Less than a twelve-month ago, Aylfrith had fought and vanquished the Welsh of Powys at Chester and this was nothing shocking. But before the battle, when two thousand monks came from their monastery at Bangor to pray for a Welsh victory, Aylfrith ordered his army to slaughter every one of them. Even as she waited for Enfrith's answer, she shuddered. If they could act with such savagery against unarmed men of prayer, they would not baulk at killing small children. She cast an anxious glance at her firstling, but Oswald was content by the fire with his favourite hounds and his little friend Manfrid, son of a leading Bernician thegn.

Enfrith pointedly followed her gaze and said, "He's safe enough. We would only worry about those who might be a threat to us."

Aylfrith chuckled his appreciation of his eldest son's joke. It was no secret what they both thought of the gentle Oswald, so blond and slim like his mother. Acha glared at Enfrith, a hard stare being the only way for her to express her disapproval, for even if she dared to criticise his belittling of her eldest boy, he would take no notice. He was bound to take his father's side, but nevertheless she hated him for it.

"This one, however, might one day come to take our kingdom from us." Enfrith reached down and scooped the baby from the floor, lifting him high so that the child's feet kicked through the air. Acha felt Nia's body tense, but little Oswii did not mind; he gurgled and giggled, his heavy little head sitting so low onto his solid little body that it looked as if he had no neck. He was forever on the move, crawling and fearlessly exploring and his father and his half-brother applauded his toughness.

Oswald moved away from the fire and came to stand next to Acha and Nia. He took in the scene with a second's stare and laid a hand on his mother's arm, giving her a tender squeeze. Acha, despite her worries, smiled. These ignorant Bernicians mistook Oswald. He did not cower next to his mother because he was a weakling; he stood by her, offering her the promise of future protection.

# Chapter Two

## The kingdom of East Anglia 615

Carinna watched the potter winding the coil of clay as the wheel slowly turned, building gradually until the shape of the lower portion of a jug began to emerge. Ever since they arrived in the kingdom of East Anglia she had been intrigued by their methods of moulding and firing their clay ware and she had plagued the potter with questions about their single-flue kilns, which baked the pottery to a strange grey colour, much harder and more durable than the pots of Mercia, which were baked traditionally on a bonfire.

She waited while the potter fashioned the upper lip of the jug, but the old man seemed to be teasing her, working more slowly now. At last he looked up and said, "Would you like to mark it my lady?"

She needed no further bidding and sat down on the ground beside him. He handed her the first of the antler stamps, carved with a simple criss-cross design and she lined it up with the lower edge of the rim before pressing firmly, as he had taught her the previous week. She suspected that her first few attempts had been surreptitiously disposed of, the clay squashed back into a lump to be re-used, because the fired piece that he had shown her a few days later looked much more skilfully worked than she remembered of her effort. Nevertheless she appreciated his patience and kindness.

There were so many more people here than in her homeland and many of them hailed from lands far away, over the sea, which in itself was a strange sight that had filled her with awe when Edwin first took her to the coast. There were rivers in Mercia, but no coastline and she was afraid, fearing that she would fall off the very edge of the world. Yet these men, some blonder even than Edwin, some with dark brown skin and even darker eyes, sailed regularly back and forth to trade with the East Anglians, while she could not begin to imagine where they went when the boats disappeared over the horizon, when even the flowers that grew on the estuary banks, the golden samphire and the sea aster, were alien to her.

The boats came and went from Ipswich, but Carinna and Edwin had settled further inland at Rendlesham where King Redwald, chief of the people of the Wuffingas, held court in a palace of magnificent proportions built a short distance away from a cluster of imposing ancient burial mounds.

Carinna had thought her own father to be a lover of grandiose displays of wealth, despite Edwin's assertion to the contrary, but the palace at Rendlesham made Cærl's look like a lowly sty in comparison.

Massive carved poles flanked the entrance, engraved with representations of ivy leaves which snaked round the upright posts from top to bottom. There were more carvings across the top of the great doorway, but these depicted snarling dogs with tails that reached and curled, intertwining with the next animal while the forelegs gripped the beast in front. The pattern of creatures, thus linked, had been made more elaborate by the addition of swirling shapes so that every space in the decoration was filled.

Inside the hall, reminders of Redwald's wealth were on permanent display. On the walls, expensive hangings that were so heavy they barely wafted when the doors and shutters were open, caught the attention of every visitor. They were woven in a style Carinna had never seen before and they shone with luxurious gold and blue threads. Wooden coffers containing vast piles of gold and silver were kept locked but always out in the open, as if to demonstrate that Redwald could afford for them to be stolen. At mealtimes the mead benches boasted gold and silver plate and Redwald and his closest kin and hearth companions drank from gold cups. They enjoyed wine and locally brewed ale but did not have the apple-wine so favoured in Mercia.

The food, too, was unlike any that Carinna had been used to. She was accustomed to the occasional meal of fish caught in the rivers of Mercia, but here she was served a menu of oysters, winkles, and mussels, until the weather got warmer and she was informed that these odd fish that lived in shells were not eaten in the summer. As she was used to having only bacon and preserved meat during the summer months unless a great feast justified the provision of fresh lamb or kid, this was no perceived hardship, but the cooks still served eels, salt cod and herring which Carinna quickly learned to loathe; although it was easier to chew than the meat she was used to, she found the flavour unpalatable.

An equally hard to acquire taste was for the strong aromatic spices brought in by the traders from overseas as gifts for Redwald and used by the cooks at Rendlesham to flavour the food.

Of the king himself, she had seen little, having met him only briefly, for she and Edwin had arrived as he was departing to the kingdom of Kent, on a peaceful mission, they were told. But Redwald was a man who made a striking impression however brief the encounter, not least because of his height, which was unusual in itself, but he was also broad and possessed of a bright white mane of unruly hair which grew not so much down as out. He prowled lightly though, for all his bulk, like a wild animal stalking prey. His chin was strong and his brow was pronounced and whilst it was hard to say that he was handsome, his looks were nevertheless arresting and when he was in the room it was hard to look upon anyone else.

When Carinna first saw him he had been wearing a sleeveless tunic and his muscular upper arms were encircled with gold bands. He wore a gold necklet at his throat and his belt buckle and hand-sæx sheath were set with shining red garnets. His wife, Bertana, was almost as tall as he was and she was slim and muscular, even though she had borne at least three children.

Carinna was still unsure if she had correctly ascertained which of the tangle of young males belonged to the royal couple, for the boys ran around the settlement in a pack. Today though, they were all in the practice yard and as she walked past, Carinna wondered how Edwin would take to having to share the space with those of a less accomplished level of swordsmanship. Edwin prepared for war every day, honing his fighting skills and keeping his muscles taut and strong.

Carinna left the potter and went to stand by the fence, intending to gather up her young ones before they got in the way and annoyed their father. The boys were all together at the far end of the enclosure beyond the great hall and for the most part they were keeping their distance from the adults. Those who were nearest in age to Carinna's boys were sticking close to their new playmates, while the older ones directed them in the pretend swordplay, although they swung their own weapons with more intent and greater strength. One of them, Regnar, stopped briefly to smile at Carinna and blushed as he did so.

She smiled back, keeping her expression friendly but maternal, aware that he had taken a fancy to her and aware that she must neither encourage nor cruelly rebuff. One thing she knew for certain was that he was the second eldest and at fourteen, was on the cusp of manhood and she knew that the first thing to burgeon to full capacity was pride.

Watching them all for a while she realised that there was no immediate need to take her boys away from their fun and she leaned against the fence rail, making sure that she could now fully identify them all and thinking how much her little Mercian charges, especially Penda, would have enjoyed making friends with all these boisterous youngsters.

Of Queen Bertana's children, Siegbert was the eldest, but he was not Redwald's son. Next was Carinna's admirer, Regnar, followed closely in age by Erwald.

Younger still and of an age much closer to that of her own boys, was the little cousin, Ænna, who seemed frail in comparison to the older youths. Carinna had noted with fondness that recently, despite his obvious weakness, little Ænna had been trying to join in with the bigger ones and prove his mettle and she knew it was because his mother had recently given birth to a baby brother, named Adelar.

Ænna and his baby brother were cousins of the royal boys, sons of Redwald's brother, who was a man who realised all chance at kingship was lost to him now that his elder brother had grown-up sons of his own, and who played his part as a rich man with no job to do with easy drunken relish. Carinna had soon learned that he was harmless enough, as long as he was more than an arm's length from her backside, and she endeavoured to keep him always in her sightline when in his presence. Perhaps he was not the best father for a sensitive boy such as Ænna, being loud and boorish and not particularly interested in his offspring beyond the act of begetting them, so she was pleased to see that the lad was trying to gain Edwin's attention and had at least not grown too scared of all the adults in the settlement.

Siegbert and Regnar had gradually moved away from the younger ones and were now edging nearer to the other end of the yard where the adults were hefting spears into sacks stuffed with straw, firing arrows into pig carcasses or refining sword strokes against a willing opponent. The boys came to stand near Edwin and Lilla, who was acting as his sparring partner, and began to match their moves, stroke for stroke. Edwin laughed and increased his effort, with more deft moves and daring angles.

They appeared not to have noticed little Ænna stealthily moving alongside them and, try as he might, he could not make them engage, no matter how much he hopped from foot to foot and tried to indicate that it was his turn now.

In frustration he decided to attract Edwin's attention and he went to stand behind him, waited for his moment and then playfully whacked the flat of his wooden sword against the back of Edwin's leg. Edwin turned instinctively and fortunately realised straight away that it was only a boy who posed no real threat. Nevertheless there had been danger, both from getting caught up in the adults' fight and from strong warrior reactions.

Edwin was clearly angry and although he stayed his sword, he lifted up his leg and gave Ænna the full force of his boot, felling the child who lay in the dust and snivelled.

Carinna climbed over the fence rail and ran over to the boy, picking him up and dusting him down. "It's all right, my sweet. Lord Edwin knows you meant no harm."

The child wiped a forearm across his snotty nose and reached out to grab her proffered hand.

But before she could lead him away, Edwin said, "And mind you don't come back in a hurry. You put us all in harm's way with your silliness."

Carinna spoke quietly. "He was only trying to be like you."

"Well that's no way to learn. Still, no wonder the

youngling is so inept. His sot of a father will never teach him anything and I doubt he'll ever make much of a man with all these strapping kinsmen around him. Best show him how to weave, since he'll be more use in the sheds with the women."

Edwin's outbursts of frustration were becoming more frequent the longer they waited for Redwald's return so that he could be petitioned about supplying troops against Northumbria, but there was scant need to take his anger out on a little boy. She would not speak to him about it now though, for to gainsay him in front of everyone would only stoke his anger and make it worse. She would broach the matter later when he had calmed down and in the meantime she was sure that Ænna would soon forget all about it and would be back playing with the others again tomorrow as if it had never happened.

A horn sounded. The long blast indicated only an arrival; short blasts, urgent, would have signalled danger, although Carinna thought that it would be a brave war band indeed that dared invade the stronghold of the Wuffingas, even when their mighty king was not in residence. She called to her boys, using the pet names she had given them; she was so confused trying to learn all the East Anglian names that she had stopped using the Deiran names that Edwin had conferred upon his sons. Ash, as she called her firstborn, and his younger brother Yvo came running to her and she held their hands and made her way to the hall.

Along the way they passed the hedgerow where the bright yellow flowers of hawkweed vied with the scrambling brambles. A sparrowhawk swooped low, flying the length of the hedge in a quest to catch smaller birds unawares. Carinna pointed out the purple flowers of the throatwort and told the children that when these flowers died away it would be time for the season to turn.

Outside the great building there were crowds of

people, but few seemed willing to go inside. Everyone was looking towards the gateway which bridged the massive boundary ditch surrounding the settlement. A procession of horsemen was making slow progress towards the enclosure and leading the men was the magnificent figure of Redwald. His ceremonial battle-helm glinted in the sunshine and the attached plume of coloured horsehair waved from side to side as he moved. Jewels and gold decoration dangled from his horse's bridle and his bright red cloak fanned out behind him, billowing in the gentle summer breeze.

Following him in the cavalcade his hearth-troops looked almost as fine, many holding aloft spears which had lengths of coloured cloth tied to them. In amongst the spear carriers there were also banner-thegns, waving the scarlet and blue cloths which depicted a snarling canine on hind legs, the emblem of the Wuffingas. Bringing up the rear were the foot-soldiers, those who were not as rich as the thegns and had no horses of their own but still fought for their king. These represented only a small proportion of the men available to Redwald in battle, but this had been a peaceful expedition and all Redwald had needed was an entourage, a showy sample of the resources at his disposal.

Those on foot might not have owned such exquisite weaponry but their shields were as brightly painted, the linden-wood covered with swirls of green and yellow, chevrons of red and blue, bordered with intricate knot-work and the central metal bosses gleaming in the sun. Never had an army looked so clean and Carinna even wondered if they had halted some miles from the settlement to wipe the dust of the road from their clothing and equipment to maximise the effect.

As the horses came to a halt in the centre of the enclosure, many of those watching began cheering. Redwald dismounted and his queen, Bertana, stepped forward and held out her hands in formal greeting. The rest of the thegns handed their horses over to the care of the stable-boys and followed the royal couple as they made their way towards the hall. Gradually the rest of the throng formed into columns of rank as the folk of Rendlesham began the process of attempting to squeeze into the great communal space, although it was clear that some of them would have to take their meal sitting outside.

As honoured royal guests, Edwin and Carinna were vouchsafed a space at Redwald's table, which meant that Carinna could afford to hang back a little and not press through the crowds in an urgent quest for a seat.

When everyone was settled at last, Redwald stood up to speak. Carinna thought that there might be an immediate ceremonial gift-giving; there was no need to reward his men in the same way as he would after a battle, but perhaps he might want to continue to secure their loyalty by offering small tokens of his appreciation for their company on his long journey. She was wrong. Redwald looked around at those assembled, grinned and spread his arms wide as presage to an announcement.

"I have come back from the kingdom of Kent with a wonderful gift. I now have a new god, called the Christ."

To gasps and mutterings, he replied with a beam of delight.

Queen Bertana stood up slowly and said, "You have done what?"

Arriving at Redwald's court, Carinna had noticed that Bertana was loved and respected and it seemed that it was largely because the woman was gruff, not quick to humour, but eminently fair, sensible and loyal. Now Carinna realised that she was also slightly feared and looking at the expression on the queen's face, Carinna pitied any man who would dare to cross her. Bertana's features had constricted into something more fearsome than an ordinary frown and her expression brought to Carinna's mind the moment when liquid in a cauldron began to seethe with activity before erupting into a boil.

Redwald appeared to be oblivious to her change of mood. Still smiling, he said, "The king of Kent has promised me life after death." He folded his arms across his great chest in a gesture that suggested he thought his point well and truly made.

Bertana gave him such an icy stare that he stepped back, almost as though an icicle had, in truth, shot from her eyes and pinned him to the wall. His grin slipped from his face and his brow furrowed into a frown of puzzlement.

"You great fool. You dare to offend Woden and Tiw by taking up with this new god? Do I not oversee the temples well enough? Life after death you say? Hah! When they bring your pieces back from the battlefield I will honour you in such a way as no man will ever forget you. Your name will live on, have no fear." She lowered her voice and muttered so that only those closest to her could hear. "And if you do not stop this silliness, you might find those hearth-songs being sung rather sooner than you hoped."

Redwald sounded less assured now. With questioning intonation, he said, "Well, there is no harm in adding another god." He closed his mouth and Carinna had to work hard to suppress a smile; he looked like her boys when they descended into a sulk after a telling-off. He puffed out one last gasp of defiance. "There is strength in numbers. I will add a shrine to the god Christ and it will sit alongside those to Woden, Tiw and Thunor. We will be better protected for having another god."

Bertana sniffed her contempt for the suggestion. "Those who worship this Christ call him a king. This will lessen your power. I do not see how this will do us any good at all." She pointed her finger at him. "There should be none but you who is called king."

The great man looked a little sheepish and Bertana fell to silence, mid finger-wag. She pursed her lips, scrutinised his face and then said, "What else?"

Her husband was looking past her shoulder and Bertana turned. Everyone in the hall craned their necks to see what was happening and it soon became clear that in their excitement to welcome home the warriors, none had paid much attention to the man who had travelled at the rear of the column. He now stepped forward and bowed low.

His garb was peculiar; he wore a long robe tied simply at the waist with a length of bare rope which held neither a knife nor a money pouch. The robe was long, reaching to his ankles and it was plain, un-dyed. As he bent forward it became apparent that the back of his head was bald. Carinna had seen many a proud warrior embarrassed by the loss of his hair, but never had the bald patch been perfectly circular while the remaining hair remained healthy and shiny.

The man straightened up, but his back was rounded and he had the stoop of a tall man permanently forced to lower his head to speak to those of normal height. His black hair was probably less unusual to those of Rendlesham who were used to seeing foreign traders come and go, but Carinna still found the dark colouring a novelty. The man's face was thin and his nose was long and curved, like an eagle's beak. Indeed, with the bobbing of the head he did look like a bird. Carinna looked away, unsettled. The strangers who jumped from the boats at Ipswich had exotic colouring and equally vibrant clothing and their whole being spoke of rich variety, other worlds, dark and enticing. But this man was deliberately devoid of colour, displaying not wealth but almost proudly declaring poverty and yet he clearly was not a slave. There was no place in Carinna's understanding of the world for such a man as this.

Redwald stepped forward and held out his arm. "This is Paulinus. He is the king of Kent's priest and he has come to tell the folk of my kingdom the good news."

"Good news?"

Paulinus smiled. "The Gospel, my lady."

Carinna inhaled sharply. This was a Christian? She had met such men, for many of the folk in the Welsh kingdoms worshipped the Christ god and had Irish holy men preaching amongst them, but they could not be identified by appearance alone.

She continued to stare, but was distracted when Bertana followed her husband in stepping forward, looked Paulinus up and down and then Carinna would have sworn to it that she sniffed him. Bertana then reached around her husband's waist and dragged him back to the head table where only her family and royal guests could hear what she said.

"Look at your hearth-men, husband of mine. Do they look as if they are about to hear some good news? They are frightened; look at your kinsman Ulf, clutching his necklace of Thunor's hammer. And see, your brother is doing the same. All this talk of life after death makes them think that there will be no hearth-tales told of their feats. Yet they have already heard you say that you have not turned your back on Woden and Thunor, so they do not understand what this new god is for. You are richer by far than the Kentish king and there are better ways to maintain your wealth and greatness. To accept this king's god is to accept this king as your overlord and admit that you are the lesser king. Send this man away, we do not need him."

Redwald's great shoulders rose and fell as he let out a loud sigh. Then he kissed his wife and grinned at her. "I suppose that now is not the time to tell you that I promised Regnar as husband to that same Kentish king's daughter?"

Carinna watched, wide-eyed, as Bertana reached between her husband's legs.

Bertana said, "Well, my love, if you have your heart set on sending one of my sons away, then I shall have to make another to take his place and that would be a shame for you."

Redwald frowned in bewilderment and squirmed beneath her grip. "Why is that, my sweeting?"

"Because I will have to bed with another, for if you send Regnar away, I will make sure you are incapable of fathering any more sons." She squeezed, released him and walked over to the priest. "You'll have something to eat before your journey home?"

The gathering laughed, enjoying the spectacle and glad of the release of mirth, and Carinna looked across at Edwin. He was smiling, but he looked wistful, as if he had been watching the scene carefully, storing the details away to hold as memories that might one day be needed as perfect recollections. She was reminded of the first day she ever saw him and then she realised why. The thoughtful expression now was identical to the one he'd worn when he first arrived and took the time to assess Tamworth's defences, but Carinna could not see the significance for Edwin in this day's events and she turned her attention to more immediate matters.

Looking across at the children, she thought ruefully that in all the excitement, Edwin had forgotten all about little Ænna and an opportunity to apologise, or simply to make the boy feel better, had been lost.

The East Anglians were newly returned from a border skirmish and Edwin was a guest at the gift-giving and tribute ceremony. Redwald was sitting on his magnificent gift-stool, carved out of a single oak tree and decorated with ornate engravings of the canine rampant, his personal emblem. He had given gold jewellery to his steadfast followers and received tribute from a representative of the tribe of the Middle Angles, who, Edwin quickly deduced, had no actual king but seemed content to rely on the strength of their most immediate neighbours.

Sombre music was being played on the lyre, a particularly dreadful dirge. Not many were listening but it added to the solemnity of the occasion. Each exquisite piece of jewellery seemed more beautiful than the last. The ale, brewed specially for the occasion, was strong and heady and Edwin felt the room begin to swim. As soon as he could, without giving offence to his host, he nodded at Lilla and Diethelm and made his way to the private dwelling set aside for him and his family, and found Carinna within.

She was sitting by the open door, using the light to sew by and Edwin suddenly felt mildly irritated by this good woman who always managed to make herself useful. Why couldn't she just for once enjoy being an honoured guest, instead of feeling that she had to pay for her bed and board?

He flung himself on the bed and crossed one ankle over the other. "If I had riches like Redwald, I could get my kingdom back in no time at all."

Carinna did not look up from her sewing but quietly said, "Don't you mean Heric's kingdom?"

"Yes," he said, "of course I did." But Heric was a little boy whilst he, Edwin, was thirty years old now and impatient to make his mark on the world.

She still retained her annoying habit of being able to read his thoughts. "Heric is a grown man and father now."

Edwin sat up, leaning back on his elbows. He worked his mouth a little while he framed his answer. "Yes, but I was the eldest male heir. Heric's father was king, yes, but he was only a boy when his father, my brother," he emphasised the fraternal connection, "was killed. Had we not been forced to flee, I would have been the next king."

Carinna looked up and peered at him. "I can see from your eyes that you truly believe this, but I think the ale in Redwald's hall has addled your thinking. May the gods see to it that you are sober come morning time."

Edwin felt his body stiffening and his arms tensed. How dare she question his integrity, he who had fought unendingly to avenge his family? "Kings like Redwald have power in wealth and trade. This is their way; they have friends in kings across the water. The king of Kent is the oath-sworn friend of the king of Frankia and he has daughters who can weave the peace and take wealth and influence to their new kingdoms when they marry."

Tears glistened in Carinna's eyes. "I recall that King Cærl of Mercia had such a daughter. I wonder what became of her?"

"She came with me to this great kingdom and found naught better to do than carry on with her way of fussing round the children." Funny, but Edwin had never before noticed how cloying her mothering tendencies could be. He shook his head, trying to sharpen his focus but the room remained fuzzy. He lay back down on the bed and slept.

## The kingdom of East Anglia 616

It might be the last occasion that year when they could plunge the linen into the river and wash it without their hands turning blue from cold. Already the days were shortening and the swallows would soon fly off to their winter home beneath the lakes. Oak-apple galls had appeared on the oak trees and witches broom on the birches. The hedgerows held rich pickings of haws, sloes, elderberries and old man's beard. The teasels would not be in flower for much longer and the cackling screech of courting foxes could be heard regularly. The stag rut would begin soon enough and already in the early morning the spider webs were silvered with dew.

Queen Bertana was amongst the washerwomen, for it was a time-consuming task and she was not above giving assistance when required. Carinna stayed to help for as long as she could before she returned to assist in the kitchens. Rarely idle, the women of the settlement were busier than usual making ready for the forthcoming harvest celebrations.

Carinna was a frequent visitor to the sacred sites, the trees, hilltops and wellsprings that marked natural points of worship for the deities of Eostre, Tiw and Thunor, where she felt a strong tie to her Iclinga kin who bowed before similar earth-shrines back in Mercia, but now she walked past Redwald's purpose-built temple to Woden and wondered what would happen over the next few days, when preparations were complete.

The festival of Eostre the previous spring had been an odd affair, with ceremonies arranged by Bertana taking place next to the newly added Christian shrine. Redwald had taken his wife's advice not to convert and thus admit inferiority to the king of Kent, and was never to be seen worshipping at the new altar, but he refused to destroy it, for reasons of expediency, and Carinna knew that it was a source of tension between Bertana and the king.

The spring festival had reminded Carinna of Penda and now, recalling the occasion, she wondered sadly once more how he was faring. She imagined that he would remain closer to his little sister than he would to his domineering elder brother but she also wondered if, at the age of eleven, he was beginning to fight back. She suspected not; little Penda had a developed sense of justice and he would only punish his brother if he felt he had just cause. Being thumped simply because he was younger might make him cross, but only a more serious injustice, probably one in which someone other than Penda was the victim, would spur him to retaliation.

She walked into the hall, intent on gathering up empty bread baskets to return to the kitchens and was almost at the head table beyond the great central hearth before she realised that Redwald was entertaining guests.

She turned her body to face the door, showing that she was not listening, but she was, nevertheless, curious. The men were foreign, undoubtedly, but they were not from over the sea. They might have been Saxons, but their dress suggested that this was not the case and they were fair-haired like most Anglians. She did not recognise the men, but with her thoughts so recently focused on her loved ones at home, she wondered whether they were Mercian messengers with bad news concerning her kin.

Redwald looked grave as he pawed his thick beard, evidently considering their words.

Carinna collected the baskets, straining her eyes by looking sideways so that she could see as much as possible without turning her head and looking directly at the group of men.

The king said, "Edwin came to my kingdom last year and within days you turned up and I sent you away. You came back again before winter set in and still my answer was no. What makes you think that I will say yes when you ask a third time?"

The visitor nearest the king said, "King Aylfrith has spent the year strengthening his army and taking tribute from yet more conquered British kingdoms." He leaned forward. "You heard, I assume, about his win at Chester?"

Redwald grunted. "I heard that he slaughtered a few unarmed monks. My youngest boy could have done as much and more."

The other man let the insult go. "He says he can offer you a choice. You can agree to hand Edwin over to us, for which you will be paid handsomely, or you can turn us away and unleash the raven of death to swoop not only over Edwin but the whole of your kingdom."

Carinna shuddered, desperate in her sadness for Edwin that he was doomed once again to fail to win support from a king who had offered him sanctuary. How far must he travel to evade Aylfrith's murderous reach? It had been more than ten years; surely this bloodlust on Aylfrith's part was dishonourable?

A defiant voice spoke newly and briefly to her, urging her to act, but she had long ago accepted in her heart the bitter truth that as a woman she could not help him. Her marriage was meant to be the seal on an alliance that would see Mercia march with him upon the north, but she had to acknowledge that her father had proved untrustworthy in that regard. Her usefulness had long ago been spent, with no purchase made.

Eyes burning wet, she turned and made her way out of the hall. All she could do was to warn her husband and help him to pack.

She found him, as always, with his companions Lilla and Diethelm, practising his swordsmanship. He was initially annoyed to be disturbed, but she made no apology on this occasion. "There are men in the hall persuading Redwald to betray you. You must leave."

Edwin cast a glance to the corner of the yard where the boys were playing.

"You need to flee with all speed," she said. "No harm will come to your sons. Queen Bertana will make sure of that. Come back for them when it is safe."

He went with her to their dwelling where she helped him to pack essential items and they were on their way to the gates when Bertana swept through the gateway. She looked at Edwin, Lilla and Diethelm, dressed for travel and then at the visitors' horses tethered nearby. "What has happened while I have been at the river?"

Carinna told her, and had barely finished speaking before Bertana said to Edwin, "Wait here." She marched into the hall and Edwin did as he had been bidden while his companions waited by the gates. Carinna stood with him, wondering if she should continue with her plan to fetch the boys so that they could say farewell to their father but decided that she would be of more use if she repeated her eavesdropping.

Bertana was in full flow by the time Carinna arrived in the hall. She berated Redwald for forgetting his earlier promise to protect Edwin. "This will bring shame on your name and our house." She reminded him of his folly in agreeing to bow to the king of Kent. "And only last month we heard that this king was already dead before the end of winter. So what good has that done you?" She turned to the messengers and told them simply to go away. As they backed off she stepped forward and grabbed Redwald's arm, raising it high. "This is the arm of a mighty warrior. The king of Kent is dead; now there is only you and Aylfrith. Will you bow to him, or will you use the strength in this arm to show him who should now be the most mighty and revered warrior king in all the Anglian kingdoms?"

Redwald scooped her up in his arms and kissed her. "I was thinking but the same thing myself, good wife. I would rather have a friend like Edwin sitting on the throne of Deira than a slimy runt like Aylfrith. I always get cross with the children when they will not listen to the word 'no'. This Aylfrith has annoyed me with his refusal to accept my answers. Perhaps I should go and tell him face to face, that he might hear me."

The autumn sun was rising in the sky behind them. The harvest was in and the East Anglians would not go hungry over the winter. Many of the women would, however, be spending those dark cold months on their own, newly widowed. Redwald's army was huge, but there would inevitably be casualties and those closest to the king and to Edwin would be most at risk. The success of a kingdom rested on the king's abilities and such a figure was always the main target on the battlefield. If they should lose, if Redwald and Edwin both lost their lives, Aylfrith would have hearth-songs sung about him forever. But for Edwin, the risk was as nothing compared to the chance to go home.

Buoyed by the sight, sound and smell of Redwald's army he began to think of the obstacle to his hopes as a tiny stepping stone, the killing of Aylfrith merely a minor task to be tackled on his way back to his homeland and the chance to gather what was left of his kin around him once more.

As he waited outside Redwald's hall on the day Bertana sent the assassins away, he had thought he heard a stranger's voice on the wind, telling him to hold on to all hope, and he had obeyed that command as he made ready for war. A stab of guilt pierced his optimism as he thought of the family he was leaving behind, fated to wait in eerie silence while the smith was away and the forge remained cold, but he could not take his wife and small sons into battle and there was no safe place for them in the north until Aylfrith was defeated. When that happened, he would send for them.

They made staggeringly impressive progress. They knew that they could move unhindered through Mercian land, since Edwin was technically their ally, even now, but Redwald revealed his wiliness by deciding to use the old Roman road rather than using the paths through areas of wildwood. Choosing speed over cover was not the obvious action and Redwald shared the Anglian wariness of all things Roman, but he saw the advantage of travelling at speed and the road from Lincoln to Doncaster was well enough maintained to allow them to reach the border a full two days ahead of Edwin's calculations. And now Edwin stood a mere river crossing away from his homeland.

On the western bank of the River Idle lay Mercia, on the eastern bank, Deira. After a dry summer and ahead of any autumn rains, the river was not swollen but they would still need to use the ford. The Romans had built a bridge by fabricating a causeway of oak timbers resting on a layer of gravel.

An East Anglian scout was on his way back from the far bank, swimming almost unseen through the water, sleek in his strokes as an otter, barely breaking the water and making no more noise than a water vole scurrying in and out of its bank-side holes. He emerged from the water and two thegns stepped forward with a blanket. Redwald walked over to hear his report and then rushed to Edwin, clasping him firmly by the shoulders.

"The gods are here with us on this side of the river, my friend. Aylfrith is but half a mile beyond the ford, waiting for his messengers to return with my answer. He has a small host of Bernician hearth-troops with him, but he is prepared only for a raid to catch a prince, not for a pitched battle."

Edwin's stomach leaped and caused a flutter in his chest. "Let's go," he said.

Redwald tightened his grip slightly. "Not so fast, young friend. Woden and Tiw may be smiling on us today, but there is more we can do to make sure we win. We know now that it is safe to use the bridge. Give me the rest of the day and half the night."

Even as he spoke, four more men were slipping quietly over the bridge, melting away in the half-light as they ran into Deira. Redwald watched them go and nodded his satisfaction. He said, "Leave Aylfrith for now. The men he awaits will float past sooner or later, if their bodies have bloated up enough by now. Meanwhile, let my men talk to the men of Deira and ask them what they would do if they knew that Edwin stands on the riverbank waiting to retake his kingdom. My guess is that when Aylfrith rushes at us and swiftly feels a need to run away again, he will find the men of Deira are holding a spear or two at his back."

Morning broke crisp and clear. Edwin watched as the sun rose on the far bank and saw, in silhouette, the outline of Aylfrith's much smaller army. The rising wind brought the clamour to him, of voices loud in consternation, the hammering of hasty repairs and strengthening in the urgently erected forge, the testing of shields by thumping the blunt end of spears against them.

Gradually the thumping became more rhythmic as men began to take up their weapons and hold them aloft. Now they banged the spear hafts against their shields, beating a steady rhythm in keeping with their war cry. Chants of "Aylfrith, Aylfrith," carried across the floodplain on the breeze, designed to instil fear into the hearts of those on the opposite bank. The only effect on Edwin was to set his already hardened heart into a solid lump of hatred. Hot angry blood pulsed in his arms and legs; he was ready to lunge at Aylfrith and tear his head from his shoulders.

Young Regnar, Redwald's eldest son and heir to the kingdom of East Anglia, came to stand next to him. He, too, was wearing a mail coat; as royalty he was a prime target and it would be foolish not to go into battle thus protected. His cheeks were flushed and his eyes shone. He nodded towards the opposing forces and said, "A good day for a fight is it not?"

Edwin nodded, but said, "Any day would have been a good day for this fight. It has not come soon enough for me."

Regnar chuckled. "A man might think that you had a reason for wanting this particular fight."

Edwin was not in the mood for badinage, but he recognised that this was probably the lad's first major battle and the gallows humour was an important preparation, a ritual encompassing the stark acknowledgement that these words might be their last. He said, "No, I have no reason. I merely see that there is a bridge to be crossed and a man stands in my way. I might have to brush him aside. It should take no more than a moment."

"Ah well, in that case, I don't suppose you will need my sword arm. Nevertheless it looks pretty enough on the far bank. Perhaps I will follow you, since I have nothing much else to do today."

A horn sounded. Men, having lined up on either side, stared at the bridge. Whoever rushed the crossing first would have the advantage, if they could clear the bridge in time, but they ran the risk of being caught on the causeway with no clear space behind them into which to retreat. Like a child's blinking contest, it was a waiting game.

Edwin squinted against the rising sun and thought he saw a glint of royal gold shining in the morning rays. Then he saw nothing but a red shroud between his eyes and the battle site and he let out a scream that was twelve years in the brewing. He felt his stomach twist, his lungs burning, his chest straining. And he ran, not pausing to see if any of the East Anglians were following him, aware only that Lilla was next to him. He raced across the bridge, heart pounding, feet stomping, then the sound was amplified and replicated and he knew that others were following.

Once over the bridge he hurled himself upon the nearest Bernician, flooring the man without injuring him. By the time the man got back onto his feet Edwin had brought his sword down onto the neck of the man who had been standing next to him, slashing down into his shoulder and severing his head from his body. The first man attempted to exact revenge but Edwin caught the motion from the corner of his eye and battered him away with his shield, the metal boss smashing into his would-be assailant's face and sending him flying back once more. Edwin would waste no more time on him and he pressed on, stabbing and slashing with his sword as he went.

Finding a moment of pause he turned to look behind him and saw the East Anglians still spilling over the bridge and that not a single Bernician had gained ground against them. Aylfrith's men were desperately attempting to force them back against the bridge. Edwin could no longer see Regnar but the magnificent figure of Redwald was easy enough to pick out, his gold trappings glinting in the sunlight and his sword dull with smears of Bernician blood.

Now the Bernicians seemed to have given up all hope of reaching the bridge and turned their attention to the East Anglians who had already crossed over. Edwin bent low and butted his way past two of them, before he had to stop and engage with the next, who jabbed and poked with his spear. Edwin was now at a disadvantage with his shorter weapon, but he waited until the next thrust and then he dropped to his knees, bringing his sword up between his adversary's legs and pushing hard. The man collapsed and Edwin moved on, slashing and slicing, wishing only that these idiots would get out of his way so that he could find his prize.

A giant blocked his path; legs planted widely apart, the man was swinging an axe and as it came round in an arc, Edwin ducked down to swing underneath it. As the momentum turned his assailant's body to the side, Edwin stabbed his sword into his flank and as the huge man sank forward onto his knees, Edwin brought the sword across the back of his neck. Booting the body out of his way, he ran on.

Sweat was trickling down from the rim of his helm and he had to stop and wipe it, for the salty stream was stinging his eyes and impairing his vision. As he wiped, he took the opportunity to assess the progress of the battle, scanning the area from left to right and then daring a glance behind him to see what was happening back at the bridge. He turned to face the Bernician camp once more.

Then from across the battlefield Edwin saw a flash of plumed helmet and knew that he had Regnar back in his vision. But Regnar was squaring up to a warrior who was kitted out almost as opulently as Redwald. Through the distance of years, Edwin recognised Aylfrith the Cunning who was now grinning at the young East Anglian prince, taunting him, daring him to do his worst.

Edwin knew Regnar's skill. He had watched him often enough in the practice yard, but he knew he was no match for a grizzled war veteran such as Aylfrith. And so it proved, horribly swiftly. Lilla, coming up from behind, ran to help but was not fleet enough. Regnar thrust his sword at Aylfrith but the older man feinted to his right and wrong-footed the East Anglian. Aylfrith brought his shield up, butted Regnar with it and the younger man lost his grip on his shield. Instinctively Regnar put his left arm up in defence as he tried to score a hit with his sword, but Aylfrith was taunting him now, slapping his left arm with the flat of his sword blade.

Edwin, watching, winced, knowing that even the flat of the blade would break the thin bones of the forearm. Regnar's left hand now hung limply. Aylfrith paced to left and right, circling back to leer at Regnar between each step, as if he were a cat trying to decide what to do with a mouse, but the decision was taken from him when a Bernician warrior, running past, turned and spotted the vulnerable youngster and thrust a spear point into his ribs. He yanked on it to free the weapon and continued on his way.

Regnar was still standing but Aylfrith had clearly tired of his game and now brought his sword round in a wide arc and with a double-handed swipe, brought the blade across the boy's shoulder where it bit deeply into his neck.

From far away, King Redwald yelled out an anguished roar that did not sound as if it came from a human thing. Regnar sank to his knees as if his legs had simply melted underneath him. His body stayed upright for a heartbeat before it tilted forward and the boy lay face down in the dirt to breathe no more. Edwin turned to see Redwald thundering past him and launching himself at Aylfrith. The force knocked the Bernician off his feet and for a while the two of them were lost from Edwin's view.

He was now the focus of interest from a group of Bernicians who perhaps mistakenly thought that Regnar was the East Anglian leader. If so, his life having been taken, they must have assumed the battle to be won and their bloodlust was partially sated. Edwin was humble enough regarding his fighting skills to know that it was their diminished interest that probably saved him. Two of them took a swipe at him with their swords as they ran, but he dodged one and returned the other, connecting with the second blade swinging towards him. There was a song of metal colliding with metal, but these men seemed more intent on pillaging the corpses behind Edwin and they ran past and bothered him no more.

When he was free to look across the field again he saw that the two kings were on their feet once more. Aylfrith was clutching his side, indicating that Redwald had inflicted a similar blow to the one which had begun the end of his son. Now the two men were engaged in sword-battle and from the murderous looks on both their faces there was no guarantee that either would survive.

Redwald shoved with his shield, smashing it into Aylfrith's face and splitting his nose. Aylfrith spat blood and teeth and tried to catch the side of Redwald's head with a swing of his sword. Redwald had not fully lowered his shield and was able to bring it up to deflect the blow, whilst at the same time he stepped forward and thrust his sword, aiming for Aylfrith's midriff. Aylfrith lowered his shield slightly to be sure of catching the blow and in less time than it took to blink, Redwald had swung his sword up and round and brought it crashing down on the exposed side of Aylfrith's neck.

Blood shot in a spectacular gaudy arc and Aylfrith staggered like a drunk before crashing to the ground. Redwald denied him the few moments' peace that a merciful stab to the heart might have brought, instead choosing to watch as the blood pumped from the Bernician's body. Yet still Aylfrith seemed not to concede defeat, struggling to rise up on one elbow and trying to grab at his hand-sæx as if he had it in mind to thrust upwards with the short blade and jab Redwald in the leg. Redwald stood his ground, watching these last pathetic attempts, until with a final twitch the Bernician's head fell back on the grass and he was still.

Edwin was still panting, his every inhalation an inadequate snatch of air that scarcely filled his lungs. As he tried to steady his breathing he knew that he had witnessed a consummate warrior bring down a foe who was no milksop boy but a worthy opponent. Redwald, by no means a young man, had plenty to teach those who might aspire to emulate him. But, impressive as it was, the skilful despatching of Aylfrith now left Edwin feeling cheated, as if it had been he who had flushed out the deer only for another man's arrow to pierce its hide.

He had but a short time to allow the thought to take root though, because as he started to walk over to join Redwald, the most powerful king south of the Humber, who now could lay claim to the whole of the north should he choose to withhold it from Edwin, sank to his knees by the body of his son and keened.

His wails caught on the wind and Edwin turned to see that all those who were still fighting on or near the bridge had stopped and lowered their weapons, aware that for better or worse, the fight was over. Redwald's head went back and he howled like a wounded bear. He threw off his helm and pulled out handfuls of his hair and then closing his fists around them, leaned forward and pummelled the earth until his knuckles bled.

Never had Edwin travelled so far north. Instincts clashed as his desire to reacquaint himself with his homeland of Deira competed with his urgent need to ride north until he found his sister.

He rode hard, accompanied by a band of Deiran thegns who had gathered to him; some of them were kinsmen of Lilla and his brother Diethelm and some were simply loyal to the Deiran royal house. Edwin feared what would happen if he stopped and he urged his horse on, not daring to pause. Bloodlust had driven him thus far and had not fully been satisfied after he was robbed of the chance to kill Aylfrith. For so many years he had been impotent, unable to do any more than dream and plan. Now he could not stop until those plans were executed and his kin were back together once more.

Aylfrith's fortress at Bamburgh stood stark and forbidding, balancing on the rocks that rose high above the sea. The approach to the timber hall was via a gatehouse above steps through a cleft in the rocks. This was the only gap in the walls, built strongly of stone. It would be hard to enter such a place unnoticed but even so, Edwin thought it lax that there were no men stationed in the gatehouse. The palace appeared to be deserted; even the stables were quiet, with no tell-tale snorting or stamping.

Edwin strode across the yard to the great hall and

shoved hard against the heavy oaken door. The mead benches were set neatly and the king's stone-carved throne had been placed carefully at the centre of the head table, but there was no one there. The hearth was cold and dead. Edwin scanned the room briefly and turned on his heel. He heard a tiny sound, like the whimper of a puppy.

He stopped, mid-step, and slowly began to unsheathe his sword. He listened and thought he detected a scuffling noise emanating from the corner of the hall. Walking around the benches, sword poised, he peered into the dark recess behind the support pillar at the back of the room. Cowering, knees drawn up in a defensive crouch, a servant was hiding, shaking with terror.

Edwin sheathed his sword and beckoned the servant to her feet. "Where are the folk who live here?"

The servant lowered her eyes. "Gone, my lord. They did not want to stay and suffer your wrath."

Edwin was taken aback. It had been such a long time since he had been addressed as a commanding warrior. For the last eleven years any deference shown to him had been as that shown to a guest of high status, but one with no real power. Now this woman was standing in awe and trembling. Edwin was also irritated. Did this person seriously believe that he would exact revenge on a lowly servant? "Aylfrith is dead, as are most of his hearth-men. Whoever stayed behind here and did not follow him into battle is not worthy of my wrath. I merely seek my sister."

The servant frowned. "Your sister, my lord?"

Edwin's impatience grew. "Yes, my sister, the lady Acha. Where is she?"

The servant's face registered such a strange combination of relief and anguish that Edwin felt a sharp cold stabbing in his stomach. "Where is she?"

Now the servant wept. "We heard that King Aylfrith had been defeated by King Redwald. We never dreamed that you would come. King Aylfrith sent men to pay Redwald to kill you. My lady was so afraid."

"But I am not dead, as you can see. And I have come to take her home."

"She... She is..." The servant could barely speak. "Follow me, my lord."

Edwin followed her out of the hall and back across the palace yard, past the well, to a small stone chamber, dimly lit with tallow lamps. Laid out on a pallet, his sister's body lay with hands serenely clasped. She was dressed in a plain linen shift and her hair had been lovingly combed. Even in the inadequate light Edwin could see a long gash stretching from her temple to her lower jaw. The wound was open and gaping, but was dry. There would have been a lot of blood, but it had been wiped away and her face cleaned. Great care had been taken to find autumn-flowering blooms and on her chest had been laid a posy of groundsel and ivy-leafed toadflax.

Edwin tried to swallow and found that he couldn't because there was a huge constriction at the back of his throat. He blinked furiously and then managed to speak. "Tell me."

"My lady was sure that Aylfrith's killers had done their work. The king went south and all we heard afterwards was that King Redwald had won the battle. My lady believed that whoever killed Aylfrith would ride north and claim ownership of all his chattels, including her. She would not suffer to be befouled again and so she threw herself upon the rocks."

Edwin nodded and reached forward gently to stroke his sister's ice-cold hand, using the time to regain control over his voice. "Where are her sons?"

"Begging forgiveness, my lord, but Lady Acha thought that their lives were at risk so she sent them away. I am Nia and I have cared for her boys since they were born. My man, Bran, he who taught them to sit astride their horses as soon as they were big enough, took them across the border with my lady's blessing. Had she known it was her own brother who was coming, then she would have kept them here, knowing that there was naught to fear."

Edwin said nothing. Staring at his beloved sister's body, he could not be sure enough of his answer. He would never know what he would have done to young boys who, whilst they were his sister's flesh and blood, were nevertheless Bernician rivals to the Deiran throne. The knowledge that he would not have to make that decision was the only relief and there was nothing else to cheer. He was home, he had won, but it was a hollow victory; he had come too late.

He went back outside and the biting wind sliced into him. He gathered his cloak around his stomach and held it tight. Stepping back into the hall he walked the length of the building and studied the stone chair, imagining Aylfrith sitting in it and forcing Acha to serve his drinks. He would order it taken outside and broken up, thus ensuring that no Bernician arse ever sat on it again.

Striding out of the great doorway he made his way to the wall-walk and stood on the wooden platform between the fence and the wall which surrounded the compound. He gazed out to sea and watched for a while as seabirds swooped and dived along the edge of a barren island a short distance from the coast. He looked down towards the rocks and imagined he knew exactly how Acha had felt before she jumped. Who knew more than he how painful it was to be bereft of all kin? At least he had found some peace, some happiness even, during his sojourn in the southern kingdoms. There had been no such respite for his sweet young sister, and he had no way of avenging her death.

Lilla came to stand alongside him. "My lord, I hardly dare disturb you but I have news from Elmet." He beckoned for the man to come forward and as soon as he was in reach, Lilla grabbed his shoulder and forced him down onto his knees. "Speak, then, if you dare, you Loides bastard."

Edwin raised an eyebrow at the rough manhandling, but Lilla said, "He thought to find Aylfrith here and came running with what he thought was good news. Now he shits himself at the thought that he must instead give his message to you."

Edwin listened, but found that he was more mindful of the snivelling courier than the faltering words he spoke. As the details spilled forth, Edwin focused on the patch of ground in front of the miserable man, finding that if he followed the patterns of the stones and concentrated sharply, the wound inflicted by the words was less intense. But the truth remained, however he chose to shield himself from its impact. Heric, his nephew and heir to the Deiran throne, was dead. That old bastard excuse for a king, Ceredig, convinced that Aylfrith would triumph over Redwald, and unwilling to be found still to be harbouring a Deiran, had murdered him the coward's way, with poison.

Lilla said, "I am sorry, my lord. This has not been the homecoming you wished for."

Refraining from commenting on the understatement, Edwin curled his hands into fists and held his arms firmly against his sides. Staring out across the water, he whispered into the wind. "Why did no one have faith in my ability to win?" Because he had been gone too long, because he had allowed himself to be distracted, and because he had waited while lesser men made promises that they took too long to keep.

Edwin, Lilla, Diethelm and a small company of battle-hardened thegns rode more fleetly than the wind as they raced across the lowlands of Deira towards Elmet, stopping only to slaughter any messengers carrying news of the battle of the River Idle, despite their instincts telling them that Ceredig would have heard the truth by now. The only wonder was that he had got the wrong news in the first place, given the proximity of Elmet to the battle site. It was Edwin and his kin who had paid heavily for this misinformation, but Edwin repeated the vow as he rode, that his would not be the only life left in ruins by Ceredig's act of cruel cowardice.

They were astounded to find that the great fortress at Leeds was undefended. They came to a halt outside the hall and Ceredig, old and bent, came out to welcome the victor of the battle, the autumn wind catching his white hair and blowing it across his face.

Taking care down the steps from the door, he only looked up when he came close enough to see the new arrivals clearly. It was obvious that he had been expecting a familiar friend; he stopped and smiled, eyed his visitors, and his brows knotted in puzzlement briefly before realisation dawned and his jaw dropped open.

Edwin shuddered, not with cold but with revulsion, stepped forward and, without ceremony, drew his sword and swung it in a wild arc above his head, bringing it crashing down upon the old man's shoulder, digging at an angle and cleaving his raddled body from neck to pelvis. He lifted his foot and shoved with his boot against the corpse, pushing it to the ground and pulling back on his blade at the same time.

"Osric!" Edwin was hardly aware that it was his own voice calling, as if his mouth was working ahead of his brain. His thoughts caught up and he began dashing between the huts, flinging back the door curtains and shouting for his cousin. In a small building at the end of the enclosure he thrust the door-hanging aside and shouted once more. "Osric!"

"He is not here."

Edwin stepped into the hut, blinking while his eyes

adjusted to the dim light within.

The woman who had spoken was sitting neatly on a small bed, her feet flat on the floor and her hands clasped in her lap. Sitting on the floor beside her feet, a small child was staring up at him, sucking on the corner of a rag of cloth and twisting the end which dangled below her mouth, tangling it around her tiny fingers.

"Where is he? Has that murdering bastard killed him too?"

The woman said, "No, but Osric feared for the life of his son and he took him to safety after my husband was slain."

Edwin stepped forward. "Your husband? Heric?"

She nodded but made no other reply.

Edwin's powers of cognition were being freshly assaulted and he shook his head as he tried to absorb this new information. "Is this his child?"

Heric's widow nodded once more, but this time she spoke as well. "This is his daughter. Her name is Hild." She gestured vaguely at a cot in the corner of the room and he saw that there was a baby fast asleep in the cradle. "That one is Haryth."

Grief merged with wonder as Edwin stared at the little girls. This, then, was all that was left of his kin. "Why did he not take these children to safety also?"

"He wanted to, but I refused to leave, and he deemed the children better left in their mother's care. Osric was such a kind man. Did you know him?"

"Know him? He was my kin, you silly…" He did not complete the insult. Exasperating as it was, he realised that this woman would never again inhabit the world in a way that would enable her to make sense of events unfolding around her. She had seen too much and decided that she would see no more.

She said, "I dreamed that they had taken my Heric away and although I searched and searched I could not find him. As I sought in every corner, I felt something below my dress and there was the brightest necklace you ever saw. It gleamed and shone and filled the room with brilliant light and I knew then that though my husband was lost to me, the gods had a purpose for my daughter. I heard a voice telling me never to give up hope. I knew then that my father would not harm my child."

"Your father? Ceredig?" Now Edwin shook his head in disbelief. His own father-in-law may have proved to be a bitter disappointment but at least he had not stooped to murdering him and leaving Carinna a widow. The thought of Carinna reminded him of the last time he was with her, waiting outside Redwald's hall to hear his fate and hearing a sweet voice of encouragement. He told the woman, "If Osric and his son are gone, then these children are all that is left of my northern kin. I will take them back to Deira with me."

Heric's widow did not shift from her prim seated posture but her thumbs parted briefly before settling back on her clasped fingers. "I have said that I will not leave."

"There is nothing left for you here. I will take the king-seat and Elmet will be no more."

She shrugged. "War is for men, but it is the women who suffer."

Her calm acceptance irritated him briefly. It was a good thing, he thought, that it was the men who fought; the women simply surrendered to their fate. Anger sent the taste of bile to his throat. He did not want to be reminded of the softness of women who stood meekly by, or who were left so defenceless that they leaped upon rocks to escape. He would fain have a sword in his hands than have any more time alone to think of such things.

"If you will not come, I shall take the children anyway."

She would barely notice the loss, he concluded. He squatted in front of the child who considered him with the same wide-eyed stare with which she had acknowledged his entry to the hut, and she did not resist when he scooped her up into his arms. He said, "I am your Uncle Edwin and you are a princess of Deira. Come with me to see your kingdom." Shifting her so that she was sitting on his hip, he walked to the cradle and picked up the baby.

He left without a backward glance. This was what men's wars did to women, it seemed; not marking them, but destroying them. Well, let the woman stew in the cauldron of madness. He would think on her no more. Bernicia was subdued, the Loides of Elmet would be eradicated, and Deira was reclaimed. Now his reign could begin.

# Chapter Three

## Mercia 624

Penda had ridden with no thought of destination and had found himself down on the southern border of Mercia, at the confluence of the rivers Severn and Avon, looking out at the Hwicce tribelands. Not wanting to stop even then, he had journeyed on to Deerhurst and had another interesting conversation with Bardulf of the Hwicce who had been only too keen to complain to him again about the West Saxons who bordered their land to the south and had increased their raiding parties recently. The meeting had been a welcome distraction and by staying the night Penda felt as if he had put yet more distance between himself and Eowa.

The argument had been merely the latest in a long series of disagreements, but the difference was that this time, when they came to blows, Penda had been the victor. Eowa had been left with a bloody nose and his claim of superiority over his nineteen-year-old brother had been proved to be spurious, but Penda still needed time to calm down. Cærl's court was stifling him and Eowa irritated him daily. A day or two spent idling in the autumn sunshine, taking in some fresh air and stretching his legs, might sate the need to kick out, and he had returned to the river crossing to waste some more time before setting off for home.

He stared at the water, flowing briskly after the recent rain, and he took a deep breath, inhaling all the scents of the freshly washed earth. The purple loosestrife was still in flower and he could see dragonflies and alderflies flitting across the surface of the water, but there needed to be plenty more rain after the dry summer if the harvest were not to fail again next year. There was barely a whisper of a breeze, so when he heard a rustling amongst the trees behind him, he put his hand to his sword hilt and stepped lightly over to the woods to investigate.

Behind an oak tree, a young girl was hugging tight against the tree trunk, hiding. Penda assessed her age and then recalculated as he noticed that she was pregnant, her stomach incongruously extending from her otherwise slim, almost skinny figure.

He did not recognise her, but thought that she might be a Saxon. Her hair was long and straight, coppery-brown and glossy. Her cheekbones were pronounced and her green-grey eyes lifted at the outer corners, giving her a cat-like countenance. She was dressed like a wealthy woman and wore a number of finger rings. Her dress was of the new kirtle style, not pinned at the shoulders but with a central neck opening, and it was edged with delicate golden embroidery. The cuffs of her linen under-dress showed at the sleeve-ends. Her amulet bag, the leather satchel which most folk wore, was made of the softest leather and embossed with animal designs. Her shoes, though, were also of soft leather and not designed for travel.

Alone and evidently far from home, she ought to be frightened, but he noted that if she was scared at all, she wasn't prepared to show it. She remained as he had found her, standing with her arms behind her, making no effort to protect her stomach. She looked at his sword, still sheathed, she glanced around, and the set of her mouth changed as she took a calming breath.

"You're not much of a fearsome warrior then," she said. "No hearth-men with you. Did you steal that fancy sword; are you a runaway slave?"

He laughed in surprise at her audacity. "Are you?"

She eyed him up and down and chewed her lip as if

deciding whether he might be trustworthy. "I might as well be."

He said, "That sounds like the beginning of a good tale. And by the look of you, you have nowhere to be in a hurry, so you have time to tell it."

She raised an eyebrow. "And since you have no hearthmen with you and are clearly not much of a lord, I doubt anyone is waiting for you, either, so you should have time to listen to it."

They locked gazes for a moment or two and then she smiled and he grinned back.

She slid down the tree trunk and he unbuckled his sword belt and sat down beside her, intrigued. "Where is your husband then?"

She laughed harshly and fiddled with the buckle on her amulet bag. "I have no husband."

Penda realised that she was not so much a runaway as an abandoned rape victim. What other explanation could there be?

She spoke again. "They killed him." She let go of the leather satchel and slid her hands between her knees.

He assumed she was being facetious and he was tempted to laugh, but he leaned across to look at her face, saw the sad bitterness in her eyes and knew that this was no joke. He said, seriously this time, "You have a sad tale to tell. I have the time to listen, if you would like to share it with me."

"His crime was not that he made me this shape," she patted her belly, "but that he was a Welshman. I can see that you do not believe me," she said, glancing across at him, "so that must mean you have never met my kin, or you would not be surprised." She laced her fingers and rested them on top of her distended stomach. "My father is kin to King Cyngil."

"Of the West Saxons?"

She nodded. "The same."

Penda looked back again towards the territory beyond the river, at the Hwicce tribelands whose inhabitants had more in common with the Anglian Mercians and yet were being subjected to attempted rule by the West Saxons. "I heard that not long ago he killed the three sons of the old East Saxon king."

"He is an evil bastard and his son is even worse. And with a Welsh bairn in my belly I was no more use to them."

Penda knew what she meant. Princesses of royal houses had value only as bargaining tools, to be offered in marriage to strengthen kingdoms and claims upon foreign lands. This young woman was no more than spoiled goods. He said, "I do not think that King Cyngil and I would get along."

She laughed mirthlessly. "If we ever meet again, I will pull his heart out through his arse."

Amused by her turn of phrase, he looked ruefully at his own scuffed knuckles and said softly, "I wish I had thought of that trick earlier."

She shifted so that she could take a better look at him. "So, slave-boy, how is it that you have so much time to spend by the water this day when you should be working hard for your lord?"

He shrugged. "My tale is lame compared with yours, but I will tell it. I had a fight with my brother and thought it best to ride away rather than stay and tear his head off."

"What did you fight about?"

"He is a self-loving little toad who thinks that telling me he is older and better than me and will one day be king is enough to make it so."

She drew her knees up and hugged them. "You win."

"What? How can a stupid fight between brothers be a better tale than yours? I am not bereaved and I am not cast out."

She clapped her hands together. "Exactly. My tale is at

an end. You have to go home and suffer your brother every day until you decide to kill him."

He stared at her and felt his heart lurch. "Well, Lady, when that day comes, I would be glad to have such a fearless one as you on the battlefield with me."

She tilted her head and scrutinised him once more. "In that case, you'd best take me home with you so I can have a look at this man who is to die so horribly."

He stood up and offered her his hand. "I am Penda."

She took his hand and clasped it with her slender fingers, allowing him to help her up, and he admired her anew. Her fighting talk and independent spirit were no pretence, nor was she merely putting on a brave face, for it was clear that she would accept help when she needed it and was not ashamed to let it be known.

"I had a name, but it was a Saxon name and I wish never to hear it again. So you can call me anything you like."

Penda grinned. "Anything?"

He lifted her onto his horse while he took the reins and led the stallion at a slow walk as they made their way back to Tamworth.

Travelling in silence, he had no urge to speak, feeling strangely content in this woman's company. Along the way they encountered dunnocks in search of insects in the hedges where the last flowers of the dog rose had given way to bright red hips and field voles were running in and out of the clover on the ground below. Buzzards glided overhead, claiming their territory, soaring in high circles with mewing cries. As the autumn sun sank below the horizon the temperature plummeted and even though they were little more than strangers it was as if they had forged an understanding and they slept, huddled together for warmth, wrapped in each other's arms under Penda's blanket.

They arrived at the royal settlement during the evening

of the next day and Penda led her on his stallion through the gateway. Outside the hall, he held out his arms and she slid easily from the horse and allowed him to set her gently on the ground.

Before Penda had the chance to take her inside, Eowa sauntered from the withy screen which hid the users of the latrine ditches from general view. His nostril still showed traces of dried blood and there was a livid cut across his right eyebrow. He paused when he saw his brother and his gait changed as he strode towards him. "Who's this?"

Penda said, "I found her in the woods."

Servants were carrying loaves from the bake-house and meat from the kitchen and folk began to gather for the main meal of the day. Seeing he had the beginnings of an audience, Eowa sneered and said loudly, "Looks like someone else found her first." He laughed at his own joke and was rewarded with a few titters from those who were close enough to overhear.

Penda's waif stepped away from his arms and folded her own across her chest as she surveyed Eowa. Keeping her gaze upon the elder of the brothers she spoke to Penda. "This is your brother? I had thought to find someone taller."

Eowa's smile fell away, but since her comment fell short of a proper insult, there was little he could say and he merely countered with a "Yes, well, it is time to go within."

They watched him shuffle off and she said, "You were wrong to ride away after your fight. You should have stayed and pulled his head off, after all."

Penda laughed. "I think you and I are going to get on, 'wood elf.'"

She looked at him, unblinking and said, "Your brother is a stupid turd. Your other nearest kin, if I understand you right, is one who in my kingdom is known as Cærl the Sleepy because he never moves. I would say that you are in dire need of a friend. I say again, my grief will lessen with time; yours has many years in which to worsen."

As they entered the hall, one of the hearth-thegns, Lothar, smiled and in a much more friendly tone than Eowa had employed, said, "I see you've caught a wanderer. Are you going to keep her?"

Penda, still affected by her blunt appraisal of his life, whistled in wonder and said, "Lothar, old friend, I do not think this woman will be owned by anyone."

King Cærl was already seated on his king-stool at the other end of the hall and Penda noticed how quickly Eowa had scuttled over to whisper in his ear. It was only a matter of moments before Cærl extended a bony finger and crooked it in a gesture of summons. Penda sighed and said, "The king wishes to meet you."

She shrugged. "It is his hall. I should not eat his food without first asking him for it."

They stood up together and made their way to bow before Cærl. Penda found himself looking at the king as if for the first time, as his new companion would see him. In front of him was an old man, who raised milky eyes to stare at them and spoke in a reedy voice.

"Who is this and where has she come from?"

Penda's sense of mischief overcame him and he said, "Tandderwen. Derwena."

But Cærl, who had never taken the time to converse as freely in Welsh as some of his younger kin, did not understand the translation of the place-name 'below the oak', or the name which simply meant 'oaks'. He beckoned the newcomer to step closer and he said, "Welcome, then, Derwena."

Eowa was, as usual, clinging so hard to the earlier bad feeling that it tightened his jaw and made his tone harsh. "How can you simply welcome her? Who will feed the child; will my brother take her under his roof? We do not know who she is, or anything of her bloodline."

'Derwena' gazed at Eowa and smiled sweetly. "What matter whose blood flows in me? You are the heir to Mercia, are you not?"

He grunted. "Huh. You would not think so to look at the way my brother behaves." He indicated his bloody nose.

Penda said, "Stop behaving like an arse then, if you wish me to bow to you. Until then you know where you can shove your…"

"Bastard!" Eowa threw himself at Penda and the force knocked Penda onto the floor.

Penda swiftly turned, bringing Eowa with him so that he was now on top of him. He punched him hard, once with each fist, before standing up and yanking his brother to his feet. He noted with grim satisfaction that Eowa now had a burst lip to go with his bloodied nose.

Eowa put a hand up to his mouth, felt the blood, wiped it angrily, and seemed as if he were about to appeal to Cærl to reprimand Penda, but the king had lost interest and was looking down, inspecting his food as if he had never seen cooked bacon before.

Derwena was looking dispassionately at the royal brothers, apparently unconcerned by the sight of the blood. She stepped closer and wiped Eowa's mouth with the end of her sleeve. "You see? No matter what flows through our veins, we all bleed the same."

*Tamworth - the kingdom of Mercia 625*
The spring sunshine had begun to warm the earth and new shoots were visible everywhere. Tight buds clung to the ends of the blackthorn branches and the fields were alive to the sounds of newborn lambs calling for their mothers. But the over-dry winter was not good news; folk might starve if the harvest was bad and newborn infants

would be especially vulnerable.

In the bower behind the great hall of Tamworth a woman's voice crooned in soothing tones but there was no screaming or cursing in response. Penda did not know whether to take this as a good sign, or if he should be deeply worried by the silence. He had no memory of his mother and knew only too well the perils and consequences of childbirth.

The woman said, "That's it my lovely, that was perfect and now push again."

Penda thought that her encouraging exhortation was followed by a grunt, but he could not be sure. He put his index finger to his mouth and chewed on the nail. Lothar, standing next to him, patted his shoulder but said nothing, his supportive gesture and the accompanying silence a perfect summation of his understanding of the sense of helplessness that Penda was experiencing.

The sun was directly overhead by the time his sister Audra appeared in the doorway of the bower and said, "She has a son. She has asked to see you."

Lothar slapped him on the back and went off whistling.

Inside the bower, Derwena was lying on the bed, holding a swaddled bundle. She smiled at Penda and he edged forward. Derwena said, "It is all right, he will not bite. She glanced down in the direction of her breast and added, "I hope."

Penda sat on the bed beside her and peered at the tiny form. It was not easy to tell in the dim light but it seemed as if there was a little bruising around the baby's face. His eyes were shut but he looked cross, as if he would rather have remained snug and warm in the safety of his mother's womb, but he made a snuffling, contented noise and Penda reasoned that if the mother and the midwives were showing no alarm, then all was well.

Overcome, he covered her hand with his own and blurted out his thoughts. "I will name the boy as my own.

89

I will raise him as my son."

She turned her face to the wall and spoke softly. "I do not need your pity."

He said, "I know that. And that is why I love you." He reached out and touched her cheek, gently pulling her head around to face him. Mindful not to squash the baby, he leaned forward and placed a soft kiss on her lips. His heart was thumping and he wasn't sure if its pounding was responsible for the fluttering movement he detected, or whether she was trembling a little.

He broke away from her and she said, "Silly."

He did not know if she was referring to his words, his kiss, or her response, but he knew her well enough not to ask. He would always consider it the greatest honour that she revealed to him even the slightest vulnerability. He would never betray her trust or diminish her faith in his ability to hold her secrets. He kissed her once more on the forehead and left her to rest.

Blinking in the sunshine he stepped free of the bower and straightened up, unable to suppress a huge grin. Lothar was waiting for him, a cup of ale in each hand. He offered one to Penda who drank the contents in one gulp. Even the sight of his brother approaching from the hall could not dampen his euphoria.

Eowa said, "So she has birthed the Welsh brat? You look moonstruck. What is she to you; is she your woman? You should say so, once and for all, if she is."

For six months Penda had kept Derwena company whilst keeping an emotional distance, respecting her need to grieve for her murdered husband and mindful of the growing life within her. Nevertheless, they had grown ever closer and his kissing her was naught but confirmation of feelings he had already revealed to her. Whether it was any of his brother's business was another matter. "No, she is not my woman, for I do not own her. But yes, I love her and if you insult her again in my hearing I will slit you from ear to ear."

Eowa tried to square up to him, but his younger brother had the advantage of height and his aggressive stance did not have the desired effect. Eowa said, "I will say nothing more. But do not hope to make me share your love of all things Welsh."

There was a clamour by the gate and the sound of raised voices drifted on the spring breeze across the yard. A band of horsemen had ridden in and were being challenged by the guards. Penda said, "We ought to go and see who they are and what they want."

Eowa sniffed. "I would rather go and eat. Send them to me if need be." He strutted off and Penda was left to discover the identity of the visitors. He handed his empty cup to Lothar and said, "I'll meet you later."

The arrivals had dismounted and Penda wandered over to where their leader was now standing giving careful instruction to the stable-boy regarding the care of his horse. Had his dark hair and the combination of long moustaches but no beard not been enough of a clue, his accent made it clear that he was a Welshman, and Penda smiled to think that had he heard Eowa's words of a moment ago, he might not have felt so sure of a welcome. Instead, Penda stepped forward and said, "Prynawn da. Croeso i Tamworth."

The man seemed at first taken aback and then delighted to be bidden good afternoon and welcomed in his own language. He said, "I am Cadwallon of Gwynedd."

Now it was Penda's turn to be surprised. "You are a long way from home."

The Welshman nodded. "Sadly, yes. I have a tale to tell and a boon to ask of King Cærl."

Penda grunted and silently wished him luck with his endeavour.

"Is he not here? Please tell me that I have not come all

91

this way for nothing."

"He is here, and he will welcome you, but if it is his help you seek, your open hand will close around nothing but air. His oaths are empty." Had they had any substance, Penda thought bitterly, Edwin would not have left and Carinna would still be here. Though he had been a child when she left, he missed her every day. "When Edwin of Deira asked for his help, he…"

"Edwin? That bastard is the reason for my plight. If he is your friend then I am not welcome here." He took a step as if to follow the groom and retrieve his horse, but Penda laid a hand on his arm.

"Wait. We would not turn you away before offering meat and drink. Besides, I would still like to hear your tale."

Sensing that the story would be better told away from flapping ears, Penda waylaid a passing servant and asked for drinks and food to be brought out into the yard for the travellers. He led Cadwallon by the elbow to a shady spot in the far corner of the enclosure and they sat down under the burgeoning yew tree. He waited while the Welshman stuffed mouthful after mouthful of freshly baked bread into his mouth and washed it down with ale.

"Your friend Edwin has been busy since he won back his kingdom. His first act was to set fire to Elmet and claim the land for Deira. Then he came further west, attacking my lands with such speed that I was caught out and had to flee. I have been living on a tiny island with only puffins for company. Edwin even took over the Isle of Man, using ships filled with his own hearth-men. When one of my teulu," he paused to see if he needed to translate, but Penda nodded, understanding that the word 'family' was used in this context to mean the same as 'hearth-man'. "When one of my teulu got word to me by fishing boat, I knew that I would need to gather some friends of my own before I could take my kingdom back." Cadwallon swallowed another mouthful of ale. "But I am wasting my time. You and Edwin are in alliance."

Penda was silent for a moment before responding. Edwin had always professed that the regaining of his kingdom was the limit of his ambition. To drive others into exile, as he himself had once been, seemed unsporting and unnecessary at best, hypocritical and dishonourable at worst. Penda had been eleven and still a boy when Edwin left Mercia bound for East Anglia. Ties of friendship could no longer be pretended, but, technically, yes, the alliance still held. "He is married to Cærl's daughter," he said, by way of explanation.

Cadwallon wiped the back of his hand across his mouth and continued chewing while he spoke so that bits of crust occasionally spat out onto the ground. "You have not heard, then? Edwin put aside his first wife, betrothed himself to a daughter of the old king of Kent and is in alliance with the new king, her brother." He continued chewing noisily.

A pain shot across Penda's forehead and drew a red veil across his sight. His fists clenched and his jaw clamped shut so forcefully that his teeth grated jarringly. He took a deep, calming breath. "Where is she now?"

"His first wife? Where he left her in East Anglia, I believe." Cadwallon stopped eating and looked up. "Was she dear to you?"

She was like a mother to him, his only refuge when his preening brother pinched and bullied him and the younger children. Later, when he fought back against the ineffective braggart who in truth couldn't even piss straight, she would have been the warning voice of reason, preventing him from beating the hateful windbag to pulp every time they fought. More than that, though, she was a good woman, with such capacity to love that no man should take advantage, even though it was so easy to do it. He said, "If he has set her aside, then he has forfeited any rights to Mercian friendship. The foe of my foe is my friend." He held out his hand.

Cadwallon took it between both of his own and shook it up and down. "I should properly speak to your king about such matters, but I have more use for swords than manners; I think I have spoken to the man who will wield any power here when it comes to a fight." He stopped talking and focused on something behind Penda's shoulder.

Penda turned to follow his gaze and saw Audra walking towards them. Reactions like Cadwallon's were not unusual, for Audra had a long stripe of white hair which ran from her crown down the front of her hair, as if it had been painted.

Penda said, "A handful got pulled out when she was a child and it grew back white." Before Cadwallon could speak he added quietly, "That's my sister, Welshman."

Audra sat down beside them and hugged her brother. "Derwena is resting and the bairn has already been feeding well. She sends to ask if she might give him the name of Merwal, to show his Welsh beginnings, if you do not mind."

"I have said that I will raise the boy as my own son, but his name is a matter for his mother. Of course I do not mind."

Cadwallon raised an eyebrow. "I had thought to find allies. I found such. But I am happier still to find a man like you, Mercian. I hope we can be friends."

Audra planted a kiss on Penda's cheek and said, "My brother is wonderful. Not only does he wield a sword skilfully, but he is not too proud to foster another man's bairn. Some might bluster and blow, thinking it a slight to their own manhood, or cast out the cuckoo from the nest. Women love him, men fear him. It is how it should be."

Penda smiled wryly. "You are my sister and as such should say nothing less. But I think King Cadwallon here might want some proof of the strength of my sword arm if he decides to stay awhile."

Audra stood up and smiled. "I will tell Derwena you agreed to the name."

Cadwallon grinned after Audra as she walked back to the hall. Watching the swing of her hips and the wobble of her buttocks, he said, "After staring at so many puffins? Oh, yes, I would like to stay awhile."

Penda knew he should be affronted on Audra's behalf, but he laughed and said, "You are so unlike my brother, Welshman, and for that alone, you are welcome here."

# Chapter Four

*Yeavering, Northumbria 626*

Edwin rolled his sleeves further up his arms and wiped his brow with his forearm. The sweat continued to trickle down his back and he called for a drink. While he waited for refreshment he stood back to admire his handiwork. The man who had been working the other end of the two-man saw nodded his approval. Signalling to a handful of others who were working on various tasks around the site, he squatted in preparation to heft the crossbeam onto the upright posts. Edwin mirrored his action and the other men caught the weight in the middle and between them they lifted the beam into place.

Aylfrith's old hall on the hill above the River Glen had been torn down. It had been of unremarkable size, about twenty-five strides long with a fenced enclosure attached to it. To the east of this, a much larger double-fenced enclosure had been used for the securing of livestock and to the west was the cemetery and Aylfrith's temple, where the floor lay strewn with ox skulls. These were old and it was clear that Aylfrith had not been here to worship for a long time. Edwin's workforce had been ordered to destroy the temple and construct a new one for his high priest, Coifi, and to replace the inadequate hall.

Now, in its place, stood not one but two magnificent new halls, joined together by a fenced enclosure. The larger of the two boasted a set of doors halfway along the long sides of the building, from which the servants could enter and leave with the food and drink. Left open, these doorways added more light to the interior, the better to see the sumptuous decoration within. Lime-washed walls boasted hangings threaded with silk embroidery and the interlacing knotwork carvings had all been painted in bright blues, yellows and reds.

Edwin had emulated Redwald's affectation and left heavy, locked coffers on display within the hall and the tree-wright was still working on his grand king-stool, whittling and smoothing the carvings on the back and arms. The opulence already rivalled that of Rendlesham and Edwin had chosen the site deliberately, deep in the heart of old Bernicia.

He had imported a Deiran population; all the folk who worked this manor were loyal to him. When he was in residence he would be assured of a good welcome and when he was absent, his imposing buildings would be a reminder of his wealth and power should anyone think of rebelling. More importantly, he hoped it would serve as a symbol of permanence and stability, especially after last year's famine when many families had perished. The hearth-songs would sing of Edwin as the founder of a great dynasty and there would be no more usurpation of the Northumbrian kingship.

Now that the crossbeam had been lifted into place, the open gateway to the grandstand with layers of wooden seating was complete. Symbolically, it was Edwin himself who had built the final section and so it was not merely a public space, but an area where men would gather for assembly in Edwin's manor and they would specifically answer to his call. This section of the settlement had a dual purpose, for Edwin had agreed that it would serve as a place where all could come to listen to the preaching. He looked out beyond the double perimeter fence to the scene by the river where from time to time shouts of happy salutation rose up.

Edwin had deliberated at length whether to accede to his new wife's request to bring the priest Paulinus with them when they travelled home from Kent, but the man had a persuasive manner and folk were flocking to be baptised in the river. Each person who was thus converted seemed to go off and spread the word and more and more folk came to Yeavering. Paulinus would speak to them, beginning each speech slowly and softly and building to a crescendo once he had captured their full attention. Then he would shout at them, admonishing them for their hitherto sinful lives before offering them cleansing and rebirth.

Edwin was still unsure about this new religion. He saw the political advantage in that it would tie him more closely with the rich and far-reaching kingdom of Kent which meant that, with East Anglia loyal, they formed an alliance which controlled the whole of the east coast, but he was doubtful as to how this kingdom of Heaven could provide any immortality over and above what the gods promised to every warrior who died a good death on the battlefield.

Certainly Redwald hadn't gained much from his brief conversion and yet he was Edwin's greatest friend and ally and had been victorious over Aylfrith at the battle on the River Idle. But now that Edwin's Kentish wife was pregnant it seemed to soothe her to have Paulinus near and Edwin was happy to allow his continuing presence.

If his wife was happy then her brother the king of Kent was happy and the alliance would hold. Edwin's previous alliance with Mercia had been broken, of course, when he formally repudiated Carinna, but Cærl's continued lack of interest in matters beyond the marchlands convinced Edwin that there would be no reprisals from the west and this had proved to be the case.

Æthelburh of Kent, who somewhat childishly clung to her girlhood nickname of Tata, was a dutiful wife to Edwin and had set about decorating the royal sleeping chambers with admirable enthusiasm, but she spent more time with her confessor than she did with her husband. Indeed, one of the rules of this new religion appeared to be the proscribing of a man lying with his pregnant wife. With Edwin's thoughts turning his mind to look briefly westward, he remembered the carefree days at the manifestly and resolutely pagan court of Mercia, and he felt a little pinprick of regret.

The servant ran back from the kitchen and as Edwin took the proffered cup of ale he took a deep draft of the cooling liquid and shook the memories aside. He was experiencing nothing more than a pang of grief for the passing of his youth. All men felt so as they grew older. He was king of all Northumbria and his reach stretched across Elmet in the south, the Isle of Man in the west and Lothian in the north. He had been present in the territory of Lindsey when mass baptisms had been performed in the River Trent near Littleborough, an act which had symbolised his overlordship of that place too. He had overcome the adversity that had dogged his youth and he had done nothing for which he should apologise.

Preparations for the feast of Eostre were nearing completion and little Hild and her younger sister Haryth had spent all morning running in and out of the temple, becoming more excited with every passing hour.

The younger girl had tired now though, and had gone to find the nurse Nia, leaving Hild to help or make a nuisance of herself, depending on one's viewpoint. The high priest Coifi had been filling her head with tales and promising that she could be at the head of the procession when it was time for the laying of gifts at the altar. At nearly twelve, she was perhaps a little old to be getting so giddy, but this year the celebrations would be more lavish, for it seemed that the Christians also held some sort of celebration which they began with a sad, solemn affair during which they mourned the death of their god, before they celebrated his rebirth.

Hild had listened, enraptured, as Paulinus told her the new stories, and she had repeated some of them to her Uncle Edwin. She especially liked the one about the Christ god riding on a donkey. Edwin's thoughts settled for a moment on the two small boys who celebrated their birthdays at this time of year. Even if there had not been a festival to remind him, the appearance of the straggly greater stitchwort along the paths at the edges of the woods and catkins of the birch, alder, hazel and oak trees ensured that even a man waking from a deep sleep would know it was spring.

The last time he had seen Penda, the boy had been younger than Hild was now. Edwin counted up quickly in his mind and was astonished to conclude that this Easter-tide both Penda and the bastard Oswald would turn twenty-one. Even his cousin Osric's little son, wherever he was residing, was nearly a man, at fifteen.

Edwin's own boys, Ash and Yvo, as they obstinately insisted on being called in deference to the mother who named them thus, were now residing with him, although at sixteen and fourteen they were too old to be playing alongside Hild and Haryth and were busy with their weapons practice. In a perfect world, they would have their cousin Oswin with them, just as Edwin himself had grown up with Osric by his side.

Edwin resolved to redouble his efforts to find Osric and Oswin and bring them home. Then, his family would be whole again. A family which was imminently to expand, if the signs were to be correctly interpreted, for Tata had been complaining this last week of a tightening across her womb.

He left the tools with the carpenters and made his way back to the hall. As he pushed open the door it was as if he had disturbed a bee hive. Mead benches had been upended to remedy wobbly legs, nails were being hammered hastily into the walls to accommodate more shields and weapons due to be hung there while the warriors feasted and kitchen-hands were scurrying to and fro with cooking implements and vessels to place ready by the huge central hearth, in preparation for the feasting which would follow the ceremonies on the morn. Edwin nodded his satisfaction and told his steward to carry on before he continued to the far end of the hall.

Heavy curtaining concealed a small antechamber, beyond which the royal sleeping quarters were hidden from the rest of the court. He found Tata lying on her side on the bed. Her long blonde hair was spread out behind her over the pillow and her face was pale. She was clutching her little necklace, the pendant shaped into a tiny cross that had come from Frankia and reminded her of her Kentish home, which had such strong ties with the land across the sea. She gazed up at him with red-rimmed eyes that were moist from the residue of tears.

He cast a questioning glance at her woman who bobbed a courtesy and said, "It has begun, my lord."

Edwin sat down beside his wife and took her hand in his. "Then I should not stay long. You are in good hands."

Tata sniffed and nodded. "I am trying to be brave, but it is a little frightening, I confess. But I will be strong, for you." Her gaze was fixed upon his face, entreating.

He patted her hand before releasing it. "I know you will."

He made to stand up but she hitched herself up on one elbow and clutched his arm. "My lord, you do love me, don't you?"

He gently uncurled her fingers and moved out of her reach. "Only from daybreak to daybreak."

She smiled and lay back, satisfied with his answer. It had slipped easily enough from his lips and she believed it. For a brief moment he remembered a time when he had said it and meant it, directed it with what he thought was sincerity at his former wife, who had been clever enough not to believe him.

Both ceremonies had gone well and now the feasting could begin in earnest. The great hall was resplendent; spring flowers adorned the beams and evergreens of ivy had been wrapped around all the upright posts. Strips of brightly coloured cloth had been cut into lengths of ribbons and tied in groups to the backs of the chairs. Someone had even thought to scatter white blossom over the tables and the great cauldron hanging over the central fire had been scrubbed to a shine with wood ash. The walls were lined with shields, hung up on the newly hammered nails by each of the hearth-men and visiting warriors to signal a coming together in peace.

The relinquishing of arms was an important symbol of friendship, although Edwin had ensured that there was a substantial guard outside the hall; he had not forgotten Aylfrith's tricks.

On any other day the loss of the brightly decorated shields and exquisite jewelled sword hilts might have left the warriors looking a little dull, but the richest of them had taken care to sport their most colourful and luxurious clothes. Edwin wore a jewelled crown and his tunic was pinned on both shoulders with a matching pair of gold and garnet brooches, intricately inlaid and surrounded by delicate filigree. On three fingers of each hand he wore rings, each set with a stone of either garnet or vivid blue glass.

The ladies were equally elegantly turned out, wearing dresses of coloured linen dyed blue, green, or red, with sleeves of contrasting coloured silken edging. Some wore trimmings of fur as if to make the point that here, so far north, it was still necessary to wear winter clothing. The ladies from Kent wore necklaces adorned with jewels and gold circles, with central cruciform shapes that reflected their Christian beliefs. Tata, with no less a penchant for dressing in her finery, would be sorry to miss this spectacle but Edwin was receiving regular reports that the labour was progressing well.

The lyre player plucked his tunes and the scop sat next to him, waiting his turn to stand up and recite tales of bravery, journeys of hardship, and to provide riddles for the audience to solve.

Next to Edwin, Lilla was sitting beside his young bride. Lilla was still slightly out of breath, having only recently returned from a sortie after rumours of unrest on the southern borders of Edwin's expansive kingdom. Having given his report he was free now to enjoy the meal and he reached out to help himself to slices of kid meat and took spoonfuls of a cereal brew made from oats and barley, flavoured with wild herbs, onion and garlic.

Edwin said, "So it was nothing to worry about?"

Lilla answered through a mouthful of food. "If anyone rode in from the south, they were bent only on trading. There has been no trouble."

The volume rose as men became increasingly drunk. The drinking horns were passed round and round. Coifi the high priest drank from his own engraved bowl and matched the fighting men mouthful for mouthful. Paulinus clutched an ale cup and appeared to drink thirstily but his actions were restrained and it soon became clear that he was sipping rather than gulping. Edwin noted how, as the drink went down, Paulinus continued to speak and Coifi listened to him, head turned to catch every word.

Within the roar of inebriation, these two holy men, ostensibly intellectual enemies, seemed oblivious to all around them, and the manner in which they leaned in towards each other suggested that they were more in accordance than opposition.

Hild, old enough to stay with the grown-ups, had

nevertheless gone to help the midwives. Ash and Yvo, always inseparable despite the two-year age gap between them, were sitting with the younger thegns, strengthening the newly formed bonds which would develop into the deep-seated loyalty that was essential on any battlefield. Tonight they were all emulating their elders and attempting to match them drink for drink.

Among the older warriors, light-hearted banter gave way to barbed comments as inebriation blocked the ability to distinguish joke from intended slight. Normally thick-skinned men became touchy and sensitive as crude insinuations about bodily endowment were met with challenges of shows of strength, ranging from the most obvious means of settling the argument by measuring cocks against lengths of stick, to board games and even open combat to be arranged at a time to suit the most aggrieved amongst them. Edwin continued his conversation with Lilla but kept a wary eye on proceedings, ready to give the order for calm if the exuberance spilled over into genuine hostility.

A voice rose above the rest although it was some moments before the hearth-thegns realised what was being said. A man whom Edwin did not recognise had got to his feet and was holding fast to the edge of the table to limit the degrees of his swaying. Slurring, he continued to ramble incoherently and the men around him began to laugh, their own humiliations, perceived or otherwise, instantly forgotten as the stranger became the target for verbal abuse.

A shout came from the far end of the table. "Couldn't hold his drink in a bucket!"

Others joined in. "My sister can hold more ale than you!"

Another outlandish claim suggested that the priest Paulinus was a better and more competent drunk.

The man seemed oblivious to the comments as he

carried on swaying and muttering, making his way round the other revellers who were still seated and only pausing when he was level with the top table. Most of the other men had turned their attention back to their neighbours and had resumed their good-natured arguments, but Edwin was puzzled. As he pondered on the reason why this face was unknown to him here in his own hall, the man reached his hand inside his tunic.

Dropping all pretence of being drunk, he shouted to Edwin. "The king of the West Saxons sends his greetings and his son sends you this." A glint of steel shone and, having reached for the hidden dagger, he rushed towards the dais.

Lilla leaped to his feet, rolled over the table and landed inelegantly in front of the stranger but, unarmed, there was little he could do and the blade plunged into his chest. The assassin pushed Lilla to one side and lunged forward across the table towards Edwin but the king had already darted sideways and the blade caught him only a glancing blow on his upper arm. By now the hearth-thegns had gathered their wits and came forward to stop the assailant. They overpowered him easily by strength of numbers and Edwin came round to stand in front of the table, kneeling by Lilla on the floor.

Lilla raised his head and spoke with jagged breath. "Lord King, be warned. I think the blade was poisoned."

Edwin cradled his head and shouted for the leech to be brought but Lilla's eyes darkened then seemed to roll into the back of his head and his body went limp. Still holding him, Edwin looked up at Lilla's young bride who remained in her seat, immobile, eyes wide in horror. A long moment passed and then she began to scream.

Above the wails of the young widow, Edwin shouted. "Bastard!" He laid Lilla's head gently down on the floor and, standing up, turned to his murderer. "Bastard," he said again. He shoved his face close to the assassin's.

"Why?"

The man sneered, defiantly not struggling against the restraint of the men's arms holding his own behind his back. He lifted his chin. "The mighty Edwin who thinks he is beloved by all is not so highly thought of by the West Saxons. This was their gift to you."

Edwin felt a line of sweat trickling down his back and he began to shiver. A griping pain began pulsing in his gut and he looked down at the seeping blood now showing through his tunic. His head began thumping as if one of the carpenters were now hammering inside his brain. Poison.

A woman wandered from the private sleeping quarters, grinning widely. She said, "Lady Tata has been delivered of a girl." She waited for an outpouring of hails and congratulations and a look of consternation crossed her face as she belatedly took in the scene before her.

Edwin staggered towards the curtains and collapsed to his knees, bringing one of the hangings down with him. He said, "Tell my lady it might be some time before I can see my daughter." The room began to move as if it were a boat on the water and his blood seemed to rush cold within his veins. The light vanished and darkness consumed him.

The procession of mourners wound its way slowly up the hill. There had always been a family cemetery up here on the ridge beyond Rendlesham, overlooking the river, and now a new trench had been dug and over the previous week a longship had been laboriously brought to the trench and rolled into it. After that the carpenters had set to work constructing a burial chamber in the centre of the ship, using huge timbers to build a gabled hut. On the floor, a wool and flax rug was then laid down and now, poignantly, a coffin fashioned from a tree trunk and covered with a flat lid had become the centrepiece of the tableau. Inside the coffin lay the body of Redwald, the great king of East Anglia who had ruled his people through the force of not only his formidable sword arm but his magnificent personal charm.

Carinna blinked away fresh tears. He had become as an uncle to her, even assigning her two Frisian mercenaries as her personal bodyguard, but her grief was nothing compared to the raw pain of his widow Bertana. Carinna had laid some of the pretty autumn-flowering sea asters when she had been privileged to witness the private family ceremony the previous evening, during which Bertana had scrambled into the trench and placed beside her husband all his personal items; tunics and shoes, a bowl, four bone-handled knives and, touchingly, a pillow and his combs. Carinna had watched, helpless, as Bertana had bent over and clutched her chest, as if her heart was physically breaking. Now, the redoubtable woman was in possession of her wits and her emotions and she was leading the stately procession with dignity, her head held high and her eyes dry.

In her arms, Bertana carried a yellow cloak, one that Redwald had often worn as he sat on his king-stool within his great hall. Bertana laid the cloak over the top of the coffin, taking time and care to smooth it flat and spreading out the corners.

She stepped back as one by one Redwald's dearest hearth-thegns placed his regalia on top of the cloak: his ceremonial silver helmet, with hinged cheek-pieces and studded with jewels over the eye holes, engraved all over with interlaced knotwork and depictions of fighting warriors and his sword, with gold and garnet ornaments, his baldric with its gold and garnet shoulder clasps and the solid gold belt buckle, a piece of fine craftsmanship showing swirling patterns of endless knots snaking out to cover the entire surface of the buckle.

At the foot end of the coffin, visiting dignitaries

stepped forward and laid out the makings of a feast as grand as the ones they had attended as Redwald's guests. Maplewood bottles and drinking horns were set down carefully alongside a silver dish. After this, a lyre for the minstrels, buckets and bronze and silver bowls came next, accompanied by three cauldrons.

Tomorrow, more visitors would arrive to place yet more gifts and pay their respects; the bishop was coming from Canterbury and would be accompanied by representatives from the kingdoms across the sea, from Frankia and Denmark, and more would come the following day, and then the roof would be closed and the mound would be built up over the burial. But for today, the last of the gifts were presented; silver spoons for feasting and against the chamber wall, a sceptre placed by the high priest from Rendlesham. Next to that, an iron pole with a square case on top of it with a bull's head at each corner, a standard for bearing trophies, was propped up by the king of the north, Edwin. Carinna stared at him while he made his offering but he did not, or would not catch her eye.

With the last of the items for the day placed within the grave, the mourners made a slow and solemn procession back down the hill to the great hall of Rendlesham, where at sundown a feast would begin and last until dawn.

Carinna watched Edwin who was deep in conversation with Erwald, Redwald's only surviving son, and now king of East Anglia, head of his father's people. She guessed that Edwin was not asking how easily this succession came about, for she sensed that Edwin was more concerned with his own interests than the tangled relationships of his East Anglian friends. He would not care to hear about the bitterness that had festered within Siegbert's heart, he who was not Redwald's son despite being of Bertana's womb.

Left behind when Edwin departed, Carinna had

witnessed the disintegration of the bonds not only between the brothers, but between father and foster son, and the resulting voluntary exile of Siegbert somewhere over the sea in Frankia. The East Anglian boys had all grown to manhood and were of such physical stature to make their mothers and fathers proud.

Those who remained, Erwald, his cousin Ænna and his two younger brothers and the various other royal kinsmen, seemed all to have agreed to live their own lives to the full and in the memory of Regnar, whose own life had been cut so short on the bloody banks of the River Idle. His death had prematurely aged Redwald but his other sons and male kin had done their best to compensate for the loss. Yet could so many strong, ambitious young men continue to live side by side in comfort? Carinna, having watched them all grow from their youth, was unsure.

Released from the shadow of his father, Erwald had already begun to speak openly about the benefits of converting to the new religion, despite Bertana's vehement opposition. There were many young men at court who would also object, perhaps violently. And whilst Erwald was apparently happy to continue the alliance with Northumbria and consider taking up the new religion of the Kentish, not all the boys were glad to see Edwin back amongst them.

Ænna, in particular, who behaved towards Carinna as a son and who had sought comfort from her more than usual following the death of Redwald, had pointedly turned away when Edwin walked past him. Ænna's brother, Adelar, had only been a baby when Edwin left and had no memory of him, and the youngest of the boys, born since the battle of the River Idle, did not know him at all.

Carinna watched all the visitors as they took their seats around the hearth in the mead hall and she lifted her shoulders before letting out a shuddering sigh. As those East Anglian boys had shed their youth, so she had lost hers.

She had waited, but he had never sent for her. Not long after news had come of his victory, a messenger had arrived from Deira, bringing beautiful horses and a request that they be rested for the return journey. But the two steeds were for her boys; he had sent for his sons, but not the wife who had borne them.

Mourning, bereft, she had weathered the blow and tried to remain hopeful, that when his kingdom was properly established, the call would come. When she allowed herself to accept that it would not arrive, she also had to face the fact that her youth, her looks and her prospects of remarriage had all blown by with the passing of the years.

She had been given a role to play as hand-woman to Bertana and was made to feel welcome and loved and had accepted her diminished status without rancour, a task made easier by the devotion of her protectors, the Frisian brothers who had sworn their loyalty to her. Amid the deep grief that followed the death of Redwald she had not cast her thoughts beyond the immediate preparations for the burial ceremony and so it had hit her like a blow to the stomach when she had seen the entourage arriving from Deira.

Now, she gathered what little was left of her courage and, bolstered by the comforting presence of Sikke and Sjeord, who, in their distinctive otter fur jerkins were hovering as always close behind her, she approached the mighty king who had once been her husband and was still her love.

"My lord," she said, bowing her head in due deference, "forgive me, but I did not have a chance earlier and it was not meet to ask, but… did you bring my children with you?"

111

He looked at her and she might have sworn that for a moment his eyes softened as if he was recalling times past. But with a blink his expression changed and he gazed at her as if seeing her anew. "Why in the name of Thunor would I do that?"

In her heart she had known that he had come without them, for she had spent much of the time since his arrival searching in case she had missed them in the crowds, but she knew that her boys, Ash in particular, would have sought her out the minute they rode into the enclosure yard.

She cast her gaze to the floor and stared at her shoes, noting that his, in comparison, were exquisitely stitched, fashioned from the softest leather, dyed red. "It is of no matter, my lord. It would have done my heart good to see them once more, that is all. I am glad at least to see with my own eyes that you are fully well and that your wound has healed."

She turned to walk away but he caught her arm. "They send to their lady mother their fondest love and kind wishes. They hope that I find you in good health."

She looked up at him. "I thank you for that, my lord. You have no idea how much it means to me to know that they are thinking of me still."

He nodded and looked as if he might say something. But he remained silent and where once she might have tried to coax his words from him, or dared to guess aloud what they might be, she knew that such times were gone forever. Their love, their life together, was now as shrouded as Redwald's body and was equally cold and dead.

She said, "I think, if you do not mind, I will go home. My sons can find me there, if ever they have a mind to ride south." In response to his raised eyebrow she said, "There is nothing for me here now; I have no reason to stay."

## *Deira 627*

The old Roman city of Eboracum had lain abandoned for lifetime beyond lifetime. Those who had come to settle York after the Romans had left were wary of the enclosed streets and stone buildings, eschewing such edifices and choosing to live in the same manner as their Germanic kin across the water, in wooden timbered halls.

Gradually the city had been patchily repopulated and some of the buildings re-employed. As a symbol of imperial power it appealed to Edwin and Paulinus and the order had been made to begin building a new church.

On a bright but breezy Easter day in April, a year after his daughter Efa's birth, Edwin knelt in the as yet incomplete church building and received baptism into the Christian church. He was wearing his finest robes, an agate ring adorned his third finger and hanging from his belt was a pouch of the softest leather, with embossed animal figures writhing around the clasp. His hand-sæx was overlaid with silver, into which was carved a trail of ivy leaves, and he wore a garnet at his throat. As he stepped back, his sons Ash and Yvo came forward and they too were received into the family of Christ.

A moment of poignancy came when Hild was received into the Church which had seemed to claim her from the first moment Paulinus had arrived in Northumbria. Edwin knew that there were no political motives for her baptism, only a heartfelt longing to set the seal on the beliefs she had held since she was old enough to understand. Conversely, it pleased Edwin to think that at the exact same time, thanks to their discussion at Redwald's funeral and the promise by Edwin to send Haryth to East Anglia as a royal bride, King Erwald, Redwald's son, was being baptised in East Anglia. There would be a Christian power block all down the eastern side of the island. Edwin, with God's assistance, was now the undisputed high king of the Angle and Saxon nations and all his foes were vanquished. His alliances were strong and he was unassailable. He even managed a genuine smile for his simpering wife.

He emerged into the sunshine and even though Paulinus had drummed into him that pride was a sin, he allowed himself the pleasure of receiving the adulation of the crowds who had turned out to see their famous king. They walked along the Roman road which led from the church, but even on such a straight and well-paved road, their progress was slow. Glee-men were dancing while musicians played their flutes and lyres and folk rushed up to Edwin to press flowers into his hands. Men were cheering while some women sobbed even while they smiled and Edwin's queen, Tata, distributed small coins, items whose value lay in their rarity, placing them into outstretched hands.

A mother called out. "I love you, King Edwin. Will you bless my child?" She thrust the boy forward to kneel in front of the procession and Edwin touched the top of the boy's head.

He opened his mouth to speak but held his words as a murmur rose from the crowd and folk began to push sideways, jostling to get away from someone. No, not someone, but something. As the throng parted Edwin saw that a raven had been menacing them and it continued now to flap and peck. It flew towards him and swooped low, almost clawing the young boy, before it screeched in Edwin's face and flew off.

Edwin raised the boy to his feet. "Are you hurt?"

The boy shook his head.

"It is an omen!" The voice came from somewhere in the crowd and was unidentifiable. "It flew in from the south gate."

Paulinus stepped forward to draw level with Edwin. "Do not listen, Lord King. Such beliefs belong to the old world of darkness. You have the light of Christ to guide you now."

Edwin raised his arms and addressed the crowd. "It is naught but a bird and if it is a symbol of anything, it shows the flying away of outdated beliefs. There is nothing to fear."

He continued his progress though the city, trying to dismiss the images in his mind of another small boy who, whilst he had never physically knelt before him, had nevertheless worshipped the ground that Edwin had walked upon and on this Easter day, somewhere in the direction from whence the bird had flown in, had turned twenty-two and was now at the peak of manhood.

## The British kingdom of Rheged 628

Oswald leaned back against the hillock and cradled his head in his arms. He crossed one ankle over the other and closed his eyes, enjoying the sunshine. It had been a month or more since midsummer and he knew that there would not be many more days warm enough to sit outside. He contemplated Brother Seamus' lesson earlier that morning and resolved to try again to read the recommended passage in the Bible.

The holy brothers, like Seamus, lived solitary lives, each having their own tiny hut where they slept and prayed, and they only came together to work and eat. Their monastery buildings were separate from the main settlement but they farmed the land and shared their produce, making cheese from ewe's milk and slaughtering the older beasts to share with the folk who dwelled further up the hill. They kept a few cows and in the summer shared the glut of milk left over after they had made enough butter for their needs.

Watching Seamus as he returned to the monastery, Oswald had noted how the monk was now bent and twisted with age. He had been the first to welcome them when Nia's husband, Bran, had arrived with the two royal refugees and he had given them shelter and sanctuary. Hoping to find his beloved Nia and, after assurances from Oswald that he had fulfilled his vow to Acha to look after her boys and see them to manhood, Bran had departed several years ago.

Oswald was indeed a man, albeit without a role to play in their prolonged exile and his brother, Oswii, at fifteen, was old enough to make his own way in the world. He tried to turn his thoughts back to the Bible passage which Seamus had spoken of, but he was aware that a cloud had crossed in front of the sun, for the warmth had gone and the orange light behind his closed eyelids had turned to black.

He opened his eyes and found that the shadow was caused by Rhian who was standing in front of him, head tilted to one side and her arms folded across her chest. She was frowning, as if ready to deliver a mock scolding. He smiled and beckoned her to sit beside him. He lifted up to support his weight on his elbows and forearms.

Rhian sat down, spreading her bleached linen dress out around her ankles and using her checked cloak as a blanket to protect her dress from grass stains. She said, "Your brother tells me that you are a spineless monk-lover whose sword is blunt. He sent me to ask why you spend your time with Seamus instead of with the weapon master."

Oswald chuckled. "What my brother does not realise is that I make sure I practise with my sword and spear on the days when he is spending time on, let us say, other business." He gave her a sideways glance.

She blushed and sought to change the subject. Tugging clumps of grass from the earth while she spoke she said, "Where is it that you go when you ride off for weeks on end?"

He hesitated before answering. Her father was the chief of these people but he might not take kindly to the knowledge that Oswald had been riding the length and breadth of this British kingdom seeking support for his planned invasion of Bernicia. So far he had found plenty who sympathised with his cause, for the British were no lovers of Edwin, but he had yet to establish enough military aid he could call upon should he decide to mount his attack. He prayed daily for guidance but knew that he also needed allies and a voice in his head always screamed caution when he thought of his brother.

He gestured at the landscape, with its hills of purple and dark green that hid lakes and tarns of deep blue between them, and said, "You live in such a wondrous land and yet you ask me why I ride out to look at it?"

She smiled. "Oswii says you go riding to speak to all the holy men and have your head filled with tales of Jesus."

It was true, at least in part. He had heard tell of a monk named Aidan who had founded a monastery on the remote island of Iona and it was his most fervent wish to meet this man and speak to him of his work. Failing that, he would find men who had met him and glean second-hand all he could of this holiest of men, whilst he also tried to inveigle promises of support if and when the time came.

He had been up and down Strathclyde and beyond into Dalriada, although he had not dared to travel into the Pictish kingdom of the northeast since he heard that his half-brother and nemesis, Aylfrith's son Enfrith, had settled there, married a Pictish princess and now had a son of his own. "I do hear tales of Aidan and his work, you are right. Better, though, to have my head filled with tales of Jesus than spend my hours filling the bellies of young women who are kind enough to give us a home."

Rhian's hand went to her stomach. She cast her gaze towards the ground and spoke softly. "We are to be wed. He has given his word."

Again he was slow to answer, not wishing to convey his scepticism. Young Oswii had discovered at a tender age what his cock was for and he tended to follow where it led, rather than stopping to think about his actions. If he had agreed to marry Rhian, it was probably more through fear of what her father would say than any personal preference for married life.

Oswald smiled at Rhian, who was little more than a child herself even though she was a few years older than the wayward Oswii. "I shall be pleased to call you sister-in-law," he said.

Rhian's cheeks remained pink but she seemed pleased with the compliment. "You and Oswii are not much alike."

He could only guess at her meaning but chose to acknowledge the most obvious. "He has our father's looks, while I have my mother's colouring."

Was that why his father had always underestimated him? That he looked like Acha, with her pale hair, lashes and light blue eyes? Oswald knew he had been a skinny, willowy child and his father had not seen him grow to be the tall man he had become. Oswii meanwhile had been, and remained, stocky, with his father's hazel eyes, short, wide nose and hair that never seemed to stay flat, even when it had been held pressed down by a helm for hours.

The differences did not end there; Oswald wondered if Rhian was alluding to their temperaments. He was no paragon but his ire was slow to rise, he was rarely riled or flustered and while his bond with his childhood friend, Manfrid, was tight, he was happy with his own company while Oswii was a pack animal, rarely apart from his friends, sons of one of the hearth-troop refugees, the brothers Elwyn and Elfrid.

Oswii was volatile, quick to anger and slower to find calm again afterwards. He was careless of his women but surely he was not violent towards them? He glanced at

Rhian but saw no fear in her eyes. Perhaps she was merely wishing that Oswii paid her as much attention when she was on her feet as when she was on her back. Even so, he resolved to keep close watch on this girl, particularly now that she had confirmed his suspicion of her delicate condition.

As if summoned by the power of thought, Oswii sauntered towards them from the direction of the practice yard. He was slightly red in the face and still out of breath. Sweat glistened on his forehead and as he approached them he wiped his forearm across his top lip and then pushed his hair back from his brow. He threw himself on the ground next to Rhian and squeezed her knee.

"You should have stayed to watch. I knocked Howell off his feet and bloodied his nose. Elwyn and Elfrid had to take him to the leech to get the bleeding staunched."

Rhian's own nose wrinkled. "I should not have liked to see that," she said, with a half-laugh.

"Caris stayed to the end. You know Caris, the one with the…" He paused to let his hands convey his meaning, bringing them down as if skimming her curvaceous hips. "She praised my fighting skills."

Rhian's shoulders slumped a little and she began a reply with a soft, "Oh…"

Oswald interrupted. "Howell will have been belittled by that; he and Caris are promised to one another. I think they are much in love."

Rhian shot him a glance of thanks but Oswii merely sneered. "What would you know of matters of the heart? There are no women around here whose legs have been parted for or by you. You might as well go and live in one of those monks' cells for all you seem to want to use your cock. I wonder what use you will be if ever we have the chance to get our lands back."

Oswald shrugged. "At least if I die in battle I will not

119

leave a trail of widows and bastards in my wake."

His younger brother scowled at that and accused Rhian. "You told him. You silly bitch."

She opened her mouth to protest but once again Oswald interjected. "She did not tell me; I guessed. And soon it will be no secret and you will have to speak to her father. Would it be too much to ask you to keep your breeches fastened up until then?"

"Only if you keep away from your monks and their arses."

"Oh don't be so childish." Oswald paused and scrutinised his brother. Of course he had been a child until recently and having newly discovered what his body was capable of, he was testing those capabilities to the full. Had Oswald been as carefree at the same age, perhaps he would have been the same. But all he had thought about since they'd run away from the victor of the battle at the River Idle was how to get home again and be reunited with his mother, if she were even still alive, and get his lands back. He found sustenance and hope through prayer and if he found someone with whom he could leave his heart in safe-keeping, he would. He had not yet met such a one and until she came into his life, he had no need for meaningless encounters.

His brother, however, had no such concerns and was merely taking what his limited life here had to offer. He was an incongruous mix of ambition and laziness, always urging Oswald, as he had just now, to go and get their lands back but never coming up with any strategies of his own. He got cross if women showed immunity to his charms but he could never be bothered to pursue them. Yet he was vicious to those whom he perceived to be his rivals and Howell now had a bloody nose, Oswald suspected, because he had secured the affections of Caris.

If Oswald had any plans for reclaiming Bernicia or ever met a woman with whom he could share his life, he would be wary of telling Oswii. Better if his little brother thought him a defiler of monks, perhaps, than become gripped by some irrational envy that Oswald had found happiness. He shook his head. "No matter. It would be a dull world if all men were the same. Let us leave it there and speak of other things."

Oswii also shook his head. "No. I bested Howell and I can best you." He stood up. "On your feet Brother, and let us settle this."

Rhian inhaled sharply. "No, please don't."

Oswald stood up, but he turned his back on Oswii and began to walk away.

Oswii shouted after him. "Fight, you lack-spine, or lose the right to tell me how to live my life."

Oswald continued walking and felt the weight thump into him as Oswii followed him and landed a running punch into his lower back. Oswald turned, caught the next punch before it made contact and, gripping tightly, twisted Oswii's arm until the turning motion forced his brother to the ground. When Oswii was prostrate, Oswald stepped forward and put his boot across his throat. "I said let us leave it there. And we will. If you want to best me, you are going to have to find another way."

## Mercia

The young man was obviously well-born and used to fighting, but Carinna could tell that he was not an Angle, more likely a wealthy Saxon. His pile of clothing included a tunic with silk borders on the cuffs, while his jewelled weaponry was protected by an embossed leather hand-sæx sheath and a sword scabbard lined with sheep's wool. His torso was muscular, arrayed with the typical scars across shoulders and forearms, garnered either in the practice yard or on the field of battle. His skin was bronzed, suggesting that he often rode shirtless.

The girl standing by his side was of a similar age, less than twenty, and her hastily arranged kirtle was dyed a rich deep red. Her hair might have been dressed with jewels earlier in the day but was now a ruffled mass of tendrils hanging free down her back. She had a stripe of pure white hair snaking through her dark tresses. She reached up and with tender care, held her lover's linen undershirt open at the neck while he lowered his head to allow her to slip it on over his neck. Before he straightened to his full height he placed a gentle kiss on her lips. He slipped his tunic on while she caught her unruly curls and brought her hair forward over her shoulder to begin braiding it. In another moment they were both fully dressed and they walked out of the grove with their hands clasped. She turned to look up at him, spoke a few words and he laughed, reaching down to plant a kiss on her temple before they walked on.

Carinna smiled and thanked the goddess that she had not stumbled upon them a few minutes earlier. She and her Frisian escorts, the brothers Sikke and Sjeord, idled a while in the grove, she picking the red-purple florets of saw-wort from their low bushes and the Frisians pretending to search for adders, making sure that the couple had long gone before they emerged, not wishing to let them think for a moment that they had been anything other than private.

In the royal settlement of Tamworth, the Mercian folk were conducting their business in such a familiar manner that if Carinna had been told that the last thirteen years had been a dream and that she had been in Mercia only yesterday, she would have believed it. Her father had passed away two winters ago, and the news had reached her the following spring, so she knew she would not find him sitting in his old chair, or wandering in the yard, but in the scene before her, she could almost imagine him still there.

The yew tree was perhaps a little taller and no doubt these were not the same children playing around its trunk, but the rules of the game of stones appeared not to have changed for they were still throwing their pebbles to see who could get nearest to the line drawn in the dirt. Smoke billowed through the thatch of the cook-house and, inside the barns, folk were busy clearing the storage platforms ready for the apple harvest in the autumn.

Carinna caught snatches of cheerful conversation and laughed when she heard the occasional curse as someone got too close within sweeping range of a besom. The familiar clack-clack of the looms wafted on the breeze from the weaving sheds and, outside the tannery, two men whom she did not recognise were busily constructing frames on which the skins would be stretched after the annual slaughter of livestock in the blood-month of November. She overheard the beekeeper lamenting that his stripey charges had undertaken their annual summer swarm in search of a new home and he was setting out to find them and bring them back to the hive.

Carinna looked across to the great hall and saw a group of well-dressed people standing by the door. Of the three men, one was dark-haired and sported a magnificent black moustache which reached below his chin. He was leaning against a post, with his arms folded. There was a young woman nearby and Carinna noticed the white stripe in her hair and marvelled at the speed with which the young girl had got back from the grove and with her composure ostensibly completely recovered. The other two men were arguing; one, taller and darker, flailed his arms as he spoke while the other was jabbing his finger to punctuate his speech. Carinna moved closer.

"Two years! Two years since Cærl died and still you do nothing. Two years since the attempt on Edwin's life." The taller man flung his hands up once more to accentuate his exasperation.

"Two more years that we have lived in peace. I do not understand what you want?"

"I want our people to be ruled by Mercians, not Northumbrians. I want the Iclingas to bow to no man in their own lands. Folk should be able to eat their food, not send it far away in tribute. We've had two good years since the famine and still not enough to see us through hard winters." He sighed, as if the words would not come out fast enough in his frustration. "And two more years that Cadwallon has been unable to get his lands back."

The moustachioed man nodded in acknowledgement, but chose to remain silent.

The angrier of the two men waved his arms once more, indicating the general direction from which Carinna had arrived. "And now the West Saxons are camped in great numbers over the border in Hwicce lands."

The young woman flushed and began to pay close attention to a perceived patch of dirt on her skirt, busying herself with scratching at it and using the task as an excuse not to look up. Carinna smiled. It was not privacy that the young couple in the grove had been craving, but secrecy.

The shorter man pointed at his own chest. "I am king, not you. I am not a halfwit and I know why you wish to go riding off to fight men who have not yet threatened us; it is to show off to your woman now that you have a son of your own."

His opponent's dark eyes narrowed briefly and then he laughed. "Yes, Brother, of course, getting Derwena with child was not enough for me but I must now go and prove my manhood by wielding my other spear. And it has naught to do with strengthening our kingdom against a West Saxon king who has already sent murderers to Edwin's court."

The sarcasm was met with a fleeting triumphant smile

before the meaning sank in. "Bastard." The smaller man curled his hands into fists.

*Now they will fight*, she thought. How little they had changed, save that the younger of the brothers had inexplicably grown to become the taller of the two. His dark features were more noticeable now that he was a man and he had grown broad across the shoulders. His elder brother, though still a young man, already had deep vertical lines shooting down his forehead to the bridge of his nose, so deep that they must be the result of habitual frowning.

Carinna stepped forward. "It is as if I had never left and you two are still peevish children."

Both men turned and stared at her. The shorter man studied her face but his own expression registered a lack of interest. He began to turn towards the hall. The darker of the brothers, though, looked at her with eyes that rapidly filled with tears. "Carinna," he said, rushing forward to embrace her. As Penda enfolded her in his arms, she saw over his shoulder that Eowa had returned and was now looking at them with a degree of incomprehension still clouding his features.

Penda whispered into her neck. "Dear, dear Carinna. I thought you were lost to us." He stood tall and held her at arm's length, looking at her. "You have suffered. And I will make him pay."

She reached under his grasp and gently took his hands from her shoulders, holding them in her own and stroking them. "He did what he needed to, to win back his kingdom. You would do no less, from what I heard a moment ago."

He shook his head. "Even after all that has happened you will not say a word against him. Ah well, none of it matters but that you are home, with us." He put an arm around her shoulders and drew her towards the others.

Eowa embraced her cautiously and said, "You have

come alone. Am I right?"

She nodded. "Apart from my men. They are Sikke and Sjeord, from Frisia." She stepped to one side and gestured to them, but whilst they came forward and nodded, they did not speak.

Penda acknowledged them, admiring their otter-skin jerkins and, after asking permission with the raising of his eyebrows, stroked the fur in one, quick, downward movement to gauge its quality. He spoke again to Carinna. "You will remember my brother," he said, not giving her time to answer and barely glancing at Eowa, "but you will not know this lady. Audra, this is your kinswoman Carinna. It was she who brought you into the world."

Audra bobbed her knee and Carinna reached out to grasp her hands. She smiled at the young woman and said, "I thought I had seen you before." The girl returned the smile but looked puzzled.

"And this," Penda said, "is King Cadwallon of Gwynedd."

Now it was Carinna's turn to bow her head. "You will not be pleased to have the mother of Edwin's children sharing the air so near to where you breathe," she said.

Cadwallon stepped away from the wall-post and raised her up with gentle hands placed under her elbows. "It was not you or your sons who invaded my kingdom, Lady. We Welsh do not take out our grievances upon women."

Penda chuckled. "No, indeed. Cadwallon shows a great fondness for women. But take that as no comfort, kinswoman, rather hear it as a warning." He grabbed her hand. "Come, you must meet Derwena."

He led her to a building behind the great hall, which though it was smaller in size, boasted an opulently carved wooden portico where a red and black banner flapped in the breeze. The solid oak door was propped open but a heavy curtain, threaded with gold, hung across the doorway to keep out any draughts.

Penda swept the curtain to one side and held it while Carinna made her way through the doorway, leaving the Frisians to wait outside. He let the curtain swing back, followed her and said, "My love, you will never guess who has come home to us."

Seated cross-legged on the floor by the fire, a woman was nursing a newborn infant while an older child slept on the floor beside her, his head on her knee. Her hair was loose and hung like a thick ribbon in front of her, covering her other breast from view. In the firelight it was impossible to discern her hair colouring and her pupils were big and circular, making her eyes appear black. Her cheekbones were high and wide and her expression serene. Carinna was reminded of the goddess Fríge. The woman was neither worn out nor ashamed of her fecundity but was a celebration of all that was beautiful about motherhood. Carinna choked down a lump which constricted her throat. Once, a long time ago, she had been the same.

Derwena smiled up at her and said to Penda, "Of course I will guess. Who else but Carinna would have you leaping about like a child who needs to piss?" With her free arm she gestured towards the bed and said to Carinna, "Won't you sit? I am so glad to meet you. He speaks of you daily and leaves gifts to the goddess every day if she will bring you home. And now she has. Welcome."

Penda knelt between them, first kissing Derwena and then swivelling on his knees to grab Carinna's hands again. He smiled at her, shaking his head. "I still cannot believe that you have come back to us." He glanced over his shoulder. "Oh, I should have said; this is my son, Pieter, and the sleepy-head there is Merwal, my fosterling. But you did not bring your boys home with you?"

Carinna inhaled deeply, taking time to make sure her

voice would be steady when she gave her answer. "No, I could not. They are with their father."

"Will he not send them back to you?"

She shook her head. "I could not ask him to do that, even if he would. Kin is the most important thing to him and he needs them there with him."

Derwena said, "It might be better for them if they stay there. Eowa lives in fear that they will one day come south to claim Mercia. They are Cærl's grandsons when all is said and done, the reason Cærl gave you to Edwin." She paused. "You got the message, yes, about your father's passing?" At Carinna's nod, she offered, "I am sorry." Then, "We heard that Edwin has had more children. Surely he could have sent his elder sons home to be with their mother?"

"I fear that my sons are part of his fighting band now; after all they are eighteen and sixteen. They are men, too old to be with their mother. And I heard that his wife's second child died within a week of the birth. She has now been delivered of a son, I believe, but she must still be grieving."

Derwena tilted her head to one side and studied Carinna for a moment. "Hmm. Penda told me that you were made not of flesh and bone, but of kindness and love. So I will say it, since you will not. Edwin is a shit and he has displeased the gods. His time will come."

Penda seemed not to be listening. "Feast. We must have a gathering to welcome you home." He planted a kiss on Carinna's forehead, squeezed her shoulders and leaped up.

He ran out, nearly taking the curtain with him, and Carinna laughed. "I have been gone for more than half his life and yet he is as giddy to see me as he was when he was a child."

Baby Pieter had fallen asleep and Derwena gently stroked his cheek. The sucking action began again briefly before ceasing and she tucked him lower in the crook of her arm and rearranged her dress. She lifted him over her shoulder and rubbed his back. "He has never forgotten you, nor has he forgiven what Edwin did. But I should thank you, really."

"Thank me? What for?"

Derwena paused while the baby let up a tiny burp and she smiled at Carinna. "He was haunted by not being able to help you, so he did all he could for me. Once he has made up his mind to love a woman, let no man harm a hair on her head."

Carinna thought again about Audra and her secret lover. "I think there is something I need to tell him," she said. But it would wait; let his smile remain for a while.

The feast, albeit impromptu, had gone well and most were either drunk or asleep. Derwena had joined them briefly but had gone back to the house to feed the baby and tuck young Merwal up in bed, although she had promised to return later. Carinna had been assigned their most comfortable guest house and after her long journey, had retired early. Penda grabbed an ale jug and slopped more apple-wine into Cadwallon's cup.

The Welshman drank thirstily and wiped his moustache, exaggerating the movement and making as if to wring out the ends. "You think you have enough men, even if Eowa's hearth-men refuse to come with us?" He passed the jug to Penda's deputy, Lothar, who poured his own drink and placed the jug on the table.

Penda drained his cup and reached for the jug again. "I think so. I am going anyway."

Cadwallon turned his cup back and forth in his hands. "Are we being hasty? After all, the West Saxons nearly killed Edwin for us. 'The foe of my foe is my friend'; that is what you told me when first I came here. Is it right to fight the West Saxons rather than holding out the hand of friendship?"

"You know I will not rest until Edwin is dead, but we must tidy our own house first before we look to another. Edwin swore to me that all he wanted to do was avenge his kin and get his kingdom back. But he went further and attacked the smaller kingdoms, yours among them. In my eyes he is no better than Aylfrith was. And the West Saxons are set to do the same with the Hwicce lands; if they establish kingship there, who is to say that they won't come here?" He barked a mirthless laugh. "Not that I would weep if they killed my brother."

Cadwallon glanced across the room to where Eowa lay slumped in a drunken stupor, his mouth open and a dribble of spittle sliding its way down his chin. "By the look of him, we could be all over the West Saxons and back before your brother even wakes up."

Penda slapped him on the back and stood up. "Talking of sleep, I had better go and see Derwena and kiss my bairns." He nodded at Lothar and left the hall.

It was only when the night air slapped him in the face that Penda realised how much he had drunk. Batting away the moths fluttering towards the light of the hall, he found it difficult to keep to a straight line as he walked back to the house he shared with his family. As he stumbled inside he put his finger to his mouth and said "Ssshh."

"Ssshh yourself, you silly man. You are drunk."

"Yes," he said. "And you are lovely."


As daylight seeped through the gaps in the shutters, Derwena watched him sleeping, trying to decide whether to chance a kiss. She thought it unlikely that he would wake, but she wanted to let him rest. His eyelids, though closed and hiding his dark-hazel eyes, were blinking rapidly and she wondered if he were dreaming. In repose there was not a wrinkle upon his face but there were fine white lines fanning out from the corners of his eyes where the sun missed when he squinted in daylight.

She leaned forward and breathed in the scent of his skin, so different from the soft milky smell of the snuffling bairn who was sleeping by his side. Sometimes she found it impossible to believe that she too wasn't dreaming. She was so thankful, not only for the child he had given her, but for the boy he loved as if he were his own flesh and blood. Widowed, bereft and banished, she had lost all hope beyond basic survival yet he had rescued her. She would be naught but a small piece of dust floating aimlessly about the earth if he ceased to exist or withdrew his love. Not that she would ever tell him, for she would sound like a daft old woman. Besides, he knew how she felt.

Reaching out, she wound a curl of his dark hair around her finger. She let it fall and traced the contours of the muscles which spread across Penda's chest and then fluttered her hand across the taut, defined sections of his abdomen, smiling to think that here was a person built from two substances, one hard as stone, one soft as blossom. He was as gentle as a whisper when he embraced her and he was loving and protective towards his womenfolk and children. But this body which she delighted in staring at was toned, honed and built for fighting. She knew his frustration with Eowa would soon spill over; Penda was patient, but he would not wait forever.

For a moment she envisaged this strong torso lacerated and ruptured and she shook the image hastily from her mind, preferring instead to take a long lingering look so that she would have the picture for her memory. Last night he had sobered enough to assure her that, of course, he would come back whole. But if, and it was only a tiny possibility, he fell under a Saxon sword…

She had put a finger to his lips. "*I know how to use a*

*knife. I will do whatever it takes to make sure that Pieter one day becomes king, even if I have to split your brother."*

*"Will you mourn me?"*

*"Not for long. I will be too busy finding another man to keep my bed warm."*

She smiled at the memory of what he had done next, after telling her that he had better give her a memory for this new man to match.

He stirred now and smiled up at her. "What, is it morning already?"

She said, "It is nearly afternoon. You should be busy gathering your hearth-men and rousing the smith to pack up his forge."

He grinned and sat up on one elbow, reaching out his free hand to stroke her mane of hair. "Have you no more use for me?" His fingers moved to caress her breast.

She slapped his hand away. "Let us see whether you put another child in my belly last night. Then I will tell you whether I need you again."

He laughed, kissed her and sat up. He grabbed his breeches from the floor where he'd dropped them the previous evening. As he dressed he said, without turning, "Did you mean what you said last night?"

"Not all of it."

"That is a relief. I was worried for my brother's balls."

"Oh no, I meant that."

He turned, grinning. "Ah, so you do love me, after all."

She licked her lips. "Let us say that I like to love you. Often."


Penda had beaten the West Saxons at Cirencester and it was clear that Eowa was furious but impotent. How could he castigate him when he returned a victorious hero? Carinna watched her kinsman as he struggled to retain his composure, his mouth working as if swilling poison round his cheeks and trying not to swallow it. They said the West Saxons had been soundly beaten and had agreed to let the Hwicce rule themselves. It was also reported that Penda had decided not to take their word for it and was bringing back hostages. After all, what was to stop them sneaking back into Hwicce lands as soon as his back was turned?

Carinna shifted her weight from foot to foot and tried to keep watching the gate, but she couldn't help noticing that Eowa was not the only one fighting his emotions. Derwena affected an air of nonchalance, playing casually in the puddle with Merwal, but Carinna knew how much her heart had been aching; she always smiled when she was with the children, but with Penda away she walked as if her own shadow had disappeared.

A cry went up; they had been spotted. Shortly afterwards, a straggly procession of horsemen and foot-soldiers came through the gateway, the hooves clattering as they passed over the wooden board that breached the boundary ditch.

Penda and Cadwallon headed the column with Lothar close behind and Carinna let go of the breath she hadn't realised she'd been holding. Her darling Penda was safe, but she was glad, too, that the Welshman was uninjured; despite his hands too often finding their way to her waist, she had grown fond of him. She cast a glance at Derwena who gave little away, but to Carinna the woman's relief was obvious. The three horizontal worry lines had disappeared from the younger woman's forehead.

Audra had been waiting by the great hall door. The girl had been a ball of misery since the warriors had left and she had been walking everywhere with a hunch, her arms wrapped round her body as she hugged herself as if in the throes of a stomach ache. Now she stepped forward into the yard, chewing her lip and staring at the group of men, glancing from one man to the next, as if searching.

The prisoners were well-dressed in what looked to be their finest gear. These were no ordinary warriors, but were hearth companions at the very least and possibly of royal blood. They had been divested of their weaponry, but the patterns on their cloaks were expertly woven and their cloak pins were golden and set with garnets.

Two of the men were older, greying, but the third was a young man, barely out of adolescence. Carinna recognised him and at the same moment, Audra gasped and ran forward. "No, you cannot! You must not…"

Penda slipped from the saddle and handed the reins to the stable-boy. His right arm went out and Derwena stepped into his embrace. He kissed the top of her head and then beckoned to Merwal, who ran into his arms and giggled to be thrown up in the air. Still clutching the boy, Penda turned to his sister and said, "What's this? Whatever it is, it is a long way from a welcome. Why do you yell at me?"

Audra's mouth moved but no discernible words came forth. Carinna stepped forward and touched her arm. "Let me," she said. She turned to Penda and pointed to the young hostage. "There is something you need to know."

Penda gave Cadwallon a quizzical look but the Welshman shrugged his ignorance. Handing Merwal back to his mother, Penda followed Carinna into the hall. "There are other things that I need to be doing…" He unfastened his cloak and threw it onto the nearest mead bench. Signalling for a drink, he flung himself into the king-seat and hooked one leg over the arm, slumping down and stretching out his other leg in front of him.

Carinna remained standing. She wanted to impart the information as quickly as possible, aware of the hiatus outside. Folk, as Penda had so rightly said, had things to be getting on with. Warriors had weaponry which needed repairing, horses were in need of a rub down and a feed and the prisoners needed to be housed. But she still needed to find the right words.

"Well?"

She took a deep breath. "The young man you have brought back in shackles is known to your sister. That is why she is upset."

His dark eyes narrowed and in the dim light of the hall, now glinted black. Scowling, he said, "Known? Known how?"

"I saw them together."

She held her breath. Penda noiselessly repeated the word 'together' and leaped up from the seat, strode outside and pushed his way through the cluster of hearthmen, grabbing the young hostage and dragging him out of the crowd. He kicked the back of his legs, forcing the prisoner to fall to his knees. He put out his arm and gestured. "Axe. Give me an axe."

Audra screamed and ran forward, throwing herself on the ground at Penda's feet. "No, please, I beg you."

Penda stooped to pick her up, bringing her gently to her feet. As he straightened, he looked past her at Derwena. He raised an eyebrow, as if inviting her opinion.

Derwena shrugged. "I know this boy. He is the youngest son of King Cyngil. Kill him if you want. It would pay Cyngil back for what he and my father did to my man. And then your sister will be as I once was, mourning a lover killed by a kinsman."

Carinna's heart was pounding so loudly she was convinced that it must be audible to all those around her. Everyone was standing silent, waiting.

Penda propelled Audra back so that he could hold her at arm's length. "You plead for this man's life. You love him?"

She nodded, gulping sobs.

He addressed the prisoner. "You love my sister?"

The young man, his tethered arms still out in front of him, struggled to his feet, using a twisting motion. He looked Penda in the eye, tilting his chin slightly upwards to stare at the Mercian who was the taller of the two. "I do, my lord."

Penda sniffed, nostrils flaring, then he seemed to exhale most of his anger. "Then take her."

Audra grabbed his arm. "You do not mean to banish us?"

Her brother looked at her. "Why would I do that? I brought him here to bind the West Saxons to their oath to keep out of the Hwicce lands. But if you and he are wed, that's as good, if not better."

Cadwallon clapped his hands and laughed. "Dywedodd yn dda! Well said."

A ripple went through the crowd of witnesses, as if all had been holding their breath and now had exhaled. Folk began to chatter and those who had returned from the fighting attended to their tasks as if the incident had never happened. Ripped tunics were presented for mending, while a reasonably orderly line formed in front of the forge. It would be some time before his fire was up to temperature, but numerous nicked sword blades, rimless shields and spears in want of new heads were tossed onto haphazard piles for the smith to sift through and prioritise on the morrow. Grooms came to take the horses from the nobles, while those of lesser rank and wealth took their steeds to the stables to attend to their horses and tack. Audra and her young man were embracing and at least three times by Carinna's count, he broke off to grab Penda's hand, pumping it up and down.

Penda said, "I have given you the most precious gift. If you tarnish it, I will kill you."

The young man nodded. "I am Cynwal. As a West Saxon I know my oath to you is worthless but I give it all the same. I swear I will love her with my very life."

Folk had started to make their way to the hall and a cheer went up from those who were close enough to hear the young man's declaration, but Carinna found that her legs were heavy and reluctant to move. This day's doings had finally dispelled the notion that Penda was simply the little boy she once knew but in a man's body. He'd sat in the king-seat and behaved like a king.

Even now, Eowa was watching, powerless but furious, from the perimeter fence; when it came to it, Penda had merely side-lined his elder brother. Carinna knew it would be a long time before she shed the memory of the look in Penda's eyes when he sought vengeance against the young man who had, he thought, wronged his sister. Her blood cooled within her veins as she contemplated what he would do to her beloved Edwin if he ever got the opportunity.

## The British kingdom of Dalriada 630

Oswald stood still, weight more on one foot than the other, ready for the next step forward.

She had pulled her currach up onto the shingle and was sitting cross-legged on the beach, tending to her net and checking for holes. Her dark-blonde hair was knotted at the nape of her neck, tucked there to keep it from falling across her face as she worked, and his fingers itched to reach out and undo the leather thong that secured it there. He loved to run his hands through the silky tresses, tuck them behind her ears and then kiss the soft spot high on the side of her throat, below her earlobe.

He did not want to intrude, but if he stayed where he was there was a chance that she would think he was spying on her. He would never wish her to think badly of him so he completed the step forward and walked down to the shore to greet her.

She looked up when his boots hit the tell-tale shingle

and she smiled before making a comical face as the sun's rays hit her eyes and forced her to squint. Laughing, she put a hand to her forehead and said, "Is it you? I can hardly see. I hope it is Emrys come to woo me."

He sat down beside her, chuckling at the notion that Emrys, the blind old man who lived in a hermit cell further down the beach, was a rival for her affections. "Will you never let me forget that he mended your net where I could not?" He plucked one of the horned poppies that grew amongst the tiny beach-stones.

She put her net down, put her hands on her knees and scrutinised his face. "He is a little better-looking than you, too."

"Ah, but can he do this?" He leaned towards her, tucked a stray tress behind her ear and pushed the poppy into her hair, then he searched with his lips for the sweet spot on her neck which felt so soft against his mouth.

After a moment, she wriggled round and with a gentle tug on his hair, pulled his head round so that they could kiss properly.

She sat back, removed the poppy and twirled it in her fingers. She smiled. "It is good to see you again. I did not think you would be back so soon."

"Nor did I." He paused. He had not been looking for love, because his campaign to recruit enough men to retake his kingdom had taken precedence over all else. And yet here he was again, the sight of her after his long journey leaving him replete, as if thirst had driven him to a river and he had drunk deeply. He was twenty-five, more than old enough for marriage and fatherhood. Dalya was not of immediate royal family but her status was not important to Oswald. Many of his companion refugees, particularly his lifelong friend Manfrid, would consider his marriage to a British girl tantamount to an announcement that he had given up all hopes for his kingdom but he couldn't help that.

He had always been determined that when he married, it would be for love and it was for this reason that he now found himself back in her homeland. He knew his hosts in Rheged had begun to whisper about his frequent absences and he knew that Oswii was curious, but he would not have his little brother despoiling his little piece of happiness so he had said nothing. For the same reason, the question he was about to put to her came with its own conditions of secrecy, and she might be reluctant.

She was still waiting for his explanation, so he said, "I came here to ask you two things. Firstly, will you be my wife?"

"Yes." It was a simple affirmation, her tone unequivocal.

"And will you agree to live on here, while my home remains in Rheged?"

She reached for his hand. "You are worried that you will sadden me. Don't be. I understand why you need to live like this. From what you tell me of your brother, he is not as trustworthy as you would like and it would be a shame if you gathered an army only to have him try to fight you for it. Best he knows nothing about your followers here and best if he knows nothing about your fisherwoman." She kissed him quickly and leaped to her feet, dragging him up with her. "Come; I have something to show you."

Her dwelling was a roundhouse built in the shelter of the trees above the beach where the sand and shingle gave way to firmer ground. Inside, she went to a wooden chest at the foot of her bed and pulled out a bundle of material. She unfolded it and spread it on the bed. The sunbeams streamed through the window light and illuminated the embroidery on the cloth. The stitches shone in brilliant hues of purple and gold and staring at it brought a lump to Oswald's throat.

"A banner for you to fly when you go into battle and

win back your kingdom," she said.

He reached out and picked up the corner of the banner, feeling it between his fingers and then he carefully folded it up and laid it on the little table. He put his hands on her shoulders and said, "Thank you. I do not know what else to say."

She put a finger to his lips. "Then say nothing. Show me instead." She reached down to entwine her fingers in his, increased the pressure of her grip and pulled him down onto the bed.

# Chapter Five

## Mercia 631

Penda was lying on his back, eyes closed against the sun. Derwena was sitting with her back supported by the tree trunk and with her legs resting across his. He could hear the children playing close by; six-year-old Merwal was busy telling three-year-old Pieter how to gut a fish. Penda chuckled to hear his own words coming from the boy's mouth, words that he had uttered only the previous day when they had been fishing. Now Merwal was speaking as if he were an expert. Penda said, "At least I know that he was listening."

Derwena called out to the boys. "Watch her; she is coming your way."

Penda opened his eyes and watched as his daughter crawled towards the boys and Merwal picked her up, turned her round and set her off crawling back to her mother. Little Carena, named for Penda's kinswoman, already had four tiny white teeth and a full head of soft downy hair, which lay in all directions and was now long enough to curl at the nape of her neck. Penda sat up and held out his arms. Carena gave a delighted gurgle and rushed to him. He picked her up and lifted her above his head. Her arms and legs continued to work as if she were still on the ground and she laughed.

Derwena said, "You will make her sick."

He put the child down and bounced her instead upon his knee. "You say so, but you do not seem overly worried."

She shrugged. "It will be your tunic covered in spew,

not my kirtle."

Penda laughed. It would be a brave man who ever accused Derwena of being an overbearing, over-cautious mother. Yet as the shout went up and Pieter came running to her with tell-tale white bumps which told of nettle stings on his knees, she swept the lad into her arms and kissed his tears away with tenderness the like of which Penda had at one time never thought to see again after Carinna had left. "Red ones are dead-nettles, my sweet, and will not hurt you. These ones sting and you must learn to stay away. Hush now, sweeting."

Through the noise of Pieter's wails, another voice penetrated his consciousness and Penda turned to see Cadwallon striding from the settlement towards them. "The Welshman's back," he said.

Cadwallon still had the dirt of the road upon him. His boots were caked with mud and there were splatters on his breeches. His face was grimy where dust had settled in the creases around his eyes and the lines from nose to mouth. He was carrying a cup and he sat down carefully in order to avoid spilling any more of the contents. "Your brother is busy preparing to send off more tribute."

"Why do you think I am out here?" Penda said. "I could not stay and watch while he gives away gold and livestock to the Northumbrian." It was rare these days that he referred to Edwin by name. As for his brother, he could barely bring himself to speak to Eowa while the king continued to announce Mercia's subservience to Northumbria by sending the best of their cattle, weapons and jewelled war gear.

"Well, I have tidings to cheer you." Cadwallon drained his cup and exhaled with an open mouth, expressing satisfaction at the brew. "I have gained oaths of support from three more of the Welsh leaders."

"That is good. But we are still not strong enough to march north. However, I have been thinking that maybe we need to start closer to home."

Cadwallon discarded his empty cup and lay back on his elbows. "Tell me more."

Penda said, "My kinswoman Carinna has told me a great deal about the East Anglians and she still hears news of them from time to time. Redwald's sons were apples that fell a long way from the tree, it would seem. The first son, Erwald, took on the new religion at the Northumbrian's behest, but was overthrown by a kinsman who wanted to rebuild the temples of Woden. But now comes news that the foster son, Siegbert, has come back from exile over the sea to claim his throne."

Cadwallon scratched his ear. "Yet another East Anglian king. What of it?"

"We have heard that while Siegbert was living in Frankia, he too accepted the new religion. It must have addled his brains because the first thing he did as king was to go and live in the temple that they call a monastery and has given his kingdom to a lesser kinsman."

The Welshman grinned. "And so you think that we, as wolves, would be wise to go hunting while the shepherd has left the flock watched only by a lame sheep?"

Derwena released the soothed Pieter to run off and join his brother. "It is the chance you have been waiting for; to weaken the East Anglians and separate them from Northumbria so that when you go north, you can face your foe without worrying about an enemy at your back."

Both men stared at her and Cadwallon whistled softly.

"What? Did you think I was so busy pushing out bairns that I don't know what goes on in the world of men?" She put her arms out to take Carena back from Penda and sat the girl on her lap. "Go. I will wait to hear news of how the mighty Iclingas beat the Wuffingas of East Anglia. And have no fear about Eowa. Somehow I have a feeling that he is about to have a terrible time gathering his tribute; someone is going to release the cattle and hide the treasure. He'll be too busy to worry about what you two are up to."

Penda supposed it was inevitable that he would think of Carinna, as he rode along the same route the following spring that she must have taken to East Anglia all those years ago. Perhaps it was a false memory but he vaguely recalled running off into the woods and making an offering in the temple of Woden, swearing that if her journey ended in misery, he would grow up to avenge her. And now here he was, no longer a child of eleven but a warrior, watching as the remnants of the East Anglian force, hastily mustered against him, scattered and fled towards the horizon.

Was revenge his only motive? It was the driving force, certainly, but the politics also made sense. He hadn't made a conscious decision, yet lately he was not only acting like a king, but the folk were also treating him as such. And while he had no interest in ruling more than his own people, he could see the danger of remaining inactive like so many of the old British kingdoms, sitting targets for those, like Edwin, who wanted to expand their territories.

Redwald had been the only king mighty enough to take on Aylfrith and win Northumbria back for Deira. Squashing the East Anglians before breaking Edwin's stranglehold on the smaller kingdoms was a logical plan and Penda was pleased to have the support of Bardulf of the Hwicce and Berengar of the neighbouring people of the Magonsæte to help him rout the East Anglians. And he wished he had done it long ago, for this once mighty land was now ruled over by a spineless, witless distant relative of Redwald who, when faced with the combined forces of the Mercian federation, had put up a mere token fight before fleeing.

Cadwallon came up to him, wiping his sword blade on

the edge of his tunic. "Shall we follow?"

Penda scanned the horizon. "Yes. This was but a skirmish, not enough to frighten them from coming to Edwin's aid when the time comes. But there is no hurry. I'm hungry."

There was little point in setting fires for cooking and Penda's thegns brought flatbread, cheese, dried meat and ale. Rumours spread through the ranks that whoever they had bested in the fighting, it could not have been the East Anglian king, and several of the chiefs came to speak to Cadwallon and Penda seeking confirmation.

Penda swallowed the last mouthful of bread and said, "He flew the banner of the Wuffingas. But perhaps not enough of Redwald's blood flowed in his veins. We will move on, deeper into the kingdom and see if we can't find a more worthy foe."

Cadwallon grinned. "After all, it would be a shame to find that we had put on our finest war gear for nothing."

They continued in an easterly direction, led by their scout who had grown up in these parts and swore to know the lie of the land as well as he knew the back of his own hand.

They camped overnight, flinging up their war tents and sleeping through the night undisturbed by any local warriors, and the only worry was that they would become complacent and that the younger men would come to believe that all campaigns would be this easy. As dawn spread across the expansive East Anglian sky, Penda was dragged from his slumber by the announcement that the scout had come back from his night-time patrol and had news of great import.

The Mercian forces lined up in the tight formation of the shield wall and along with the sound of the buffeting wind was the rippling noise of murmured voices waving along the massed ranks, as man after man gasped with astonishment to see that the information had been correct. Penda had been no less incredulous than the men, but he had no choice other than to believe his own eyes as he stared across the meadow at the advancing army.

The scout had told them that they had earlier fought with the East Anglian kinsman charged with ruling the kingdom. He, realising that he was no match for the Mercians, had fled to King Siegbert's monastery to beg him for assistance, which had promptly been refused. Siegbert had been bodily removed from the building and brought reluctantly to the fight but had decided that as a holy man he would ride to battle unarmed. Penda had laughed so hard that his stomach muscles were still aching. But now, staring at the rider leading the opposing army, he could clearly see that the man was indeed wielding nothing more than a staff.

Cadwallon and Lothar came to stand beside him. Lothar said, "What in the name of Fríge's tits does he think he is doing?"

"He seeks to inspire them and to show them that they are protected by their Christ."

Cadwallon grinned. "He is my Christ, too."

Penda sniffed. "I would sooner have Thunor's hammer than a stick, but let us see what the day brings."

Less than an hour later Penda stood over the body of King Siegbert and thought dispassionately that his Christ god had done naught for him this day. This new religion promised so much and yet Siegbert was dead, his people were defeated and there would be no hearth-tales sung to keep his name alive. What was the point? If this was the god to whom Edwin now prayed, Penda's next task would be equally easy.

He looked around and was pleased to see that not only had they cut the head off the snake but hacked most of the body to ribbons too. Of the corpses strewn across the meadow there were few Mercians and even among the wounded, most seemed to be East Anglian. Penda nodded with grim satisfaction. This was the message they had intended to impart; that any interference from East Anglia in matters north of the Humber would result in their annihilation.

Cadwallon touched his arm. "There is a kinsman, a nephew of Redwald, who wishes to speak to you."

The Mercian leader and his Welsh ally followed the messenger through the gates of the royal settlement of Rendlesham. Penda noted the shadowy burial mounds on the hillside across the river and wondered again how such a noble people who so fastidiously honoured the old gods and the ways of death had allowed themselves to be seduced by such a false new faith.

In the great hall there was an abundance of riches, exhibiting devotion to both the old and new ways of worship, with pieces of gold, fashioned into the cruciform shape of which the Christians were so in awe, placed directly next to older articles dedicated to Woden and Thunor.

Seated on the king-seat, where once sat the greatest of the Wuffingas, a small man was waiting, agitated fingers smoothing a beard over and over in a seemingly subconscious repetition. The messenger told them that this was Ænna, a nephew of Redwald.

Beyond the hearth, a younger boy was sitting with a girl of about fifteen or sixteen. She was sniffing and periodically her shoulders went up and down in a shuddering motion and it was clear that she had been crying. Penda wondered if she were grieving for the dead on the battlefield, but she bore no family resemblance to the boys here in the hall. She wore a head covering which he supposed was an outward symbol of her Christian faith and he wrinkled his nose as he imagined Derwena with her beautiful coppery hair hidden from view in such a way.

Cadwallon looked from the children to the slight young man seated on the king's chair and muttered under his breath. "This is the best of what's left?"

Penda stepped forward to speak to the lad, guessing him to be about eighteen. "Are there no grown men of the Wuffingas left here?"

Ænna smiled ruefully. "You think me young. I am twenty-one." He stopped playing with his beard and looked Penda full in the eye. "I never thought to be king. I had so many cousins and kinsmen who were all stronger, fitter and older than me. But here we are and they are all dead. Now the kingship passes to my father's sons, of whom I am the eldest." He nodded in the direction of the younger boy. "My brother, Adelar. We have a younger brother also."

Cadwallon said, "And the girl?"

Ænna made an odd snorting sound. "Haryth of Deira, promised by Edwin as wife to any one of us who wanted her. Maybe he thought that she would do for Siegbert, or even me. I do not think Edwin cared overly much who had her. Now what am I supposed to do with her?"

"Wed her?"

Again the strange noise gurgled in Ænna's throat. "I do not want her, or any symbol of Edwin's peace."

The younger boy, Adelar, stood up at that and came forward. "It does not mean that you have to be cruel to her. She is far from home, alone and frightened."

His elder brother said, "Oh shut up. I tire of your bleating on her behalf. What is she to us? Nothing."

Adelar looked as if he wanted to do murder, but whilst his hands curled into fists, he held them by his sides and then sat back down.

Ænna turned his attention back to Penda. "I wish to rule here. It is my guess that I will be king only by your leave. Do you wish me to bow down to you?"

Penda, struck by the revelation that it was not only

Mercians who lacked brotherly love, held up his hands and spoke pointedly, looking at the young Adelar. "I am not a king, for I have an elder brother." He was finding it hard not to be distracted by all the wealth which was so openly on display.

"Then we were both wrong. You thought me still a youth, while I mistook you for a leader. Do you seek, then, to be king here instead? Is this why you have come?" Ænna stood up and stretched out his hands in supplication. "Let me rule it for you. I will send tribute and hostages to stand for my oath. Ask me anything and I will give it in return for your acknowledgement of my right to wear the king-helm."

Penda motioned him to sit back down. "I have no need of tribute, nor do I wish to be king here. I will take some of your gold, though, since you seem to have plenty to spare. As I said, I am not king in my own lands and I could make use of a little wealth that my brother has no knowledge of."

Relief washed over Ænna's features, smoothing the petulant frown lines of moments before. "Take what you want."

Penda was not a greedy man, but only a fool would decline such an offer. He shouted an order for bags to be brought into the hall and took items of the greatest weight, regardless of the images they carried, so that as many gold crosses went into the bags as did objects more familiar to him as a worshipper of Woden. He held each piece in his hand for a moment, assessing its worth as a lump of metal, before deciding whether to add it to the booty.

When it came to some of the larger crosses, he and Cadwallon brought their own weight to bear upon the metal, bending it so that it would more easily fit into the bags.

Tossing a piece into one of the larger bags, Penda

turned to Adelar and the girl and winked. To the boy he said, "Younger brothers can still cart off bags of gold. It is not always a grim life. We who are not firstlings can find a way to get what we want. Never lose heart." To the girl he said, "The mother of my children was once like you, alone in a strange land. I hope that one day you, too, find the same ease of heart that has soothed her."

Adelar took hold of Haryth's hand and spoke to the Mercian. "Thank you for your kind words. It means much to us."

When they had packed all that they needed, Penda turned to leave but left Ænna with a warning. "As soon I can, I am going north to fight Edwin. You have seen what I can do to a foe. I will leave no man here still breathing if you ride to help the Northumbrian."

Ænna scowled and his voice rose in pitch. "The only reason I would ride north would be to see that bastard's head on a stick. If you kill him, feed his heart to the wolves."

Penda raised his eyebrows. He said, "To do that I would have to find his heart and I am not sure he has one." He chuckled softly and resolved to ask Carinna why it was that this youth hated Edwin so much. Without a backward glance he strode away from the dais, past the central hearth and headed for the doorway.

Ænna called out after him. "You say you are not a king yet you act like one. Either your brother is a mighty warrior, or you are a fool."

Now it was Cadwallon's turn to laugh. "Indeed, this youngling is not what we thought when first we saw him. And he's not wrong. You are a fool to stand in line behind Eowa."

Penda grunted and hefted the sack of gold over his shoulder, assured by its substantial weight that at least now, when this was added to the tribute which Derwena had liberated and hidden, he had independent wealth even if he never gained his own kingdom. "One thing at a time. And you know whose notch is next on my carve-stick."

The sun was strong enough still, but it sat lower in the sky and Oswald knew that this would be his last chance to travel to Dalriada before the winter arrived. It still pricked his conscience that he had told Manfrid nothing beyond the half-truth that he was journeying to rally yet more men willing to fight for him and to speak in depth with the holy man Aidan.

If Manfrid knew, he would of course suggest that he and Oswald move their household to Dalriada, but however enticing the prospect of living with Dalya, Oswald could not shake the feeling that it was better for Manfrid to remain in the Rheged settlement during Oswald's absences, to remind the hot-headed Oswii that he was a younger brother and not the immediate heir to any throne.

He lifted a hand to brush the hair from his eyes and hunched his cloak up around his neck in an attempt to breach the gap and stop the autumn breeze working its way under his clothing. His fingers pressed inadvertently against the vestige of the bruise across his collar bone and he thought back to the previous week's fight.

It had started over nothing more than a spilled cup of ale and Oswald had won easily. The difference on this occasion was that while it was Oswii who had challenged him, somehow it had been Elfrid who had thrown the first punch and Elwyn the second, with Oswii sitting back as if he had accepted that he would never be able to beat his brother in a fair fight and so had unleashed two faithful hounds instead.

As he rode further away from Rheged and travelled through the kingdom of Strathclyde, the border of Dalriada came ever nearer and thoughts of his troublesome brother receded with each mile. Men of Strathclyde greeted him, offered him hospitality and bade him stay awhile. One man, Selyf, had become a particular friend and made his usual request. "Stay the winter this time and come hunting with us. The stag you brought down last year fed us for weeks."

Oswald chewed his bread and washed it down with a mouthful of mead. He said, "I would like to, but I cannot linger too long on my way to and fro any more. I have more reason than usual to hurry north."

Selyf frowned in puzzlement briefly before his features spread into a wide smile. "Unless my memory plays me false, last time you came through would have been long enough ago to have planted…"

Oswald held up his hand to interrupt. "Yes, she is with child. Now you know why I must not tarry."

Selyf slapped his knee. "That is good news indeed. I am pleased for you. But will you not wait for your hearth-man to catch you up?"

Oswald reached for another chunk of bread. "What do you mean? I came alone, as always."

"Oh, I must be mistaken then. There were reports of a horseman riding not too far behind you as you crossed from Rheged into our lands. But there are many men out on the roads at this time of year before winter closes in." He stood up. "So, you will stay the night with us and you must let me know if there is anything you need before you set off in the morning."

Oswald was honoured with a coveted space near the hearth. He barely slept, getting up at first light, but even though he rode hard, he did not arrive in Dalya's settlement by the sea in time.

Emrys, the blind old man with superior net-mending skills, shouted out to him as Oswald ran along the shore. "A manchild, born seven nights ago. Sláinte mhath. Good health!"

Oswald rushed into the house and found her sitting by the fire, with what looked like a bundle of rags in her arms. She lifted the blankets away from the warmth of her body and showed him the tiny face. Oswald was overwhelmed. "My son."

She smiled. "He came easily into the world. He will be strong, like his father." She lifted her face.

Oswald leaned forward and kissed her. "What name have you given him?"

"I haven't. I wanted to wait to ask you for your thoughts on it. He should have an Anglian name, I think, if he is to be a king one day."

"Indeed. Œthelwold is a good name for a king."

She tried it out. "It is not an easy name to say, for a Dalriadan."

He laughed. "You're right. And I would fain call him Udo."

"Udo. That is easier. What does it mean?"

"In my tongue, it means 'little child'. It was my mother's pet name for me."

He stayed with her for as much of the fading year as was practical, leaving only for short periods to visit the revered Aidan and to meet those who had promised him armed warriors if and when the time came. His first call was upon an elderly chieftain, a bear of a man, with grey moustaches and few teeth. He had fought with Rhian of Rheged's forebear Urien and was always keen for news of Oswald's adopted homeland.

"I thought you had come last week," Domnell said. "There was a horse with a Rhegedian bridle tied to the rail by the gatehouse, but it was not yours after all. I am old and my eyesight is not what it was, but if you came more often, I would not be so eager every time a rider came in from far-off lands."

Oswald followed the older man into his house and gave him all the news he begged for, but found that all he really wanted to do was to return to Dalya and his son and when he got back to her little house by the sea, he vowed not to leave them again until the weather dictated the timing of his return to Rheged.

## The kingdom of Mercia 633

At Tamworth the preparations were well underway. The forge glowed night and day as the smith made, mended and sharpened the weaponry. Spear hafts, newly turned by the tree-wrights working on their pole-lathes, were stacked in bundles, waiting for blades to be attached. Sitting cross-legged in the enclosure yard, the smith's younger children attended to the warriors' shields, attaching metal decoration and piling to one side any shields in need of a new metal rim.

Outside the cook-house, carts had been rumbled into position to allow the cooks to bring out supplies of flatbreads and dried meats to be loaded directly onto the carts.

By day, the population expanded hourly as more and more men from the surrounding villages arrived to answer the call to muster, and Mercians from further afield shared the last part of their journey with those who had been sent by subsidiary territories: the Hwicce, the Magonsæte and several smaller tribes. The Welsh warriors had set up camp beyond the boundary ditch, where fires from braziers and temporary forges glowed and every day another batch of tents was erected as yet more arrivals joined the camp.

By night, the great hall filled up quickly and men sat on makeshift benches outside, servants working quickly to bring food and ale to them, while the walls of the hall seemed to pulsate to the sound of laughter, music and shouting within.

Penda whistled softly as he walked in front of the stables, stopping briefly to check that all the tack was being properly scrutinised and that any bridles too badly worn were being identified and put to one side. Satisfied, he strolled on, thumbs tucked through his belt. In the great hall he warmed his hands by the fire for a moment before greeting his brother. Eowa was sitting in the king-seat, nursing a cup of ale and chewing his bottom lip.

"I hear that I am an uncle once more," he said, barely looking up.

Penda released the broad grin that he had been trying to subdue. "Derwena has given me another daughter, named for our mother, but to be known as Minna."

Eowa remained grim-faced. "Should you not think again before leaving her now?"

Penda sat down next to him and reached for the ale jug. "She gives birth as easily as you or I take a shit. She would hurt me badly, I think, if she thought that I had abandoned my plans in order to play nurse to her. She will not be abed for long." He thought, but did not add, that it was a good thing, for it meant that she would be more able to keep an eye on Eowa while he and Cadwallon were away.

"Well, I have not changed my mind either. I am not coming with you, nor will I put my name to this madness. I have sworn to Edwin and I will keep sending tribute. As long as I keep my word to him, he will not send his sons back here to take my throne. If you lose, at least I will not have a Northumbrian storm brought upon my head."

Penda could not keep the contemptuous tone from his voice. "He abandoned our kinswoman."

"Good. It means his sons aren't here to challenge me. If you see them, kill them for me." Eowa frowned and stared at his cup, twirling the gold vessel in his fingers.

Penda stared at him, but the words had come as scant surprise. Eowa would not wield the blade himself, for he was too much of a coward, even though he lived in terror of Carinna's sons returning one day to claim his throne.

And so he continued to send tribute in the hope that it would be viewed as payment of board and lodging for the rival claimants and that Edwin would keep them in the north.

Penda suppressed a snort of laughter, wondering if Eowa was brooding over the knotty problem of the loss of huge portions of that tribute which he was raising so diligently. Cattle had been miraculously released before they could be herded as far as the border and the treasure regularly robbed. Penda had added to Derwena's stockpile when he brought the riches back from East Anglia but he had no doubt that she had more secret hiding places that even he did not know about.

He stood up, pushing his chair back with his legs. "Well, Brother, this might be the last time we meet. Live well and long." It was an habitual phrase, said without thought, and they both knew he did not mean it.

Eowa grunted in reply and Penda left him, wondering how it would be to spend a lifetime looking inward, never outward. And did Eowa even like what he saw, given that he rarely smiled?

Penda went to look in on Derwena, opening the door as quietly as he could.

"I am not sleeping," she said. "Come in and look at your children."

She had not said 'for the last time' but he nodded, stooping to pick up his eldest daughter Carena and kissing her. She wound her chubby arms as far around his neck as they would reach and returned his kiss with sweet gentleness and accompanying it with a 'mha' sound.

He set her back on the floor and she walked to the bed, clutching his hand and tugging to make him follow. "My sister," she said.

He reached down and stroked the soft baldness of the newborn's head. "She is lovely," he said softly. Taking a seat on the edge of the bed he stared at Derwena for as long as he could, trying to burn the image into his head. "Goodbye, love."

She sat up to kiss him and with her free arm touched the back of his head, running her fingers through his hair. Sitting back she said, "Go. And think not on me until you ride home again."

Outside, he went to see the boys and found them, as he'd expected, in the practice yard, receiving instruction from Lothar. Merwal towered over Pieter, who, though tall, was after all still only five years old. Merwal paused in the middle of demonstrating a slashing action with his wooden sword and raised the weapon in salute to the man he had always called 'Father'. Penda waved back and was about to drop down to clamber between the fencing rails when he sensed a presence behind him. Turning, he saw Carinna standing in the yard.

He took a step towards her, but she shook her head and made to move off. Calling after her, he said, "You know I must do this."

She did not turn, but only said, "Yes."

And, knowing as he did that she had left gifts in the temples both for himself and for Edwin, Penda let her go.

Edwin came away from the private bedchamber of his palace at York as hurriedly as he could without his actions being deemed unseemly. Every child was the living proof of his fruitfulness and God's blessing upon his endeavours, but he much preferred them when they were grown entities and not self-serving squalling infants. The newborn seemed sickly to him, its pallor redolent of the child born to them years before, dead within a week of baptism. But these mewling cries had been drowned out by the wails of his five-year-old son, who had taken unkindly to his mother's attention being robbed from him by the new arrival. Waiting in the hall, his eldest sons greeted his arrival with eyebrows raised.

"Yes," he said, "you have another sister but she is weak."

Ash stepped forward and placed a hand on his father's shoulder, no doubt also remembering the grief of the previous occasion. Yvo looked down at his shoes, clearly unsure what to say for the best. They were good, dutiful sons and their sorrow and sympathy needed no words, for Edwin was assured of their respect and love for him. His daughter Efa, though, was the blinding light in his life and she approached him now, dipping in a reverent bow as she did so, before taking up his hand and placing a kiss upon it.

She asked how she might serve him and he felt hot tears stinging the back of his eyes. At seven, she was but a child still, yet she walked the world with such grace and softness that whenever he doubted his life's actions, all he had to do was to look at her and know that she truly was God's gift, born on the night he survived an attempt on his life. "Go to your mother," he said.

As she moved to obey his command, the low October sun poured through the doorway, lighting the fluffy hairs around Efa's crown and giving the effect of a halo.

Edwin sighed and sat down by the fire, hooking a stool with his foot and resting both feet upon it. He rubbed his knee, working away at an ache which seemed recently to have taken up permanent residence there. It annoyed him, for he felt like he was still a young man, particularly as his wife was still giving birth to his children. But as he looked at his boys, adults now at twenty-three and twenty-one, he had to remind himself that he was now only two years from his fiftieth birthday. Perhaps it was time to give some thought to his successor; given that he had never managed to find Osric and his son, the only heirs were Edwin's three sons.

He looked at his eldest boy, and knew that should anything happen to him and the throne pass to Ash, then

Northumbria would be in good hands and his work would be continued. He allowed himself the sin of pride whenever he took time to look back on his achievements.

His rule stretched from Bernicia in the north to Elmet and the British territory of Lindsey in the south and as far west as Gwynedd and Man. He was over-ruler of East Anglia and Mercia, although it seemed that they needed a reminder, and he'd already begun plans for a march in retaliation for Mercia's unwarranted attack on East Anglia. Many folk had him to thank for bringing stability and unity to the whole of the northern kingdoms. Yes, he had grown rich, but hadn't they benefited too from his protection? He had built monasteries, he had made the roads safe to travel, his young wards, Hild and Haryth, were well provided for and he had sired six children, four of them healthy.

He looked across to Ash's younger brother. Probably it was time, too, for Yvo to strike out and claim Mercia through his mother's line and he resolved to speak to him about it. He sighed. If he had but one regret, it was perhaps the forgoing of the abiding companionship offered by Carinna. She had told him once that he would be grateful for those years she gave him and the opportunity they afforded for him to rest awhile. It was indeed a sweet memory, but however many times he brought it to mind, he could not see a way in which he could have brought that sweetness with him and been able still to fulfil his destiny.

Ash came to sit next to him and, misinterpreting his air of sorrow, said, "If it is God's will, the bairn will live. Have faith."

Edwin patted his arm. "You are good to say so. You put me in mind of your mother, who was wont to give such comfort in trying times."

Ash said, "You have always spoken kindly about my mother. It has kept my memories alive and fresh as if I had seen her only yesterday. I am grateful that you allowed me to go by her pet name for me. I pray that one day I will…"

They both turned at the sound of a messenger rushing in. The runner caught the edge of a mead bench with his hip as he hurried to the end of the hall, setting the metal plates and jugs rattling and clanging. He rushed to the hearth, gasping for breath. "Lord King, there have been sightings of a massed army riding north to here. The banners are of dragon and raven."

Edwin stood up. "Christ on the cross." For so many years he had been followed by shadows that lurked in the gloom and never allowed him to forget. They were reminders of the two boys, the young pretenders who one day would come to wrest the king-helm from his head. They were so close in age: one the bastard product of his sister's rape by Aylfrith, the other a Mercian lad who once idolised him. At least Edwin knew now which one it was who was coming to confront him. And he was more than ready.

Hatfield Chase was a bleak, forlorn place. Penda thought that if either of them had to die this day, it was a fitting place for what would undoubtedly be a grim death. The day had dawned slowly, for at this time of year the sun itself seemed drowsy and the further north they travelled, the worse the weather and the darker the days. But there would be enough hours of daylight for the task in hand.

They had watched Edwin's forces arriving in straggly groups as if they had been summoned in haste, and Penda was grateful that Edwin's scouts had not spotted their advance sooner. The aim had been to march on York and they had been pulled up short only about thirty-five miles south of their target.

The land was flat, giving advantage to neither one side nor the other, but Penda and Cadwallon had the strength of numbers, the benefit of preparation, and they were both younger men than their adversary. It was of no matter. Penda's bloodlust was driving him and he would fight to the death, as would his friend and ally and, no doubt, Edwin. This was what they all, ultimately, lived for: the opportunity to win glory in battle or die in such a manner that hearth-tales would be sung forever about their courage and battle strength. He was sure he was not alone in feeling this way and it made him question, not for the first time, his brother's ability to sit on his arse when such chances were his for the taking.

Behind him the clattering of metal and wood told him that the shield wall was coming into formation as his forces lined up, shoulder to shoulder, behind the protection of their shields. Penda had made his offerings to the gods before they had embarked, but now he could hear the soothing tones of Cadwallon's priest, bringing comfort and doling out promises of absolution to those fighting in the name of the Christ. Penda grunted. How was the Christ god going to decide which of his followers would be victorious? With Edwin on one side and Cadwallon on the other, it seemed to Penda that the Christ would have to declare a favourite. He had the feeling that, offerings and prayers notwithstanding, the victory would probably belong to whichever side proved the stronger.

The priest had worked his way along the massed ranks and now came to Cadwallon, who knelt to receive the blessing and then crossed himself. He stood up and smiled at Penda. "I know that you do not approve."

Penda shook his head. "A man's beliefs are his own business. His actions, however, become my business if he behaves wrongly. It is not Edwin's faith that has earned my hatred, but the man he has become and the things that he has done. It does not sit right with me and seems to go against the teachings of your Christ god."

Cadwallon's smile turned into a wide grin. "We'd best go and kill him then."

Penda began to bang his sword hilt on his shield and the men behind him took up the beat. They moved forward, clusters of the doughtiest warriors out in front, the majority in a tight shield wall formation following closely.

Edwin's forces mirrored their actions and it was not long before the shields were subjected to a greater force, as the great rounds of linden wood smashed into each other.

The fighting began in earnest, each warrior using his shield to protect his neighbour while they were temporarily vulnerable by attacking with their sword, shield or axe.

The Mercians were greater in number which equated to superior pressure and it was not long before the Northumbrian shield wall began to fragment. Smaller groups formed but each breakaway huddle of Northumbrians faced a band of Mercians double in number. Lothar was fighting well, leading a group which had already smashed into three of those breakaway formations.

Penda and Cadwallon exchanged a look and both nodded. It was time for them to separate so that they did not offer a concentrated target for the enemy. Rarely did a battle end without the death of a king and they needed to maximise the chances of at least one of them surviving.

Cadwallon took two of his most trusted deputies and peeled off to the left of the enemy shield wall, smashing at it with all his might in an attempt to break it up completely. Penda took a moment to take stock, staring across the field to assess how much ground they had already covered. And then he smiled, thanking Tiw for the gift.

A few short paces away, Edwin was engaged in hand-to-hand combat and he had become detached from his band of hearth-men. Penda ran forward, yelling, as Edwin despatched his adversary. Edwin looked up at the shouting and frowned.

Penda had him at a disadvantage; he remembered Edwin and although the blond hair had whitened with age, he was recognisable as an older version of the full-grown man whom Penda had known twenty years before. He, on the other hand, had grown from boy to man in those intervening years and whilst he might look familiar, it was clear that Edwin was slower to realise who was charging towards him. To be sure there was no doubt, Penda shouted his own name as he ran and the threatening call alerted a young man fighting near Edwin, who immediately turned and came to Edwin's aid.

Edwin shouted, "Ash, no!"

The tone of the appeal suggested that the young man was dear to Edwin but the name meant nothing to Penda; besides, Penda could not have stopped if he'd tried. He crashed into the young man who, to his credit, managed to stay upright. There was a moment of inertia as each man pushed with his shield. Then the Northumbrian, already unbalanced by the initial onslaught, took a step back to support his stance and Penda shoved with even greater force. The man went down and Penda brought his sword down across his body, slashing him open from neck to groin. He stood up to find Edwin staring at him.

"Penda." It was not a question, but a statement of recognition.

Penda had been waiting for nearly twenty years for this moment and he sensed that, for different reasons, Edwin had been waiting too. But this was not a time for words. He swung his sword in a great arc, but Edwin blocked it with his own blade.

Time and again they came at each other with shield up and sword slashing, but each met the other's blow. They came together, pressing shield to shield, pushing, then using the opportunity to rest, before they broke away and repeated the sequence. But with each successive thrust Penda felt the power in Edwin's arm diminishing and he knew it was only a matter of time before he would be able to overwhelm the older man.

He waited until the blade became too heavy for Edwin to lift to the same height and the force of his slashing was further reduced. Penda raised his sword high, Edwin countered with a sword that would not lift and brought his shield up instinctively to protect his face and neck. In that moment, Penda, with arms still fresh and strong, swung his sword back round and sliced across Edwin's torso.

Edwin lowered his shield and his sword hung down. He looked at the wound and dropped his weapon. He was too seasoned a warrior to fight on when he knew he was mortally wounded. He looked Penda in the eye and did not avert his gaze, even as Penda brought his sword up one more time to shoulder height and, holding now with both hands, brought it sharply across and severed Edwin's head from his body.

He stared at Edwin's remains and tried to recall the man he had once known, the man who had dandled him on his knee, played games with him and taught him the rudiments of swordplay. This man, lying dead on the ground, had once been openly loving to Carinna, not caring who saw them caressing, so much in love with her that he had persuaded her to travel to Redwald's court because he couldn't bear to leave her behind. Penda could only conclude that whatever had happened to change him had happened there.

Was it, as Carinna had hinted, the lure of gold and riches? What caused him to abandon the gods and embrace the Christ god, if not the promise of yet more power and control? Whatever the enticement, much good it had done, for now he was on his way to feeding the worms and no one would sing hearth-songs. Only the Christian monks and priests would tell stories about him and who would listen to them? Not the Mercians, nor the British and Welsh kingdoms who could now rule themselves and keep their gold and cattle to help feed their own folk instead of Edwin's warriors.

The fleeing Northumbrians were mere specks on the horizon now, although some of the Welsh warriors were still giving chase. Penda hailed Bardulf of the Hwicce to give the order for the Mercians to rally under his banner. Let the Welsh harry as much as they liked; they had a grievance which hurt far more than his. Overrun, forced into exile by Edwin, a man who'd known the same such pain, the Welsh would pursue, slash and burn for a long while yet before their anger cooled.

Cadwallon came to stand beside him. "You are leaving?"

Penda turned away from Edwin's body and nodded at his friend. "I have done what I came here to do. And now I think it is time I made a stand for the kingship against my brother. My deeds this day must show him that he should have been here, that if he wishes to rule Mercia he must wipe the rust from his blade."

Penda, with Lothar and the rest of the hearth-troops, was almost at the border and with each mile his thoughts turned a little away from the carnage he had left behind, as he began instead to envision the scene that awaited him at home.

Derwena would be back to her daily routine and preparations for winter would be already ongoing. Apples would be harvested, stored in the roof spaces of the storage barns, or pressed into a pulp to make the apple-wine that would quench their thirst during the long dark months. The women would be tending the leek beds and before long it would be blood-month, when animals were brought in from the fields to be slaughtered and the meat dried for preservation.

He was looking forward to the long dark evenings around the fire, of tales and riddles and drunken laughter, of watching his growing children while they slept, and nights spent in Derwena's embrace.

There was shouting from the back of the group and he turned to see that they were being pursued by a lone horseman. He was a young man but the splattering of blood on his clothing and a gash across his forehead told of his role in the battle. Penda tugged on the reins to turn his steed about and rode back past his men to await the stranger.

The horseman drew rein beside Penda and panted until his breathing became less ragged. He said, "I seek the lord Penda."

"You have found him."

The stranger leaned a little closer, peering as if trying to see the face more clearly beneath the battle grime. He appeared to have been unsuccessful, because he shook his head and sat upright again.

Penda said, "Have we met?"

"A long time ago, yes. But I do not know your face, nor will you remember me. My name is different, too, from the one you will have known. I am Yvo, Carinna's son."

He was at least sensible enough not to introduce himself as Edwin's son, but the facts could not be ignored. "I killed your father, and, I think, your brother, too. Why did you not come at me with an axe?"

"I will understand if you do not believe me, but I do not come for vengeance. My father and brother are dead and I have naught left but my mother. I would see her again, before…"

Penda held up his hand. "Your mother is in rude

health. I will take you to her."

They rode on and Penda took the time to consider how best to play this new game. Ostensibly, he was bringing the only surviving member of her immediate family back to Carinna and his gift would assuredly ease the pain of losing her eldest son and lifelong love. But Yvo had admitted that there was nothing left for him in Northumbria and the death of his brother had conferred the claim to Mercia on him. This cuckoo in the nest would need careful watching if he were not to push all others out of the tree. Such considerations would wait for another day. As they rode through the gates at Tamworth, the sight of Derwena waiting to welcome him was eclipsed, for a moment, by the experience of witnessing the look on Carinna's face and the familiar lopsided smile when she saw the identity of the man riding alongside him.

The midsummer sun shone its intense midday heat onto the dusty ground; an unusually dry year in Rheged had parched the earth and lowered the level of the lakes. Now the massed horses kicked up showers of dust as they circled and jostled in the open yard outside Oswald's sleeping quarters. He took one last look round to make sure he had not left anything; one way or the other, he would not be returning. A shadow cut a patch out of the sunlight streaming across the floor and he turned to see his brother Oswii standing in the doorway, blocking the light.

"What in hell's name are you doing?"

Oswald felt his shoulders tense. His brother seemed to have embraced Christianity merely to add more blasphemous oaths to his repertoire. "I am going to get my kingdom back." He slung his sleeping roll over his shoulder and stepped towards the door.

Oswii folded his arms across his chest and widened his

stance, making sure that there was no room for Oswald to pass. "Who says it is your kingdom?"

Sighing, Oswald released the blanket roll and placed it on the bed before sitting down. He hesitated, wondering why he should have to explain to a man who never bothered listening to intelligence when it came why he was not fit to be a king. He counted each piece of information off on his fingers. "Firstly, Edwin is dead. Secondly, our father's eldest son, Enfrith, went to claim Bernicia and he is now dead. Thirdly, Edwin's cousin, Osric, went to claim Deira and he is now dead."

Oswii stepped forward. "Dead how?"

How could the lad not know this? It had been discussed often and loudly since the news arrived. "Enfrith brazenly went to Cadwallon to make peace, taking only twelve men with him. Cadwallon killed them all. He went back to his stronghold in York and Osric besieged him there. Cadwallon broke out with no warning and obliterated his army."

"And now you are going to win against Cadwallon where these men failed?" The scorn in Oswii's voice was so thick that the words made his lip curl into a sneer.

Oswald stood up and retrieved his pack. "Yes."

His younger brother grabbed his arm. "Why you?"

"Who else? My father was Aylfrith of Bernicia. My mother was Acha of Deira, sister to Edwin. All others from both houses are dead." He clamped his mouth shut, to keep the lie in place. Best to say naught of their half-brother Enfrith's son, growing up somewhere in the Pictish kingdom. Nor to mention Osric of Deira's son, who had not been counted among the dead at York, and yet had not come forward to claim his birthright. Of Oswald's own wife and baby son in Dalriada, Oswii knew nothing. It was safer that way.

Oswii scowled at him. "You forget, Brother, that my father was also Aylfrith and my mother, too, was Acha."

As his elder brother tried to push past him, Oswii said, "I am the one most like our father. And I am the one who has children. My son even has a good Bernician name, after our father."

"Yes, indeed. The young Alfrid is a living reminder of our father. That is why the Deirans will never accept you as their king. But if you feel that you will fare better than I, then feel free." Oswald yanked his arm free and stood close to his brother, staring down into his eyes. Now, directly in front of him, he could barely pick out Oswii's features, silhouetted in the darkened doorway, but he kept his gaze evenly upon him as he finished his proposal. "If you can get them to follow you, my men are outside. You will need to kill me first, of course, since I am the elder brother."

For a moment there was nothing but the sound of breathing, Oswald's measured and slow, Oswii's fast and laboured. Then without another word, Oswii stepped aside, walked out into the sunshine and past the horsemen without looking at them. Oswald followed, mounted up next to the British recruits from Dalriada, and gave the order to move off. There was no question that Manfrid would accompany him but he was surprised to see Elwyn saddled up and ready to go, whereas his brother Elfrid, as expected, was not.

Elwyn turned as if aware of Oswald's scrutiny and said, "I am homesick."

Oswald needed no other explanation.

Riding eastward, through British territory, flying Oswald's banner of purple and gold that Dalya had made for him, they had come to Bernicia from the north and found that God had chosen to occupy Cadwallon in Deira, so Oswald journeyed more slowly through his birth country, gathering loyal men to his cause and swelling the ranks of his army which remained, even so, relatively small in number.

There was no need to issue a challenge to Cadwallon; there were so many migrants fleeing both ways during this period of hell on earth to pass the news from settlement to settlement that word would reach the Welshman soon enough.

Oswald was still north of the old Roman wall when word arrived that Cadwallon had mustered his forces at York and was marching to meet him. "We will await him, then."

He had been away for many years and had only been a child when he had been swept westward to safety. Malger, a Bernician thegn and distant cousin of Manfrid who remembered the princess Acha with fondness, had put himself forward to fill in the gaps in Oswald's geography. Oswald spoke to him now. "Malger, what is this place?"

Malger kicked his heels to bring his horse level with Oswald's. "My lord, it is most strange and wonderful but over there is what some men call the Heavenly Field. It was a holy place to the Romans and to those of the old gods."

Oswald smiled at the germane detail. "Then it will become a holy place for us, too." He asked Manfrid to organise a hole to be dug in the field and then rode round to the tail end of the war band, where the few baggage carts were being guarded while men awaited the order to either unpack or move on. "Empty this one," Oswald said, pointing at the lightest laden cart. "And break it up."

Stunned, one of the carters opened his mouth to protest but Oswald held his hand up. He reached into the next cart along and selected a length of rope. "Do it. And then bring me two of the planks."

As the sun began to set and the smell of simple food, cooked over basic fires, wafted on the evening air, the carter brought the lengths of wood and placed them on the ground outside Oswald's tent. Oswald took the rope and placed one of the planks at right angles across the other, lashing them together. Pulling the cross upright he dragged it to the middle of the field and placed the longer end into the hole. Holding the upright post, he called to the nearest men and waited as they pushed the disturbed earth back into the hole and around the base of the cross. When it was stable, Oswald let go and took a few steps away.

"Hear me, all of you. Kneel with me and pray to God that we will win on the morrow. We are few, but we will be well rested. Sleep and while you do so, draw strength from this most holy ground, knowing that this cross will guide the hand of God to put His blessing upon us."

He knelt, offered up his own silent prayer and stood up again. The symbol of the crucifixion would comfort and encourage the men who were newly converted. To those who still worshipped the old gods, the cross, so roughly constructed, would serve as a totem of the world tree. The fact that this field had been sacred ground for so long would appeal to men of all faiths and beliefs.

Manfrid nodded approvingly. "Few we may be indeed, but these men will follow you unto death and beyond."

Oswald brushed soil from his hands. Turning to look south over the wall he said under his breath. "Now, let him come."

Oswald made sure that all but a few sentries had as good a night's sleep as possible. Their unhurried progress and the early sighting of Cadwallon's forces had already given them the advantage. His scouts informed him that it would have taken twelve days or so to march from York and the Welshman's forces would need their rest. Oswald was determined to deny them their sleep and as soon as he was alerted by the lookout that Cadwallon's forces had arrived and were pitching camp on the other side of the wall, he sent out the command for his men to get up and arm themselves for battle.

As the dawn gave way to full daylight it became clear that it was not a battle but a rout. The Northumbrians and their allies poured over the wall, taking the Welsh by surprise and slaying a great many there where they stood. Those who ran were pursued, run down and slaughtered, caught by men with fresher legs and fuller bellies. Cadwallon fled too, for several miles, before being brought up short by a fast-flowing burn. By the time Oswald got to the scene, the water was running red and the mighty Cadwallon was no more than a carcass.

After the victory of Heavenfield, Oswald made slow progress through Deira and was humbled by the warm welcome he received there. An old woman came out into the road from her dwelling to stand in front of his horse. He dismounted and she stepped forward to kiss his hands. "Your mother was like a goddess and her story broke my heart. Mend this land and let it thrive once more. Enough blood has flowed."

The scene was repeated in similar circumstances along the way until he returned, reassured, to his birthplace at Bamburgh. Here a messenger from Rheged was waiting with the news that Oswii had abandoned Rhian and sailed to Ireland. Oswald did not know how to react except with relief.

Opportunities for plunder and adventure would probably keep his little brother happily employed. The Welsh would not rally, especially against the man who felled Cadwallon. Oswald would demand their oaths, but his boots would be lighter than Edwin's and he resolved not to trample over any of the subjugate peoples. The old woman was right when she said that enough blood had flowed; now was the time for peace.

There was a newly built stone chapel in the courtyard of the fortress and Oswald went to pray and give thanks for his victory. It took a few moments for his eyes to adjust to the dim light within and only then did he see a young woman, kneeling before the altar. She turned at the sound of his footsteps and stood up slowly to face him.

She was of marriageable age, perhaps twenty or so and her hair was white-blonde, tied loosely and brought forward over one shoulder. Her robe was simple and she wore no jewellery and yet Oswald felt that this woman was of noble birth. He wondered if this could be Edwin's widow but the woman's words relieved him of the notion.

"If you seek the lady Æthelburh, known to some as Tata, you are too late. She fled with Paulinus to her home in Kent and she took her children with her. She said that it was her husband's wish, should anything happen to him. He told her she must not be here when the murdering pagan bastard arrived."

Oswald raised an eyebrow and twitched a smile at her coarse explanation. "I see," he said. "It is a shame, though, that he got it wrong. As it turns out, I am not the murdering pagan bastard that your lady was expecting. I am the avenging Christian bastard."

Now it was the woman's turn to raise her eyebrows. "You are Oswald?"

He nodded.

She said, "I think, then, that you and I are kin. I am Hild. Edwin was my father's uncle. Acha, your mother, was my father's aunt." She took a step closer and looked him up and down. "Christian, you say? Well, if you can prove it to me and help me in my work, I will let you stay."

Oswald was not known for his levity. These summer months of preparation had, in some ways, been his darkest days. Plotting and planning and prayer had consumed his every waking thought and occupied his dreams too. Now it was over, he was undisputed king of all Northumbria and a slip of a girl was laying down a

173

fresh challenge and offering to grant permission for him to remain in his own kingdom. He threw his head back and laughed until the tears rolled down his face and slid down his neck into his hair.

# Part Two ~ The Time of Kings and Princes

# Chapter Six

## Tamworth 634

Penda was almost blinded by the pain. His temple throbbed until he thought that his brain was about to push through his skull. He'd had headaches before, but not like this one and he knew it was born of pure anger. "That bastard killed Cadwallon. Why have you submitted to him?"

Eowa affected to look comfortable, leaning back on his chair and cradling the back of his head in his hands, but underneath the mead bench, his foot was tapping rapidly. Nevertheless his speech was assured. "We cannot hope to win against them. They fight among themselves yet still they come; sons and more sons and cousins come crawling from under stones. To make peace is to live in peace."

"So you will carry on sending our cattle and food and gold to Northumbria and never mind if our own folk face a harsh winter? I did not kill Edwin so that we could stay on our bended knees and bow to another Northumbrian king. And what if Oswald asks for more than we can give?"

Eowa's cheeks flushed, infused with a rush of blood that could not be explained by the heat of the fire, since he and Penda were not sitting particularly close to the hearth. "Oswald will not be displeased with us."

Penda stared at him. He had known this sad waste of a skin all his life and he could tell when he was hiding something. "What have you done?"

While he waited for the reply, which he expected to consist of some shifty half-truth, a commotion broke out in the yard, sending the sound of screaming and wailing bowling into the hall to assault his ears. Men were shouting and women were crying and Penda jumped to his feet, but was halted by the realisation that Eowa remained seated, staring at the floor. Penda leaped forward and grabbed his brother by his tunic. "What have you done?"

Eowa would not meet his gaze and he spoke quietly, sulkily, like a child trying to justify stealing bread from the kitchens despite not being hungry. "He was a threat to my throne. He was a threat to Oswald's. If Oswald had learned that we were harbouring him…"

Penda took another handful of tunic in his fist, twisting it until Eowa made choking noises. "You have slain Yvo? He was under our protection. He was our kinsman. You little shit; the one time in your life you think to raise your sword, you use it against your own kin. How could you be such a…"

Eowa mumbled his reiteration. "He was a threat to my throne."

"Will you kill me too? Right now, I am more of a danger to you than he ever was."

Eowa looked up defiantly but said nothing.

Penda could feel his brother trembling beneath his grasp. He spoke slowly, spitting each word. "Boneless, gutless, you foul the air with your very breath." Penda reached down to his belt and pulled out his hand-sæx. He pulled his arm back, ready to slice the blade deftly across his brother's throat.

"No, stop, I beg you." Carinna came running into the hall and grabbed Penda's arm.

Penda stepped back and let go of Eowa's tunic. "You wish to do it? It is your right." He held out the knife and waved it as he spoke, pointing it first at Eowa and then offering it, handle first, to Carinna.

Her face was wet, but she cried silently. Slowly she

shook her head and closed her hands around Penda's, pushing the knife back towards him. "No. There has been enough blood shed in my name. I cannot have brother set against brother." She squeezed Penda's hands. "Please."

He glanced at the usually stolid Frisians and knew from their pinched expressions that they shared his thoughts that his brother should die at Carinna's hand. Penda looked at her face, lined with wrinkles which had formed too early and which bore witness to every heartache she had been forced to endure. He sheathed his knife and drew her into his arms. Holding her while she sobbed, he said, "I swear that as long as you walk the earth, I will not kill him."

They buried Yvo with all the ceremony and deference due to the son of Edwin, the grandson of Cærl. As they filled the grave with all the accoutrements he would need for his life in the next world, including a small golden cross in recognition of his conversion, Penda thought of his friend Cadwallon and wondered if Oswald had given him any kind of burial, or whether he had nailed his remains to a tree in some forlorn scrubland. Edwin's defeat, when it finally came, had come too easily and yet cost too much.

As memories of fighting, drinking and laughing side by side with Cadwallon crowded round his head, crashing and colliding, Penda knew that he was no further on. He was honour-bound to kill the Northumbrian king, his brother was still sending tribute and Carinna was still in pain. Nothing had changed.

Derwena, standing next to him, slipped her hand in his. She had arranged a good funeral. It was part of her role as the senior royal female; kings were the physical protectors of their people but queens were keepers of the spiritual realm, interceding with the gods and goddesses and ensuring that each man, woman or child, had a safe and proper journey into the hereafter. That Derwena had consulted the Christians to find out which grave goods they included in their ceremonies showed that it was she, not he, who was the resourceful one.

The youngest of the children, the girls Carena and Minna, had not come with them to the burial ground, but Merwal and Pieter were standing next to their mother, heads bowed in silent respect. Bardulf of the Hwicce and Berengar of the Magonsæte had also come to make their farewells to a young man who had borne his status of impoverished refugee with dignity. Beside them in the long grass, bumblebees scanned the low ground, looking for nest sites. The smell of woodruff carried from the woods on the gentle spring breeze and it seemed too benign a day for such a sad occasion.

Bardulf said to Penda, "This will not do. Eowa has become yet another king who murders those whom he has promised to harbour. We will not bow to him any more, nor will we offer up our portion of the tribute."

Penda continued to stare at the fresh grave. "Will you go elsewhere to make your alliances?"

"No, you mistake my meaning. I say only that we will no longer bow to Eowa. In our eyes, it is you who should wear the king-helm."

Penda opened his mouth to protest but closed it almost straightaway. Moments ago, had he not been thinking of his role as king and of Derwena's as queen? Bardulf was perhaps only giving a name to something which had been fact for some time.

Derwena had moved away and now had her arm around Carinna. She led the older woman away to her bower and Penda watched as his kinswoman struggled to place one foot in front of the other. Grief had finally worn her down; she was only forty-three but her hair was grey and her back was bent. He said, "I swore to her that I would not harm Eowa as long as she walked the earth.

On the day she dies, he will breathe his last."

## Bernicia 635

The sound of hammering was rhythmically soothing yet exhilarating too, for it declared the ongoing process of rebuilding and rejuvenation that seemed in concordance with the spring blossom. The palace at Bamburgh was gleaming after its protective lime-wash and the carpenters were working hard in the chapel, fashioning seating to accommodate all the worshippers who now came for the daily services.

Oswald looked out to the island and watched the industry there. The wooden chapel was complete and there were now several huts for the monks. Earlier that week he had been privileged to watch as the scribe from Rome had set up the scriptorium and shown him how the stretched and treated calfskin vellum was marked by scoring it with a knife point to give lines to follow, and then how they mixed their pigments, grinding some to fine powder, leaving others gritty so that they retained their colour, and explaining how the colours could be damaged by the gold used for illumination, so the gold was always applied first.

The British and Irish monks had been scornful. *"Overuse of gold spoils the look of the page by making it too shiny. We do not like it."*

In their fussing and fidgeting they had reminded Oswald of so many agitated bees. Looking over the water at the site now, he spotted that the hives were ready and one of the monks was watering the recently planted butterbur, in the hope that the plant's rich nectar would attract the industrious insects. He smiled and hoped that peace had been restored in the writing-house.

A few of the brothers were bringing baskets of fish up from the water's edge and a white plume billowed from the smoke-house roof. Oswald took a deep breath and savoured the smell of salt and seaweed in the air. The onshore breeze not only brought the familiar aroma but it also lifted his hair and he shook his head, enjoying the cooling effect of the wafts of clean air.

He jumped away from the wall and bounded down to the far end of the compound to a small, newly constructed dwelling. He called out to announce his presence and when he received the reply, he opened the door and went inside.

Nia raised her head as he approached, even though she had lost most of her sight now. The light, a rush core dipped in fat, kept the small house illuminated only for guests. Oswald bent to kiss cousin Hild's cheek and whispered his enquiry. "She is warm enough?"

Hild indicated the thick blanket tucked around the older woman's lap and nodded.

Nia said, "You children are so kind to me."

"It is as nothing, given what you have done for me and mine." He sat down next to her and took her hand in his, stroking it.

Tears glistened in the old woman's eyes. "I never thought to have one of my little charges home again. Your poor mother…"

"Ssh now." The forward march of time never seemed to put enough distance between him and the past, and he still found it painful to think upon the day he discovered that his mother had taken her own life only hours after seeing him and his brother safely away from what she thought was the aggressive grasp of Redwald. The joy of finding Nia still alive was equalled in intensity by the knowledge that Bran had never made it back home to her, after having discharged his duty to the boys by seeing them safe to Rheged. The reunion between Oswald and his former nurse had therefore been bittersweet. No, there was no task he would not perform for this gentle lady who had sacrificed so much.

Hild said, "We have been speaking again about the Lord. Nia is ready to receive baptism. Will he be here soon?"

He smiled at his kinswoman, grateful that she had phrased her question delicately. Would he come in time; that was what she wanted to know. Nia was old and tired and her health was failing. He and Hild were concerned that her soul was in jeopardy if she should die before being received into the Church. "I will go and find out if there is any news." He ran back to the hall, calling for Elwyn, newly appointed as reeve.

Elwyn was standing with a group of thegns recently returned from the outer reaches of the kingdom and who were now delivering their reports. Elwyn touched the arm of the man speaking to him, to indicate that he should hold his account for the moment. "Yes, Lord?"

Oswald had come to rely on Elwyn, frequently leaving him to administrate when he, Manfrid and Malger were away from the centre of the kingdom. The man's Bernician credentials and support of Oswald had helped to smooth the way for the kingship and to remind the older men who had lived through Edwin's tenure that here was a successor in whose veins flowed the blood of both the royal houses. He was at pains to point out at every opportunity that the sons of Aylfrith the Cunning were the natural heirs to Northumbria.

Oswald was grateful to him, not least because it was a reminder that Elwyn had always been closer to his younger brother than he had been to Oswald and had been under no obligation to travel with him back to Bernicia. He beckoned Elwyn to a chair. "What news?"

"He is nearly here, Lord. He has been sighted less than a day's ride away, although he is on foot so…" He held up his hands, his expression eloquently conveying his thoughts on the stupidity of walking from the western shoreline all the way to the eastern edge of the island.

Oswald rubbed his hands together. "Good. I think we are ready, are we not?"

Elwyn raised an eyebrow and gestured with his arm in a sweeping motion, indicating the finely decorated hall, the cauldron hanging above the fire, the newly carved king-seat and the side tables stacked with gold cups, enormous earthenware ale jugs and aurochs drinking horns. "Unless you can think of anything else, Lord?"

Oswald laughed. He picked up a wooden spoon, thumbed the intricate carving along the stem and put it back down, adjusting it until it was at a perfect right angle to the table edge. "I am like a child, I know." He had, indeed, been given a chance to live his life anew and it had imbued him with an exuberance that he'd never previously possessed. Some might argue that he had taken all that was now his, but he chose to see it as a gift from God and now, as if that were not enough, that holiest of men, Aidan, was travelling to Bamburgh to take up Oswald's invitation to become the first bishop of Lindisfarne. Accompanying him were Dalya and her son. Their son. Soon, they would all be together and his life would truly begin. He leaped up. "I shall go over to the island as soon as the tide lowers."

Elwyn lifted both eyebrows this time in an expression of disdain. He had often made it clear that he thought the time spent checking on the progress of the monastery was demeaning for a warrior king. "Would you not be better going to the…"

"And until then, I shall be in the yard, honing my weapon skills." Oswald walked off, smiling to think that behind him, Elwyn was probably making yet more faces at his back. Let him not be mistaken; Oswald was a man of faith, yes, but he was most definitely a king, too.

The travellers from Dalriada arrived in time for Easter and Reeve Elwyn ensured that the feast rivalled none for its sumptuous food, the free-flowing of ale and entertainment in the form of music, dancing and riddles. Bishop Aidan attracted many curious glances, commanding attention by moving very little, talking only with his mouth and not his hands and assuring attentiveness by speaking softly. Warriors who were used to shouting to make themselves heard over the babble of exuberant revellers were awed by the quiet stillness of this man. While his manner was restrained, his appetite was not and his appreciative consumption of the food that was laid before him endeared him to the men of Oswald's hearth. He had cleared his plate and a servant was piling more spit-roasted lamb onto his silver platter when Reeve Elwyn came to stand behind him to say that the poorer folk were outside asking for food.

"They usually wait for scraps and leftovers but they have heard that a holy man has come amongst us so…"

Oswald's plate was also full, but only because he had not touched a morsel. He spoke without looking up. "Take it," he said.

Elwyn was hesitant. "My lord, are you sure?"

"Take the plate, too. Let them melt it, sell it, tell stories about it. I don't care."

Elwyn had the sense not to say any more. He took the plate and moved away.

Aidan spoke in soft low tones. "It is a kingly thing you have done, to sit through this feast tonight and to remember the poor even in the midst of your…"

Oswald did not catch the final word. What had he said? Anguish? Despair? It did not matter; he was fairly sure that Aidan was wrong, for it seemed to Oswald that he was feeling nothing at all. In the centre of his body there was naught but a gaping hole where his heart had once beat time only to mark the contrast between a resting rhythm and the giddy speed induced by her presence. Now there was barely a dull thud, an unwelcome reminder that he was still alive.

Aidan repeated his earlier statement. "She did not suffer. Nor did she die unshriven. You must take comfort from that."

For her sake, for her soul, yes, he could rest his worries. But what of his pain? When it came, as it surely would after this initial numbness, it would be of almost unendurable intensity. And the question would swirl forever unanswered in his mind: why?

She was an experienced fisherwoman, she knew the tides and she was a strong swimmer. Why would God allow her to drown when the water was so calm, why would He be so cruel as to snatch her from this world days before she was due to begin her journey to Northumbria, and why would He abandon Oswald to rule his new kingdom without her wisdom to guide him?

The boy was safe, it having been decided at the last moment that he should not accompany his mother on the fishing trip but should spend the day playing with friends whom he would not see again for many years. Elwyn had been circling around the boy, surprised, wary, as if the child had come too close to death and was somehow contagious.

Little Udo had said nothing, barely recognising his own father, and now he was curled up beside the fire, sleeping with his head in Nia's lap and taking comfort from her grandmotherly embrace.

There was no such succour for Oswald and so far he had evaded Aidan's attempts to lead him to prayer. Of course he was grateful that the boy had survived but he could not thank God for taking the lad's mother from him; Oswald knew all too well what it felt like to be motherless at a young age. No, it would be a long time before he understood God's purpose.

He glanced up to see Elwyn by the open doorway, handing the plates laden with food to the folk waiting outside and their astonishment that they had been given leave to keep the silver platter too. Let them have it, for he had no need of it. Just when he had thought his life was beginning anew, it was over.

## The kingdom of the West Saxons 635

At Dorchester on Lammas-eve, Oswald knelt in prayer, expressing gratitude to a gracious Father whose assured love had given him strength in his grief and rewarded his hopes for the future. The church was not complete, but the old temple that had previously stood on the site by the wellspring had been torn down and Oswald felt that he could speak to his Protector here and be heard.

He had established his rule successfully in Northumbria, so much so that he had felt secure enough to leave his realm in the hands of Reeve Elwyn and travel south. King Cyngil of Wessex was feeling the hot breath of the Mercian renegade Penda on his neck and had made overtures to Oswald.

There had been a few matters to resolve though, not least of which was the sending of assassins from the West Saxon court to make an attempt on Edwin's life. Edwin, despite being Oswald's uncle had been his enemy; nevertheless, Oswald did not feel happy dealing with folk who employed such tricks. But Cyngil, roundly defeated once by Edwin and then by Penda, was now feeling politically isolated and needed a strong alliance.

The bargaining had begun, the agreement swiftly concluded and the terms suited Oswald very well. Cyngil had promised to submit to Oswald as his overlord, thus giving Oswald power in the south and, albeit as surety, he had agreed to convert to Christianity with Oswald standing as godfather, and he had offered his daughter as a wife for Oswald.

All of this was more than acceptable in terms of political expediency but now, having arrived in Cyngil's lands, Oswald was giving thanks because it turned out, beneficially, that the son who had ordered the assassination attempt against Edwin had died and therefore the problem of how to treat with a murderer had been neatly resolved. Furthermore, Cyngil's daughter was an attractive girl with a sweet nature who seemed personable enough to understand that she would never occupy Dalya's place in his heart but was willing to be companionable.

He made the sign of the cross and stood up and walked out of the half-built church through the gap where there would, eventually, be a door. The spring sunshine was warm, although he doubted that this would be enough to heat up the icy waters of the river into which Cyngil would have to plunge later on that day.

The dignitaries were gathering and all were in their best outfits, scarlet cloaks worn over richly dyed tunics with neckbands studded with jewels, and on their breeches, leg-bindings of gold ribbon.

The women had plaited brightly coloured ribbons and gemstones into their hair and wore necklaces threaded with coloured glass that reflected the sun's rays and dazzled at their throats.

A combined baptism and wedding was enough to excite even the most jaded. Although it would be a solemn affair there would be raucous feasting and merrymaking afterwards and Oswald sought out his bride-to-be, hoping to spend a few moments with her before ceremony overtook them.

He found her sitting on a rock on a sandy bank down by the water's edge and he stopped a few steps away, wondering if he should disturb her. Princess Cyra was small and slightly built. Her skin was delicately pale and her collar bones jutted out and emphasised her lithe frame. With her white-blonde hair cascading around her shoulders and framing her high cheekbones and wide set ice-blue eyes, she looked to him like an ethereal creature, more an angel than a mortal being.

She was talking softly to herself as if to silence any last-minute doubts and fears. Such bravery was so instantly endearing that it saddened him to think that this fearless and beautiful girl was about to leave her home and kin to travel north with a man whom she hardly knew and who could never love her.

Cyra would make a worthy consort, for she had expressed an interest in converting to Christianity, but had requested instruction from him and from his bishop when they went north, so that she would fully understand the teachings of the gospel rather than have hurried lessons before they left. With such willingness to devotion she would soon find herself under Hild's wing and the notion gave him some comfort even if the thought of that lustrous hair being covered up was, he thought irreverently, something of a shame.

She turned and saw him standing there and with supreme effort she bestowed on him a brilliant smile which reached to her eyes.

"I sought to have a few moments with you alone," he said. "Are you feeling brave?"

She continued to smile, but could not quite meet his gaze. "I am, my lord. At least, I keep telling myself that I am, so that I might yet believe it."

"And that," he said, "is true bravery. Don't worry, for I am as frightened as you are, but we will have a long time to get to know one another on our way north."

She raised her head and dared to hold his gaze.

Oswald stared back at her and found that it was his turn to feel shy. He was perturbed that a warm sensation was working its way from the pit of his stomach downwards. He coughed and looked away. "Yes, well, we should perhaps go to stand with your father now."

The holy man, Birinus, was charged with performing

191

the baptism and Oswald had agreed with Cyngil that when the church building was finished, Birinus would become the bishop of Dorchester and would have a centre from which to work his mission to convert the West Saxon kingdom. This day was significant; if the king received baptism, then his subjects would follow, and yet another territory would move to stand under God's protection as well as Northumbrian rule.

King Cyngil was dressed in finery that would outshine a kingfisher. His cloak, which was to warm him after his wetting, was made of brilliant fox fur. His tunic was dyed the brightest blue and edged with silk and stitched with golden thread, but all the silk in the world could not disguise the fact that he was now an old man, bent and grey. The recent loss of his eldest son had etched lines upon his face and robbed him of his balance. His younger son stood a little way behind him, with the woman whom Oswald presumed to be his wife.

She was a striking figure, not only because of her beauty but because of the pure white stripe of hair which ran the length of her tresses. Oswald had noticed her the moment he first entered Cyngil's hall but today her hair was loose, with no band or ties, and she was holding her head in what looked like an uncomfortable position, in order to keep a part of her cheek hidden. She kept her gaze towards the ground in a submissive pose and Oswald looked again at her husband. Cynwal was looking straight ahead and not at his wife and there was nothing strange about this, but something in his expression, not frowning, but thin-lipped, suggested that he was angry.

Other couples were standing with arms linked and beatific smiles upon their lips, but these two were standing apart, bodies slightly turned away from one another, and Oswald was convinced he was looking at a man and woman who had recently argued. If it was a bruise hiding under the veil of hair, then this man was beneath contempt.

Oswald knew that what happened to his mother at the hands of Aylfrith the Cunning had coloured his view of men who were violent towards their women, but he was not alone. Men who abused their women were not welcome in most mead halls. Leaders who did so would find their hearth-troops less than loyal.

It was not Oswald's place to interfere and he had no proof, but he mused that if this woman's kinfolk discovered that she was badly treated, Cynwal's royal status would not protect him. He made a mental note to question his bride about it to see what, if anything, she knew and whether he needed to act, in his new capacity as overlord.

The baptism was not the joyous occasion it might have been, for Cyngil slipped in the cold water and lost his footing, emerging spluttering and coughing. For a moment he looked as though he might give vocal expression to his anger before remembering how much he stood to gain and he fought to retrieve his composure, while Oswald struggled to suppress a grin. Next came the wedding and Oswald could feel Cyra trembling slightly although he could not be sure it was any more than the breeze rustling her gown.

The food laid out at the feast showed Cyngil to be a wealthy and generous king and it was quickly forgiven and forgotten that Cyngil had made the sign of Thunor's hammer over the food at the beginning of the meal, lifelong habits being hard to break.

There was lamb and kid meat, spit-roasted chicken and leavened bread served with butter and ripe fresh cheeses. The gleemen played their lyres and drums and danced wildly, turning somersaults in the air, leaping backwards to land again on their feet and flying across the floor in imitation of a rolling cartwheel. Bawdy riddles were offered to the gathering and the suggested answers matched them for filth and innuendo.

Cyra seemed to have relaxed now that the ceremony was over and she ate and drank heartily, regularly holding out her glass palm-cup for a refill of wine. She did not risk an answer to any of the riddles but at one point she giggled at the suggestion proffered by one of her father's hearth-men. "I did not think it was possible to use it thus," she said.

"No indeed," Oswald said, "I think it would bring a tear to the eye." He laughed and she joined in and he saw that her cheeks were a little flushed, either from the drink or the lewd comments. He said, "This is a fine feast and the welcome here is warm. Your father's hall does him proud."

She smiled and accepted the compliment. "He has done his best for you, but I have to say that on most nights there is something noisy going on. I sometimes crave a little stillness so I often go and sit down by the river."

"To be at one with your thoughts?"

She nodded and made a small affirming noise. "Mm-hmm. The trickle of the water flowing over the stones helps me to think."

He said, "I know what you mean. At times it seems as if the loudness of the hall gets into my head and I need to go somewhere where the sounds are more soothing." He was pleased that they had so quickly identified an area where they were a little alike. "But," he said, "do not tell my men for they would tease me unceasingly."

She gave him a conspiratorial nod. "I will keep your secret in here." She made a fist and placed it upon her chest, smiling, and then looked up to meet his eyes, blushed, and quickly made a show of inspecting the meat left on her plate.

Oswald, warmed, he thought, by the ale, smiled too before he joined in with yet another toast and raised his cup high.

Across the room, on the mead bench running parallel, Cynwal son of Cyngil also raised his cup, but there was no smile upon his face and he did not join in the exhortation for all men within the hall to 'be hale'. He put the cup to his lips, drained the contents in one draft and reached for the jug to refill it.

His wife, the woman with the white stripe in her hair, laid her hand upon his arm as if to stop him but he shook her off and spoke in hissed whispers out of the corner of his mouth. She glanced around as if checking to see if there were any witnesses to the exchange and then lowered her gaze to stare blankly at the food in front of her. She picked at it and between mouthfuls she spoke to her husband without turning to look at him.

He replied, but he too kept his gaze anywhere other than upon her face and his own features were fixed in a scowl. As they continued to argue, surreptitiously because they were wary of being overheard and were aware of social niceties even whilst gripped in the throes of passionate disagreement, Oswald needed to hear no words to know that this was a couple at war.

Much later in the evening, Oswald could hold onto the contents of his bladder no longer and he made his way from the hall to relieve himself. Outside, the night was quieter and he could hear the wheezing calls of juvenile tawny owls emanating from the nesting sites and the nocturnal birds known as goatsuckers were darting around in search of insects.

Standing by the kitchen, a young man, possibly in his mid-twenties, was chewing his way through a loaf of bread. He looked up and saw Oswald and hurried away. Oswald was puzzled; the man's garb suggested that he was a wealthy noble and yet he had not been at the feast. Why would such a well-dressed man need to beg for scraps at the kitchen door and why would he run when spotted?

Oswald looked around the hall often and carefully after that, and at every opportunity before he left Cyngil's court, but he did not see the young man again. He began to believe that he had imagined the whole scene and resolved not to ask Cyra about it for fear that his new wife would think him a madman. Instead, as they began their long journey northwards, he quizzed her about her brother and his wife.

"It is a shame," she said, "For they were so much in love. But they have been wed for seven years and have no children. He blames her and it is hard for my father, too, for having lost one son he is keen to know that his line will carry on after him. It has been simmering for a while but boiled over when my brother died, leaving only one young son."

"Does he ever strike her?"

She shook her head. "I do not know. She would not say anything even if he had ever struck her, for she is deeply in love with him still."

"Her kinsmen would not be pleased to hear it if he is mistreating her."

She gave a strange little laugh. "I think that is why she keeps it to herself. Her brother is known to take swift and terrible action against any man who shows cruelty to his kinswomen. Audra would not wish to bring her brother's wrath down upon my brother's head."

Oswald nodded. He could only respect such a man, who would fight to avenge his kin, especially defenceless women.

They rode on in silence. Cyra stared at the changing scenery and occasionally looked behind, as if seeking the comforting view of her homeland. Oswald was transported then for a while to his own memories of fleeing from his birthplace and travelling westward for many days and nights until Bran, their faithful servant, deemed it safe. Oswald had been younger than Cyra but he could still feel the lump in his throat, the longing for his mother's embrace, the comfort of the hall.

He leaned across and gave Cyra's hand a gentle squeeze. "I know you are fearful and I know how it feels to yearn for home. I will make it my life's work to see to your happiness. There is my son, too, who despite the loving care of my old nurse, still needs a mother. And my kinswoman Hild is waiting to welcome you. She is a gentle Christian woman and she will care for you when I am away, for I will have to be gone into Deira often and when I do, Hild will be company for you. "

But when they arrived at Bamburgh, weary after many days riding and many nights spent sleeping in hastily erected tents and using blankets for mattresses, the scene that greeted them was far removed from the picture Oswald had painted of calm welcome and warm greeting. Reeve Elwyn was waiting by the steps and he ushered his lord inside. "You have come back not a moment too soon," he said.

Oswald put a hand to his sword hilt. "What is amiss?" He cursed himself for a fool, realising that it had been a mistake to leave his kingdom so soon.

Elwyn sighed. "They are at it again. I cannot get between them."

In the hall, the servants had respectfully lowered their eyes as they continued attending to their tasks. They brought cups and platters from the side tables and set them upon the mead benches without once looking at the far end of the hall, and the little boys tending the fire did so whilst staring studiously at the flames.

Old Nia was winding yarn around Udo's outstretched hands and even though it was common knowledge that she had barely any sight, the two of them locked their gazes upon one another so that they could not be found staring rudely at the spectacle at the end of the room.

Hild was standing with her hands on her hips, berating Bishop Aidan who had bowed his head and was listening in silence.

"I have told you I care nothing for the ways of the Irish. My baptism was by Paulinus, sent to these lands by the pope. He speaks God's word on earth and I will listen to no other."

Oswald spoke to Elwyn. "What is it that has upset her?"

The reeve shrugged and sighed a second time. "It is beyond me, my lord. They are at odds regarding the date of Easter, with one saying it should be on the day the Roman pope observes it and the other standing by the ways of the Irish Church." He shuffled his feet, betraying his discomfort. "I do not know what to do. Never have I seen a row that cannot be decided by the blow of a sword. I am at a loss."

Oswald smiled. At least there now seemed no need for him to act as translator, for the Irishman and the Englishwoman were managing to understand one another, even if they could not reach agreement. He said, "There may yet be blood spilled. But I think these two are well enough matched. Let us leave them to it." He turned to attend to Cyra and found that she was wide-eyed with surprise at her first taste of life in the north. He said, "It is not always like this."

"If you say so, then I believe you," she said, in a tone of voice which gave the lie to her words and conveyed only doubt.

They buried Nia that autumn in the cemetery on Lindisfarne and Oswald wept openly. Her decline had been temporarily arrested by the arrival of the boy Udo and for a while she had lived her life with renewed purpose, but there were some battles which could never be won and as the summer faded away the chill seeped back into her bones, lowering her defences and allowing a fever to take hold.

She was the last link with his childhood and with no word from Oswii since he went to Ireland, Oswald felt bereft of kin, too. It was time to break ties with all things from the past, he decided; to show the people living north of the Humber that peace could prevail and that in such times, folk could prosper.

He took Cyra on a progress of his lands in Deira, hoping that he would be welcomed there as the son of Princess Acha and the nephew of King Edwin. His Deiran name would no doubt help, but credentials would only take him so far. He needed to win these people over and that could not be done by sitting on his king-seat in Bamburgh.

When they arrived in York, it became clear that he need not have worried. The first woman who greeted them as they entered through the gateway fell to her knees and blessed them, saying, "You are the image of your mother, my lord."

The reeve took them to the place of Edwin's baptism and then to his palace, the hall he'd used when he was in residence in Deira. On the way, Oswald was distracted by the sight of one of the old Roman buildings and turned to point it out to Cyra, but she was walking with hunched shoulders, looking at her surroundings but moving only her eyes, keeping her head still as if she were frightened. He had the sense that she had shrunk, grown smaller somehow in response to the unfamiliar and imposing environment.

She said nothing, but nodded with forced enthusiasm as he pointed out some of the architectural detail and the yellow-green flowers of the ivy curling through a window opening. Oswald was moved by pity but also admiration and on an impulse, reached for her hand, squeezing it tightly. She responded by moving closer to him so that her upper arm brushed against his elbow with every step.

In Edwin's hall, they were fed and entertained and the leading Deiran thegns came forward to swear their oaths of loyalty to Oswald. Their steadfastness brought a tear to Oswald's eye and he thanked them profusely, first with words, then with gifts of gold and silver and ornate ceremonial weaponry.

The reeve spoke, he said, for all the Deirans when he announced their welcome for, "The king who killed Cadwallon and saved us from his savagery. We welcome, too, a king who is of the house of Deira through his esteemed mother."

Oswald was warmed by both the sentiment and the alcohol. He sat back and surveyed the scene before him. Men were sitting, legs splayed, hands on knees, displaying a relaxation that spoke of trust in their king to keep them safe. They had sworn to him and all were content.

A little over a year ago he had stood on the edge of his dreams, poised to make them reality when he was cruelly snatched back into the world of disenchantment by the tight grip of grief. Now, with distance, he could see that God's guiding hand had led him through his mourning and helped him to keep a steady course to ensure that the kingdom did not also fall victim to that vicious bereavement.

He became aware of the sound of soft giggling and turned to see his wife engaged in conversation with one of the leading Deiran thegns and saw that the man was entranced, leaning forward and speaking with the sole purpose of making the queen laugh.

With a rush of belated humility, Oswald acknowledged that not only had he been shown a path through his grief and a way to continue to function as king, but he had been given an opportunity to rebuild his life as a man. He reached for Cyra's hand and said, "Ride with me tomorrow."

She kept her head turned towards the thegn, rewarding the man's efforts by continuing to laugh at his jokes but her answer to Oswald came with an unambiguous squeeze of his fingers.

The morning broke clear and cloudless and Oswald set off with Cyra and a minimal guard led by Manfrid, giving instructions for the rest of the hearth-troop to follow, since they were going to ride north and thence homeward. With a head start on the main contingent of Bernicians and with Manfrid riding at a discreet distance behind them, Oswald and his bride were free to indulge in private conversation.

Evidence that the year was coming to a close was all around them with grey bonnets sprouting atop chestnut stumps and the hedges heavy with hop vines and blackberries. The trees lining the path were dotted with hazelnuts, wedged there by nuthatches, and the hawthorns had been stripped of their fruits by mice and voles.

Watching Cyra as he rode alongside her, Oswald was reminded of a question which had occurred to him the previous evening. He said, "You speak little and yet I know that you are not shy. Do you think that I will not be interested in what you have to say?"

She laughed in such a way as to suggest that she had been expecting his comment. "No, my lord. But I am the daughter of a king who is known as a treacherous murderer and that is merely how his allies see him. His foes call him worse. I have always thought it better if I do not draw too much attention to myself. I would rather be known as Cyra, mild woman, than Cyra, daughter of Cyngil."

He said, "All I know of you is that you showed the bravery of a warrior on your wedding day, the fearlessness of a sailor when you set out from your home and the kindness of an abbess when you smiled at that drunken fool last night. There is nothing there that would remind me of your father."

She smiled, accepting the compliment. "I am glad. Children can grow to be like their mothers or fathers, but sometimes it is better to decide to be like neither. I like to walk in the sunshine, not lurk in the shadows."

He was tempted to tell her that she had certainly brought the light back into his life, but he sensed that she would cringe at such sentimentality. Instead, he waited until they stopped for a meal and to empty their bladders.

After they had shared a flatbread, apples, and some dried hazelnuts washed down with a flask of ale, he moved to sit up close beside her and draped an arm over her shoulders. When she did not shake him off, he exerted gentle pressure on her shoulder to draw her body towards his and when she turned her face he bent his neck and kissed her. He felt her body relaxed and compliant within his arms and he laid her down upon the ground, hoping that Manfrid had turned away, but too consumed by his passion to care.

Night was drawing in as they continued their journey northwards up the great Roman road and Manfrid rode up to join them. "We should seek shelter for the night," he said.

Oswald nodded. "On you go."

Manfrid rode off ahead in search of suitable accommodation and Oswald slowed the pace. It was time to ride altogether as a group, as darkness began to descend and give hope to any would-be assailants.

Before long, Manfrid returned, accompanied by a thegn who introduced himself as Hunwold of Gilling.

"Lord King, I have a hall nearby. It is not used often and only when I am hunting, but it is yours for the night and as long as you choose to stay."

They followed Hunwold as he led them away from the road and down paths, through meadowland and then to a small riverside settlement which had the look of a disturbed anthill, with folk running hither and yon in hasty preparation for the king's imminent arrival.

A groom rushed forward to take Oswald's horse and Oswald held out his hands to allow Cyra to dismount. He made sure that she was safely on the ground before he released his grasp from her waist. As he turned, she reached for his hand and held it as they walked into Hunwold's hall, stroking his palm with her finger.

Oswald looked round the small building, noting sadly that it was unlikely a private bed could be found for them at such short notice. He felt like a pimply youth, unable to master the self-restraint required while waiting before he could be alone again with his beautiful wife.

## Bernicia 636

All was well in Deira and now he needed to mend any residual hurts in his homeland of Bernicia and to that end, he rode to Yeavering as soon as the spring weather allowed and gave the order to burn down Edwin's great hall. As a symbol of domination it had no place in this new world that he was trying to build. His rule had begun with a battle, but he saw no reason to keep fighting.

The British kingdoms had remained quiet thus far, the East Saxons had restated their neutrality, and the kingdoms of Kent, the West Saxons and the East Anglians had all converted to the true faith. The resolutely pagan Mercians were still sending tribute, albeit sporadically. Eowa of Mercia had given assurances that he would keep his adventurer brother under control, although Oswald had had to flex his muscles and send armed soldiers occasionally to remind the Mercians who was in charge.

Nevertheless, he thought he was acting fairly and not applying undue force and in this way he hoped that peace would indeed prevail, and that there would be time now to focus on building churches, establishing monasteries, expanding trade links and getting on with the business of living.

The smith had been to see him and shown him the latest product from the forge, an exquisite sword, made by the process of pattern-welding strands of iron, in this case, six strands, to create a blade of beauty and strength. He had also brought a commissioned piece, made to Oswald's specifications, and the king held it now in his hands.

It was a gift for Cyra, an intricate working of gold, fashioned into the shape of a small beast, with limbs curling and intertwined so that the hind legs and tail were indistinguishable. He held it against the side of his hand; with the head level with his little finger-end, the tail barely reached the knuckle. It was small and beautiful and Cyra, he was sure, would treasure it. It was a sign of political stability that the smiths could now be employed in such ways, crafting ceremonial swords and pieces of jewellery.

Reeve Elwyn had other ideas. "If you do not fight, men will think you weak."

"But should I fight if there is no need? Is it right to spill blood unnecessarily? I saw enough of that in my youth and I would not go back to those dark days." He glanced at his boy and knew that Udo's future was dependent on his actions now.

"I would still keep my blade sharp if I were you, my lord. Men of the north know only three things: fighting, drinking and…" He broke off and bowed his head.

Oswald turned to see his wife standing in the doorway.

Elwyn smiled and said, "Still, it is clear enough that you know how to do the third of those things."

Cyra came into the hall, walking slowly and with her hand protectively on her belly.

Oswald helped her to a chair and pressed the gold beast into her hand. "For you."

She gazed at the piece, turning it in her hands and stroking the smooth, cool metal. "It is lovely. Thank you." She grimaced and clutched her distended stomach.

He knelt down beside her. "Are you well, my love?"

She nodded. "My ladies tell me that it will be born within the next few days. I hope they are right, for it would be good to see my feet again."

As the evening wore on it became clear that the babe was going to grant her wish sooner than expected. Several times, Oswald looked over and caught her wincing and shifting on her seat. It seemed as if the frequency increased throughout the night until she began to moan and sigh each time her abdomen contracted.

In the quietest dark of the mid-night, when it seemed possible to hear a dormouse feeding on flowers, she cried out and asked for the midwives to be summoned. Oswald waited until they arrived and then he went to sleep in the hall with his hearth-troops. He had no reason to assume that much would happen before dawn, for he remembered that firstlings usually took longer to enter the world. He decided to get as much rest as he could, secure in the knowledge that sometime during the morning, he would become a father again.

As the morning sun rose high enough for its beams to shine through the window lights, the hall came to life. Servants bustled about, stoking the fire and working round the slumbering bodies to place cups and jugs of ale on the tables. The great cauldron was lifted down and filled with bowlfuls of steaming broth brought from the kitchens. Once it was full it was hoisted back above the fire where the broth would remain warm until required.

Oswald sat up and looked around, taking a moment to remember that he was in the hall and not in his sleeping chamber. The baby had likely been born. He stood up and went through the curtains at the back of the hall, passing bed boxes containing the sleeping forms of children of various ages and then through another curtain which kept the king's private space hidden from the rest of the community. There was little to be heard except the sound of soft moaning, the same noise which Cyra had been making the previous evening.

Oswald went to stand by the bed and frowned. His wife was still on her knees, leaning on the bed for support, and there was no baby. One of the midwives was asleep on a chair, while the other was leaning over the queen and rubbing the labouring woman's back. She turned to look up at her king and stood up, massaging her forearms.

"It is taking longer than we would have hoped, my lord."

Cyra let out a piercing yell and Oswald flinched. The midwife took him by the elbow and led him to the far end of the room. Lowering her voice she said, "The bairn is the wrong way round and we have not been able to turn it. We can keep trying but..."

Oswald coughed to test his voice before he spoke. "But?"

"She has been at this too long and she is getting weaker and weaker. It might be better to try to birth the little one feet-first." The slight stress of the word 'might' and the trailing off to almost a whisper indicated that this was not a welcome alternative.

"Are there risks?"

She sucked her lower lip and gave him a compassionate smile. "Yes, Lord. I cannot lie. Both mother and bairn might die and there is no doubt that she will be..."

He held up a hand to stop her. He did not need to hear the words. His wife would be torn, ripped, and the risks of bleeding to death would increase considerably. But midwives were not in the business of letting mother or baby die if they could help it. "Do what you must," he said.

Another day and half a night passed and Cyra grew weaker until she barely cried out. Her quietness was more alarming than the sporadic screaming.

Oswald, aware that he could be of little use, nevertheless opted to stay in the room, holding Cyra's hand and offering comfort when he could. Like most newborns, the child seemed to sense that the darkness was complete and in the middle of the second night it made an appearance.

There was an awful moment when both mother and child were silent. Oswald held his breath until the babe gave a pathetic little cry but the midwife shook her head sadly in response to Oswald's optimistic smile. Now all attention turned to saving the mother, with both midwives kneading Cyra's abdomen, working hard to expel the afterbirth and trying to staunch the bleeding. Oswald had never seen so much blood, even on the battlefield, and he knew that they were wasting their time.

Cyra, her face pale and her brow dotted with tiny beads of sweat, looked up at him in supplication and he dismissed the women. Kneeling down beside her he brought his ear close to her mouth and she said the same word over and over: "Sorry."

He shook his head and put a finger gently to her lips. "No. Hush now. Save your strength."

She became agitated and clutched his arm, drawing him back down to listen. She spoke in broken sentences and quickly, as if she knew her breaths were numbered. "My son, dead. Yours so little. Was scared to tell… Father sheltering Oswin. I know now you are a forgiving, Christian king. Name Oswin as heir… Forgive me."

He dropped her clammy hand as if he had been scalded. The shifty-looking nobleman skulking by the kitchens on the day of the wedding had been Oswin, son of Edwin's cousin Osric of Deira, and rival claimant to Oswald's throne. Cyngil of Wessex had been harbouring him even while he pledged his allegiance to Oswald, and his daughter knew all about it.

Dear God in heaven, was nothing as it seemed? Could he do as she asked and forgive her? It took but a moment to recall the happiness she had given to him and he knew the answer. Leaning forward he picked up her hand to kiss it and then reached his face to hers, but her eyes, open, were unseeing.

Standing up, he made the sign of the cross and folded her arms across her chest. Not bothering to wipe his tears, he spoke the words even though she could not hear. "Yes, my love, I forgive you." But he knew that he could not accede to her other request; his heart was already hardened against the perfidious West Saxons and he could not contemplate leaving any portion of his lands to Oswin. His own son might be little, yes, but that gave Oswald time to build up an inheritance for him. Not only would he follow Reeve Elwyn's advice to keep his blade sharp, he would keep it soaked in the blood of his enemies and any man who would not bow to Northumbrian rule.

Hild rushed in. "Dearest man, they told me she was ailing. I am so sorry." She reached out to embrace him and then stepped back. "You are angry."

He sniffed and wiped ineffectively at his tears. "She told me something, about her West Saxon kin."

Hild nodded but did not seem surprised. "It was a heavy burden for her. She wanted to tell you but she was not sure how you would take it. He killed Edwin, who was your kin but not your friend, and she wasn't sure how you…"

Oswald shook his head. "What are you talking about? What does Edwin's killer have to do with it?"

She seemed less assured now. She frowned and when she spoke, it was hesitantly. "Cyra's brother is wedded to Penda's sister. Is this not what she confessed?"

He stared at the holy woman and her eyes grew wide and fearful. She took a step back, as if anticipating a blow. He probably appeared terrifying to her but at that moment he did not care.

So, the Mercians were in alliance with the West Saxons who had so utterly betrayed him. His fists were curled so tight that he felt his nails digging into his palms. Yes, he would secure his son's inheritance and then when he had raised a big enough army he would take the fight south and wipe out the Mercians on his way to destroying the West Saxons. He would speak to God, but he cared not for the answer, for he would do this with or without divine assistance.

*** 

"I had not thought of any girl's names. I was so sure that it would be a boy this time." Derwena smiled down at the tuft of dark hair covering the back of her baby's head. "She is dark, like you, anyway." She stroked the soft hair. "A dark little Mercian, aren't you, my little starling?"

Penda smiled. "We will simply have to call her that, Starling, until you think of a name."

Derwena grunted. "I might have to stop letting you anywhere near me. It seems as if you only have to sneeze at me and I end up with child."

He laughed. "I think not, these days. You are slowing; it took almost a day to birth this one and that is a long time for you."

She held out her hand and he reached for it, sitting down next to her and kissing her fingers before he released her.

She said, "You might be right. I think I will take a day or two to rest. You will need to tell me all the news while I am abed."

He shuffled back until he was comfortable and she

leaned in against him. He kissed the top of her head. "There is not much to tell. Oswald of Northumbria rode away from the West Saxon kingdom with a bride, and I hear that she is now heavy with a child. No doubt he will drink to its health with a silver cup sent by my dear brother."

"Ah, now, since you speak of it, I must tell you where to hide the latest haul before Eowa has a chance to send it on. You know, I was thinking on Oswald's wedding and I wondered if you and he are now kin? Your sister's husband's sister is his wife." She poked him playfully.

"No," he said emphatically, "we are not kin and I would not wish it so."

"They say he is a good king who is ruling wisely."

He wrapped his arms tightly round her and squeezed. "You are teasing me, woman. The bastard killed my friend. And if this Oswald is so great, tell me why he does not yet have any children with only one on the way while I have five strong children?"

She wriggled to turn, and put a hand upon his cheek. Serious now, she said, "You are the better man. You say 'five', when Merwal is not of your seed. And I will never forget the day you took my sorrow and dried my tears for me."

He looked down at his fingernails. "Hush. You and he mean the world to me, you know that. I..." He looked up at the sound of his brother's voice penetrating the quiet of the yard. "I will go and see what he is shouting about."

Penda kissed her again and went outside. The first exchange between the brothers was indistinct, but as they raised their voices it was audible enough for her to hear every word.

Eowa said, "Oswald has gone mad and sacked the British kingdoms and he will come here next if we do not send the tribute."

Penda grunted. "Let him try."

"Your friend Bardulf will not be moved on this. He has only given a small amount of gold and silver when I know he has more but he will not release it to me. You have to come and tell him."

"Why? I am not the king, you are. Tell him yourself."

"I have tried. He will not listen."

"Use different words, then. If you wish to be a king, then you need to behave like one. Thunor's balls, you tire me. Derwena has only now finished giving birth and she could rise up from her bed and be a stronger king than you. Do it yourself or stand aside and let me take over."

"Bastard. Never!"

Derwena lay back against her pillow and rocked her little baby gently while she listened to the sound of fist colliding with jaw and the sharp exhalations that followed the connecting of knee to midriff.

Perhaps Penda should have simply told his brother the truth, that Bardulf of the Hwicce had delivered the remainder of the tribute to Penda and that she had already hidden it. Let Eowa rant and curse, it was all to the good. Penda and Cadwallon built up the strength needed to defeat kings and Penda was almost destroyed by Cadwallon's death. But the Hwicce and the Magonsæte now openly supported Penda and more would surely follow. Messages had come from Cadwallon's successor in Gwynedd, too, confirming alliance and promising the support of the Welsh of Powys. It would not be long before Penda once again commanded an army the size of that which defeated Edwin. Eowa's days were numbered. And then Oswald's would be measured and counted.

# Chapter Seven

## Ireland 638

Oswii called for more ale and settled back contentedly. His brother had undeniably ruffled some feathers and had in the process made Oswii's own life so much easier. Oswii hadn't taken to the new king of Gwynedd but he supposed it took an untrustworthy man to spot another. The Welsh were nervous, that much was clear; Oswald had struck the British kingdoms and there was no knowing when he would go west. The Welsh were hedging and might not support Oswii if and when the time came, but at least he and they had come to some kind of understanding which might prove useful. Now, almost as soon as they had ridden away, emissaries had arrived from Bernicia.

Two of them had come, one known to Oswii, the other a stranger. They were dressed in dowdy travelling clothes, their cloaks a dull brown and held fast by simple clasps, giving no clues to their status. The steam rising from their clothing as they sat by the hearth told of a long ride through the rains, and the mud splattered up their leg bindings confirmed it. They had arrived too late for the evening meal and so a plate of cold meat had been brought to them and placed next to a full jug of ale.

The man who was unknown to Oswii and his name was Malger, drank the last dregs in his cup and held it out for a refill. He had told Oswii that they were in Ireland on official business but he seemed anxious. Manfrid, whom Oswii knew from their days of shared exile in Rheged, seemed no less worried.

Oswii said, "So, you have come from my brother?"

Malger took another long draft of ale, clutching his cup as if courage could be found in the bottom of it. "No. Yes. Well, that is to say, Lord Oswald does not know we are here. Reeve Elwyn bade us come."

Oswii said, "Ah, so you are Elwyn's man?"

Malger seemed affronted. "No." He looked down at his clothing as if assuming that Oswii had based his question on his rough appearance. "I am Manfrid's cousin and Oswald's man and a landholder in my own right. But I am worried, and so is Manfrid, and when we spoke to Reeve Elwyn he said we should ride and tell you what is going on."

Oswii leaned forward. "Tell me more."

Manfrid held his hands out and rubbed them in front of the peat fire. "You remember what he used to be, what kind of a man he was. He went on the rampage in Lothian and Lindsey. Both these British kingdoms were already Christian but he marched in there anyway, almost as if he had nothing better to do that day. I was with him at the Heavenfield and he was different there. He has changed. He is careless. He thinks to go next to the West Saxons, ploughing through Mercia on the way. But in Mercia he will come face to face with Edwin's killer."

Oswii spat on the floor. "Penda and Cadwallon did our work for us. I would have killed Edwin myself had I been there."

"Indeed. Nevertheless, Oswald will seek that vengeance and it might be the end of him. Reeve Elwyn bade us come to ask you to raise men and make ready to return, because sooner or later someone, maybe the Mercians, maybe someone else, will kill Oswald and Oswald seems not to care." Manfrid hesitated and tilted his head to one side as if weighing up the advisability of his next statement. Then, with a deep breath, he said, "And if you will forgive me, Lord Oswii, you seem not to care much about this situation either."

"Huh. Would you like me to come and kill him for you? Calm yourself, man, don't choke on your drink, I didn't mean it. Even I am not so stupid as to think the folk would hail me as king if I murdered my brother. No, I will wait and let someone else do it for me."

Brigid came in and sat down beside Oswii. Oswii slapped his hand down upon her thigh and said, "My wife here is daughter to the O'Neill king. When the time comes I will have many men to call upon. Tell Elwyn he can count on me. He will know what I mean. Tell him that his brother Elfrid still dwells in Rheged and between us we control who comes to Northumbria from any of the western kingdoms." He smiled as he sank back in his chair and stretched out, arms above his head.

Manfrid's frown conveyed his disappointment and he said, "I understand," in a tone which suggested that he did not. He put his cup on the table and seemed to have given up when he jerked forward and tried one last time. "Will you sail back with us? You are not an exile any more, but the full brother of the king. You can return whenever you like."

Oswii smiled. "The soil here is good. The cattle are strong. There is always someone to fight and somewhere to raid. The food is plentiful." In truth, among the Irish, hospitality dues were important. They took their role as hosts seriously and one could always expect a good meal and a decent bed for as long as they were required. "And as for the women, well, you can guess how well this one warms my bed. Why would I come back while Oswald lives? Send for me when he is dead." With that, he turned to look at Brigid and tilted his head, indicating the curtains behind the mead bench.

She nodded and stood up and they left Manfrid and Malger to their ale.

In the bedroom behind the curtains, Oswii unbuckled his belt and pulled down his breeches, while she watched him from the bed. Kneeling on the mattress, he lifted up her dress and shoved his hands between her thighs, prising them apart. She wondered casually if every man was as abrupt but she had no complaints, for though Oswii had no sweet words for her or gentle kisses, his hands had the ability to turn her body into a writhing wreck and she always welcomed him inside her.

He once told her that he had always practised this skill as diligently as he did his swordplay, having begun both at a young age. She knew, having gleaned snippets of information from the other women of the court, that he was exceptional in that he nearly always kept his cock there long enough for her to experience a tide-swell of exquisite sensation. Afterwards, she was sometimes left craving a little tenderness but it was never forthcoming. Generally he would roll away from her and all too soon the gentle rhythmic breathing would signal to her that he was asleep.

Tonight though, he stayed on top of her a while after he had finished and even kissed her, and she wondered if it had something to do with the messengers and what they'd had to say. She did not know what had passed between them she had heard one of the men offer to take Oswii away and her husband had refused. She was relieved, but knew that if she could get with child she had even more chance of making him stay with her.

She tried a touch of playful flirting, wriggling while he remained inside her and hoping to rouse him again. She said, "It would be lovely, wouldn't it, if I could give you a son? Your first child; think on that, my lord."

He grunted, pulling away from her and turning his back. "Not my first. My first wife gave me two children, one son, one daughter."

She was nonplussed and then, when she had thought it

through, she was mortified. "I am so sorry. How did they die?"

He was pillowing his head with his arm and his voice was muffled. "Not dead. I left them behind, that's all."

The warm, residual tingling in her loins abated and she felt her blood flowing more coolly through her body now. "I do not understand."

He turned to lie on his back. "I left them behind in Rheged. Didn't need them. I might call for them if I do. Now, let me rest. I have much to think about."

She was not stupid enough to disobey so she remained quiet and let him rest. She would not risk making him angry because then he might be certain to leave. And Brigid knew that for all he was a rude, lazy and inconsiderate man, he satisfied her too well for her to contemplate letting him go.

## Tamworth 640

Penda joined in with Lothar's shouts of encouragement, although it was meaningless since he favoured neither one combatant over the other. Merwal turned full circle before bringing his wooden sword down in a killer blow only to find it blocked by Pieter's shield. Pieter shoved with the linden board and swung his sword, aiming for Merwal's shoulder but he too found his thrust blocked by a shield. Their father, chest puffed out with pride, whooped and cheered. Merwal should have had the advantage, being, at fifteen, three years older than his half-brother, but his natural father had obviously been of stockier build and Pieter now matched him for height. Merwal, however, was of cheerful disposition and unusually for an elder brother, at least in Penda's experience, held no grudge whatsoever towards his younger brother.

Penda grinned at Lothar and put his hand to the rail, preparing to swing over the fence and join the boys, but paused when he saw Carena approaching from the house. She came to stand before him and gave a little bow. He kissed the top of her head. "How is your mother?"

His daughter was growing into the image of Derwena with the same coppery-brown hair and high cheekbones. She said, "She is well and bids me send her love."

"And your little brother?"

She beamed a radiant smile. "Minna and Starling cannot say 'Wulfhere' so they call him Wulf." She tilted her chin skyward and stood up straight. Their inability to pronounce his name affirmed her place as the eldest girl, important when she was now the third of six children.

Penda knew about childhood pride and he indulged her. "They are little still, but they have you to teach them."

He signalled to the boys and while he waited for them he said to her, "And now you must take an important message back to your mother and tell her that your brothers and I have gone to the moot." She bowed again to receive his kiss. It was such a habit for them both, he sometimes wondered how long she would stand thus, waiting for him to stoop and kiss the top of her head. "And tell your uncle…"

She looked up at him and her face was wide-eyed with convincing innocence. "I shall tell him that I have not seen you all day."

Chuckling, he watched as she went back to the house and then he put his arms around his sons, resting his hands on their shoulders, and they set off with Lothar for the meeting ground.

They walked through grassland, among meadow saxifrage and cuckooflower and onto the beechwood, where up in the tall oaks the caterpillars of the purple hairstreak butterfly were feeding on the leaves, and gall wasps buzzed around the trunks, while yellow catkins hung down from the beeches. Patches of tree bark were missing, the tanners having taken it. The partially shaved trees towered over the profusion of holly at the shrub level. On the ground, bluebells provided colour whilst the woodruff puffed out its warm, enticing scent. The flowering of the swallowwort indicated that the swallows had returned from their winter under the water.

At the mound, the area of raised ground in a clearing towards the southern edge of the woods, where the men of Mercia had gathered for meetings regularly since their forefathers first settled the area, representatives of the Hwicce and Magonsæte had already arrived. Bardulf and Berengar were deep in conversation but they turned to greet Penda and his sons.

Bardulf touched Penda's elbow and guided him to the other side of the glade, taking care to circle round the cluster of sacred trees that served as a temple to Thunor, god of sky and thunder and a friend of the common man; it was no coincidence that the moot gathered in this place.

Penda was profoundly moved to find himself hailing leaders from many of the tribes who lived in the lands bordering the Mercian kingdom. Groups had come from the Wreconsæte in the northwest, the Arosæte whose lands nestled north of the land of the Hwicce, and a delegation had even travelled from the lands of the Chilternsæte in the southeast on the border with the kingdom of the East Saxons, even though the East Saxons had declared time and again their neutrality as a small kingdom looking to live in peaceful autonomy and therefore being no threat to the Chilternsæte.

Beyond these tribelands, much of the territory that stood as a buffer between Mercia and Northumbria was British rather than Anglian and Penda noted that today there were even men from Elmet who had come to have their say at the moot. The bindings of common cause were pulling tighter than ties of common blood.

It was not long before the discussions turned from the irritations of border disputes, petty raiding and other minor transgressions to the ongoing payment of tribute and the ineffective leadership of King Eowa. Penda pointed out that he had returned most of the livestock and a fair portion of the treasure, and he made no secret of the fact that he was stockpiling much of the Mercian gold so that he would have a big enough treasury from which to reward warriors who fought in his name when the time came.

"That is all fair enough," said Bardulf, "but we question why we are sending any tribute at all. Is this Oswald of Northumbria such a fearsome warrior?"

Penda shrugged. "He killed the Welshman. But, for what it is worth, I do not think that means he is a mighty foe. If Cadwallon had not been so weary, having been fighting and marching for so long beforehand without rest, I doubt that he could have been bested so easily."

Berengar nodded. "Yet Oswald's reach stretches ever further. North and south, up into Lothian and down into Lindsey. The Loides of Elmet have already been downtrodden by Edwin and have no wish for it to happen again. How long before he strikes into the Welsh kingdoms and comes from there to attack us here in the middle lands?"

The leader of the Chilternsæte said, "And we will be hemmed in; Oswald will tell the West Saxons to attack from the south."

Berengar grunted. "That is true. The lady Audra is wedded to Cynwal, but as long as his slimy snake of a father is still king, we should watch our backs."

Penda agreed. He had allowed the marriage in deference to his sister but he had never been convinced that such a bond would hold the West Saxons tight enough; more likely was that their marriage alliance with Oswald would prove the tighter. All this had been done in the name of Christianity and he still wasn't sure how this new faith fitted into a world where fighting, glory and hearth-songs brought meaning and purpose to life. If Oswald represented a new way, then Penda wanted none of it. Others were free to choose and to follow their own conscience but he would not be moved. He grunted. "Maybe I should offer one of my daughters to wed Oswald's son, while he is still in the cradle, and thus tie a bond of friendship of our own."

Elidyr, the leader from Elmet, said, "Have you not heard? His bairn by Cyra of the West Saxons was born dead."

Penda dipped his head. "Then I am sorry for him. But I have to be glad that he remains childless."

"Ah, but he is not childless. His son by his British wife still lives. I believe he is about ten years old now."

"What?" Penda cocked his head. Where had this son come from? What British wife? So, Oswald was naught but another steaming hypocrite who, like Edwin before him, had put aside his wife the moment the king-helm was on his head, and taken a Christian bride to strengthen alliances. What was wrong with staying with a woman for love, no matter her status?

Merwal's voice broke into his thoughts. "If Oswald has no rights over us, then why don't we stop sending the tribute? And if he comes south, then we can fight him. As my father said, he has never been tested in a fair fight. We might beat him."

They all turned to look at him and Merwal flushed. "Have I said something wrong?"

Penda shook his head emphatically but it was Bardulf who explained. "No, Lordling, you have not misspoken. You have come to the heart of it. It is simply that…" He glanced at Penda, who gestured that he should continue. "It is simply that we owe the tribute firstly to King Eowa. So while he lives, whilst we can gather like this and talk,

221

there is little that we can do."

Merwal looked at his foster father.

Penda let out a weary sigh. "I cannot kill him. Believe me, nothing would please me more, but I gave my word and how many men would follow me, knowing that I would break an oath not to slay my own brother?" He spoke directly then to Berengar. "And as for Oswald, I have reason enough to feed his body to the crows, but last time I went north, as you know, for you were there, I had Cadwallon and all the Welsh with me."

Berengar said, "You took on Edwin without your brother's say-so. Why is this any different?"

Penda spread his arms out. "Are those who are here today a big enough number to take on the might of Northumbria? If you think so, then gladly will I ride north."

Bardulf nodded. "Give us a little time and we will bring you the men you need."

## Tamworth 642

She had a thick head after the Yule celebrations but her nausea was not due to excessive imbibing. Derwena knew the signs. Her breasts felt swollen and she had difficulty keeping her food down, but this time all the symptoms were worse than usual. It had been over two moons since she last bled and only a little longer since she had weaned baby Wulf. The pattern was familiar and she was sure that it was not possible to get with child while she still had a babe at the breast. Now that her first act upon waking was to throw up, she knew for certain and accepted the inevitable consequences of weaning her youngest.

Instructing Carena to watch the little ones, and cursing her fumbling fingers which had grabbed her only cloak not designed to be fastened with a brooch, she clutched the edges close to her body and set out to find Penda to tell him that come harvest time he would be a father again.

She had thought to find him in the stables, where he had gone late last night to tend to his favourite mare and watch her while she foaled. But Emmett, the horse-thegn, told her that the lord Penda had left some time ago, shortly after the foal was born. Derwena assumed that Penda had chosen to sleep for what was left of the night in the hall, so she went to look there for him, but the hall was empty save for the servants.

She went back outside, past the practice yard where Eowa was throwing his sword and his weight around. She scoffed inwardly, wondering why on earth he was bothering. She moved on past the weaving sheds, smiling to find that her step fell into tempo with the rhythmic clacking of the looms. He was not in or near the bake-house, nor was he down at the forge. Might he have gone fishing? She made her way towards the gate and stopped for a moment to watch a half-brown, half-white stoat dashing in and out of the woodpile. Starlings were leaping over one another as they probed the hard ground in search of food.

Derwena leaned against the old oak, keeping her clothing away from the algae covering the north-facing side of the trunk, saw the Frisians Sikke and Sjeord emerging from prayer at their temple, and remembered one last place where she had not looked.

Walking to Carinna's house, she slowed her step. The elderly woman had not been well and Derwena did not want to startle her by arriving noisily. As she approached, the door of Carinna's house opened and Penda stepped out. One look at his face told Derwena more than she wanted to know and she put her hand to her mouth, shaking her head. She rushed towards him and he stepped to meet her, accepting her offered embrace and butting his head against her shoulder. She said, "She has gone." It was a statement, not a question.

He nodded without lifting his head from her shoulder. In a voice broken by suppressed sobs he said, "She had a terrible life."

"No, my love, she did not. She had a husband whom she loved and sons who returned her love and she had you. She was not unhappy."

She knew from the ragged rhythm of his breathing that he was losing the fight against tears. "Come," she said, coaxing, "come with me." She took him to his favourite spot in the woods and sat with him while he succumbed to his sorrow and bellowed his grief.

The sun was high in the midday sky before he had regained his composure and still they sat, in silence now, drawing comfort from one another and he, she was sure, taking time to indulge in memories of an astonishingly loving and generous woman.

Sounds of shouting carried on the wind and Derwena looked up to see Merwal running towards them. "Father, there is a messenger from the West Saxons."

Derwena had so long ago hardened her heart to King Cyngil that she was not sure whether she felt anything at all at the news that he was dead. Kinder folk than she had told her it was simply because she was still mourning for Carinna that she felt dull inside, but she was not convinced. Her first husband, his murder at Cyngil's hand and her running away were all episodes belonging to another life and not scenes which she often revisited in her thoughts, for to do so would seem like a threat to unpick the stitches of her life with Penda. Any 'what ifs' would involve imagining being without him and she could not do that, so she had learned to leave the past in its place so as not to disturb the present.

The death of the king of the West Saxons had no impact on anyone else and while she busied herself with the arrangements for Carinna's burial, life went on much as usual. Thus the arrival of Penda's sister Audra on the day of the funeral came as a surprise to the whole community.

Penda was grey-faced, his eyes red-rimmed, and even Eowa was displaying uncharacteristic sense and staying out of his way rather than taking every opportunity to goad him. The arrival of their sister could only signify bad news and Derwena reached supportively for her husband's hand, fearing that his emotions were stretched too far, and worrying that he might not be able to control the reaction should his ire be pricked. Perhaps, somehow, Audra had received word of her kinswoman's death and had come to pay her respects. Derwena held her breath, hoping to have her wishes confirmed, but, unlike the children, the gods were not playing nicely today.

Each piece of information came as a separate knife thrust: Cynwal had decided that he would embrace Christianity. He and Audra had not managed to produce any children. Now that Cynwal was king he had declared the need for issue so he had put Audra aside and married another.

Those who were close enough to hear the news now found other places to look, either at the ground or their fingernails. Some decided it would be better to remove themselves from the scene altogether, no doubt convinced that Penda would erupt and give full rein to his wrath, and this group included Sikke and Sjeord, whose grief over the loss of their lady had engulfed them so completely that they would probably have been drawn in to any fight.

Derwena felt Penda's shaking and winced as he squeezed her hand so hard she thought her fingers might break. But she could only commend him as he managed to master his rage, stepping forward instead to embrace his sister and see her entourage settled. Audra was invited to join them at the head table for the funeral feast and

Penda sat down and drank, eating little and saying less.

Derwena had observed enough men deliberately trying to get drunk to know that it was well-nigh impossible and so it proved this night, with Penda remaining sober no matter how many cups of apple-wine he drank. She let him be, knowing that he was wrestling with his thoughts and that when he had grasped them and put them into order, he would share them.

When most had drifted away or bedded down, he spoke. Directing his words to his sister, he said, "I told him that if he mistreated you, I would kill him. Those West Saxons are not trustworthy. They killed Merwal's father, they sent murderers to Edwin's court and now my sister is put aside. Cynwal couldn't help himself, evil is in his blood, but he is no fool and he won't wait for me to come and skewer him. So where will he go? Oswald wed his sister..." He paused, head tilting first one way then the other as if he were weighing up the possibility.

Audra said, "Cynwal and I met Oswald, when we attended his wedding. I recall his staring at me when I was trying to act as if Cynwal and I were still in love. I swear that he knew all along that Cynwal was wroth with me." She fell silent, thoughtful, and then slapped her hand on the table. "He spent a long time talking to Cyra while she kept looking over at us. I swear it was me they were speaking about. She must have been telling Oswald all about it."

Penda's voice was quiet, every word coming after a pause as if each was carefully measured. Derwena knew this to be a worse sign than explicit anger. He said, "So, these Christians preach love, and yet they treat their women thus. And the biggest Christian of them all saw it happening, and did nothing. Of course the Northumbrian will shelter Cynwal." Then his anger began to take over, propelling his words with more speed and volume. "Oswald is no different from all the others. He took a

Christian wife as soon as he became king, putting aside his first wife. Small wonder then that Cynwal would do the same." He punched a fist into his other palm. "Why can't they wed for love?"

Audra said, "What will you do?"

Again, Penda paused. He looked around the room, his gaze resting briefly but pointedly on each of his sons. He spoke slowly. "I am going to right some wrongs." He turned to Derwena. "What say you?"

Derwena thought about the baby in her belly, the babe whom Penda knew nothing about, for she'd not had a chance to tell him. She said, "I say that if you would not go, I would kick your arse until you did go."

Now he leaped up and called for a rider to go to Bardulf and another to Berengar. "Tell them to come, with as many men as they can muster." He despatched a third man to Gwynedd to send a message to Cadafael ap Cynfeddw, Cadwallon's successor in Wales. He watched them stride out of the hall and then he went to where his brother lay slumped in his king-seat.

He kicked Eowa's boot to wake him. "I swore to Carinna that I would spare your life while she lived. She is dead. Now heed me, Brother, and tell me which of these things you will do: ride with me against Oswald and Cynwal, or give up the kingship. If you choose the latter, I must advise that you go as fleet as a wolf, for I will run after you and if I catch you I will kill you."

Eowa stared at him, wide-eyed. "You are moonstruck. You cannot take on the might of all Northumbria."

"Oh yes I can."

Eowa pushed him out of the way and stood up. "Oswald is my overlord and he will not let you take my kingdom from me." He began to walk out of the hall.

Audra called out after him. "Brother, where are you going?"

Eowa spoke without turning round. "To Oswald."

Derwena raised an eyebrow.

Penda said, "No, let him go. I know what you are thinking, that he will warn Oswald. It doesn't matter. We will be so many in number we could not hope to march without him finding out." He raised his voice and shouted to his brother, "If I see you on the battlefield, I will kill you." Under his breath he muttered quietly, "In a fair fight, I will kill you."

Eowa rushed from the hall and the door banged behind him.

Derwena placed a hand on her abdomen and closed her eyes while she tried to calm her breathing.

## The Welsh kingdom of Powys

At last, Oswald understood God's purpose for him. His destiny was never to be content, nor even to establish a dynasty. His role on this earth was to build a kingdom, one which served Christ. Two marriages, two dead wives and only one son to show for it; this had been God's way of humbling him, showing him that men cannot assume that good things will come but that a man must reach out and grasp them.

Now he had something else to be grateful for, because the men from Powys had risen up and given him another chance to spend the summer on campaign instead of thinking. And if he couldn't think, then he couldn't question God's will.

Since Cyra's death, he had immersed himself in aggressive aggrandisement, assured that he was doing God's bidding, comforted by having a reason not to stay at home and brood. When he was done, when the whole of the mainland was under his rule, then he would stop. Then he would take time to mourn. For now, he would welcome every opportunity to fight and here, in Powys, was the chance to do just that. But while he did not, would not, dared not question God's plan, he did wonder about the man who was riding next to him.

Eowa's appearance in Northumbria had presented a conundrum, not the least part of which was the odd assumption on Eowa's part that Cynwal of the West Saxons, who had not even travelled north for his sister's funeral, should be at Oswald's court.

Eowa had further stated that his brother Penda was on the march precisely because of the belief that Oswald was harbouring Cynwal. Did they not understand betrayal, these Mercians? How could he think of giving shelter to a man who had hidden Oswin from him?

Then here was the strangest part of Eowa's continued presence: the suggestion that there was a huge army heading north, because so far all that had happened was that the Welshmen of Powys had risen up in rebellion against Oswald's overlordship and he had spent the summer dealing with small pockets of insurrection on the borderlands between their territory and his own heartlands.

Along with Eowa, Oswald's loyal deputies were by his side. Manfrid, who was, in truth, never far from Oswald's side, and Hunwold, the thegn who had offered them shelter on the journey back from York, represented the unity of Northumbria, one from Bernicia, one from Deira, each with his own kinsmen and hearth-troops. Banners flapped in the breeze, with Oswald's shining purple and gold, and Manfrid's red and Hunwold's green and gold adding to the collage.

The latest skirmish had seen the Welsh scuttling back to their hideouts to lick their wounds and the mood among the Northumbrians was buoyant. Hunwold seemed to have only one phrase in his vocabulary and regularly repeated that there was nothing to worry about. Reeve Elwyn kept his ear to the ground and knew that there was no real threat and didn't this latest rout prove it? Oswald thought that the man was too relaxed, too reliant on intelligence, but he had no reason to doubt Hunwold's information, since it came direct from Elwyn, even if, as Manfrid pointed out, Elwyn had stayed behind at Bamburgh, citing an infection of the gut.

They had given chase after the fleeing insurgents but the Welshmen had disappeared into the sheltering camouflage of the woods. It was assumed that they would make their way thence to the hills, and the Northumbrians were a few miles into their return journey to their camp and perhaps, onwards to home if there were no more skirmishes. Oswald said to Hunwold, "What is this place?"

Hunwold shrugged. "We are not far from the monastery at Bangor."

Oswald said, "We will stop there for the night. I would like to pray." While he was on his knees giving thanks for their victories thus far, he would also beg forgiveness for his father's atrocity all those years ago. Oswald had been only a small boy but he remembered his mother's revulsion when the news came that Aylfrith had slaughtered so many innocent monks before the battle of Chester.

The monastery was built to the same design as that in which Oswald had spent so much time during his sojourn in Rheged. In the centre of the compound was a small wooden chapel and, outside the church, a stone cross, etched with swirling patterns, dominated the surrounding buildings. Clustered around the church were a few simple cells and there were several more, situated further away by the river. The abbot greeted the war party with obvious trepidation but Oswald assured him that his troops would camp outside the enclosure and that all he required of the abbot was permission to kneel in his church and pray.

Inside the church there was little in the way of decoration and no seating. Oswald walked forward and knelt in front of the simple altar, crossed himself and began to pray.

He was still on his knees in deep meditative repose when Manfrid came clattering in, holding Oswald's helm out for him. He was already wearing his and his hand was on his sword hilt. "Lord, they are coming."

Oswald stood up, rubbing his knees. He took the proffered helm but did not put it on. "Who is coming?"

"The Welsh, Lord. Hurry."

Oswald saw no need for haste. If it was another small skirmish party they had little to fear and had the strength in numbers against any such war band. "The men of Powys do not know when they are beaten, it seems."

Manfrid danced in agitation. "No, Lord, it is not only the men of Powys. Reports have come in that a great army is indeed marching from the southwest. The raven banner flies over them."

Oswald inhaled sharply, whistling air through his teeth. "Penda. So he has come, after all."

"He not only has the Welsh with him, but many tribes from the south as well."

Oswald nodded. "The West Saxons and Oswin, come no doubt to take the king-helm from me."

Manfrid frowned. "No, Lord, no one has spotted a West Saxon banner."

Oswald let out a harsh laugh. "So, he thinks I have Cynwal and I thought he had Oswin. How could we have got it so wrong between us? Is there even any need now to fight?" He put up a hand to silence Manfrid's attempted answer. "Whether or not he is helping Oswin, he is still a pagan savage who killed Edwin and attacked East Anglia for no reason, and clearly he cares nothing for the bonds of kinship. He has risen up against his own brother, for God's sake." He walked to the doorway and looked outside. The sinking sun was washing a blush of red across the sky, promising a fine dawn. "And it looks like the morrow will bring a fair day for a fight. So why not?"

His gifts to Woden and to Tiw the war deity had been extravagant but the price had been worth paying. Penda squinted against the hot summer sun, shielded his eyes with his hand and stared up into a cloudless sky. This fifth day of August seemed to be an auspicious day for a fight. If he and his allies lost the day, they were fools and deserved to die. Either that or it would prove the power of Oswald's Christ god. So, he thought, let it be decided, once and for all.

Cadafael ap Cynfeddw, king of Gwynedd, came to stand beside him. "I told you the men of Powys would prove useful. Not only have they kept Oswald busy while we gathered our strength, but the raiding has confirmed that the West Saxons are not with him."

Penda lowered his hand and made a rippling pattern with his fingers, moving them in a fanning action from fully outstretched to fist and out again. This was the smear that took the sheen off his good mood and he did not welcome the reminder. He would have relished the opportunity to get Oswald off Mercia's back and wipe the bastard Cynwal from the face of the earth all on the one day.

Cadafael said, "There is however a Mercian banner flying alongside Oswald's."

Eowa. So there was still a chance to pluck two thorns from his flesh this day. Even so, Penda felt uneasy, and it was not only a sense of anti-climax following the disappointment of discovering that Cynwal was not among Oswald's war band. He found that he didn't much like Cadafael, who was not cast from the same forge as his predecessor Cadwallon.

It also offended his sense of honour that they were about to fight a man so hopelessly outnumbered. Oswald appeared not to have got the message that a massed army was advancing north; he seemed ill-prepared and Penda couldn't understand why. Surely Eowa would have told him they were coming? But the time had come and it was an opportunity that would not come again. His federation of Mercians offered the last point of resistance against Oswald's ambitions and they would be wiped out if they did not fight. The fact remained that Oswald, outnumbered or not, was a hypocrite who took actions as a Christian that made him less honourable as a man.

Penda turned away from the Welshman and went to speak with his own hearth-troops. "We have clear sight over the field to Oswald's army. The ground is not flat, but neither are there hills or rivers to worry about. There are one or two trees but there is plenty of open ground between them. We are greater in number, they will have the sun in their eyes and I think we can win easily. Merwal, fight with me, Bardulf and Berengar, but stay between us. And stay close to Lothar. Pieter, stay well behind the shield wall. It is for you to watch and learn, not to get killed in your first fight." He could see that his boy was disappointed but he was proud that the lad made no vocal objection. A nod from Sikke the Frisian was enough to assure him that his boy would be in no danger.

Over such even ground, the only strategy required was that of a simple but effective shield wall, pushing forward and giving a protective barrier for the men at arms behind it. With each side calling their war cries the two armies advanced towards each other until with a splintering thud, the two walls collided.

The pressure was intense, equal forces pushing and resisting until one side finally weakened and gave way. Then the fighting began between smaller groups, each man trying to best the opponents closest to him with the sole intention of reaching and killing the enemy leader. Loyal hearth-men clustered around the kings who were the main targets in any battle and Penda was grateful to have Lothar and Sjeord alongside him. Whenever he had the chance, he stole a backward glance to make sure that his sons were safe, and he could see that although Bardulf and Berengar were doing their best to protect Merwal, the lad was responsible for almost as many Northumbrian men lying face down on the ground as were the older, more seasoned warriors. Another glimpse behind confirmed that Pieter was doing as instructed and keeping to the back of the ranks.

Penda could not afford to take his focus from the battle in front of him now, since several Northumbrians had broken away from the wall and were running towards him. He planted his feet firmly, took the blow of the first man clattering into him and saw him fall away after Lothar's sword cut through his chest. Penda thrust his shield forward to meet the next one and the force knocked the man onto his back. Penda stood over him and despatched him with a single sword thrust through the heart. He stepped over the body and continued on his track towards Oswald.

Beyond a scrubby tree a banner was flapping red and black, and he recognised it and knew that his brother was nearby. Breathing quickly and deeply, his lungs hurting with the ferocity of the inhalations, he made his way to the tree, sword aloft and ready to make an end to Eowa. Someone in the Northumbrian ranks had actuated the bowmen and Penda had to duck behind the tree to avoid a shower of arrows.

As he waited, crouching, he saw one of the Magonsæte, a hearth companion of Berengar, rush forward, shield over his head to protect him from the arrow fire, and grab Eowa by the neck of his tunic. Without ceremony or the slightest pause, he drew his hand-sæx across the Mercian king's throat and dropped his body to the ground, moving on while the blood still pumped from

Eowa's neck.

Penda stared at his brother's carcass and felt nothing but grim satisfaction. He felt not the least bit cheated; the slimy coward was dead and it did not matter who had dealt the mortal blow.

The bowmen appeared to have run out of arrows and Penda leaped up and ran on.

He could see Oswald now, but the Northumbrian king was surrounded by his hearth-troops. A group of men had gathered to a banner that shone green and gold. He was close enough to hear their cry, although at first he thought he was mistaken, but no, their howls, not of "Oswald, but "Hunwold, Hunwold," rang out above the battle clamour, and more men were running back to enforce the protective ring around the king. They were returning from skirmishes nearer the Mercian line and Penda now found himself being overtaken.

As the Northumbrians ran past him, some of them noticed him and he realised that they now stood between him and Lothar and Sjeord. Three of them turned and advanced towards him and he gripped his shield more tightly while swinging his sword in a wide arc. His shield smashed into the first while his sword made contact with the second, but it caught only a glancing blow and it was still two against one. He braced himself, aware that he was now fighting for his own life even as he came so close to taking Oswald's. He heard a cry from behind him and a flurry of movement as Merwal came to stand alongside him and now it became a fair fight.

Merwal launched himself at the wounded Northumbrian leaving Penda free to despatch the other man. It was over in minutes and father and son stood panting for a moment. Penda patted Merwal on the back and ran on, determined to reach Oswald, knowing that unless Lothar, Bardulf or Berengar could catch him up it was futile, for the king was too well surrounded.

He could not be sure and there was no time to ponder on it, but it seemed to Penda that as he leaped towards the group, the thegn whose troops were gathering under his banner and who rallied to the call of 'Hunwold' stepped back at precisely the right moment to allow Penda to lunge forward and get his sword point through the gap in the wall, where it penetrated Oswald's mail.

The king was wounded and was down on his knees. Penda's forces had caught up with their leader and Lothar and the hearth-troop were engaged with the remainder of the Northumbrian war band, finishing off the residual members of the broken shield wall and picking off any stragglers who had run forward and returned too late to get behind what was left of the wall. Penda stood still while the fight continued around him, staring at the wounded man in front of him.

The king looked up at him and said, "Penda?"

Penda nodded. "Oswald."

"Will you draw it out? Do you wish me to suffer a painful end?"

"No. I am fiend and foe and do not care how you die. But I cannot say what these men will do with your body afterwards."

Oswald said, "I care not for my mortal remains. I know my soul will rise to heaven."

Penda sighed. Why did such men clutch at their nonsense, even at the point of death? He stepped forward. "There will be no hearth-songs sung for you, Christian." He took a step forward, swung his sword in a wide arc, brought it round and took Oswald's head from his body.

He would have liked to stamp his authority over the Northumbrians by riding in triumph to the royal centre of control but he remembered too well the fate of Cadwallon who had stayed, burning and plundering, and had tarried too long to get out of the way of an avenging successor. Those of Oswald's followers who had survived the battle were divested of their weaponry and left in no doubt what would happen if they rose up against Mercia or even attempted to raid the borderlands.

Penda insisted on pressing northeast as far as the nearest royal manor and was gratified to have his instincts vindicated. Oswald had spent all summer dealing with Welsh raiders, making sure to travel with plenty of gold and silver with which to reward his campaigning warriors. Penda pointed to the wooden chests and said, "Load them up."

At the end of the room there was a table, but this one was not laid with napery, or food and drink. There was a flask on one side of the table and in the middle was a gold cross, set with a round bright garnet in the centre, where the two arms of the cruciform shape were conjoined. Oswald had carried something similar into battle, for it had been found near his body and was now in a cart awaiting transportation back to Mercia. They might as well have this one too. "Put that in as well."

Lothar hefted the cross, whistling silently at the weight and said, "It is rather big to fit in a sack."

"Bend it up, then."

While he watched, Penda was approached by a man dressed in a simple floor-length tunic tied at the waist with a length of twine. He knew from memories of the priest who accompanied Cadwallon into battle that this was a holy man. "Yes?"

The monk said, "You are Penda? You will go to hell for what you have done. Where is my king? What have you done with his body?"

Penda sniffed and waved a hand in the vague direction of the battlefield. "He is still on the field, or should I say on the tree, if you wish to go and fetch him."

The monk gasped and repeated his warning. "You will

burn in hell."

"So you say, but right now, I am alive whilst your king is not. What matters is not where a man goes after death but what men say about him. No one will speak of my spineless brother and no one will sing of your king."

The monk was indignant. "The scribes will write of his life."

Penda studied him for a moment. "In a book?" He thought of the huge Bible hauled around by the priest who periodically touted his wares at Tamworth in the hope of gaining converts. "Who will look at that?"

"Who would not? At Lindisfarne the scribes are already busy working on a new book of Gospels that will amaze all those men who look upon them. The gold lettering, the inks of such bright hues…"

Penda held up a hand to silence him before the monk burst into tears of ecstasy. He was aware of movement in the corner of the room and he turned to see a young boy of maybe twelve or thirteen, fumbling in one of the chests, looking, perhaps, for a knife. He resembled the man whom Penda had so recently killed on the battlefield and Penda guessed that this must be the son of Oswald's British wife. The boy was trembling but he straightened and stood with his chin up, signalling his understanding that defiance was the best way to conceal fear.

Penda went to stand in front of him and said, "Are you Oswald's son?"

The boy shot a glance to left and right before nodding.

"Do not fear me, boy. I killed your father, I will not lie to you. But I killed him because he wronged me, not because he was a Northumbrian. I have no quarrel with you." He spoke to the monk. "Who will care for this boy now? His mother?"

The holy man shook his head. "I am sad to say that his mother died when he was a small child. Not long afterwards, his foster mother died. Now you have killed

238

his father."

The last of the chests had been removed and Penda said, "I'm taking your gold, I'll have some cattle as well, and some food to feed all my men. I can take the boy, too, if you like. I have children of the same age and he will be made welcome."

The boy spoke, in a quivering voice that threatened with every syllable to crack. "I will stay. That is to say, I will go back to Bamburgh."

Penda shrugged. "As you wish. You know you cannot be king, don't you?"

The boy opened his mouth to protest.

"You are too young. For the time being, at any rate. You will have to wait. In the meantime, go home, hone your weapon skills and learn how to be a king. Have you no other kin at all?"

The boy looked at the floor and shook his head.

The monk stepped forward and said, "He should not even be here. He was left in the care of the reeve, but that reeve took flight some days hence. I brought the boy here to tell his father but we were too late. When we arrived, they had already made the line for battle."

The boy said, "Reeve Elwyn never liked me anyhow."

Penda knew that Derwena would never forgive him if he did not try to help this young lad. "Come with us," he said. When the youngster shook his head and took a step back, he added, "I swear to you that I will not be unkind."

The boy was resolute. "I must stay. There is a woman, Hild, who has been kind to me and if I am going to be king one day, then I need to stay in my own kingdom."

The monk said, "What will become of us? Who will be king now?"

Penda said, "I cannot answer. Let any man who craves it take the king-helm of Northumbria. But let him be warned that if he thinks to rule Mercia too, I will come back and turn this kingdom into a land of fire and fill its rivers with blood."

He rode through the gates of Tamworth in unseemly haste. Why, though, should he act as if he were in mourning? He'd hated his brother and that was common knowledge. To pretend otherwise would be hypocrisy. No, Penda would not profess sadness. On the contrary, he felt as if a massive stone weight had been removed from his back. Mercia was free from the yoke, subservient no more to the Northumbrians. Christianity had been exposed as a false faith and Eowa had met the fate he deserved, indeed had woven for himself. All Penda desired now was to see his love.

He jumped from his horse and ran across the courtyard to the hall, but Derwena was not within. He went instead to the weaving sheds but she was not in there either. A cursory glance the bake-house and the kitchens told him that she was not employed in cooking activities that day. So where was she? They must have had word that the host was returning. Never before had he ridden home and not seen her in the yard, waiting for him. A cold coil of fear began to twist in his stomach and he did his best to ignore it, but in doing so he found that the disquiet merely moved, so that his mouth dried and he encountered difficulty in swallowing.

A serving-woman passed by with a pile of linens in her hands and he touched her arm to halt her progress. "The lady Derwena?"

"Still abed, I think, my lord."

He felt a cooling flushing sensation as if the blood was leaving his body. "At this hour? Is she ill?"

"No, my lord, but…"

He ran to the house and shoved open the door. Inside, all the younger children were playing, apart from Carena, who was sewing. She looked up and beamed, bowing her head. In his agitation Penda almost forgot the ritual, but he stepped forward and kissed the top of her head distractedly before stepping over to the bed. Derwena was lying there, asleep, ill, dead, what? What was amiss?

He heard a small snuffling sound and he turned to look at the cradle. Was that it? Had she had another babe while he had been gone? He peered into the cradle and was astounded to see not one, but two tiny bundles lying in their swaddling.

"Ah, you have come back." Her voice was sleepy, but strong.

Penda felt as if he could weep with relief. "I could not find you," he said, still staring at the tiny sleeping forms in the cradle. "I thought you were unwell or…" He shook his head and turned to look at her. "Twins?"

She smiled and reached out a hand, clutching his and pulling him gently to sit down next to her. "Both girls. Born early. I did not want to tell you before you left. You are such a soft-heart that you would have worried. And a soft man is no good to me."

He laughed and kissed her forehead. "When?"

"Nigh on three weeks ago."

He counted back on his fingers and mouthed the rest of the numbers. "On the day of the battle. What a good omen."

She said, "Ah yes, the battle. You are alive, I see. So who is dead?"

He sobered for a moment. "Oswald." He paused. "And Eowa."

She looked at him and simply said, "Good." She lay back on her pillows and closed her eyes. She smiled and briefly opened one eye. "Children, your father is home. Come and crawl over him, he will like that."

They needed no more prompting, and leaped onto the bed. Little Wulf, at only two years old, giggled and waited to see what his sisters would do. Six-year-old Starling and nine-year-old Minna plunged straight into the rough and tumble and even Carena, a young woman now at twelve, joined in by grabbing Penda's feet to stop him escaping while he cried for mercy through his laughter. From beneath a bundle of cuddles, tickles and play-fighting, he heard Derwena's voice, the question casual but the tone less relaxed. "Did you bring my boys home with you?"

Penda pushed the girls away gently and scooped Wulf onto his knee, stroking his tufty head and wondering how to tell her. "Pieter's horse went lame and he wanted to settle him in the stall and into Emmett's care but said he would not be long. Merwal is, er, well he…"

Derwena sat up, gathered her hair forward over her shoulder and began braiding it as she stepped her feet into her leather slippers. "Take me to him. How badly is he wounded?"

He put out an arm to steady her. "No, my love, he is not hurt. Rather he is…"

All in a moment it was as if her heart had shattered, spreading cracks of pain up her body and across her face. She clutched his forearm with desperate force. "No!"

He moved away slightly and braced himself. "No. Rather there is, erm, a young lady whom he wanted to see. They have gone to the woods to be alone for a while."

The blood loss after the birth must not have been too great, for as the lines of worry smoothed, Derwena's face flushed instead with anger. "Who is she? Who is it who thinks she is good enough for my son?"

He braved a pat on her knee. "Love, he is a man of seventeen summers. He has fought in a great battle. His needs are not what they once were. He has a new kind of itch and it is for others to scratch it for him."

She took Wulf from him and cuddled him tightly. "I shall remind you of your words when it's time for that one to wed." She nodded her head in the direction of

Carena, who had quietly gone back to her stool by the fire and taken up her sewing.

He coughed. "Yes, well, that will not be for many years yet."


The bond between a man and his lord was always tied at both ends and thus service was repaid with gifts and public recognition of bravery and loyalty. Even as Berengar of the Magonsæte knelt and swore an oath of fealty, Penda bestowed on him a ceremonial sword, its hilt and pommel decorated with tiny inlaid garnets and the gold setting polished until it was gleaming, as reward for his bravery on the battlefield.

Derwena was sitting in her own queen-seat, hastily constructed by the tree-wright the day before the ceremony. It was as yet crudely carved but Penda insisted that she take her place beside him. She stood up now though, stepped forward and gently raised Berengar to his feet, not because she had adopted a superior manner, but because the leader of the Magonsæte was ageing and as with all older men, kneeling down was easier than getting back up again.

Penda shook his head in admiration. She had engineered the move in such a fashion that to all onlookers it would have seemed as if Berengar had merely stood to embrace his queen and none was any the wiser concerning his arthritic knees.

After Berengar had returned to his seat the rest of them came up one by one, announced by the scop who, later at the feast, would sing their praises and present a new poem about the battle of Maserfeld, the field where Oswald died. Swords, shields and all other manner of war gear were handed out to those who had shown fearless disregard for their own safety in the battle. Decorated swords, finely worked sæx hilts laced with delicate filigree, and silver helm decorations made generous gifts for brave warriors. Other items, like the crosses and the horse, had been shut away with the rest of his growing treasury, to be melted, reworked or handed out as gifts at a later date. Penda doubted, though, that the horse would ever leave his possession, for his daughter Minna was entranced by it.

He had found it among Oswald's personal belongings, fixed atop a large ceremonial staff. The monk had told him of little horse creatures that could be found living in the sea and when Penda recounted the tale to Minna she took to sitting in the treasure house and staring at the gold horse head. It was decorated with filigree, used to mark out its face and snout, and its neck was filled with lines of more swirling filigree coils. It was a beautiful piece, but no use to his men and he was still smiling to think of the expression on Minna's face when she heard the tale.

He reached out for another sword hilt decoration and was slow in looking up to see who had stepped up to his chair. His hand hovered over the pile of gold weapon accoutrements and his fingers closed around air. This was no warrior, or leader come to swear oaths, but his sister Audra.

She knelt before him and took his hands, mimicking the part of the oath which the men swore to him where the clasping of hands symbolised the bond between the men. She said, "I have come to beg for my husband's life."

Penda's back teeth came together as his jaw tightened. Cynwal was still in hiding and Mercian scouts on the border with the kingdom of the West Saxons, poised to send word of his return, had seen no sign of him. Penda had reckoned up the number of tribes whose leaders were loyal to Mercia and knew that should he choose to, he could safely ride out from his heartlands, leaving Derwena not as figurehead but as leader in his absence;

he would need have no concerns for the wellbeing of his kingdom while he chased the length and breadth of the mainland in search of the faithless Cynwal.

A glance across at Derwena gave him no clues as to her thoughts. He wondered, frivolously, whether she would favour another prolonged absence over the prospect of his lingering presence. No doubt she would berate him if he stayed to put another child upon her, and the notion had the effect of relaxing his jaw.

He looked around him, at the throng of loyal supporters, at his hearth-men and at his children. Perhaps it was time to stay awhile and enjoy his home and all that came with it. He looked into his sister's eyes as she implored him with her silent stare. He had avenged his kinswoman Carinna and then had to watch as the grief bent her double and then destroyed her. What kind of man was he that he could not learn from life's lessons?

He sighed as he fought hard to suppress the natural instincts that screamed at him to raise his sword in vengeance. He brought Audra's hands up to his mouth and kissed them. "I will not seek him out, on that you have my word, but if I should find him on my road…"

Audra freed the tears that had been threatening to spill. "Thank you, Brother."

Penda allowed her to squeeze him in an embrace and over her shoulder he looked at Derwena, who gave a quick nod of approval.

Adelar of East Anglia hurried from the dwelling at the far end of the settlement of Rendlesham, disturbing a foraging party of chickens and affronting the geese which had decided to take the centre of the pathway and objected to his overtaking them. He strode into the great hall, searching among the revellers for his brother the king. He found Ænna sitting with a serving girl on his lap, his hand up her skirts. Adelar glared at the girl and she sat up and moved away.

Ænna looked at him, frowning as if cross to be disturbed. "Well?"

"Our brother is ill and the leech thinks it unlikely that he will live more than another night. Haryth is with him but we need to consider what will become of her and their son if he…"

The king shrugged. "You had better wed her then. Oswald is dead and we can't send her back. Best to keep on the right side of whoever rules Northumbria next."

Adelar was struggling to contain his rage. He clasped his hands together behind his back, squeezing with effort in order to refrain from landing a punch on Ænna's weakling jaw. "I will not wed my brother's widow before his body is even cold. I doubt Haryth would even have me anyway. Besides, you have more to worry about than the next king of Northumbria. If Penda of Mercia ever finds out what you have done after swearing an oath to him…"

"And who is going to tell him?"

"I will, if you ever give me cause. Now, I ask you to go and see our brother in his hour of need and comfort Haryth with assurances that she and her boy will remain welcome in your hall and at your mead bench."

Ænna stood up, but only slowly, moving with dragging steps from the table towards the door at the far end of the hall. As he passed Adelar he said, "I still think that you already sheath your cock in your brother's wife every night."

This time Adelar could not restrain himself and his fist slammed into Ænna's smirking face and then he turned his back on his brother the king and walked away.

Ænna shouted after him. "You had better sleep with one eye open from now on."

Adelar said, without turning, "You also, Brother, you also."

He kept walking, for an hour or so, until he was clear of the boundary of Rendlesham and had passed the sleeping giants of burial mounds where his ancestors lay and where, no doubt, one day he would reside. Beyond the last of the barrows, he stared at the open grassland between the burial ground and the farmland, where fat pigs were snuffling on the ground for beechnuts and acorns.

The year was drawing to a close; the presence of waxwings and fieldfares was testament to that, as was the abundance of berries ripening on the holly bushes. And as the year was dying so too, it seemed, was his younger brother.

He could forgive Aldric for being the one who finally won Haryth, more so than Ænna could forgive either of the brothers for being closer to each other than they were to him. Maybe Adelar would one day wed Haryth, after they both had finished mourning. In better times, he might fantasise about a life lived simply but well, with the company of a good woman such as Haryth, but for now, as he nursed his throbbing knuckles, all he could wonder was how much longer he could suffer his elder brother's rule.

Manfrid of Bernicia had evidently ridden hard, though his clothes were stained not only with salt from the sea crossing to Ireland but also with marks that looked more like dried blood than mud from the road. He was staring at Reeve Elwyn as if he had seen a dead man rise from his grave and Oswii chuckled.

"So my daft brother went and got himself killed, did he? Elwyn has been telling me all about the battle."

Manfrid glowered at the reeve. "I am sorry to have missed that. I would like to hear what he has to say about a battle in which he took no part."

Oswii said, "Elwyn and I have been friends since

childhood. He thought it best to come to me as soon as he saw which way the wind was blowing. I believe the Welsh had a big part to play in my brother's downfall." This information had been the most interesting, for it showed he had been right to court Cadafael of Gwynedd. All men could be turned, if the price was right. He indicated the mead benches and said, "Be seated. Help yourself to ale and I will be back shortly. Then we can leave."

Manfrid glared at Elwyn again before he addressed Oswii. He said, "Will you not need a little more time to gather your kin and hearth-men?" He lowered his voice and said, "And those of us who are but newly arrived here would like to rest before we start the long ride home."

Elwyn concurred. "There is no rush, Lord. And there is something I need to tell you…"

Oswii held up his hand for silence. He had waited long enough already. Other men, through their greed, disloyalty or because they were driven by the need to settle bloodfeuds, had killed his brother for him and handed him a kingdom. Why should he wait? He scanned the room. "There is none here who would come, nor is there any man whom I would ask. And I'd like to cross the sea before winter takes hold."

Manfrid said, "But your wife?"

"She has become a mother since you were last here. I crave but a moment."

He swept aside the curtain which separated his private quarters from the communal space in the hall and Brigid barely looked up as he began to gather his possessions. He threw open a chest and picked up a handful of tunics, his antler-bone comb, his arm rings and belt buckles. Arms full, he kicked the lid of the chest back down and scattered his haul on the bed and began stuffing the items into a saddle bag.

Brigid said, "You are leaving." There was no emotion in her voice. Good girl, he thought, you are learning.

He had never professed any love for her, never fed her any lies or soft half-truths in the candlelight. He felt a little sympathy for her, being left with the boy, but he had never made any secret of the fact that he considered his children to be largely an irritating by-product of one of his favourite leisure activities. If he could find a way to stop them happening, he would. His children all had good Bernician names and were of high birth, their mothers being British and Irish princesses, and if they wanted one day to come and claim their inheritance then good luck to them. To do that, princes did not need to be with their father throughout their childhood; was he himself not proof of the truth of that? No, he had no need of children running around getting underfoot.

Still, he thought with regret, Brigid was a comely little thing and it would be a wrench to leave her. If only she hadn't caught with the child, perhaps he could have taken her home with him, but time was of the essence and he needed to set off. He bent over her and gave her a long, lingering kiss. God but she was beautiful. He felt a stirring in his breeches and wondered whether she would be up for one last roll on the bed for old times' sake, but the baby was grizzling and it broke the mood. Shouldering his pack and blanket roll, he made his farewells and went back into the hall.

"Let's go," he said.

He had nothing but optimistic plans as he journeyed, exultant, across the sea and then overland through British Strathclyde. He avoided Rheged, partly because he was in a hurry and the more direct route took him north of Rhian's homeland, and partly because there was no point in stirring them up. He'd said his farewells to his first family when he sailed for Ireland. Only a fool stepped on an ants' nest when he knew of its whereabouts.

Oswii and his travelling companions made up a small band and he expected that as they got closer to Bernicia more men would join them, but gradually his good mood evaporated as it became clear that no one was coming to bolster their ranks.

Elwyn was becoming tiresome, always trying to get him alone, away from Manfrid, but Oswii thought it better if they continued the pretence that they had not been in touch in recent years. And all vestiges of his hitherto cheerful outlook disintegrated when he arrived, travel-weary, at his father's great fortress on the rocks to be greeted on the steps not by a welcoming party, but by a messenger from York who told him that the Deirans had not waited for him, nor were they willing to love him as they'd loved his brother but had sent instead for Oswin, he who was the son of Osric, Edwin's cousin. Oswii was king, yes, but only of Bernicia.

The wind, laced with salt spray, had lashed his hands and he was shaking with cold, which came not only from the appalling weather but the frostiness of the welcome. He listened with mounting rage and caught Manfrid looking at him. It was nothing short of a smug gloat.

"Go on," Oswii said, "say it."

"You should have come back when I asked you to return. If you had served as hearth-thegn to your brother, much as Osric did when he and Edwin were thegns at the Deiran court, then maybe you would be king of both kingdoms now."

Oswii made a fist and got ready to punch the satisfied grin from the bastard's face, but Elwyn touched his arm.

The reeve said, "The Deirans welcomed Oswald, it's true, and it was partly because he was so like Edwin and Acha in looks. He rescued them from the Welshman Cadwallon who was ravaging their homeland so they loved him for it. They did not suffer so much at Penda's hands; from what I hear he merely stole some gold and then went home. But do not worry. They can be won round in time and I know of one or two who would be willing to see things the way we do."

Oswii was still sorely tempted to cuff Manfrid around the head, but he could see that the man was not in the least cowed. He kept his fist by his side and said, "Well aren't you clever with all your wise words. Better yet if you'd tell me what I should do now."

Manfrid slid his tongue across his top teeth. "You're going to hate me for saying this, but you're going to have to think like your brother did."

Oswii grunted and pushed him aside. Oswald's thinking had got him killed.

He marched towards the great hall, muttering under his breath as he went. This was not what he was expecting, nor was it what was owed to him. He was Aylfrith's son. Those who had known his father went so far as to say that he was his walking image. His father was known as the 'Cunning' and Oswii had already employed some of that inherited skill.

In the hall, waiting for him, was a middle-aged woman, dressed in simple garb. She stood up when he entered and walked across the floor to meet him. She was holding a glass beaker full of ale which she offered to him. "I am your kinswoman, Hild," she said.

Oswii unclasped his cloak and swirled it round his head before flinging it on the nearest bench. He grabbed the beaker from her, holding it above the intricate claw-shaping at the base. "Where are all the folk? Bad enough that they shun me in Deira, but I had hoped for a better welcome than this here in my father's hall." He had already decided that he was officially in a bad mood and knew that whatever her answer, it would not soothe him. He deserved a sulk and he was going to enjoy it.

But it seemed that the shrewish woman had no

intention of trying to placate him. She put her hands to her hips and said, "I was not blessed to ever meet your mother, but those who knew her have always spoken fondly of her. Your brother was a good and Christian king. I find it hard to believe that the man who sits now before me shares any of their blood or mine. You want to know where the folk are? They are hiding, scared of the new king, for he is not known to them. The tide has turned and now Northumbria bends its knee to Mercia. You are king, yes, but only of a small kingdom, one that is beholden to another, mightier, realm. Your folk are beaten and bruised. Instead of feeling sorry for yourself, you should be thinking about how to win their hearts."

He looked up at her and agreed with her on one point. His brother must have been a good and patient man indeed if he put up with her without throttling her. Dear God; was this what it was to be a king, to have every man and his hound telling you what to do?

He put his feet up on the table, crossed them at the ankles and snapped his fingers for another drink. He recalled watching his father and half-brother Enfrith sit just so at this very table and whilst it was a long time ago, it all seemed familiar. There was even a young boy cowering in the corner, much as he remembered his brother Oswald was wont to do whenever his father shouted at him. He peered at the youth, thinking that he had seen him before, but then he shook his head and spoke to the interfering woman who claimed to be his kin. Pointing at the boy, he said, "Who is that?"

Reeve Elwyn shot forward so quickly he nearly stumbled over his own shoes. "I have been trying to tell you…"

Hild moved nearer and gestured to the boy to come forward. Propelling him by the elbow she brought him to stand in front of Oswii and said, "This is your nephew, Œthelwold, known as Udo."

Oswii shook his head, thinking now that the woman was quite mad. He had no nephew, unless she meant Enfrith's son, but he was far away in Pictland and was, in any case, much older than the sapling now standing in front of him.

Hild said, "This is King Oswald's son. I can see from your face that you did not know about him."

Oswii glared at Reeve Elwyn. "No," he said, "I did not think that my brother had a son still living." He emphasised the last word and Elwyn's cheeks coloured. "I had heard that he died along with his mother."

Oswii peered again and now it was obvious why the lad looked familiar. He had the look of Oswald, with his pale face and white-blond hair, right down to the willowy stance that made him seem as if the slightest breeze would knock him over. Oswii sniffed, took a long draft of ale and wiped his mouth with the back of his hand. "Well, there is no mistaking whose whelp you are. And I don't want to be reminded of my lack-wit brother too often. So keep out of my way and we'll rub along nicely." He hid his frustration by burying his face in the ale cup and drinking thirstily. This was another problem he had not foreseen, and he realised instantly that with Hild snapping round him like a vixen with a cub he would not be able to deal with the brat any time soon.

She spoke now and he had to look up. "When will your own children be arriving?"

He looked at her for a moment and then decided to ignore the question. He stared at the boy, who met his gaze with a bravery that was belied by his shaking torso.

"So, this is what passes for your mother, is it, boy? What happened to the West Saxon woman?"

Hild gave the answer. "You know then, that Udo's mother died before she could set out to make her home here. Bishop Aidan was with her at the end and gave her the last rites and a Christian burial. When Oswald became king he took a second wife, the West Saxon to whom you refer. She was a good, god-fearing woman whose father was also a king. It was a great day, for as well as giving his daughter away to wed, the West Saxon king accepted baptism and Oswald's overlordship. Her name, God rest her soul, was…"

Oswii put a hand up to silence her. He had already decided that he could not bear the sound of her voice. But more than that, he was beginning to piece together a solution to his immediate problem. If force was not an option in building up an empire to rival that of his predecessors, then he would have to find another way. He had been vexed since his arrival and was thinking now about what Manfrid had suggested. He said, "I think I might do not as my brother did, but as our father did. Reeve Elwyn, send out to find me a wife."

Manfrid made a face which irritated Oswii, a sardonic lift of the eyebrow. He said, "Does my lord have anyone in mind?"

Oswii shrugged. "Get me a Deiran princess. Don't care which one."

Reeve Elwyn, who had been standing with head bowed like a child caught out having not performed its chores, looked up now and said, "Good thinking indeed, but I'm sorry to say that there aren't any in Deira."

"Shit."

"But, if my lord will allow, I do have an idea."

Oswii nodded and dragged Elwyn to one side. He spoke softly so as not to be overheard. "It had better be a good one. You are going to have to work hard after your brother Elfrid let me down all those years ago. I was supposed to be the only heir left when that boat sprang a leak in Dalriada. Lucky for you that the throne has come to me while that brat is still only a child."

## Bamburgh 643

Efa was born in turbulent times, on the night of the attempt on her father King Edwin's life, and she was a child of seven when her father's head was hacked from his body and she, her mother and baby brother fled to her mother's homeland of Kent. Her mother, whose pet name was Tata, had subsequently sent her little brother over the sea to Frankia and had retired to a monastery. Efa had assumed that she, too, would take that route and become an abbess in due course.

Abbeys offered a spiritual service, caring for the souls of the dead, much as the pagan women had done, but with proper, Christian rituals rather than heathen incantations. Efa knew that women enjoyed the highest rank within the church while the men were too busy with war, and their supreme holiness added mystique and status to the royal houses.

Her mother's brother, the king of Kent, had died three years ago and his son, Efa's cousin, was a loving kinsman. So it was a surprise when he agreed to the request from Northumbria and allowed entry to the armed escort which arrived to accompany Efa back to her birthplace, there to become not an abbess, but merely the wife and queen of King Oswii of Bernicia.

She was seventeen years old and all she knew of her future husband was that he had been a rival to her father's throne and that he had been born when her father was still a young man. She had prayed for strength, for patience and fortitude and the wisdom to steer a noble path in her role as peace-weaver. She had also prayed that her much older husband was still in possession of his teeth.

Now she was standing in the great hall at Bamburgh and staring at a man who, whilst admittedly was past thirty, not only had a full set of teeth but also a fine head of hair which appeared to defy any attempts to make it lie flat. He wore his hair in the longer, British style, and his trousers were an odd shape, much wider than those worn by the Kentish. His shoes were ornate, also in the British style, and highly decorated. He was not tall, being stocky with a thick neck, and his eyes were a little wide-set. His smile though, when it came, was at first cheeky and attractive and then bordering on lascivious as his scrutinising gaze travelled down her body and back up again.

"You will do," he said, but in a tone which suggested rather more satisfaction than was normally contained in those three small dismissive words.

Efa was taken aback, having heard that this man was a baptised Christian, albeit in the Irish and British tradition. Perhaps there needed to be some changes in Bernicia; Northumbria seemed to have lapsed since Paulinus had left its lands. She fingered her pendant, the cruciform jewel given to her by her Kentish mother, and looked around to see that the Northumbrian women still favoured the gaudy wearing of multiple finger rings, and rows of beads rather than a single ornament at the neck.

A swishing of skirts announced the arrival of another woman and Efa turned and found herself taken up in a tight embrace while the woman who had attached herself was sobbing into her neck. Efa extricated herself as best she could and leaned back a little in order to see the face of her emotional assailant. She looked for a moment, attempting to focus at such close quarters and then with faltering recognition she said, "Hild?"

The older woman clasped Efa's face in her hands and nodded, while the tears continued to stream down her own cheeks. "My little love, I can hardly believe it is you."

The two women remained then in their embrace, laughing and crying, until Oswii made a loud tutting noise. Efa looked up to see him glancing towards the ceiling as if exasperated, before making his way to the mead bench, taking with him a platter of meat and a cup of ale.

Efa was horrified. "What is he doing? We are still in Lent."

The king belched and shook his head. "Easter Sunday yesterday."

Efa sought confirmation from Hild. "How can this be?"

Hild pursed her lips and said, "Welcome to the land of the British Christians." She worked her mouth as if trying to rid it of a horrid taste. "They will not hear sense and they observe Easter at odd times." Turning to look at the bishop she said, "Now we will see who is right and who is wrong."

Bravery came with this unexpected opportunity to instruct, and Efa heard forcefulness in her voice when she said, "I think I have come back none too soon."

Aidan sighed and the king looked heavenward once more. "God help me, now there are two of them."

It was not the scene that he had imagined. Instead of a grand, victorious procession, it had been barely more than a covert mission, involving a ride through lands which, whilst not openly hostile, were nevertheless reluctant to extend the hand of friendship to the new king of Bernicia.

On a windswept patch of ground the recent turbulence was still evident and the grass had grown back in uneven clumps, betraying the spots where the vegetation had been torn up by hooves, boots and grounded axe blades, or died away completely underneath the weight of bodies, left to rot. Now, those partly decomposed bodies and skeletons had been removed, save one.

What was left of Oswald's body still hung from the crude cross where it had been nailed by the victors of the battle, or perhaps by the hand of a lesser warrior in a moment of exuberant vindictiveness. The severed head had been stuck on a branch near the neck and shoulders.

Oswii had always thought that he had a strong stomach but he was swallowing frantically in an effort to keep his gorge from rising. He had brought only a handful of men with him, seeing no need to draw attention to himself in his diminished status. All of those men now looked at the ground, hoping no doubt that he would not select them to attend to the corpse. Oswii was aware of his faults, for he had been told about them by all those around him: his brother, his wives, the churchmen and women whose role in life it was to torment him. But never had any of them suggested that he was squeamish.

He slipped from the saddle and unsheathed his hand-sæx so that he could work at the nails and cut through the fraying rope that had been used to bind the limbs. As he worked away at the fetters, he felt compelled to speak softly to the brother who had never been a friend yet had been of his blood. "Who would have thought it would come to this, Brother? Let me show you how it should be done. A strong sword arm is a fine thing to have, but our mother's bloodline was not enough. Our father's cunning, that is what is needed." He had to pause while he sawed away at a particularly recalcitrant piece of rope, swollen and then contracted by the harsh winter weather.

As his blade finally came all the way through, he said, "I have wed Edwin's daughter. Clever, no? I have no doubt that your soul is with the Lord; watch me from there, Brother, as I get all of Northumbria back again."

At last he was in a position to signal for the box to be brought forward and he loaded his brother's grisly remains into the coffin. "Come then, let's get you home. I will not have you forever in a foreign land."

They rode back, skirting the border of the lands of the Pecsæte, the most northerly members of the Mercian federation, and travelling quietly through Elmet and Deira, striving always to remain inconspicuous and camping well away from any settlements, other than at Gilling where he received a warm welcome from Hunwold.

Safely back in Bernicia they made their way home via the blackened skeleton of Yeavering and at last the great silhouette of Bamburgh stood stark against the darkening evening sky. Oswii was met at the gates by Bishop Aidan, who was openly weeping.

"Have you brought him?" He rushed forward to the cart and put his hands on the lid of the wooden box.

Oswii called out. "I wouldn't if I were you. It is a grim sight."

Aidan rolled his sleeves up. "No matter. We will clean and bleach his bones and give him a fitting burial."

Oswii left him to it and went into the hall.

Hild and Efa were together, heads bent over some book of scripture. Oswii ground his teeth together and then rubbed the back of his neck to ease the tension. After a hard ride he wanted a better welcome than this. He had no choice but to tolerate Hild's presence for she was an important symbol of continuity for the Deirans, giving them faith to convert to Christianity and being a high-ranking member of the royal family. They had Oswin, but he had Hild and Aidan and now he had Edwin's daughter, too. He must keep sight of the political advantage thus held, but at times it was difficult to see beyond the flash of long robes and to hear above the constant hum of prayer.

Even if Hild was of the Roman tradition, he had to concede that she was nevertheless an important figure for the Deirans, who still lit candles to the memory of Edwin. The arrival of Efa would serve only to magnify the presence of pious Deiran women at the Bernician court and thus elevate his own status.

He watched them twittering and fussing over the brat Udo and hoped that he would not come to regret his decision. He sat down heavily and called for drink. Leaning back in his chair he closed his eyes, but he was not ready for sleep and the drone of pious voices was jarring rather than soothing. He jumped up again and shouted across the hall. "Wife, come with me."

Once upon a time Efa had hoped to devote her life to Christ by retiring to a monastery but had been called instead to serve as queen of Bernicia. Already there was talk of Hild establishing such a house with Aidan's help and when that day came her role would be elevated further. She saw no particular hardship in her life as Oswii's wife, regarding it as simply another way to fulfil God's purpose for her and allowing her to spread the gospel. It helped, of course, that he was less of a brute than she had imagined, being tolerable of countenance and fit and active.

Her duties in the marital bed were also part of her service to a higher lord and master and she had been prepared to endure whenever required. It was fortunate that she felt no shame, for he was anything but subtle; indeed he seemed to delight in announcing to the gathered company whenever he fancied taking a tumble between the sheets. He was coarse in public and somewhat detached in private, rarely speaking to her or even kissing her. But even as a nervous virgin bride she had quickly discovered that there was nothing to fear, no reason for dread. At her home in Kent, among the other royal and noble ladies, she had heard enough to know what to expect, but from the first night Oswii had employed tricks that would make a harlot blush.

The act itself, between husband and wife, was no sin, but she knew that what Oswii did went far beyond the imagination of those who wrote down God's laws in the Bible, even going so far as to put his head between her legs and since she felt certain that this would not beget a child, it must surely be a sin, especially as she found it not unpleasant.

He was an ignorant man, boastful and lacking in any finesse. He was appallingly behaved towards his kin, particularly his nephew, and his convictions on matters of scripture were dubious. They argued; she dared to scold him, enlisting Hild's help and then whenever he had had enough of listening, he took her to his bed and silenced her, leaving her writhing and flushed and wanting more. He was blunt in his honesty. He loved women, he told her, but only when they were bare-arsed in his bed.

Today though, something was amiss. He had been gone for over two weeks and she knew that she would be called upon the moment he returned, but she had not expected the intensity which in any other man might have been mistaken for passion. He had cried out as he shuddered and she detected more than a mere physical release. What he had seen when he went to fetch his brother's remains had clearly left its mark upon his eyes, for she was convinced he still saw the horror when he closed them.

She wondered briefly whether to try saying anything to soothe him, but before she could formulate the words, he said, "Turn over."

Obliging, she knew that words would never comfort him. She could pray for him, but he would fight his demons alone.

# Chapter Eight

## Tamworth 644

Derwena cradled her newborn close to her body as she walked across the enclosure yard towards the hall. Little Ethelred, nicknamed Noni because he was her ninth child, had caught her by surprise. Nearly twenty years after her first child was born she had supposed that her fertile days might be behind her. Her twins Edith and Eda toddled along with her, each holding on to her skirts, making walking difficult. Every now and then they paused to rummage among the hens' nests, having learned even at such a tender age to make the most of the nutritious seasonal treats while there was still a spring glut of eggs.

Progress slowed even further when the cooks called the children over to sample some buttermilk and handed them each a wooden bowl as big as their faces, so Derwena decided to leave the girls in the cook-house and made her way with the baby to the great hall which was not looking its best, but stripped of dignity like a great noble lady caught in a state of undress while the tree-wrights were employed in making the whole structure bigger.

Penda had decided to enlarge the hall to give more space for gift-giving and to increase the number of private sleeping areas. Within the yard, the open spaces were becoming cramped as more and more buildings sprang up. King Penda's court was an attractive place to be and folk were moving in as fast as houses could be built. Trade expanded, foreign visitors began to appear and Derwena noticed that yet again, for the third day running, the funny-looking missionary from Ireland was sitting outside the bake-house, enjoying begged bread and entertaining the youngsters with stories from his book that he called the Bible. Penda would have nothing to do with the man, so much so that Derwena wondered he did not hiss at him as he went by, but it was to his credit that he would not prevent those who wished to listen from so doing. Yesterday, she had seen Merwal, Pieter and Carena sitting in rapt attention but she had not mentioned it to Penda, fearing that to be a step too far for him.

With trade came coins, and they were now stored in a new building, a much larger treasure house with space to hoard all the booty and expropriated tribute which she and Penda had amassed over the years. Members of various tribes came and went and the extension of the hall was also a nod to the high status of the Mercian court, denoted by the quality of its guests.

These people came willingly with tribute, but Penda had seen too much given away to northern overlords to demand any livestock or food from his subsidiaries and allies. Nowadays he dealt almost exclusively in gold and jewels and the word soon spread that to give military service to Penda was to be richly rewarded.

The treasury was her destination this morning, for she had seen among the piles of recent collections a small ceremonial dagger, a fine piece with a decorated handle worked from antler. She wished to use it to make a sacrifice of a lamb, to thank the Goddess for little Noni.

At the door, she met Merwal, who stroked his little brother's downy head before planting a kiss on his mother's cheek. "Little Noni. Is that it, now, Mother, will you simply give them each a number from now on?"

She raised a hand in playfulness, as if to cuff his ear, although truth be told it had been many years since she could comfortably reach up to his head. He towered over her and was the only reminder of her old life, for he was the living breathing double of his father, with his sharply defined jaw, speckled grey eyes and tawny hair. He even had the same distinctive tooth formation which made one of his dog teeth stick forward slightly. The girl who had been no more than a tumble in the lush grass when he returned from Maserfeld was now a permanent presence in his life. Any day now she would make Derwena a grandmother, a fact which seemed at odds with the silliness of his mood this day, but might nevertheless account for his giddiness. He grinned and looked past her and she turned to see his even taller but younger brother standing behind her, hand raised in mimicry of her stance.

"Back, fierce warrior woman," Pieter said. He spoke to his brother. "Worry not, I will save you."

Derwena sniffed and gave a mock scowl. "Have you big lumps nothing better to do?" Baby Noni snuffled in her arms and she rocked him gently. "More sense than the two of you put together."

Pieter clutched his chest. "Mother, such harsh words. I am wounded."

She stared up at him. When did he become a man? Because, for all his childlike raillery now, he was most definitely an adult. He, too, was a replica of his father, except that his face was a little wider, giving him a more innocent expression in repose, but the beaming smile was identical and radiated at the exact same temperature needed to melt her heart. Yet, for all that innocent appearance, there was a shadow in his eyes that marked him as a man; it had been there since Maserfeld. Even her darling Carena had left childhood behind, having come running to her mother only a week ago to announce that she had begun her first monthly bleed.

"Mother, are you all right?" Merwal, serious now, peered at her, frowning.

"Hmm? Yes. I was only thinking. I came for a knife, the pretty one with the bone handle."

"Lady Derwena!" Sikke the Frisian came running from the half-built hall. "The king has asked for you and Lord Merwal."

Derwena looked at Sikke's face and said, "This is not good news." She thrust little Noni at Pieter and said, "Take him to your sister."

She and Merwal followed Sikke to the hall, taking care to pick their way over the pile of ready sawn planks, old supporting beams, abandoned hammers and two-man saws, once propped against the walls but knocked over by careless passers-by.

Inside, sitting among the detritus, Penda was cradling his head in his hands. He looked up when they approached and it was obvious that he had been weeping.

He said, "Berengar of the Magonsæte has died."

Derwena found tears stinging her own eyes. It was not unexpected news, but he was a good leader, a loyal friend and a fearsome fighter. She sank to her knees at Penda's feet and clutched his hands. "I am sorry, my love."

Penda lifted her hands and kissed them. "The Magonsæte have sent to me for a leader." He nodded at the messenger, who stepped forward.

"There is no one else," the envoy said. "As I have told Lord Penda, Berengar had no sons of his own and among his kinsmen there is none who is better placed than the others. We have no tradition of kings, only leaders, but…" He shrugged and looked at Penda.

Penda said, "I have said that I will give them a kingdom and a king to go with it. Merwal, will you wear the king-helm and lead the Magonsæte?"

Derwena gasped. "Do you mean it?"

Penda nodded. "In time I will need to see all my sons seated firmly on a king-stool. Merwal is the eldest, so it is him to whom I offer it first." He looked at his foster son. "Will you take it?"

Merwal seemed punch-drunk. His mouth was working

but no sound was coming out and he was swaying a little. He steadied and then he, too, sank to his knees and bowed his head. "I will Father, thank you. I will."

Penda touched the top of his head. "Go then. Take your wife and unborn child and lead your folk well and wisely."

Derwena could hardly breathe. The pain in her chest came in sharp stabs and hurt all the more because of her swollen heart. Swollen with love and pride, because she would see her boy become a king, honoured thus by a man who never had any obligation to treat him as his own, but did. And pain, because her boy was not away enjoying a grope and a fumble, but grown to adulthood and about to leave and take her grandchild with him. She did not know whether to kiss Penda or slap him.

## Bamburgh 645

"Is he not the loveliest thing you ever saw?" Efa showed him the tiny pink creature and beamed with delight, but all Oswii could see was a scowly-faced little crosspatch whose quivering bottom lip signalled another imminent bout of squalling.

He stood up and looked round the room. Where did all these people come from? His wife was surrounded by her retinue from Kent and he was sure that she had not brought that many people with her when she first arrived back in Bernicia. Was she bringing more in on a daily basis?

Some of the Northumbrian women still wore a peplos style of dress, strings of beads and larger hairpins, but the Kentish women favoured the kirtle, individual pendant stones and smaller, single brooches rather than pairs of shoulder brooches. Their headdresses were held in place with finely decorated pins. The men eschewed the shaggy outer garments woven from the wool of double-coated sheep and wore striped cloaks pinned at the right shoulder. In contrast to Oswii's beautiful shoes, theirs were simply fastened with toggles, but looking around he realised that these foreigners were not all Kentish.

It was his elder brother Oswald's legacy that the place nowadays was filled with pilgrims and traders, and Oswii hated the constant reminder that he had not been able to emulate that reputation. More than that, the disdain that these visitors showed him was an eloquent expression of how unimpressed they were with his recent waging of war against the British kingdoms. Oswii had tried to break the alliance between Penda and the Welsh and had been unsuccessful because he could not yet raise enough men who were prepared to fight under his banner. Well, ballocks to them. The battlefield was not the only place to defeat enemies.

His wife was still waving the child at him.

"Will you name him?"

She was persistent, he would give her that. "Ecgfrith."

Hild dared to interject. "That is a Bernician name and a fine one, but would a Deiran name not sit a little better with those whom he will one day hope to rule?"

Oswii said, "I do not give a shit."

Efa said, "Lief, then. He shall be known as Lief, because he will be loved."

Oswii showed how little he cared by changing the subject. He spoke to his wife. "How long before we can get rid of all these folk and I can er..." He walked his fingers along her thigh so that there would be no mistaking his meaning.

She slapped his hand away. "Not until I have stopped, you know..." She whispered the next word. "But be that as it may, it is Lent and so there will be none of that."

Oswii's head began to hurt, as if a band of thread had been wound around his forehead and pulled tight. "God's teeth, woman, I have told you before. Easter is when Bishop Aidan says it is and not when you Kentish madwomen say it is."

He was about to shout for Aidan to confirm the truth of his words, but was reminded that the date of Easter was, in fact, the only thing upon which he and the bishop agreed. Aidan had no respect for the members of the court and was at that moment in the middle of rebuking them all for having more interest in their fine clothes and jewels than in the starving folk outside. Oswii sensed that he would receive no support from the bishop that day. And now a nobleman and his wife were presenting their fourteen-year-old son Wilfrid, for Efa's patronage.

To be approached in such a way and asked to foster a child was an important function of royalty and a compliment to Efa that she had been so readily accepted as queen. Oswii knew the credit was all his, for it had been his idea to wed the girl, but he felt no pride now, merely irritation that they could not see his skill as a statesman.

Efa spoke ingratiatingly to the parents, agreeing to sponsor the boy and to pay his keep while he went to Lindisfarne to train as a monk. "And I will say special prayers for him this evening."

Oswii felt as if he might spew. He pushed past the throng of women and made his way outside, taking gulps of fresh sea air. No doubt all these children of his would come in useful one day, but for now, the birth of this latest had proved to be as irritating as all the others, preventing him from indulging in his favourite pastime. He unsheathed his sword and stomped off towards the practice yard, intending to take his frustration out there.

On the way he spotted the youth, Udo. The lad was leaning against the outer wall of the enclosure, staring at him. Always staring. It riled Oswii at the best of times; it was as if his brother was haunting him, reminding him daily of how little he had managed to achieve as king and warlord. Now, in his thwarted rage, he bellowed at the boy and swung his sword at him. "What do you want, huh? Get away, you lanky by-blow."

Udo stood up straight, pushed his weight away from the wall, doing as he was told, but moving with deliberately slow steps.

Oswii watched him go, wondering why the lad refused to show him any respect and then he went and stabbed and slashed at a straw sack until he had expelled all his anger.

## Tamworth 646

Penda and Lothar were at the forge, assessing how many weapons had been damaged. The heat of the smith's fire was fierce and Penda stepped back and wiped the sweat from his brow even though the ground beneath his feet was frozen. A recent February snowfall had sent the lapwings and fieldfares away from the fields nearest the settlement in search of clear ground and the snow on the ground was marked with tracks of five-toed badger paws and fox prints showing four neat pointed claw marks.

Lothar looked at a sword blade, turning it over in his hands. He said, "Not too bad, really. For Welshmen, they were not a mighty threat."

Penda nodded in agreement. "I do not think their hearts were in it. But it does no harm for all to keep their battle wits sharp. A few thick heads and a few bent blades and we have all built up a good thirst. No harm done."

Pieter, standing close by and evidently keen to learn, said, "Are you not worried that the Welsh rose up?"

Penda shook his head. "It was a small war band from Gwent. After a long winter we all need to hone our skills and they thought that while they were at it, they would help themselves to some of our cattle. There was no more meaning in it than that." He dropped an arm over his son's shoulders. "Now, about that thirst..."

The three men made their way to the hall but stopped

at the sound of commotion at the gates. The numbers of people coming in and out of Tamworth had increased considerably in recent years and the guards needed their wits about them, but it was usually evident from the person's garb, level of weaponry and number of companions whether they posed a threat to the peace. There was no one standing at the gates whose appearance marked them out, yet the guard was clearly agitated.

Penda slipped his arm from Pieter's shoulders and walked over to the gatehouse. "What is amiss here?"

The guard jabbed his spear towards a young man, of maybe sixteen or seventeen, whose companion was an even younger girl, wearing a head covering the like of which Penda had not seen since he encountered Haryth of Deira at the East Anglian court. An older boy, a servant or hearth-man, hung back at a slight distance. He also looked as if he had yet to see his twentieth birthday.

Penda was incredulous. "These? These are children. Look at them."

The guard was unabashed. "Yes, Lord, I can see that. But he says they are the children of Oswii of Bernicia."

"Really?" Penda stared at them, wondering why anyone would say this if it were not true and concluding that if they wished him harm, they would not have stated their identity so openly.

The boy was solidly built, with spiky reddish-brown hair and the girl was darker, with eyes that shone with honey-coloured flecks of gold. They had brought little with them, for the packs on their ponies were small. The ponies themselves looked like the breeding stock so favoured by Cadwallon of Wales and they were finely attired, with bridles decorated in the British style. These youngsters had evidently travelled far and had a tale to tell.

He extended a hand in welcome and said, "Come into my hall." With that, the guard signalled and two grooms took the ponies. The visitors stepped forward. Penda let them go past him and whispered to Pieter. "Fetch your mother."

In the hall, Penda waited for them to settle comfortably and looked frequently at the door, wishing Derwena would hurry up. After what seemed like an age, she rushed in, with Pieter close behind her. It was clear from her expression that Pieter had told her everything. She sat down next to Penda and he turned to the young man. "Well?"

The young man chewed his mouthful of bread and washed it down with ale. He looked as if he would rather finish his meal, but seemed aware also that he should not keep a king waiting. In a British accent, he said, "In English, or yn Cymraeg?"

Penda shrugged. "I understand both."

So the young man began his tale, sometimes in faltering English, sometimes in the language of his homeland, so close to the Welsh of Cadwallon that Penda could follow it. "I am Alfrid and this is Ava. Our father is Oswii of Bernicia and our mother was Rhian of Rheged."

Derwena stopped him. "Was?"

He nodded. "She died last year."

Derwena put a hand on the girl's arm. "I am sorry for you."

The girl smiled her gratitude and swallowed, the little lump at her throat moving up and down.

The lad continued. "She was the last of the line of Urien, king of Rheged. She could not have been more high-born and yet our father left her alone with two small children, sailed to Ireland and married another. He did the same there and left the O'Neill princess with a child when he went back to Bernicia. Last year we heard that he has since had a son with his Kentish wife who is kin to Edwin of Deira. Thus the two houses of Northumbria are bound together once more. My mother knew then that he would never call for us and I think it hastened her death."

Penda sat back in his chair. "Yours is a sad tale, indeed. But I wonder why you have come here?"

Alfrid met his gaze and spoke without emotion. "One day I would like to claim Rheged for my own. But I know I can do nothing for the time being, being young and with no hearth-men to speak of, apart from Aneurin here." He gestured at the young man who had accompanied them. "I have no hope of ever being acknowledged by my father if, indeed, I even wished for such a thing. I cannot yet make my own way so I have come to offer you my sword, in the hope that one day Mercia might help me to a kingship."

Penda took a moment to let the information sink in, although he did not think there was much to analyse. He had been presented with a set of facts and no reason to question them. He shrugged again. "The foe of my foe is my friend." He sat forward. "Welcome to your new home. You will be a hearth-thegn, along with my son, Pieter." He indicated his boy, sitting on the mead bench behind the newcomers and noticed that Pieter was staring at the girl, who was repaying his scrutiny with a shy smile.

Derwena chewed her lip as she made her way between the traders' stalls, round the back of the piggery and up the small track which led to the tannery. The tanner said he had seen him, but he had moved on some time ago. Derwena berated herself for her cowardice, because the information was welcome and meant that she had a few more moments before she had to impart her news. She had warned him that this would happen one day, but even she could not have predicted the manner in which it occurred. She thought the shock might strike him down. After all, Penda was past forty now and no longer in his prime.

She caught up with him down at the far end of the

town, in discussion with the fletcher, organising the forthcoming winter hunts and working out the number of extra arrows required for the bowmen.

He turned and smiled at her and she attempted to do the same, but was sure it would have presented more as a grimace than a grin. She grabbed his arm and dragged him away, across the field and on to their favourite spot in the woods. The first chills of autumn had seeped into the ground so, rather than sitting, she leaned against a reassuringly solid oak trunk, with her hands behind her, protecting her skirts from the bark, looking up at the caterpillars in the leaves and listening for a moment to the song of the starlings. A moment longer was all she needed, a moment when the world stayed the same because he didn't know.

He had kept his silence while they rushed to the trees, but now he said, "What is it? You are worrying me. Are the children all... Ah, I see. There is another on the way, is that it?"

To be pregnant again would be the worst news for her, but right now she wished that were the nature of her problem. How to begin? Which would be the worst part for him? She took a deep breath. "How would you feel if the houses of Mercia and Bernicia were to be bound by a wedding?"

She watched as his expression changed from surprise, to disbelief to anger.

"The girl was in your care. How has this happened?"

Defensive now, she said, "She is old enough to wed. If you opened your eyes to see her, you would know that."

"Why would I look at her? What is she to me?"

Derwena had her mouth open ready to respond but his answer was not what she was expecting. "What do you mean, what is she to you?"

He seemed affronted. "If my son wishes to fawn all over some slip of a Rhegedian girl, then that is his business. I like my women a little older."

She stared at him, trying to understand what on earth he was talking about. Then realisation dawned and she felt momentary relief until she remembered that for him the truth would be far worse.

She reached out and placed what she hoped would be a calming hand on his arm, even going so far as to step back in case she needed to step aside and let him punch the tree. "Not Pieter. It is Carena. Alfrid wishes to wed her and she has agreed." While the information sank in, she increased her grip on his arm and spoke quickly. "And she has also agreed to take on his religion and become a Christian."

He stood and watched as his baby daughter became the wife of a boy who probably still had the cradle marks on his arse. His wrap-over ceremonial brocaded coat was heavy and itchy. His knuckles still hurt, bruised and torn from where he had repeatedly punched the oak tree and his jaw ached, although he could not be sure if that was a result of the tension, or because Derwena had clouted him with a punch of her own when she felt his tantrum had gone too far. He had to smile, though, when he thought of how they had spent the rest of that afternoon, undisturbed in their little spot of woodland. His grin was perhaps inappropriate for the setting and he assumed that was why Derwena now gave him a surreptitious kick.

His daughter looked beautiful; he was sure that Carena understood no more of the priest's Roman than he did, but she was smiling serenely as if every word had special and significant meaning for her.

That morning she had come to her father and bowed her head. As he bent to kiss her he'd realised that he barely needed to stoop to reach the top of her head, and had to concede that she was now a woman and not a little girl. Where had the time flown to? His firstborn daughter was sixteen and wearing the Christian head covering, Merwal was a father and Derwena had streaks of grey in her hair, not that he was fool enough to mention it.

He looked around. It was a grand turn-out and he was almost at the point of forgiving Derwena for sending out the news before she told him of the impending wedding, for it had given many distinguished guests the time to journey to Tamworth in time to witness the ceremony.

Merwal had come with many of the Magonsæte, along with his wife and child, and so too had members of the other tribes of the Mercian federation. Penda saw British and Welsh, too, among the crowds and was pleased with his decision to extend the great hall, otherwise he would never have been able to accommodate all these guests. As they took their places for the feast, Derwena squeezed his hand and reminded him that all these folk had come not because they owed tribute but because they looked to him for their safety. They were under his protection, not his yoke.

He grunted self-deprecatingly. "Huh, try telling that to the men of Gwent."

"I think you told them well enough when you sent them running home. Ah, look at the little one."

Little Merchelm, son of Merwal, had been released from his mother's arms and was tottering from mead bench to mead bench, clinging to the edge of each board as he progressed along the length of the hall.

Elsewhere, too excited to sit down, two-year-old Noni and the four-year-old twins were running in and out of the gaps between benches and crawling under the tables to hide. Wulf, six now, seated near his elder sisters, looked on wistfully, as if he wanted to join the younger ones in their play, but feared he might be judged harshly if he did. The girls Minna and Starling, meanwhile, were staring into the middle distance with their chins up and their shoulders back, trying to emulate the poise of their married sister and, no doubt, hoping to replicate her success at catching a husband. Well, they could wait.

Derwena leaned in and jabbed him in the ribs. "It won't be long until they are wed."

"Oh yes it will. Though it took me some time to see it, I know Carena is smitten with Alfrid. But those two girls have no one in their sights and whoever does come along will have to step on my corpse before he takes one of them."

She patted his knee and said, "Yes my love," in the mollifying yet simultaneously dismissive tone that she more usually employed for the children when they were whining unnecessarily.

He sighed and sat back. "I think I would rather be a young man on the battlefield than suffer all this worry. At least I know what I am about when I have a sword in my hand." He caught sight of Alfrid grinning at him and raised an eyebrow in query.

There was a clatter of bowls knocking onto the floor as Noni, pursued by a laughing Edith, scrambled underneath the main table. Alfrid waited until the clanging noise of tableware spinning to a halt subsided and then he responded to his father-in-law's questioning glance. "If any man asked me why I came here instead of going to Bernicia he need only look round this hall to find the answer. For in King Penda they will find a man who knows the true meaning of kin."

Penda took the compliment for what it was. But as he looked out across his hall at all the young faces sitting where he and his peers had once sat before they moved to the benches reserved for the older, known as doughty, warriors, and at the Christian priests who seemed now to have settled permanently in Mercia, he began to feel a little like an old stag; the leader of the herd and still respected, but one that would probably lose if any young buck chose to challenge him.

Pieter knew that the clamour at the gatehouse would alert those within that the war band had returned. He saw his mother with the younger children and his sister Carena, who was looking anxiously for her husband. Alfrid was riding alongside Pieter and Emmett and as soon as Carena saw him her frown melted away and she smiled broadly. Pieter turned his attention to her companion and was gratified to see that she was returning his smile.

Ava had blossomed since her arrival at the Mercian court. In the last two years she had grown from a girl of fourteen with little to say into a young woman, taking her place in the weaving sheds and helping to serve at feasts. Pieter was four years older, but somehow always felt like a tongue-tied idiot when in her presence. While he grinned at her, Alfrid brought his horse in nearer and leaned across to speak.

"That's my sister you're making moon-faces at."

Pieter laughed in response to the mock threat. "That's right. Shall I take a warning from one who is wed to my own sister?"

Alfrid nodded to concede the point. "She is young, though."

"She is sixteen, the same age as Carena was when she wed you. But I hear you and I understand. She had an upbringing that has left her less sure of herself and she is still more shy than my sister ever was. I am in no rush." He did not add that he would stutter over the words if he ever managed to find the courage to approach her.

Alfrid dismounted and handed the reins of his stallion to a waiting groom. He walked over to Carena and scooped her off her feet in a showy embrace. He set her back down on the ground and Pieter noticed that she put a hand briefly on her belly. Whether this was confirmation of a pregnancy or a sad acknowledgement of an as yet empty womb, Pieter could not be sure and he would not enquire; this was a private moment between man and wife. He slipped from his own saddle and gave his horse over to the care of Emmett, the only one whom he trusted to take care of his mounts. Rubbing the dirt of the road from his face, he made his way to the hall but was waylaid by his mother.

"I have had news that your brother Merwal has become a father for the second time." She reached up on tiptoe and kissed his cheek. "Your father says you fought well against the West Saxons."

Pieter shook off the praise. "He was the one who fought like Thunor. He makes much of being old, but there was no man there who could match him."

Derwena hugged him. "He said the same of you. You both make me proud." Releasing him, she nodded in the direction of Alfrid. "How did he fight?"

"Like a whirlwind. There is no fear but…" He paused, settling on a thought which had not hitherto occurred to him.

Derwena pressed him. "But?"

"It is an odd thing. There is no forethought either. He rushes in sometimes with weapons that he has not checked beforehand. A good fighter, but maybe not a good leader, for he makes no plans."

His mother nodded. "He sees what he wants and he takes it. He met and wed your sister in little over a six-month. It is not wrong to act on a whim, but if it borders on recklessness…" She shook her head. "He makes her happy and I know he loves her. Your father and I were not so different, I suppose." She put her arm around his waist. "Come. Sit with me in the hall and tell me how you put Cynwal back under the rock he crawled from."

Pieter looked around but saw no sign of his Aunt Audra. He suspected that she had retired to her house rather than learn the fate of her erstwhile husband sung in loud and deprecating tones by victorious Mercian warriors. In truth, they had humiliated Cynwal but they hadn't completely squashed him. Penda had kept his promise not to kill the West Saxon king but had laid waste to vast swathes of his fertile farmland, taken hostages, and increased the amount of tribute due. Pieter was not experienced in the art of politics but it had seemed to him that Cynwal was a man much diminished now in ambition and looked like a man defeated, and no longer defiant. "I do not know much of these matters, but I do not think he will rise up against my father."

Derwena snorted. "Can there be a man left on earth who thinks rising up against your father will end well?"

They went into the hall and Pieter could only concur with his mother's assessment of his father's invincibility. Among the members of the war band there had been representatives from the tribes of the Hwicce, the Magonsæte, Wreconsæte, the Chilternsæte and Arosæte and he knew now what was engaging his aunt, for Audra was warmly welcoming the return of an Arosætne thegn whom Pieter remembered fighting bravely during the campaign in the southwest. But here in the hall were also men he had never seen before. "You have been busy while we have been away, Mother."

She smiled triumphantly. "Here you see men from the Westerna, the Herefinna to the east and the Sweordora and the Spalda from even further east. All have come to swear to your father as overlord. With the East Saxons swearing to none and the East Angles tamed, now that Cynwal has been put down, there will be no more threat to us from Northumbria."

Pieter said, "Then I can make your smile even wider. Father has received pledges from the Hendrica who live on the border of the West Saxon kingdom. Oswii will think twice before he tries to act like his forebears and lay claim to kingdoms not his own. There is none who will stand for it."

Derwena stooped to scoop Noni up into a cuddle, admonishing the child as she did so. "You are giddy because your father and brother are home, little man, I understand. But you must calm yourself or you might get trodden on." To Pieter she said, "Now tell me that the gods do not smile on us. Our kin thrives and our lands are free from threat... But I am wasting my breath, for you are not listening."

"I am, Mother, I swear." But it was true that he was no longer looking at her, because Ava had walked in with her brother and Carena.

Noni wriggled free from his mother's arms and ran off, singing. "Pieter loves Ava, Pieter loves Ava."

## Rendlesham, East Anglia

Hild the holy woman was standing with her hands on her hips and a facial expression that could have frozen a puddle on midsummer's day. "Why was I not told before I left Kent? Does no one in Rendlesham know how to send a message?"

Adelar was cleaning his sword and he put his head down, pretending to be absorbed in the work, bringing the cloth backwards and forwards over the blade, but moving quietly so that he could listen.

Ænna's response was less than cordial. "Your sister went to the Frankish monastery barely a week after she had told us of her plans. It was not my duty to send to you and let you know; I am not Haryth's keeper."

Hild took an audible gasp of breath. "I have ridden from Northumbria, I have been to Kent to see my kinfolk there and now I have ridden here with the sole purpose of accompanying my sister across the sea to the monastery, and all you have to say is that I am too late?"

Ænna said, "It is nothing to do with me. Do you want to take her whelp? She left him behind."

Adelar laid his cloth down and stood up. He sensed

that poor little Adulf was about to get another tongue-lashing or worse from the intolerant king. The lad was still a child, who, as recently as March, had been entranced at the sight of five fox cubs in their earth and knew so little of the world of men.

Ænna had grown cocksure since the news came that Penda had subdued the West Saxons and taught Cynwal his lesson. It had been some time since the East Anglian king had bidden farewell to his prestigious long-term guest and there had been no reprisals. Ænna had begun to act like a wild beast with no predators.

Now the king was shouting out to Adulf. "Come here, show yourself. Let the woman have a look at you, though I doubt she'll want you." As Adulf came forward reluctantly, Ænna stood up and pulled him roughly by the tunic neck to force him to stand in front of Hild. He jerked him to make him stand up straight.

Hild folded her arms across her chest. "Stop it! How dare you treat a child in such a manner? It ill behoves a king to act like a churl. Never mind telling anyone to stand up, you should be down on your knees praying for the Lord's forgiveness."

Adelar sat down again. He had been praying only that morning, giving thanks that finally the sweet-natured Haryth would find some peace, and asking God to grant her safe passage across the sea to her new home in the monastery. Now he knew that God worked in more mysterious ways yet and had sent this angel-warrior to scold Ænna and remind him of his duty.

Hild had travelled with a small retinue. It did not take long to settle them at the mead benches and Adelar ordered wine to be brought, guessing that Hild might have a taste for it. She did not treat him to a telling-off but nor did her features break into any approximation of a smile. She was courteous, but no more. It was with relief that Adelar saw a messenger arrive. He could have been bringing an announcement that Penda was at the gates with an army of wolves and bears; at least it would have been preferable to the doomed task of entertaining this woman.

The messenger was sweating and splattered with mud. Still out of breath, he rushed forward and said, "I seek the lady Hild."

King Ænna flapped an arm in Hild's general direction before returning his attention to his ale cup. The messenger approached Hild and bowed low.

"I have been following you from Kent, my lady, hoping to catch up to you before you rode too far east. Bishop Aidan bade me fetch you home."

The blood in Hild's face drained away and she stood up. "What is wrong? Is it the bishop, is he ill? Little Wilfrid then; but he was settling in so well. Oh dear God, not the lady Efa, please…"

Adelar revised his opinion slightly. It was touching that this sour-faced woman should love her kin and dear ones so deeply.

The messenger shook his head. "No, my lady, everyone is in good health. Bishop Aidan had a message not long after you left that the lady Haryth was leaving and that your journey would be wasted. He begged me to bring you back home to head the monastery at Hartlepool." The man sank onto the bench and leaned his arms on the table, snatching his ragged breaths as his torso heaved up and down.

Hild patted his back and said, "We will leave. But not until you are rested." She looked up at King Ænna. "And only when I am sure that this poor child will suffer no more."

Ænna said, "Lady, I must warn you that if you do not cease your whining I will make you sorry."

Hild glared at him. "You do not frighten me. It is not I, but you, who will one day suffer the wrath of God."

Adelar's life had not been suffused with much joy. His father drank himself to death not long after his mother died in childbed and before the family had chance to bury her and the dead babe. He barely remembered the illustrious days of Redwald and his magnificent court and only knew of his great warrior queen, Bertana, from hearth-side tales. Adelar held no strong feeling for Edwin and was unmoved by the news of his death, but while he retained fond memories of Edwin's deserted wife Carinna, her heart had radiated such sadness at her abandonment that Adelar knew this was the reason he had grown up to be a sombre boy, not prone to laughter.

Haryth's plight had moved him, and he had grieved deeply for his brother, her husband. He had lived with his elder brother's caustic temperament for so long that his normal reaction was to lash out when his patience had been tested too much by Ænna's lack of humanity, but now, as he watched the holy woman confronting him and barely blinking while she called down the reproving hand of the Almighty, Adelar's reaction was simply to throw back his head and laugh.

# Chapter Nine

*Bernicia 651*

Oswii felt the familiar constriction around his forehead as the headache took hold and he felt the vein pulsing in his neck as his shoulders tensed. He had long held the opinion that if he heard one more tale of Oswin of Deira and his saintliness he would probably vomit. Yet here he was being subjected to another yarn of faultless godly behaviour. Bishop Aidan, accustomed to and famed for walking everywhere, had accepted the gift of a horse from Oswin of Deira, only to give it away to a poor man begging for alms. Oswii's comment was surely the last word on the matter. "Fool of a king to give it away. And fool of a churchman. That horse would have been worth a fortune."

Reeve Elwyn sniffed. "Indeed. Yet Oswin did not berate him for giving it away. Instead, after warming himself by the fire after a long hunt, he gave his sword away to one of his thegns, so humbled was he by Aidan." He sat down and clicked his fingers for a serving-boy to help him pull off his muddy riding boots and bring some soft slippers.

Oswii was incredulous. "And the folk of Deira love this king? Why would they keep their oaths to such a weakling?"

Elwyn jabbed his finger in the air. "Well said, Lord. I think even Bishop Aidan thought as much. Hunwold of Gilling, for it was he who told me the tale, said that afterwards, Aidan began weeping, saying that Oswin was not long for this world, that he would be cruelly killed, for the kingdom did not deserve such a king."

Oswii scoffed. "How right he was. But perhaps not in the way he meant. And yet, if they love such a man as this then maybe they are well met."

"It does make a beggar of belief, my lord, I agree. Oswin, it seems, is fine-looking and well-loved and in the eyes of his folk he can do no wrong."

Oswii made a fist and punched his other hand with it. Why was it that some men effortlessly inspired such devotion? Why was he being denied that which Oswald had enjoyed, the power that Penda now wielded?

He looked up and caught a glimpse of his nephew, staring, as always. It unsettled him at the best of times but at this precise moment he would brook no reminder of his saintly brother; rather look to his own father whose name was a synonym for slyness. He lowered his head to speak more quietly to Elwyn. "It is time, I think, to show the Deirans that there is another king, mightier than their precious Oswin, who can make manifest the premonitions of holy men." Glancing again at his nephew, he continued, "It is time I took what is owed to me. This Hunwold; he is a Deiran, yes, but he is your friend too is he not? Can he be relied upon?"

Elwyn dipped his head. "All men have their price, my lord. His is lower than most."

She stepped quietly in her soft leather slippers yet he sensed that she was coming, for it was almost as if he could feel the heat of her fury. Good; he loved nothing better than a fight as a precursor to sex. The angrier she was, the more intense their love-making afterwards. He smiled and turned to face her as she marched into the bedchamber.

"You have overreached yourself, my lord. Tell me it is not true and that this wickedness is a lie." Her face was contorted with rage. "Bishop Aidan is distraught. He tells me that Oswin was lured to the house of a Deiran thegn who, acting under Elwyn's orders, killed the king and the man who was with him. This is naught to be proud of, my lord."

Oswii puffed out his chest and said, "He was a weak king. My brother ruled both kingdoms as did your father before him and my father before that. They would not share. Neither would I. One of us had to die. Surely you'd rather it was him than me?"

She took a step towards him and poked him in the chest with a sharp finger. "Oswin was my kinsman. His father and my father were cousins."

"You never met him."

"What has that to do with it? You cannot go killing men whenever you feel like it. He never so much as raised a fist to you, never mind a sword. You should be on your knees praying for forgiveness."

"I am sorry, Lady, but you do not understand the ways of men. I will make it up to you, I swear." He nodded towards the bed. "Won't you let me see if I can't make you feel better?"

She folded her arms across her chest. "Oh, be assured, you are going to put this right, Husband."

He stepped forward and undid her arms, pulling them down and pinning them to her sides while he kissed her neck and throat. "Yes, my love, whatever you say."

Her breathing speed increased and her body moved towards his. He took advantage by pressing his pelvis forward so that she could feel the bulge of his cock through their clothing.

She wriggled one of her arms free and began to knead the swelling. She said, "You will give Deira to your nephew."

He stopped kissing her and looked up. "What?"

"You heard me. The Deirans will never accept you as their king. You owe the boy something after the way you have treated him."

"No, I will not do it. Deira is mine now."

She shifted her grip, grabbed his balls and squeezed. "Do it. Let him rule in your name."

"All right," he said, biting her lip gently, "I will. As long as he does what he is told and swears to me as overlord."

"In that case, I too will submit." She released the pressure and he grabbed handfuls of her skirts, pulling the material up until he could reach between her thighs. As his fingers crawled higher and higher and then started to knead and tease, she began to whimper softly. All the more remarkable then that between that point and the moment of exquisite mutual release, she had also managed to inveigle out of him an agreement to build a monastery in which daily prayers were to be offered for the soul of the murdered Oswin.

Alfrid had never ridden at the head of so many troops before and he did it now with mixed feelings. Excitement was tying knots in his stomach and exhilaration was making him light-headed. Darker emotions were at work, too, the strongest of which was suppressed rage against his father. He was far from sure whether he wanted to meet him after all this time, but the opportunity had been too good, too ideally suited to him, to pass up.

When news had come of Oswin's murder, Penda had been incandescent with fury. It was a crime, but not one, he concluded once he had calmed, which warranted aggressive retaliation. After all, the Deirans were nothing to Penda and his only concern was to put Oswii back in his place and ensure he got no ideas to attempt to expand his territory further than Northumbria.

Thus it was decided that a message would be sent, with demands for hostages to ensure his good behaviour from now on. The message would be accompanied by a show of force and the band of warriors would need a leader. Alfrid had heard the words almost before he had thought them. "*Let me go.*"

They had all stared at him then, although none was unduly surprised, for he was aware of his reputation for impulsive behaviour. He had always believed in seizing the moment, for if he hadn't, would he and his sister ever have found their way to Mercia? Besides, as he spoke on, his thoughts had coalesced into a cogent argument. "*If I am ever going to meet my father I would like it to be now, when I do not have to beg but am riding with a message of admonishment. Murder has been done and it was a foul deed. Nevertheless there is now a Northumbrian kingdom without a king. If I ride north and show myself as the son of Oswii yet the son, also, of Rhian of Rheged, the Deirans might welcome me.*"

He had never hidden his ambition to claim one day a portion of his birthright, and Penda conceded that much when he armed him, gave him enough men and sent him off on his mission with full blessing, with only one caveat: if he was successful, he must send for Carena within a month, before winter prevented travel, or Penda would come and find him.

Now they were within sight of Bamburgh. He had heard many tales of this great fortress on the rock but never really believed them, since most of the stories were passed on at second or even third hand and rarely from one who'd seen the place. It was impressive, they had been right about that. He wondered if living there imbued the inhabitants with a sense of invincibility; would he be challenged when he tried to enter?

There was nothing but a minimal guard at the gate and Alfrid and his hearth-men, Reinhard and Hraban from Mercia as well as Aneurin from Rheged, were admitted. It seemed as though the Bernicians had abandoned all notion of belonging to a warrior society, for the only people in the enclosure were lowly folk, going about the chores of the day, making preparation to gather in the last of the harvest by clearing out the grain barns, laying straw in the storage lofts and smoking the last of the summer cheese.

The stables were virtually empty, marcescent leaves dangled from the scrubby tree in the yard and Alfrid was struck by the contrast between this sorry place and the grandeur and bustle of Penda's settlement at Tamworth. This fortress, battered by seas, winds, and waves, seemed forgotten and forlorn and he could only imagine how vibrant and vital it had been in the glory days of Edwin and Oswald. To all his ambivalent feelings towards his father, he now added both contempt and pity.

In the great hall, a man and two women were sitting at the head table beyond the hearth. Alfrid recognised the man straight away; he had only vague memories of his father but they had been enough to sustain an image of his features that would confirm his identity should they ever meet. Now, he put them to use, comparing the recollections of the thick neck and scruffy hair.

The younger of the women, no more than a year or two older than Alfrid himself, was a Madonna-like figure, with cascading hair showing beneath her veil, the blonde tips brushing the pale blue of her dress. There was a small child sitting next to her, a girl of maybe three or four. By the fire, playing with a small wooden carving of a horse, was a boy who was slightly older, perhaps five or six.

The older of the females was a holy woman and had a face that looked to Alfrid as if she spent her life chewing on bees, rather than eating honey, with deep drawn lines radiating from her pursed lips. She was the one who stepped forward to receive him and after the formal greetings she said, "You find us in mourning. Our beloved Bishop Aidan has died, less than a fortnight after the death of King Oswin." She cast a glance towards her own king and it was a hateful look at odds with her religious garb.

Alfrid looked again at his father and, robbed of all his

saliva, found that he could not swallow. He could feel his heart hammering in his chest and his hands were sticky, though not from the sweat of travel. He wiped them on his breeches as he walked the length of the hall, trying to catch his breathing and bring it under control. He sensed that his companions had fallen back to allow him to greet his father alone. He took a deep breath and said, "I am Alfrid."

Over the years he had played out this scene in his mind many times, imagining the moment when he would meet his father and tell him all the things he had never had a chance to say, words which would by turns rage and question but, whatever he had rehearsed, it had not included the reaction from Oswii which now met his declaration.

Oswii seemed hardly to acknowledge him, much less realise who he was. He made an odd movement, putting his head briefly to one side and then righting it, as if to say, "What of it?"

Alfrid fought hard now, to prevent regression to the world of a little boy, feeling lost and abandoned. He was not that boy any more, but a man, a man at the head of a war band which represented the most powerful king the world had ever known. He inhaled again, so deeply that it was audible. He hardened his heart and delivered his message.

The details were stark, the instructions clear. Penda was not pleased with Oswii's act of aggression, he wanted him to desist and if he did not, Penda would ride north and annihilate him. Furthermore, Oswii was to give up hostages as surety of his future good behaviour. Again, if he did not comply, Alfrid was charged with wreaking maximum damage to Bamburgh and the surrounding area before he left.

Oswii received the news without visible reaction.

So, after all these years it had come to this. His father

was a weak, broken man who did not respond when threatened. Alfrid wondered whether such hostages were even necessary, for he saw nothing here that would persuade him that Oswii was a danger to anyone.

The woman in the blue dress spoke. "You can take Oswii's son, my firstling."

The older woman stepped forward. "You cannot!"

The younger one waved away her objection, holding her hand up for silence. "Look at him, Hild. Here is his grown-up son and he does not greet him, even after so many years parted from him. I offer to give away his youngest son and he does not flinch. His children mean nothing to him and I am frightened for my Lief after what has happened."

The woman called Hild dared to interject. "My lady, you do not mean it. I understand that you said it merely to goad the king, but to hand over your son, this is madness. If you must, give him to me for safekeeping at the abbey."

The younger woman, whom Alfrid assumed was Oswii's wife, Efa, shook her head. "I did not do it merely to bait him. It may be that giving up my boy will see to it that if the Deirans rise up to avenge their murdered king then Penda might come to our aid as our overlord. And I believe that my boy will be among his half-siblings, who would not harm him. I know that Penda of Mercia is a pagan and so, too, is his wife. But my husband does not see the worth of his own kindred." She spoke to Alfrid. "You know Penda and his heathen wife. Is she a kind and loving mother?"

Alfrid, stunned by Efa's confirmation that Oswii's attitude to his offspring remained unchanged after all these years, merely nodded.

Oswii grunted. "Huh. A man who loves his sons before all else betrays a weakness that other men will use to their own ends."

Alfrid opened his mouth to protest, but considered the words and saw a faint trace of truth in them. It reminded him of his primary purpose. "I have come to take my rightful place as king of Deira."

Efa said, "Deira has a king. Œthelwold, son of Oswald and known to those who love him," she looked pointedly at her husband, "as Udo, has been given the king-helm by the Deirans. They will brook no other and it would be unwise to try. Udo has grown up in Northumbria and I think that is important for them, too." She smiled at him, kindly. "I am sorry if you have come all this way in hope. This land has a history of trouble and unrest. The Deirans are my folk and I know that they crave peace above all else."

Alfrid took a moment to say farewell to his dream and then fixed his mind to his task. "Reinhard, give the boy some time to make his goodbyes and then ready him for the ride south. Lady Efa, I will let it be known in Mercia that your willingness to give up your son has made the peace which my father-in-law is keen to uphold."

There was no more to be said. He would not witness the leave-taking of a mother and her son and so he turned his back.

Only then did his father appear to wake up. "Wait."

Alfrid returned to face Oswii and his anger finally spilled over. "What? You had the chance to speak to me and you did not take it. I came for a kingdom and there is none here to be had. I have nothing to say to you."

Oswii glanced over to the hearth where Efa and Hild had enveloped the boy in a blanket of embrace and were crying openly. He stood up and touched Alfrid's elbow, leading him to the far corner of the room. Away from eavesdroppers, he said, "I cannot offer you a kingdom. Yet. I am still counting the cost of Oswin's killing and as you can see, I am overrun with women who have taken up the role of keepers of my soul. Udo is king now of

Deira and he is my nephew, but not my friend…"

Alfrid knew how the sentence would end. A fool could see that Oswii was isolated and needed an ally. Alfrid needed a kingdom. Penda had been good to him but he had an uncrowned adult son and two others besides. He would confer lands on them before Alfrid was given any scraps. Here, at least, there was a chance. "You want me to stay? As your son?"

Oswii shrugged. "If you like. You look to me like you have a useful sword arm. You will need some time to think about it."

"No, not really. Yes, I do have a good sword arm and I will stay and use it in Bernicia's name."

He turned on his heel and went to consult Reinhard. "I will not be coming back with you but tell Penda that he can send Carena to me; I will keep my word to him about her."

Reinhard said, "You are going to be king of Deira then?"

Alfrid hesitated. "Something like that."

The lady Efa had recovered her composure and she stood up, patted her son's head and watched him run off to gather his possessions. She said to Alfrid, "I hope you have your own reasons for doing this. If you think that Oswii welcomes you as a son, you are sadly mistaken."

Alfrid could not suppress the instinctive defensiveness. "Why not? I am, after all, his son and he is my father."

"Oh yes. And his father was known as Aylfrith the Cunning. Oswii is simply using your need and feeding off it. He knows you want acknowledgement as his son and he knows that you want a kingdom. This is all he needs to keep you as his friend instead of his foe. Oh, do not worry. He will keep his word to you, but if you are holding on to any hope that he will be as a father to you, let it go now before that hope crushes you."

Alfrid said, "And yet you stay with him, even though

you send your son away."

She gave him a rueful smile. "What can I tell you? He is a bad father but he is a good husband. By sending my son away I am trying to be a good mother and in staying, I will be a good wife."

Alfrid found this puzzling. He had no memory of his father's relationship with his mother but he knew his Mercian hosts and guessed that if Derwena ever felt compelled to send her own child out of harm's way, she would leave Penda too, or kill him. Yet Queen Efa recognised Oswii for the uncaring brute he surely was while opting to stay with him. This was not the act of a rational woman.

The reeve wandered past and smirked. He sidled up to Alfrid and said, "They hate each other. She spends all day on her knees in prayer or scolding him and he curses her every breath. Then at sundown he takes her to bed and pokes her until she shuts up."

Alfrid was astonished. "Against her will?"

Elwyn chuckled. "I think not. Wait until tonight; you'll see him beckon her to bed and off she'll trot, eager as anything. I daresay she thinks we don't know, but there's no mistaking a bitch on heat."

Alfrid's thoughts were swimming around his head like bewildered minnows. The shock of seeing his father, of being rejected all over again only to be invited to stay; all this would have been enough to sift through, but now he had to reconcile the sight of a demure young lady dressed in modest clothing with the idea of her being a rampant wife who could barely wait until dark to be ravaged by her husband. And now, finally, he had to acclimatise his sensibilities and familiarise himself with a court where the inhabitants frowned on Penda as a pagan savage, yet used coarser language than ever tripped off the Mercian king's tongue.

He wondered for a second whether it was a suitable

place for Penda's daughter and considered rescinding his summons for her to join him, but he dismissed the notion instantly. If he did not send for her he might as well hack his own balls off and send them on a platter for her father to feed to his hounds.

## Tamworth 653

The people known as the Middle Angles had no tradition of kingship and when they came to Penda asking for a king he was happy to offer them his son, Pieter, and to create a new kingdom whose neighbours would be the West Saxons to the south, the East Saxons to the southeast, East Anglia to the east, Lindsey to the north, Mercia to the northwest and the Hwicce to the southwest. It would be a small realm, but it would consolidate the lands of the central tribes into one cohesive unit, loyal to Mercia. Penda had often had reason to give thanks to the gods for his wife's fecundity and here was another of those occasions. Ask him for a son and he could provide one.

Indeed, there were enough children and grandchildren running around Tamworth in the spring sunshine to ensure that he could furnish many lands with kings and princesses for years to come. He looked around at the family group, gathered together to witness Pieter's marriage.

The youngest of his offspring were in their best clothes and on their best behaviour. Noni and the twins were barely young enough still to be called children and Wulf, at thirteen, would reject the description out of hand. Starling was hoping to wed her Hwiccan love later that year and Penda might have regretted the passing of time which took with it their childhood, were it not for the existence of Minna's baby girl, born last spring and, praise be to Frige, the arrival four years ago of Audra's son. His sister, so cruelly abandoned by Cynwal the West Saxon, had defied chance and expectation and found a man who hailed from the Arosæte and birthed her babe with ease despite having passed her fortieth birthday.

Also here for the ceremony were Merwal with his two elder children and the little baby Merfyn. Looking at them, Penda's satisfied smile slipped a little. Merwal had been left heartbroken after the death of his first wife and had wed again.

Little Merfyn's mother was Efi, a princess of Kent and a Christian. First Penda had watched his daughter Carena take the new faith upon her marriage and then, with Merwal's conversion, Penda knew he must concede that the world around him was changing. The theological debate continued to rage all around them, with the missionaries establishing their centres of worship close, and sometimes adjacent, to the older temples.

The price of marriage to Ava for Pieter had been baptism and the lad, ever mindful of the feelings of others and who had waited so long to become husband to the girl he had loved since she was fourteen, had asked his father's blessing. No one who had witnessed Pieter's cautious wooing of the girl could have thrown any more rocks in his path and Penda had agreed, telling his boy that each man must be free to follow his own conscience. Derwena had complimented him for accepting that which he could not alter. Wistful though he was, his smile righted itself as he recalled how she had comforted him then, reminding him that only in the Christian world was it wrong to fornicate without the intent of procreation and thus they had spent a pleasant afternoon indulging in some very unchristian practices.

The memory caused him to turn to look at the last of his extended brood, standing next to Derwena as if she were his own mother. Lief of Bernicia had been made as welcome as possible and no doubt he filled a hole in Derwena's heart which had opened up with the realisation that she was unlikely to have any more children of her own.

It was to be hoped that Oswii of Northumbria feared that his son would be mistreated, but in reality, Derwena could no more permit harm to come to a child than a fish could walk on the earth. Her dedication to all the children in her care was but one of the things that made him love her and it was all the more poignant now because it was one of the reasons that they were now estranged. It seemed, after all her wise words, that it was she who would not accept that which could not be altered.

The marriage ceremony, conducted in the Latin which Penda still found harsh to his ears, was nearly over. He had no need of the new faith; the gods had blessed him with plentiful progeny and success on the battlefield while the Christ god had not always looked after His faithful. He might be unconvinced by this new religion but he was sure these marriages between his children and Oswii's were beneficial in keeping the Northumbrian in check. Not only was his little son Lief in custody, but Oswii would be a fool to rise up in rebellion while Carena resided in the northern kingdoms. As a father, Oswii would know that to jeopardise the lives of children would be foolish indeed.

Whilst Penda might accept that the world was changing, he didn't have to like it and he was relieved when they were allowed to leave the chapel and return to the hall. Here, he was master; this was where he dispensed justice, rewarded service and sent out orders for the governance of his territories. Here, his word was law, not that of some unseen and yet somehow all-knowing god.

He sat down on the king-seat and gave the nod for the feasting and toasts to begin. He made the sign of the hammer, but the rest of the order of ceremonies was overlooked. Today, it did not seem appropriate to expect

Derwena to serve his drink. His son Pieter solicitously patted his new bride's arm and then made his way to stand by his father.

"Father, may I take Emmett with me when I leave?"

Derwena pulled a mocking face and said, "What, would you leave me with no one to keep my bed warm when your father is away?"

Penda looked at his son's expression, listened to his nervous giggle and then he himself gave way to harsh laughter. "If ever I find time to think myself some great leader of men and begetter of children, along comes your mother to cut me down."

Pieter gave a little half-smile. "I was worried about leaving you and this does nothing to allay my fears."

Derwena's tone was indignant. "Worried about leaving me? Why?"

His reply was in the manner of gentle admonishment. "Not you, Mother. I was worried about leaving my father with no grown-up male kin to take his side."

As if to prove his point, the children began to run around, chasing after a feather blown by the draught from the doorway.

Penda grunted and looked for solace in his ale cup. After draining it, he set it down and began to twirl it round in his hands. "Boy, when you next come home you will find me sitting in a corner, dribbling, while your mother rules the whole of the Mercian lands, cutting off the cocks of any who dare to gainsay her."

It was clear that their son was feeling uncomfortable. He tried to arbitrate by giving them each a compliment. "Father, you must stop thinking of yourself as an old man. What about last month? After that border raid there was no doubting who was king around here. And Mother is often left to guard the kingdom when you are away. From small beginnings hiding Uncle Eowa's gold, she is now so adept that she rules when you are not here. I have heard you wonder aloud how mighty she would have been if she had not been taken to childbed every year or so."

If he hoped to placate either one of them, he had failed.

Penda said, "Oh indeed. A man argues with your mother at his peril."

Derwena clutched her cup so tightly her fingers went white. "And a woman wastes her time having bairns if she thinks her man won't send them away when he has done with them."

Now it was Penda's turn for anger. He slammed his hand down upon the table. "Enough, woman! I cannot blame Alfrid for wanting to stay with his father. I would not begrudge him one last chance at a family life and it is right that he should send for Carena to live with him in the north. It strengthens the likelihood of keeping the Northumbrians where they belong, in Northumbria."

She glared at him. "Hah! There speaks a man who has learned nothing. Each time a kinswoman of yours has left Mercia, it has been to suffer at the hands of a king in a far-off land, yet you send your own daughter to the same fate. You are no better than the Christian kings who pick a bride merely to expand their kingdoms."

She was wrong, for he prided himself on learning from his mistakes. He also knew that marriages made for alliance could come undone. The truth was that his female kin had all married for love.

Derwena could not know the anguish he had suffered before deciding to let his daughter go. Thinking back to the times he had faced similar situations he'd concluded that it would have been better for him and less painful if his kinswoman Carinna had left when he was older, but at least, being a child, he'd been helpless to stop her, and thus had avoided earning her hatred.

He was a child no longer and he might have tried to

stop Carena, too, if he had been given any real say in the matter. It was, in any case, not being sent away but subsequent abandonment that had caused the heartache for her namesake and for Audra. It would have been futile to have withheld his permission for his daughter to leave and, even as he tried to kiss the top of Carena's head, she had tilted her chin as if defying him. She was too much like her mother; stubborn.

His sister Audra's marriage had promised political advantage, yes, and yet it had turned sour. But what man, who saw them that day cooing at each other like doves, could have foretold that Cynwal would turn into a replica of his father? Indeed, of all of them present that day, it was Derwena who knew what the West Saxon royal family was capable of and yet she had not objected, because she saw that Audra loved her West Saxon. Penda valued his balls too much to remind Derwena how she had supported the marriage, but it meant that she remained angry with him and he did not know how to fix it; more proof, if any were needed, that he was lost when it came to fighting without weapons. He muttered into his ale cup. "A husband should be with his wife."

She laughed harshly. "Speak your own thoughts; mine differ."

"For the love of Woden, do you not think it wrenched my heart from my chest to see her leave? I did not want her to wed him in the first place, if you would choose to recall it. But she wanted to go. We have Oswii's son; no harm will come to Carena, I swear to you."

"Why? Because all men love their children like you do? Yet how can that be, when you send them away to live with our foes?"

He looked into her eyes and spoke more softly. "Not all women suffer at the hands of kings when they are driven to leave their homeland."

She held his gaze for a moment and then said, "That

301

was a cowardly blow."

"Nevertheless, it is true. I gave my heart to you."

She drained her cup, set it down on the table, gathered the little ones and stood up to leave. "And you have ripped mine out."

The hall at Bamburgh was gleaming, inside and out, newly whitewashed, and all repairs had been carried out. Efa had been a tiny child when her mother had fled the great fortress but her memory was of an imposing palace, with riches on display and the great space of the hall filled with beautifully dressed people drinking from gold cups or delicate glass palm-cups, the men dressed in fine tunics with gold edging and the women swathed in dazzling silks of bright blue and red, with gold and garnet jewellery hanging from their necks and pinned upon their garments.

Over the past few days she had watched with excitement as the wall hangings were dragged outside into the cleansing warmth of the summer sunshine and given a beating to remove the dust, dried herbs were brought from the kitchens to be strewn across the floor, and the tree-wrights tested rickety chairs and repaired any creaky joints. Wooden bowls were piled high with wild strawberries and honey biscuits.

Efa looked now at her hall with satisfaction and knew she had done Oswii proud. While he was wooing the eminent guest, she enjoyed the surroundings which more closely matched her predilections and hugged her body, smiling to recall the words of the messenger from Mercia.

The lady Derwena had sent her good wishes and would like the lady Efa to know that her son was flourishing, that he now matched young Noni for height even though he was a year younger and he was diligent with his weapon lessons. Such news would nourish Efa for weeks and looking across at her husband, she realised that her good mood would need to sustain them both if his strategy failed.

Alfrid stood up and wandered over to sit next to her by the hearth. She smiled as he approached. She had grown fond of her husband's eldest son; they were close in age, she having been born but three years before him. She said, "I told the messenger that when he goes home to Mercia he must let them know that Carena is well and thriving."

Alfrid said, "Thank you. Her mother will welcome the news."

She nodded towards the head table. "How goes it?"

He sighed. "King Sigi's speech is hard to understand and that does not help."

She smiled. What he meant was that Oswii was growing impatient with the king of the East Saxons and it probably had little to do with the man's thick accent. "I daresay this would be one time when my husband would welcome the presence of Abbess Hild."

He chuckled. "You might be right, but I think he would die before admitting it."

The sound of laughter wafted through the window opening and while her little girl's voice always came to Efa's ears as music, today it saddened her. "I wish my daughter were older and not still only five. Had she been a woman she could have been wed and then all this would not have been needed. I fear it will not end well." A marriage of alliance between the houses of Bamburgh and the East Saxons would have left both kingdoms feeling less isolated in the face of Penda's supremacy, but Oswii's tactics were more provocative than a mere wedding and she wondered if Penda would see it as an act of aggression.

Alfrid feigned incomprehension. "What is wrong with a Christian king inviting another king to receive baptism?"

She raised her eyebrows and looked at him as if he were one of her naughty children caught out in a brazen lie. "If King Sigi embraces the faith then I will give thanks. But all this?" She flung her arm in a wide arc to indicate all the wealth on open display. "This is half-show, half-threat. When Sigi comes out of the river, he will then have to bend his knee to Oswii as his new overlord." She lowered her voice. "And then we will all need to pray."

Alfrid laid a hand upon her knee. "Are you worried for your son?"

She remembered the words of Lady Derwena's message. "No, I am worried for my husband, because a man who does not care about the lives of his children will be more reckless with his own life."

The Picts spoke a different language from Alfrid's mother tongue, but his British seemed to be understood. He had tried to explain, speaking slowly, not only his purpose in being this far north but also the family connection. Talorgen's father was Enfrith, son of Aylfrith the Cunning. Alfrid's own father was Oswii, son of Aylfrith the Cunning and therefore he and Talorgen were cousins. The man looked at him warily and past him to his hearth-troop. Alfrid was glad that he had brought only Aneurin and a handful of men with him so that he could not be mistaken for an aggressor.

Talorgen clearly did not welcome the mention of kin, for he said, "My father left me here when I was a child. He went off to get a kingdom and he never came back. Why should I speak to you about such things?"

Alfrid was surprised to find that he had to swallow hard before he could reply. He let out a little cough to test his voice and said, "It was the same with me." He glanced around at the unknown and yet oddly familiar buildings, rounder in design than the Anglian constructions in

Northumbria and Mercia. The plaid patterns of the woven clothes were reminiscent of the raiment worn by his childhood friends, even though these Picts were darker and, on the whole, a little shorter than his Rhegedian relatives. Many of the men were shirtless in the midsummer heat.

Talorgen said, "So we were both forsaken by our fathers. What of it?"

"My father is going to give me a kingdom and he wants to do the same for you."

Talorgen laughed harshly. "A man will treat his nephew the same way he treats his son? I think not."

Alfrid said, "I can see why you would think that. But Oswii is not like most fathers. He needs me and he needs you. All you have to do is take the king-helm and swear to him as your overlord."

"How can I take the king-helm? Another man happens to be wearing it right now."

Alfrid leaned in closely. "All you need to do is be ready. And while you are waiting, make it known to all who might have forgotten that your mother was of the royal line here and your father was king of Bernicia, even if only for a brief while."

"Be ready? For what?"

"The king of the Picts is going to die soon."

"Is he ill?"

"No, but nevertheless he is going to die. You need do nothing but take your chance when it comes. And if ever you come to Bamburgh, be sure not to say anything to the queen, lest she start putting up monasteries for yet another fallen king." He suppressed a smile then, for it amused him that Efa exerted such pressure upon Oswii to be a good Christian, whilst he continued to act upon the principle that what she did not know, she could not denounce.

Alfrid turned to the members of his hearth-troop and

beckoned two of them to come forward. "These men are going to help you. They are Elwyn and Hunwold."

The sun was low in the sky and yet it was only mid-afternoon. The year was old and soon the winter rains would cause flooding and the vale of York would be sodden, the roads impassable. Udo of Deira looked again at the defensive wall and knew that it could be a prison as well as a fortress. If he waited he would be safe, for if he could not get out then no one would be able to get in either, but could he hold his nerve? If he was going to run then it would have to be soon.

He walked over to one of the fence posts and grabbed hold of it, trying to wobble it. It held fast. He had doubled the guard, his hearth-troops were ready and he knew they were loyal. The Deirans would never yield to the yoke of a foreigner, be they Bernician or otherwise. They would fight for him, he knew it. But over the border, Oswii was building up his own federation of territories loyal to him and hostile to Mercia, and Udo was under no illusion, for he knew that he was only king here because Oswin was murdered, slain by a man who had taken great delight in bullying Udo.

News had come that the king of the Picts had died suddenly and in unusual circumstances. Details had been patchy but the scenario did not seem to differ significantly from that which hastened Oswin's end.

King Sigi of the East Saxons had converted to Christianity and accepted Oswii's overlordship. If Oswii came now to Deira, he would demand servitude at best, blood at worst. Udo had been, ironically, safer when he still lived in Bamburgh, for he was right under Oswii's nose and under Efa's protection. She would have witnessed any attempt upon his life. But she couldn't protect him out here.

A moment of bravery saw Udo standing up tall and deciding that he would fight the bastard and kill him, jeer over his dead body and stare at his lifeless eyes. Then he recalled how he used to quiver when his hulk of an uncle came up to him, putting his face up close to his, calling him a by-blow or worse. His uncle had never forgiven himself for not being Oswald and he had never forgiven Udo for being the image of his father. Udo knew he was no match for Oswii, even with the advantage of youth on his side. He looked again at the darkening sky and ran inside to pack his belongings and rally his hearth-troop.

Ænna was pacing up and down his hall, twisting his rings around his fingers, pausing to chew his nails, then resuming his anxious prowling. Adelar watched him and knew he was being uncharitable but he felt little sympathy. Ænna had sown and now he must reap.

But the king was blind to his own hypocrisy. "First Penda takes the land of the Middle Angles and gives them a Mercian king right on our border and then he agrees to harbour a Deiran. It is like Edwin all over again."

Adelar had heard the mordant criticism of Edwin many times over and it washed over him. He bit into a crisp apple, freshly fallen from the tree. He had been but a babe in arms when Edwin marched with their Uncle Redwald and his only memories of those times were of Edwin's wife, Carinna, and her warm embraces and exciting bedtime stories. His heart was whole and not twisted like his brother's. Now he dared to admonish him, waving the apple as he spoke. "You are a fine one to whinge about men giving shelter to other men."

Ænna was barely listening. "Oswii of Bernicia has no love for the Deirans. I am going to swear to him and then he can help me against Penda."

Adelar was incredulous. Holding the apple to his mouth but not biting he said, "You are going to fight Penda? Are you mad?"

"He has killed two East Anglian kings."

"So why would you want to take that tally to three? He has never threatened your kingship."

"We are going to be stuck on the edge, friendless, when Oswii rises up. The East Saxons have sworn to him, the Middle Angles are sworn to Mercia. Who will swear to us?"

"I think you should reconsider. Penda is the better ally. Think of the boy."

Adelar was fond of the boy, but his status was important, too. He was the only male offspring of the East Anglian brothers, but he was a different creature in Ænna's eyes, being Haryth's child and therefore partly Deiran and thus kin to the hated Edwin.

Ænna's voice was shrill in response. "Oh yes, I must think of the boy. How can I not? He is the one who reminds my wife every day that she only was able to have girls, the boy who reminds me every day of his mother, Edwin's kinswoman, the boy who earned me a telling-off from that god-awful woman Hild. Why do you care so much anyway? You always made moon-faces whenever Haryth was around. Is that it? Is it that you are really the boy's father?"

He charged over to Adulf and picked the lad up by the scruff of his tunic neck. "Who is your father, eh? What has been going on behind my back?" He shook the lad who remained mute through fear and then flung him across the room.

"Stop it!" Adelar threw the apple to the floor, rushed forward and shouted at his nephew to get out of the way. He lunged at Ænna and grabbed him by his throat. "Stupid bastard. Take on Penda and you won't even live to regret it. I'll swear to him before I swear to you. At least he is not cruel to children."

He shoved his brother back into his chair and left the room.

Outside, he called for a messenger and when a rider

presented himself he drew him to the furthest point of the royal enclosure and said, "Take a message to King Penda. Tell him who it was who harboured Cynwal of the West Saxons. And tell him that same man, Ænna of East Anglia, plans to rise up against him with Oswii's help. Go, now, and ride hard."

# Chapter Ten

*Tamworth 654*

Penda wondered if the rage would ever evaporate. He had felt it boiling inside him since the rider from East Anglia delivered the message. The sun was shining on a clear spring morning and now at last the ground was firm enough for his army to ride and he could give vent to his wrath.

Derwena had been to the temple to leave gifts and she came to him now, telling him that the priest said that the omens were good. He did not care if they were not; he would ride today or burst from fury.

Despite the sunshine, she was shivering, and he pulled gently on the edges of her cloak and drew them tighter around her body as he took her in an embrace. He bent down and sought the little indent where her neck met her shoulder and breathed in deeply, trying to fill his body with the scent of her skin so that he would have enough to last him for the journey and beyond. "You're cold," he said. "Come inside."

She did not acquiesce, but stood staring up at the cloudless sky. "Do you not feel it? A storm is coming."

He laughed. "Are you mad, woman? The lambs are out in the middle of the fields when last week they were huddled by the hedge for warmth. Noni's shoes are dry already though he was in the river but yesterday. There is warmth now in the sun and winter is behind us."

She shook her head and he had to work hard to stop an icy pool of fear from sloshing around in his stomach.

"What then? Have you seen the Wild Hunt?" The sight

of Woden riding in the hunt foretold the death of the men riding with him. Had Derwena seen him among the riders in her dreams?

She sighed and rested her head against his chest. "I have no fears for your life, but for our peace. It is no longer one king set against another; every king in the land has taken sides now. I wonder where it will all end."

He knew he should not goad her, but bitterness buried only in a shallow place rose up now to work his tongue. "What do you care? You have cursed me to shrivel and die every day since Carena left."

She looked up and said, "And I have cursed myself for a fool who has suffered a cold bed for every one of those days. I will waste not one more day of those I have left. Will you forgive me?"

He put a finger to her lips. "I love you. No more needs to be said, save that I am sorry for any hurt I gave you." He bent his head and kissed her, then whispered in her ear. "I have missed you." He straightened and said, "And I will answer you; it will end in some marshy bog in East Anglia with Ænna's guts wrapped around a withy hurdle and his head on a stick."

Pieter came from the stables and, overhearing his father's comment said, "I like the sound of that. When do we ride? The horses are ready."

Derwena smiled and Penda wondered, not for the first time, how much it cost her to do so at times when she must feel like weeping instead. She said, "Soon, I hope. My hall is bulging with men and I'm itching to get rid of them. They smell bad."

Penda could only concur. Her comment carried the sound of forced jocularity but there was truth in it too. Merwal's hearth-troop had swelled the ranks of the Deirans who had travelled with Udo. All week, men had been arriving from neighbouring territories and outlying settlements and even the extended hall was full to capacity. Penda was grateful for Pieter's decision to travel with only a handful of men. They would gather the rest of the Middle Angles on their journey to the east. As the three of them turned to go into the crowded hall, the sound of hurried footsteps caused them to stop and turn.

Wulf was running to catch up with Pieter and he had his saddle in his hands. He thrust it up for inspection and said, "Look, the strap here is worn through. It will need to be mended before we leave. I thought you and Emmett had looked at them all."

Pieter, causing a lump of pride to lodge in Penda's throat, ignored the reproachful tone and acknowledged the weakness in the leather strap. "Forgive me, Brother, but I did not think you would be needing it."

Wulf's chin jutted out and he glared at his elder brother. "You mean to leave me behind."

Pieter's voice was gentle and soothing. "I mean that if you are to stay here and protect our mother and sisters then I hope you would not forsake them by going off riding to see one of your young women."

Wulf stood taller and said, "Yes, well, I do not have any… But you are right. Mother needs me."

Penda smiled his gratitude to his tactful son but his smile faded when he saw Derwena scowling at him. He pulled her away from the others and said, "What? I thought you would be pleased. He is only fourteen and I thought you would shout at me if I took him."

He was confused. She had been this way with him when he had conferred the highest honour he could on Merwal and given him a kingdom. And with Carena's leaving still a source of tension between them until a moment ago, he would have been foolish to risk her wrath regarding yet another of her offspring. Or so he thought.

She said, "Of course I want him with me. But now I know that you are more worried about this fight than you

313

will admit."

He flung his arms high and then slapped them to his sides. "Women! If I live to be one hundred years old I will never understand."

She relented a little and nudged him in the ribs as she walked past him and into the hall, speaking as she went. "And what on earth makes you think that I need anyone to stay and look after me?"

His prediction had not been so very wrong. He had indeed dismembered Ænna's body, but in the end it had not been in some vast swathe of boggy marshland, but on the road out of Rendlesham, heading north. Whether or not it was true that Ænna had appealed to Oswii, no help had been forthcoming from that direction.

Either Oswii did not wish to send assistance or he had not been able to get his army so far south in time. The fact that Penda found the East Anglian king so close to his base suggested that Ænna had been banking on Northumbrian support to come and rescue him before he needed to come forth and fight.

Penda would never know, nor did he care. The oath-breaking little shit was dead and that was an end to it. Old man he might be, but Penda still had the strength to strike a mortal blow to cowards.

He had never understood the need for lying, or for flattery. He had lived his whole life by the sword, which spoke eloquently, solved arguments and only hurt those who deserved the pain. He was mindful, like the Christians, of the afterlife, but he knew that he had done enough to ensure the nature of the hearth-songs that would be sung of his life. Meanwhile, he would leave those who cared to bury what was left of Ænna; he must tidy up another aspect of the mess his Mercians had made in East Anglia.

At Rendlesham, Penda found Adelar. He said, "I thank

you for your warning but you know I am going to have to shrink your kingdom and take your power from you?"

Adelar nodded.

Penda gave the order and this time his men stripped the hall of Rendlesham of every last piece of gold and silver. While the men filled bag upon bag of booty, he questioned this strangely calm man, whose treachery had resulted in the killing of his own flesh and blood.

"Why did you help me against your own brother?"

Adelar said, "You were kind to me once. Your kinswoman Carinna was kinder still. From bairn in the cradle to a twelve-year-old boy, I had her love. Though her own sons were taken from her, she was like a mother to me. My brother recalled only the cruelty of Edwin and it twisted his soul. The sadness is that in the end, he was not so different from Edwin. The boy here will tell you as much."

Adulf nodded. "I hated him. He knew what cruelty can do to a young man when it is meted out by an older man, yet he did the same to me."

Udo of Deira stepped forward and put a hand on Adulf's shoulder. "My uncle did the same to me."

Penda grunted. "Why do men do it? A child is a child. Men should be kind to them, even if they are not their own sons."

Udo shrugged. "My uncle is a turd. Do you not think it must have been bad indeed for me to crave shelter with the man who killed my father? You were kind to me, too, when I was young and I never forgot it, even after Maserfeld. Believe me when I say that Oswii is the most loathsome of men and being his son is no protection, I can assure you."

Adelar said, "My brother sent to Oswii for help. I do not know what the answer was, but make no mistake, Oswii is massing forces against you. He has enlisted the Picts and the East Saxons and by now he will have taken

315

over Deira. You should do what you did to my brother and take him by surprise."

Penda shook his head. "He would not be so stupid. My daughter lives with his son. His youngest son is my hostage. He would have to be mad to pick a fight with me."

Udo said, "I watched him for years. The only thing that drives him is the need to get out of the long shadow cast by my father, Oswald," he nodded at Penda, "and to have what you have, my lord. He cares nothing for his children. He lives in his hall on the rocks and has to listen to the chatter of the women who pray endlessly and read the Bible. He wants to prove himself and he is not above doing murder to get what he wants."

"All right then," Penda said. "If he wants a fight, he shall have one." He looked at Adelar. "Be ready to come when I send for you."

The East Anglian frowned. "Are you not going now?"

Penda laughed, though not with any unkind intent. "No, lad, I am going to go home and raise the biggest army ever gathered. Then I will go north and wipe the Northumbrians off the earth for ever."


## Northumbria

It was as if the November rain had filled the sea to overflowing and now the ocean was throwing the excess water up onto the beach and hurling it against the rocks beneath the fortress in an effort to bail out the surplus.

The moaning wind carried it higher until from inside the fortress it sounded as if they were in a boat on the high seas, not a great hall. Hild was sanguine about it, saying that it was God's way of beating back the marauders, but Oswii was beginning to feel penned in. The weather kept them indoors, the invaders kept him from venturing beyond the fortress walls.

Men who were old enough to remember were proclaiming that soon the rock would be an island, as it was in the days before Aylfrith's time.

Elwyn said, "Why not simply give him the tribute and then he will go away?"

Oswii slammed his cup down upon the table and began pacing the floor. "That heathen bastard has already taken tribute from the settlements that he flattened on his way here. The only thing stopping him from setting my land all to fire is the pissing rain."

He stomped to the end of the hall and then back again. "And the weather is the only thing stopping him from calling me out onto the battlefield. When the rains stop…"

He came to a halt near his wife's chair, but she was busy with the baby and barely looked up. Even if she had anything to say it would be to disapprove. She had never completely forgiven him for Oswin's death and lately, particularly after the birth of this latest daughter, she had cooled towards him in bed, thus removing the only moments of marital harmony from their lives.

Hild, sitting next to Efa, chucked the baby under the chin, looked thoughtful for a moment, chewing the inside of her cheek, and then said, "Give the child to me. For the abbey, I mean. Dedicating this girl's life to God will atone for all your sins and absolve you from any killing in the forthcoming battle."

Oswii snorted. It was a good job that he didn't value his children overly much, for no doubt Efa would accede to the request and Hild would get her way as usual. Both of these women had, in their own way, been overtly hostile to Oswii, supporting him only when he made Christian overtures, complying with his wishes only when they deemed his actions to be in God's name and almost forcing him to be a good Christian.

The argument over Easter still raged; Aidan had been

an ally, albeit an improbable one, and he was dead. Oswii was hopelessly out of his depth in matters of scripture and had come to realise, belatedly, that the Bible study for which he had so often teased Oswald, had perhaps not been so pointless after all.

Oswii found lately that, occasionally, he missed his pious elder brother for a fleeting moment, before he grew angry again that he was still living in the shadow of one whom he considered to be a weaker man. Oswald would have prayed and found a different answer than to simply pay Penda to go away. It was always a tacit acknowledgement of supremacy when one agreed to pay tribute but only a fool would offer pitched battle against a stronger king. And yet... He turned and walked the length of the hall again. Yes, he decided, he was ready for a fight. The time had come for him to prove himself.

Was Hild right? Would God let the battle go his way in return for his child? Perhaps, but he would still do well to count up his allies. His son, Alfrid, was ready to fight for him, and the Picts under his nephew Talorgen had pledged support. The East Saxons had promised to ride north and some of the lesser British territories could no doubt be coerced. Was it enough? Probably not. Penda would annihilate him in a fair fight.

He beckoned Elwyn and drew his reeve further into the shadows behind one of the great supporting timbers. There, he idly picked at the carving of an ivy leaf, working the grooves deeper with his thumbnail. "Is the gold bagged up and ready?"

Elwyn nodded. "It is. Shall I send word to Penda that we will pay up and that he can call off his hounds?"

"No. I could pay him and he might not go away. Then I would still have to fight him and I hear that he has nigh on thirty kings and chieftains riding with him."

"We would be outnumbered, that is true." Elwyn chewed his lip. "What to do then?"

"Send word not to Penda, but to Cadafael of Gwynedd. You once told me that every man has his price and he hinted as much to me many years ago. Find out how much it will take for him to turn."

Elwyn grinned. "Good thinking, my lord. This is you at your best. Anything else?"

Oswii felt the familiar stirring of excitement that tingled somewhere deep in his bones when he was planning any kind of intrigue. "Yes. Get word to my spineless nephew of Deira. Remind little Udo of his life at Bamburgh and suggest what it will be again if he finds himself on the losing side."

Penda wondered if he would ever be dry again. Surely the sky was empty now? The water found its way through everything, in between tiny gaps in clothing, dribbling down the back of his neck, leaking into his boots and through the stitch holes in his breeches.

His cloak had ceased to be any protection against the weather and it had been three days since they had seen anything approaching daylight. The heavy rains kept the sky iron-grey, and ensured that the sun remained a dim memory.

As water dripped from the end of his nose and he wiped it with a sleeve that was so sodden it simply made his face wetter, he lost his patience. "Enough. We are going home."

Bardulf said, "Are we not going to fight him?"

Penda stared out across the bleak landscape and thought of a friend who had died somewhere near here, partly because he stayed too long.

Perhaps if Cadwallon had withdrawn sooner instead of ravaging Deira, they would have had supremacy earlier and Oswald would never have gained a foothold. His friend would still be alive, and he would not now be standing in this grim place, so far from home.

"If Oswii wants to face me in battle, I will not run. But for now, let us get nearer the border before we stand and make our shield wall."

Elidyr of Elmet was close by and Penda beckoned him over. "I would like to get our men back over the border and wait there for a while. If Oswii follows us, we can fight him there. If all goes badly, it will be easy enough for those still alive to make their way home, be it to Middle Anglia, Wales, or any of the tribelands."

Elidyr said, "I agree. You are shrewd to say it and besides, it will be good to see my homeland again after all these weeks."

Penda nodded. "Let us go then." He rode along the lines, giving the instruction to each of the leaders and kings, relaying the information that they were withdrawing as far as the southern border of Elmet.

It took them another week of riding over ground which was now more quagmire than road and Penda wondered not for the first time why, when Northumbria was so large, its leaders had ever craved more land at the expense of other kingdoms.

At last they came to the place where weeks earlier his massed ranks had forded the river from Mercia into Elmet and he saw with dismay that the river had burst its banks, turning the surrounding area into soggy marsh. Whether he wished it or not, he would have to wait before he could cross the river and if Oswii came to them, the battle would be fought here.

They took what shelter they could, erecting their tents in a brief lull where for an hour or so, the sun came out, but it was too near the end of the day to do much good and all that was wet, remained wet.

In his tent that evening, Penda sat on a stool which immediately sank into the ground. He stood up and cursed. "This is no place for a fight. Let it please Thunor to lift the clouds and let us away across the river before the Northumbrians come. At least we have strength in numbers."

He looked around at the gathering of leaders. Bardulf, Pieter, Merwal, Elidyr of Elmet, Adelar of East Anglia, Udo of Deira and leaders from various tribes of the Mercian federation and representatives from British Lindsey. "Where is Cadafael?"

Merwal said, "I will go and find him."

"Yes, do. He should be here while we all talk."

Merwal opened the tent flap and had to hold it open for Udo of Deira, who had stood up and followed him to the entrance. Udo dashed past him and moments later they heard the sound of retching and vomit splattering onto the wet ground.

Penda said, "Is he unwell?"

"I rode with him today," Pieter replied. "He was doleful, and spoke at length about Oswii, asking me what I thought his uncle would do if he defeated us. I told him that Oswii will not win, but he kept talking about how Oswii used to beat him when he was a child and threatened to kill him. He even hinted that his uncle tried to have him murdered before he ever left his birthland."

Penda said, "That tells me much about this Bernician king. I hope that Alfrid does not live to regret riding off to be at his father's side, that same father who thinks so little of his sons that he rides against me knowing I have his youngest boy as my hostage."

Pieter said, "Ava hears from him often. She says Alfrid believes their father is truly sorry for what happened to Oswin. The Christian faith is hard for you to understand but it helps men forgive."

Penda sniffed. "Better if they do not behave like that at all. It does not matter how a man prays; if he's a bastard then he's a bastard. There are men among us, you to name one, who bend their knee in prayer. It is not the sum of who you are and what you are as a man."

A slip-slap sound announced the return of Merwal. A squelching sucking noise betrayed his struggle to come to a halt outside the tent flap, and his face as he came through the opening told a story of disaster. "Cadafael has gone."

If Pieter had harboured any doubts as to whether he could bring himself to kill his wife's father in battle, they had been dispersed when he looked across at his own father and saw him fighting an inner battle where boiling anger was colliding with reluctance to believe.

Pieter had been but a small boy when the man he thought of as an uncle, King Cadwallon, had been a welcome and frequent guest at Tamworth, but his successor Cadafael had never matched up to those faint memories, and Pieter knew his father had never developed the same deep friendship.

To have his reservations vindicated by Cadafael's treachery must have brought little comfort. His subsequent grim summation that they still heavily outnumbered the Bernicians remained true enough, but Pieter couldn't help glancing over to the Deiran section of the line, where Udo was leaning on his spear, holding it for support while he bent over and retched once more.

The shield wall was longer than Oswii's and when the two lines clashed, it would be a simple matter of bending their line so that it outflanked the Bernicians and then they would be able to infiltrate their ranks and pick them off in hand-to-hand combat.

Pieter turned to look behind and saw the bowmen lined up, ready to do their job of firing arrows down on the enemy from a distance, causing a nuisance that would impede their progress.

The rain, thank the Lord, had finally stopped and a weak watery sun made fleeting appearances in a sky that was pale, as if it, too, were exhausted by the rainfall and was now weary and spent. The banners of the Bernicians flapped limply in a breeze that barely had the power to blow them and Pieter thought grimly how strange it was that in the calm after the storm, the earth quietened and yet men were about to unleash another maelstrom.

The enemy were fewer in number, his father had been right about that, but they had been travelling for less time, they were nearer home and had used up less of their energy getting to this place. And they were not suffering the morale-sapping effect of having had part of their contingent desert in the dead of night. The two sides were much more evenly matched than any of them had initially supposed.

The command was given for the shield walls to move forward. Pieter waited for the singing sound that announced the loosing of the heavy spears which would be thrown moments before the walls crashed together. These would potentially cause a break in the opposing wall, or weigh down the enemy shields and render them unwieldy.

At the moment of impact each side would let out their war cry, wasted if the two armies were too far away from each other. Let the Bernicians quake at the sound of so many different cries, bellowing up from the combined ranks of so many who were united in their intent to halt Oswii's ambitions.

Pieter went to work with his sword, slashing at his opposite number and remaining aware of his neighbours, readying himself to close any gap which might appear in the wall.

The axemen began their assault on the Bernician spearmen, hacking at the hafts, while federation spear carriers protected the axemen, who were left vulnerable each time they took a swing with their heavy blades. Pieter settled in. This formulaic pattern would continue awhile, until one side or the other found a weakness and pushed through the wall.

Slicing, thrusting and pushing with his shield boss, he was surprised to feel the tell-tale slackening which suggested a break in their own ranks and he chanced a glance down the line, to see Udo of Deira finally lose his grip of any remaining courage and withdraw, inciting the Deirans to follow him.

Pieter had time to note that although he had removed himself from the wall, Udo had not run off to join his uncle; in the end he was brave enough neither to defy his uncle nor betray Penda and was seemingly going to attempt to sit the battle out.

Pieter turned his attention back to the battle, and the more pressing problem that he was now being forced backwards and the ground was slippery underfoot. One mishap and he would be flat on his back in the mud and one step nearer death.

It was impossible to keep the tight formation; even if they managed to stay on their feet, the Mercians were being forced back towards the swollen river. He shouted the order to break the wall. They would have to take their chances.

It had been some time since he had seen his brother or father but up ahead he could see Bardulf of the Hwicce engaged in one-on-one combat with a Bernician spearman. He had known Bardulf as long as he could remember but only now did he realise that the very longevity of the relationship meant that Bardulf was therefore an old man.

Bardulf fought with a sword and he was having difficulty getting near enough to the spearman to make contact. The Bernician jabbed with his spear and Bardulf held his shield aloft and stepped backwards. His foot slipped in the mud and he went down on one knee.

The spear tip punctured his mail at the top of his shoulder and Bardulf of the Hwicce sank down to the ground, never to stand up again.

Pieter turned away, lashing out at the next adversary who approached him, bringing his sword across in a sideways arc and cutting deep between shoulder and neck. It was vengeance, of a sort, but it did not ease the hurt of witnessing the death of a friend.

Anguished calling from behind him alerted Pieter to danger. He turned round to see Adelar of East Anglia backing towards the river. Forcing him nearer the water was a Bernician ordfruma, a point-leader, who had manoeuvred himself to the front of a wedge-shaped formation. His fearlessness had encouraged others, as it was designed to do, to follow him in singling out a prestigious leader.

One of Adelar's followers had managed to get between him and the river and add his sword arm to the defence, but the ordfruma was bearing down on Adelar and his axe blow was deadly in its accuracy.

Adelar fell backwards, his sword arm went up but momentum carried it back over his shoulder and another of the attackers was able to push his sword into the king's exposed armpit.

Pieter let out a yell as he tried to fight his way over to the river, rallying the Middle Angles and hoping to re-establish a battle formation.

By the time he reached the sloshing bank of the river, Adelar was floating face down, his body bobbing as the current picked him up and began to carry him downstream. It would not take him far; already the river was damming with the bodies of dead Mercians and their allies.

It was always the fate of kings to be targeted first in any pitched battle but Pieter did not expect to see so many leaders going down so quickly.

He looked about frantically for his father and brother and quickly located Merwal, fighting in a tight huddle with his Magonsæte close by him, making short work of a contingent of Picts. The northmen were easily recognised by their war cry of "Cruthni" and their use of hounds, trained to respond to commands in the heat of battle, but Merwal and his hearth-troop had despatched the animals without ceremony. Pieter nodded. Merwal was in no immediate danger.

He ran round to the edge of the fighting, tucking and rolling out of the way of an East Saxon axe-hammer and battering the assailant with his shield boss as he came to his feet. The effect was greater than he had hoped when his foot slipped and he toppled, crushing the East Saxon underneath him.

While he was on the ground, Pieter reached down for his hand-sæx and slit the man's throat before he had a chance to recover his senses.

Scrambling back upright, Pieter took a moment to gain perspective, searching for the banners of either his father or Oswii. And then he saw them both, just as the Bernician king's standard bearer sank into the mud and the banner was trampled underfoot by Lothar.

Penda had his back to the river, he was too close and had no escape, but his hearth-men were holding their ground. Pieter allowed himself the luxury of hope for the first time since battle had been joined.

Smiling, he turned and saw a shield boss aimed at his face coming towards him at powerful speed and he lost sight at the same moment as a flash of pain exploded in his head.


The ride south was a race, not least against the weather. Winter was closing in and all men were eager to get home before the roads got any worse. But it became clear that the southern kingdoms had not suffered the same amount of rainfall and the roads were still good and passable.

After such an energy-sapping battle, not many words were spoken and he was able to take refuge in his own thoughts.

So many dead kings. The scops would be singing for years about this fight, the battle which had finally ended the long-running dispute between Northumbria and Mercia. There were no more contenders for the coveted throne. It was over. Merwal had turned off the road with his Magonsæte some miles back to go home to his wife and children and the surviving members of the Hwicce and Arosæte had gone, too, so now he was riding alone, wondering how he was going to find the words to tell Derwena.

He felt her pain already, had been carrying it in his own heart since the battle. He had to hurry, but he didn't want to. He would have promised anything not to have to bear such heart-rending news to her door.

He could picture how she would receive him, relief at his survival writ large upon her face, even while she clutched her younger children to her, shoring herself up in anticipation of the devastating blow she instinctively knew was coming. He had never been able to fool her; she would know before he opened his mouth.

As he neared the familiar gatehouse of Tamworth, the place which had been his home all his life, he knew that he was about to alter her life forever. Could he linger for one moment more? No. That would merely be for his own benefit.

She would have heard by now the outcome of the battle and she would be expecting their return. To leave her wondering how many of her menfolk were going to ride through the gates would heap cruelty upon misery. He was known as a fearless warrior; now he must be a brave man.

She came running, saw him and knew. She shook her head and began to keen.

He slipped from the saddle and into her arms. "Mother, I am so sorry. King Penda is dead."

Derwena thought that she heard the noise her heart made, as it shattered into tiny pieces. The shards lodged in her chest, pricking her bones, her skin, her being. They would never be excised and she would carry the hurt unto death. Had she ever told him that she loved him? Had he known, at the end, that she had truly forgiven him for sending Carena away? Did he know that once he breathed his last, effectively she had ceased to exist as well?

She stared into the face of her anguished son and knew how much it had crushed him to be the bearer of such a heavy burden. His face, so like that of her own dear beloved, was contorted with pain. She touched his cheek, thanked Frige that he at least had survived and then she attempted to speak. Sound emerged, nothing coherent, or so she thought, but he understood.

"Merwal is safe and has ridden to his home." He clutched her hands. "Mother, listen to me. I have had longer to grieve than you and I wish I could give you time, to go to the temple, give thanks for his life, have the scops prepare their words. But you must get away."

She nodded, trying hard to listen. Oswii was marching south, he said. The Bernician had given Pieter leave to remain as king of the Middle Angles because he was Oswii's son-in-law, but Penda's other sons had been offered no such guarantees. It would be better if she were to flee and take the younger ones with her...

She knew she should be concentrating but all she wanted to do was sink to her knees. A voice went round her head, all but drowning out her son's speech and it was a voice which knew no song except the ballad of her love. It wailed its haunting lament and she knew that if she lived to old age it would send her mad. It rambled through the verses of her life, pausing at the moments of tenderness, at every begetting of a child and every lingering kiss. Its tempo increased as it marched through any sadness and then it rested on each exquisite touch and every moment of triumph, slowing down to savour the memory of every hour spent alone in the woods and every minute of shared laughter until the melody became a dirge and taunted her with the song's abrupt ending.

Then Lothar was at her side, serving his leader beyond death by taking it upon himself to act as protector to Penda's wife and children and reminding her who her man had been, who she was. She knew then that she shamed his memory by indulging her grief. He had been a leader, a warrior, a proud king. What would he need her to do?

She clutched Lothar's hand and led him to the treasure house. "Pack what you can. Take only the sword fittings and some of the gold crosses. We will need it to pay our way and gather new hearth-troops."

She ran to the hall and gathered her children to her. Minna and Starling were married women and would be safe enough. Even the most vile and cruel bastard would not take retribution against womenfolk and they could not be identified beyond their status as wives of hearth-thegns. Telling them that their father was dead was hard; bidding them farewell was nigh on unbearable. "One day," she told them, "one day, we will all be together again."

Sikke and Sjeord were already mounted and waiting by the gate. The small group set out on the oldest, most shabby horses in Penda's fine stable. Pieter, always jealous of his breeding stock and fine mounts, was appalled and Emmett voiced his dismay, but Derwena craved anonymity on the road. Wrapped up against the winter wind, Wulf and Noni and the twins rode on smaller ponies. Only the Bernician hostage, Oswii's son Lief, rode a stallion befitting his status.

They rode out of Tamworth and took the Roman road until they came to the path which would take some of their party to safety in the Welsh kingdoms. Here Derwena felt the sharp points stabbing her chest once more as she hugged her elder sons and said goodbye. To Wulf's hearth companions she said, "Look after him. One day, if the gods are willing, he will return to reclaim his father's king-seat."

She watched for a while, long after the fading light and the bend in the path had robbed her of the sight of them and then she said to Lothar, "Come with me." Not far up ahead, she turned her horse off the road at a place where thick woodland hid a steep bank from anyone unfamiliar with the territory. Climbing up through the trees, they came to a hilltop of scrubby heathland. She gestured for him to bring the treasure. "Bury it over there. We will come back for it once we have given the boy back to his father."

She scrambled back down the bank and spoke to Noni. "Mark this spot well. If we do not get back to it later this night then one day you must come and dig up the gold. Your father and I spent a lifetime gathering it. It may come in use to you or Wulf when the world is righted once more." Her ten-year-old boy blinked sleepily in the cold dusk and she wondered if he even truly knew where they were. No matter; all she could do was to try. Try to save what was left of her family and try to honour the memory of her beloved man.

Lothar slithered down the bank and said, "I have hidden it as best I could. With more time and ground less hard I could have dug deeper but..."

A rider appeared on the road ahead.

Derwena said, "Whatever you have done will be good enough. And none too soon."

The horseman approached and made himself known as Harmand of Breedon. Derwena shivered and drew her cloak around her but she knew it was not the cold which had set her teeth chattering. "You have news?"

"Oswii is at Lichfield and I am sent to bid you meet him there."

Often-times, women were known as peace-weavers, fulfilling that role through marriage. Now though, Derwena had to weave a different spell. Gathering her twins, her youngest son and her hostage, she led the procession as it rode under darkening skies in the direction of Lichfield, there to barter their lives for the return of the heir of Northumbria.

\*\*\*\*\*

*On 5th July, 2009, a hoard containing gold pieces, mostly weapon decoration and folded up gold crosses, was found just off the ancient road known as Watling Street, between Tamworth and Lichfield. No one is sure why it was buried there, where it came from and what purpose it served, but two things are certain: it was buried close to the royal centre of Mercia and whoever buried it never returned to claim it. Perhaps it was hidden there by a woman who went to bargain with a king, believing that a man's love for his child would be strong enough to allow her to go free…*

# Author's Notes

There is documentary evidence for almost everything that happens in *Cometh the Hour*. The main source of information for this period is Bede's *Ecclesiastical History of the English People* and many of the anecdotes in *Cometh the Hour* can be found there: it was Bede who recorded Æthelburh of Kent's nickname, although I changed it from Tate to Tata. Bede gives us a physical description of Paulinus and a concise assessment of Oswin of Deira's character. Bede describes how Aidan gave the nobles a telling-off, he gives us the colours of Oswald's banner and tells us that Edwin made the roads safe to travel.

Were it not for Bede it is doubtful we would know that the inhabitants of Elmet were, in fact, British. A document known as the Tribal Hidage lists them as the Elmedsæte, as if they were another midland Anglian tribe, but at the time of Edwin's reign it seems that they were British and so, to differentiate them from the other tribes which came under Mercia's banner, I have referred to them by their possible British name of Loides.

We also have Bede to thank for the stories with more of a religious aspect: Oswin giving away his horse, the giving away of the plate, and Oswald making the cross before the battle of Heavenfield. Heric's widow is recorded as having dreamed about her murdered husband and predicting Hild's future as an abbess, while Edwin is said by Bede to have heard a heavenly voice when awaiting Redwald's decision about the assassins' plea. It must be remembered that Bede was a Northumbrian Christian and as such was more interested in saintly behaviour and the miracles associated with the canonised kings.

It has been pointed out that Oswald must have had

something other than an impeccable religious conviction to have been a successful king, but Bede glosses over any darker incidents, such as Edwin's widow fleeing in fear back to Kent.

However, this bias allows us to take seriously Bede's comments about Penda; he called him a heathen idolater, but it was Bede who said that "Penda did not forbid the teaching of the Word, even in his own Mercian kingdom, if any wished to hear it. But he hated and despised those who, after they had accepted the Christian faith, were clearly lacking in the works of faith. He said that they were despicable and wretched creatures who scorned to obey the God in whom they believed." To be described as "a man exceptionally gifted as a warrior" is praise indeed from a cleric with northern and religious bias.

As well as the written sources, archaeology also provides a great deal of information and useful detail: at Bamburgh, the gold 'Beast' and the six-strand pattern-welded sword were found during excavation. There is archaeological evidence for the stone walls and the steps in the cleft of the rock, and there was, in all likelihood, a stone chapel. Similarly, the description of Yeavering is based on extensive excavation of the area, which also showed evidence of the hall having been burned around the time of Oswald's reign.

The description of the Sutton Hoo grave goods is based on the archaeological finds. It is assumed that this famous ship burial commemorated Redwald, although no body was ever found.

The Staffordshire Hoard is the largest collection of Anglo-Saxon gold and silver metalwork ever found and totals more than 3,500 items that are nearly all martial in character, including an extraordinary quantity of sword pommel caps and hilt plates. Many feature beautiful garnet inlays or animals in elaborate filigree. There is also a beautiful gold horse-head which does indeed look very like a sea-horse.

Some of the scenes depicted in the novel have been built up around fragmentary evidence. I invented the character of Dalya, but it seems unlikely that Udo was Oswald's son by Cyra, because they did not marry until 635 and if he had been born no earlier than 636, he would have been incredibly young when given the kingship of Deira: only fifteen in 651. Oswii married twice while living in exile and there is no reason to suppose that Oswald didn't do similarly. Nowhere do the sources say that Udo was Cyra's son, only that he was Oswald's. Cyra's historical name is given as Cyneburh but only by one, much later, source.

The known history always leaves gaps for the novelist to fill and it has always struck me as odd that Oswii installed his nephew on the Deiran throne, rather than one of his own adult children, and furthermore that the same nephew would fight against him in 655. I had to find some way of explaining this. I began to believe that Oswii had scant regard for any of his children; he was certainly brave or foolish to fight Penda when his youngest son was a hostage at the Mercian court, so perhaps he took the same cavalier attitude to the rest of his issue.

Penda's wife is also named only once, by Bede, as Cynewise, which suggests that she was a West Saxon, so I gave her a fictional back story, with reference to Merwal. There is some conjecture as to whether Merwal was Penda's son, because his historical name, Merewalh, actually translates to something approximating "Welshman". (It seems not uncommon that kings adopted the children of their wives; there is good reason to suppose that Redwald's 'son' Siegbert was, in fact, a foster son and that rivalry was the cause of his self-imposed exile after Redwald's death.)

I have no proof that Edith and Eda, whose historical

name was Eadburh, were twins but, given the number of children accredited to 'Derwena', it seems not impossible that at least one of her pregnancies might have resulted in a multiple birth.

It is possible that Penda and Eowa were nephews of Cærl and I have shown them as such on the genealogical tree; but there is a great deal of uncertainty regarding the Mercian royal family and with this in mind I have been cautious about referring to Carinna as their cousin, although in all probability, this was the relationship.

I have also had to make 'best guesses'. There is some doubt as to the precise years of Penda's reign. It is unclear whether he ruled alongside or after his brother, but Eowa was killed at Maserfeld and there is good reason to suppose that he was fighting on Oswald's side. No one knows the cause of Maserfeld. Bede is relatively uninformative about Oswald, citing only his saintliness and the miracles associated with his cult, but he certainly had his enemies. I have no evidence for the existence of Oswald's first wife, much less that Oswii arranged her murder, but there is no doubt that Oswii was not above bumping off his rivals, displaying a ruthlessness which appears to have been lacking in his elder brother.

Bede was a Northumbrian, and the Anglo-Saxon chronicle was mainly written by West Saxon scribes. There is no comparable Mercian chronicle. Historians seem to agree that had such a document existed, Penda's name and reputation would rate alongside that of other 'great kings' and we might know a great deal more about the Staffordshire Hoard. It is stated that Adelar of East Anglia was 'the cause of the war' (the battle of 655 in which Penda died, and which some believe was fought on the banks of the River Aire) although this is now presumed to be a mistranslation. I was intrigued, though, and wondered how Adelar might have been the cause of the war.

By the time I wrote that particular chapter, it had become abundantly clear to me that Adelar, as I had written him, would have become thoroughly fed up with his brother's antics. It is recorded that he fought on Penda's side in that battle, as did Udo of Deira.

Sources disagree about the tribute raised by Oswii in 655; some say that the Welsh accepted it, some say that they refused it, some say that Penda accepted it. It has been suggested that this might even have made up the bulk, if not all, of the Staffordshire Hoard. It is true, though, that Oswii promised his daughter to the abbey at this time.

I have only knowingly altered the chronology twice, although no one can say with any certainty exactly when Penda's attack on East Anglia occurred. I brought it forward to occur earlier than most estimates because it suited my narrative, but it is recorded that King Siegbert really did face Penda's forces armed only with a stick. I altered the date of Cynwal's exile and return which is usually given as 645-648, but again, it suited my story to have him running away when he became king and at the point at which he took a new wife.

Readers who are familiar with this period will know that I have altered the names of many of the characters, but I hope I will be forgiven, because some of the Anglo-Saxon names are very hard on the eye and sometimes don't offer too many clues about pronunciation.

The four kings' names, Edwin, Penda, Oswald and Oswii are as documented, although Oswii is sometimes spelled in the sources Oswy or Oswui. I gave Ænna a diphthong because his recorded name, Anna, looks rather too feminine to the modern eye. For those who are curious and to aid identification, there is a list below of the main characters, and their historical names if they have not been mentioned in the story prior to the introduction of a nickname.

There were some names which I had to invent. Penda's wronged sister is not named by the sources, so I gave her a name which seems to suit the Mercian tradition: Audra. Oswii's Irish bride was given a fictional name of Brigid, and Redwald's wife, though obviously influential, is also not named by Bede, even though he mentions her on several occasions, so I chose the name Bertana for her. Conversely, there are members of the royal houses whom I have not mentioned; one source suggests that Aylfrith fathered seven boys upon Acha, all with names beginning with 'Os' and there was a sister, Æbbe, who became a rather notorious abbess.

The East Anglian brothers Ænna and Adelar actually had two younger brothers and Edwin's son Ash had a child, Yffi. But I have not brought these people into the story because of the confusion of similar names and because they did not contribute to the narrative.

I did not mention the sons of Eowa, as they played no part in this portion of the story, neither did I include another possible son of Penda, Osweard, who, whilst mentioned in two charters, and in the *Life* of Saint Ecgwine as a brother of Ethelred (Noni) cannot be positively identified as Penda's son.

All of the main characters in *Cometh the Hour* existed. I invented a lot of the secondary characters, such as Lothar, the Frisian brothers, Manfrid, and Nia the servant, but Reeve Elwyn (Æthelwine) existed and was named as a conspirator along with Hunwold the Deiran in the murder of Oswin; I filled in his back story.

Similarly, Lilla really was a thegn of Edwin's and was murdered by the West Saxon sent to assassinate Edwin. The holy men, Aidan, Paulinus and Birinus are all named by Bede and St Wilfrid really did begin his ecclesiastical life after being sponsored by Oswii's queen.

## Real historical names

Adelar - Æthelhere
Adulf –Aldwulf
Aldric - Æthelric
Alfrid - Alhfrith
Ash – Osfrith
Ava - Alhflæd
Aylfrith - Æthelfrith
Cærl - Ceorl
Carena - Cyneburh
Carinna - Cwenburh
Cyngil - Cynegils
Cynwal - Cenwealh
Efa - Eanflæd
Enfrith - Eanfrith
Erwald - Eorpwald
Haryth – Hereswith
Heric - Hereric
Minna - Cyneswith
Oswin - Oswine
Pieter - Peada
Redwald – Rædwald
Regnar - Regenhere
Rhian – Rhiainfellt
Siegbert - Sigeberht
Sigi - Sigiberht
Starling – Wilburh
Yvo – Eadfrith

The feud between the Mercians and the Northumbrians did not end with the death of Penda. How could it, when his sons were still alive…

# Other Novels by Annie Whitehead

## To Be A Queen

The story of Æthelflæd, Lady of the Mercians, daughter of Alfred the Great, and the only female leader of an Anglo-Saxon kingdom. Born into the royal house of Wessex at the height of the Viking wars, she must fight to save her adopted Mercia from the Vikings and, ultimately, her own brother.

"Well-written and well-researched. A remarkable novel."
~ Historical Novel Society

## Alvar the Kingmaker

A king's reign begins with scandal, and his young life is cut short. Can Earl Alvar keep the throne secure for his even younger successor? And when another king is murdered and civil war ensures, can he protect his loved ones whilst also ensuring the queen's safety?

"Ms Whitehead knows her stuff - A must-read for anyone interested in the early Anglo-Saxon period."
~ Helen Hollick, author of The Pendragon Trilogy, Harold the King, A Hollow Crown and the Sea Witch Series